Soul Kiss Tantric Tales of Mahamudra

Where are you my love?

By: David Houghton Revelle Hauser

You can find and ongoing show Soulkiss.tv on Youtube, Facebook and
www.Soulkiss.tv This is the first book in a trilogy
The Writer can be contacted on Facebook

Acknowledgement:
All photos by Vogue Images
Photographed by Pennie Donathan (my oldest friends whom I love so much)
Hair Roderick Jackson
Make up by Pedro Vela
Art Director David King
Models Jodi Rae Love, Mr. X and Shelby Lewis

ISBN: 978-0-9968234-0-1

Dedication

Dedicated To: My Mom and Dad Who Tripped the Lights Fantastic

Contents

Foreword

By Poet: Vinita Agrawal

I read your book word to word...in fact was un-put-down-able once I had picked it up.

Your book is a stunner David, an absolutely breath-taking blend of love, sensuality and spirituality. I loved the way stories are interwoven into the fabric of the protagonists' lives. The allusions to famous personalities, legends and characters gives a splendid depth to the narrative. It elevates the novel from depicting a man-woman attraction to an artful rendition of the concept of love, viewed in its highest form.

You have bared your soul in this novel. No wonder it cut through my heart like a spear. The descriptions of giving and receiving love are so profound that they moved me to tears with their intensity. Such amazing insights, such spiritual depths and such divine heights! Wow!

You have pulled off something few would dare to conceive even in the private realms of the mind. And you have done so with enviable ease and aplomb. Worldliness rubs shoulders with Emptiness in your book and the result of that friction is a profound liturgy of pure emotions. The odd thing is that people who relish pulp fiction are going to grab your book just as eagerly as those who lean towards books on metaphysics. Tantric Tales of Mahamudra has got that magic!

Keeping this in mind, please market your book well. Please allow it its place in the limelight which it so genuinely deserves. Your command over the language is beautiful, very creative, very poetic, very unique. Never have I experienced such a volume of epiphanies on reading a novel as I did with yours. Mythology-wise all the details are in order...the Hindu and the Buddhist. Not that it was ever under any doubt because you are so enlightened and well read and well travelled. Before I end, a small suggestion: Where are you my love? would make a lovely subtitle for your book.

I have lots more to share about the book but will do so later. For now suffice to say that the book will steal the hearts of its readers, just as it did mine.

Preface

This book of spiritual fiction was the result of my observations of a cultural yearning to reunite with the cause of love. I had noticed that there was a hunger for books that dealt with redefining male and female in todays social paradigm. I wanted to make sure that our collective delve had a book that represented a more exalted version of the most precious experience we can have, "Love."

This nebulous concept has been shaped in our unconscious mind throughout the history of humanity. Over the last hundred years the capitalist have made love into something to make profits by. Identifying it with our bodies, sexuality, or even preferences in an attempt to steer our thoughts away from the mere fact that love is something that happens inside our hearts. While we can never identify love, love is something that we all feel in ways we can't really describe. I have attempted to not only describe it but rebrand it as divine.

This book was an outpouring of everything I've learned about the deeper meaning of love throughout my life. While it isn't autobiographical there is so much of myself etched into the pages of this work. Primarily I'm a researcher but I am also an adventurer, world traveler and explorer who viscerally embraces this marvelous jewel called earth. Mystical connection and higher romance is possible but without the knowledge of its existence we are lead to believe that sex is all there is to making love.

Love is that multifaceted experience where we as spiritual beings have the ability to unite as one. This ability while almost a lost art has not been completely abandoned by our inner voice. We need to talk about it with each other and teach those we love how to feel and connect again. This book is a guide for that rich in a lost language we all still recognize. I want this book to empower women so they can empower men with the knowledge that there is so much more to existence on this planet.

Love is the only reason for manifesting into the material universe. It is the only substance of worth and certainly the only thing we leave behind in each of our short stays here. It is imperative that we rediscover this higher love and share its truth with all that will listen. It is our only hope for a future where all souls will be welcomed onto this planet and their gifts recognized and cherished for the cause of love to flourish.

I've described consciousness as an entity in the book and purposely draw the line for awareness to be its collective reflection. It's only through awareness that we can direct consciousness's gaze as it seeks out understanding of its own existence and the meaning of it. I wanted to do this because of the idea of collective consciousness where awareness is the rudder that sends consciousness in trajectory towards love's essence. Otherwise consciousness goes where our massive unattended thoughts send it to delve into the minutiae of every detail ruthlessly. If war is on our collective minds then war will be examined in the greatest of details. However, with our collective awareness we can reprogram consciousness to examine the refinements of our exalted divine love.

I would like to thank the poets, philosophers, scientist that have all dared to understand love's deeper meaning. Their works and all the love stories throughout history have been an inspiration to me and this book. My sincere wish is that this book reaches the eyes of all those whose hearts have not be satisfied with what our culture has framed as love. That divine female and divine male awaken through our conversations and discussion of my work. That more and more of us have the opportunity that my two characters had to experience the cathartic epiphany of that divine love. It is now up to each of us to change the tide and embrace the cause of love as the only thing worthy of existence.

They Meet

A chalice groomed to be filled with love's appeal, each drop a miracle that stirs and feels un-cautiously remiss in innocence where dreams are made of magnificence.

Business had taken me from Reno to my friend's beach apartment. It was right next to a place of great spiritual significance to me. Years ago, I had many dreams of this location as being the birthplace of the final apocalypse of our planet. Hundreds had this dream and called it in. There was no Internet, fax, or home computers to archive them with the newly formed Para-Psychology department at UCLA under Dr. Thelma Moss. She appeared on TV and radio, discussing the paranormal, dreams, and Kirlian photography. She asked the public to participate by calling a hotline in the event they had any unique and investigable experience. I really don't know what happened to all the data she collected, but I have met a few people who have had this catastrophic dream. In the dream, Malibu and Santa Monica Beach were the site of a huge explosion followed by several tsunamis. The dream continued for many years and from time to time, still comes up in my dream realms.

Tsunamis have been on my mind recently because of my travels to La Palma, Spain, a territory in the Canary Islands that's surrounded by the rim of an extinct volcano. Because the rim rises sharply from the sea, up to six thousand feet, scientists claim one side will eventually fall into the Atlantic Ocean, creating a tsunami and wiping out New York City. It was an ominous vibe getting off the plane in the Canary Islands, and tonight I was feeling that energy on Santa Monica Beach, as if something prophetic was about to happen. I couldn't put my finger on it. Was it just symbolic or was this the night the big one was going to roll to shore? This had been an odd day of gathering forces of weather, travel, and people. Right now, for me, I was here to meet a fellow writer. She was flying in from Michigan to discuss collaborating on a writing project about spiritual love.

Night came quickly after my friend Gina, a warm and chatty writer, landed at LAX. She was so excited that she was in the land of movers and shakers. After a few text messages, I finally figured out where she was. She was finally visible, standing on the curbside, so I stopped and picked her up. No sooner had I got her bags in the trunk and her in the car that the first thing on her mind came racing out, "Where are we going?" While there is always something going on in the City of Angels, especially on a Friday night, I really didn't think about where I was going next these days.

I surrendered in the year 2012, and that meant everything, including making plans. Somehow plans are always made for me in a coincidental way, if you know what I mean. When we got to my friend and host for the weekend, Todd's, apartment, he had gotten off work early and had already started to drink, celebrating another Friday freed from work. He suggested we head right to a hotel bar at Fairmont Miramar for some more drinking and fun, so we followed him on foot over there. Really, when you live in Santa Monica Beach, everything is accessible on foot. Todd knew where all the great places were because he was single, a player, and always looking for love in all the wrong places. He also was always looking for a new target to try out his sweet words on, attempting to find that perfect someone. Gina was on his interest radar along with whomever he'd focus on during the night.

Stars began to emerge over the Pacific Ocean through parting clouds. Warmer temperatures gave a gathering of strangers a reason to imbibe and celebrate another beautiful evening in Southern California. Gina, lit up by this new world that might as well have been another country, thrilled by the feelings of adventure, was taking in this non-virtual socialization. Her animated sexuality was also on the prowl, feeling her oats, and wanting to make contact with some celebrity or important industry person. I was just enjoying the moment, having learned that it's no longer me that guides my path. Whatever the night brought, it brought. Gina finally abandoned the notion of making a contact after a few hours, and we started to leave this beautiful evening at the beach. However, the universe had something else in mind, when we noticed the smiling face of actor Cuba Gooding Jr. He was out at this exclusive, yet accessible to regular people, nightspot. He was more than kind with his time, letting my colleague take a picture with him and seemed genuinely interested in our stories. Chatting like friends on this beautiful night, I let him know that I was a writer and had a Broadway musical that would be a perfect vehicle for him. To my surprise, he told me to send it to his agent.

Well, that is the universe for sure, making moves for me again, another sign to let my awareness stay on track. Of course I have no expectations; I am just here to serve a higher good and that also goes for this adventure with Gina. She definitely is enthralled by the illusions of this world of smoke and mirrors, where the reality of the human spirit somehow never outweighs the trappings of this material world. Hey, this is the home of Hollywood! Who wouldn't be bubbling about those flickers of light that make movies move, entertain, and inspire us. Cuba and his entourage wanted to move in closer to the bar and start some serious fun. As they were leaving, he asked if we wanted to go with him. I really didn't want to intrude on his friends and fans that were clamoring after this American legend and let him head into his night. After a while, Gina couldn't take it anymore. She had to go find him and chat with him further. Maybe even meet his friends! I stayed away and let her naïveté have some fun among the sharks out on the prowl; they were on their last chance to connect for the holidays on a Friday night at the beach.

Some time went by and I began to worry about Gina. I felt responsible since she was just a visitor to Los Angeles. So, I went looking for her several times and came back to where Todd was hanging out with a couple of beautiful blonde surfer girls. He looked at me, saw that I was upset and told me, "Brother, I've known you since I was eighteen years old and I think I know you well. You have to stop helping people that don't care about your help. Look, Gina is just using you. You don't have to stay here waiting for her. She is not coming back dude, she has Hollywooditis, they have her now, just let her go."

"Todd, I know you're right, and that she's star-struck, but I somehow feel that I need to help her in some way. Gawd! I have known her for so long on Facebook, it seems like we've been friends for a long time, but you must be right," I lamented.

"Look, you know me too and right now I am very drunk, I've been drinking all day long. That's why I got off work early! But I'm here for you. I'm glad you're staying with me at my house, it's the least I can do for all the help you've given me over the years."

"Yeah, I really know how to pick them. I have no idea what I was thinking, but I work too much and thought I would give this a chance," I sighed sadly. "I'm gonna wait for her a little longer."

"Okay, well, my friends are heading into the club anyway and I'll talk with them, but we should go to the other bar soon," Todd suggested.

After another hour of her not being found, she finally returned with stories to tell, contacts, and business cards, all after a little friendly groping. Todd, happy about the drama being over, pointed us to another bar to party at. We all left and headed to the top of the Penthouse Restaurant in the Huntley Hotel. We were on a personal hunt for fun on this wild Friday night! It was beautiful, overlooking the Malibu shoreline and all the lights of Los Angeles from the eighteenth story. We had a gander at what was going on, checked out the scenery, had a quick drink, decided there was nothing there for us, and started to leave. On our way down, Gina felt like someone was checking her out, so, not wanting to miss out on another chance to flirt, she insisted we go back up. Todd, who was feeling his drinks a bit too much, told us he had to go home. He quickly left to walk back to his nearby house.

So it was just the two of us at that point and she needed someone to admire the hard work she had been putting in to her feminine charms. Unfortunately, the ones who were checking Gina out were now somewhere else, leaving her sad and without an audience to titillate. I noticed there were several expensive looking Churchill leather chairs next to a very elaborate gas fireplace made of glass beads over in the corner of the bar. With a changing of the guard, people who had been dining got up, and we sat down to enjoy the warmth on this now chilly evening.

It didn't take long for the other two chairs to refill with new players in this midnight dance of conversations and preconceived notions. One of the new players was a beautiful blond woman. I wasn't really surprised to see her, since just days earlier, a psychic predicted I would meet her. I glimpsed her from the corner of my eye as she and her girlfriend sat down opposite me. I pondered in disbelief, "Could this be her?" I had had a subliminal anticipation for this moment of possibilities and manifestation for the last few days thinking, "Okay, where is she?" At the same time, I'd been apprehensive. Like everyone else, I had been stung before by women you meet at bars.

It seemed my year had been nothing but surfing on a crest of possibilities, taking me literally around the world to write and experience. I somehow felt something directing me on this quest due to the positive contacts I've made. Being here on this stunning night was just icing on the cake of this amazing year of self-discovery. My only complaint was not being able to share the wonders I had discovered on my journey with somebody I love. Listening to the woman talk with her friend, I realized how intelligent she was as well as cultured, by her graceful mannerisms. Could this beautiful unknown woman be the one that joins me on the quest for Prometheus's fire of enlightenment? I was curious if she would have some answers about the light of awareness she obviously had already found. After all, unexplained consciousness and existence itself can only be found in solving the Oracle's riddle of 'know thyself.' I really think it takes two people to fulfill riddles; creativity needs a mirror to reflect off of. People who are filled with the excitement of an electrified mind roused by spiritual connection and unexplained coincidence are amazing riddle solvers.

I silently waited in my observations, looking for a sign to direct my view into a course of events that may have been written among the Akashic long ago. In the meantime, the simplicity of worldliness and adamant conversations about mundane day-to-day life would suffice. Surviving and being untainted by materialistic dogma, or the fraud of a reasonable facsimile of your heart's desires, were obviously occupational hazards in this quest for solving love's puzzle. I am always open to life's DJ, MC Universe, with my dancing shoes on. I'm ready for my moment to trip the lights fantastic among the stars. Oh, those special stories written in the hairline fractures of our soul, only emerging when fate and destiny intersected at any given moment. Sometimes it was hard not to be skeptical even for me, but I am a patient man and would be waiting to see why the universe brought me here tonight.

Okay, I admit it, when I first saw her, I was enchanted, and so I continued to observe her to see if she realized I was there. She was in a conversational tug-of-war with a man that was obviously attempting to make the rest of his evening interesting. I waited for some intervention where I could look into her eyes. Maybe share my voice to see if it would stir in her awareness. Her admirer was not letting up and she and her friend became engaged with him as the grains of sand slipped through the hourglass at an alarming rate.

A romance writer showed up out of the clear blue sky and we got started in a conversation about women, a welcome diversion. He, of course, was looking to make his evening more stimulating also and saw my frustrated friend looking to flaunt her stuff. I guess he figured he would find out if she and I were together by chatting me up first. We started talking about the art of writing, about love, sexuality, and what it all means in the grand scheme of things, the struggle to make contact between men and women, and what the ramifications could be on our collective hearts on a spiritual level.

Befitting for our gathering of strangers that somehow the universe brought together in wishes of love. Tonight was the night that Venus passed over the new moon, which promised magnified amorous inclinations to top off this night's energy. My enchantress' entourage began to rise as the lights came on in the bar and the evening came to its lofty conclusions. My heady expert on romance had moved on from me a while ago. He was now trying to make his last ditch effort to win a prize; he was now talking to Gina who was very excited to talk about herself with him. He, not knowing her intention was to attract, was quite willing to be charmed before his night's exercise in futility to meet someone was also over.

Seemed the cards worked out for them. Not so lucky for Todd, as his imbibing spirits outweighed his ability to close any deal. So it was my turn to see what cards were being dealt by the universe. I tempted fate with a passing comment about something I can't even remember. She turned her head towards me and we started to talk about something trivial, like where we were from. I mentioned I was born in Iowa and learned she had spent some time there. I found it interesting that I had once stepped on the same ground as she. I found it interesting that anyone would spend any time in the Midwest in these days of city life and corporate work.

Truly, our adventure had finally started, and each of our swarming knowledge bases started to percolate into conversations instantly. We both could feel a surreal magic forming around our physical presence just as the sky bar started to close. And then, suddenly, we spoke to each other for real, looking deep inside each other for a split second. We spoke about the magic a night could hold, where two souls could meet and talk with substance. With that little caveat, she asked for my email address, to the disturbance of her new admirer, and we all started to leave.

It truly was a beautiful night next to the glass fireplace, as tonight turned back to a cold November. The big city of Los Angeles from a bird's eye penthouse window was awesome to behold next to the ominous darkness of the Pacific Ocean. Romantic in so many ways, with a feeling that we are all such small specks of energy connected to something much bigger than the tip of a flickering flame. Arriving back at Todd's house to sleep, I began to experience the subtle ebbs and flows of a universal cradle, letting me know another piece of the puzzle fit. She felt so warm, rich with understanding where no earthly boundaries could thwart our next meeting. The gift of this epic story would continue.

For now, however, her sweet lips simply smiled as she dissolved into midnight's blanket of stars, cool air, and the sounds of crashing waves from the nearby ocean. As for Gina, well, she drifted off into the night holding onto the arms of her romance novelist. I didn't hear much from her for the next few days. So much for collaboration, but I was happy for her; her adventures were something every writer needed to have. Todd had long been asleep when I entered his place and I paused in silence, meditating before I fell asleep, contemplating what had transpired in this prolific night. The dawn of a new day was approaching quickly and it was time for me to shut my weary eyes and trust the stellar winds to take me to my destination. Before dawn, I entered the realm of dreams to confront the Oracle's divination among the spinning wheel of Dharma. I drifted off and set sail into a cosmic void to see what stories were conjured in the morning mist. These brewing psychic connections intoxicated my dream state, carrying my awareness into a tidal pool of cosmic soup and infinite possibilities.

As I exited from this physical world and entered a pure land of dreams, fire grew within my Bodhisattva awakened state, sorting out its consequences in retrospect. Even though I had crossed over into

12

this realm of dreams, everything seemed so real and tactile. I'd noticed my senses felt highly active. Curiously, all my senses felt like they were being experienced for the first time. Graceful pleasures of senses felt as if they were suckled from a flower's nectar, full of heartfelt and sensuous convergent delights. Still, my lamenting dream identity craved silence to be adrift in darkness, achieving nothingness, and perfect rest. It longed to be within the throes of eternal void where somber sleep is soothed in ebony ripples. Suddenly, multiple emanations appeared, rising slowly in my mind's eye, like the morning sun. This was impossible in a dream, I reasoned, whose lurching light grew brighter. Somehow I had an understanding that this was the beacon that guided my weariness through the dark night of the soul. These emanations become an opening. A gigantic, pinkish-white lotus beckons my will to enter and taste its multi-dimensional ambrosia. An ear piercing squeal turned into Hindu melodies, tearing a membrane between our two dimensions and letting me enter its immense chamber.

* * *

Entering this chamber of exquisite endlessness, home of apparitional manifestations of bliss and emptiness, I sense that I am not alone. Many unknown entities surround my holographic skin in this cavern, but suddenly within its pixilation, a Dakini brushes her fiery fury against me. This touch gives me an inward rush of feminine scented ethereal vapors. The Dakini's exaltations swiftly envelope my sultry cognizance, feeling her amrita rinsing my tenuous coronium fibers, nuzzled by her sweet elixir. She cascades along my luminiferous dream structure in little ionic hydrogen drops plummeting our collective essence into water from a misting auric fog. Our perception grasps at our unity in iridescent tumbling, reconfiguring, intertwining, illuminating blissfully by some unknown design. I continue to drift sleepily down, forever with her femininity adhered to my very essence guiding me to our next destination. We

13

ride like passengers on a fertile river where life forms with each ebb and flow of our energetic procreating undulations. I hear harmonic symphonies swelling in emotional peaks that hurtle our luminosity into a crucible of unlimited frequencies stirred in boundless light.

In a hush of timeless quiet I ask, "Is it you my torrid love? Have we been carried back into the mist of creation where we emerged from the eternal void?" I remember grappling together through emptiness, clinging to our transforming naked auric flesh. We were unafraid to risk any consequences while our spiritual crescendo allowed gravity to imminently form us in statically charged holographic dust. Our manifested proclivities dip and wane their praying grace through cosmic nebulas, conjuring impossibilities in our fall from vacuous timelessness. Rudimentary substances coalesce as we quiver through the crevices folded into time space as our molded identities hold on to reality's haven.

Our hearts compose a harmonic soliloquy, songs propelled along rippling waves across dense air to our awaiting ears. You fill my spirit's palms with water, bidding me to listen to a precious droplet that sings your name into my awareness. Each liquid molecule splashes against our lucid embankments where my love lays on its shore listening to your sweet whispers, "This is not a dream." Familiar melodies and poems speak clearly of those unfathomable dimensions where our presence has always resided. I remember in our eyes where we belong in this song of unspeakable enlightenment and unfathomable love that chimes with joy.

Consciousness weaves its magic in these orbs of dream gardens, where our ghost-like skin suddenly plummets into a planet's desolation, reaching out in all directions. Oxygen blows wildly on this parched Earth, gathering dust from primordial residue swirling in the manifestation of our beings being created. Our identities inhale and are discovered in hydrogen rich moistened dirt as our forms coalesce with oxygen in static charges. It raises our pneumatic phenomena into earthen clay. All the elements of exploded stars come together to be our rivers of blood, our frame of bones and muscle, our temple of our emerging awareness.

Unknown paradigms stimulate unknown sensations that graze over our newly formed follicles with an aura of anonymous grooming strokes. Tissues become wet, as un-parched particles have erected our structures, visceral in the midst of passion played in the rage of elements, surrounding us in a storm of creativity. Rain falls ferociously, warmed by perdition that brews flames. These flames ignite our newly arrived beings with an animal nature of unequaled lust, ready for its prey. A fever of hormones flush through our brains in a mammalian frenzy of cravings focused on visual tactile elations.

Our faces now inundated with water, I can see shimmering images of eyes, noses, and lips with lightning crashes and the fury of the wind, the first sound our ears begin to hear. We are now completely animated with electricity and muscle. With purpose, we lunge toward each other, our glistening, rain-drenched bodies to touch in marvel. Splashing upon contact with slippery skin adorning ourselves with each other's yearning limbs, we finally behold. Lips meeting in unabashed contact, plunging desperately in a language infused with abandon, stricken with a desire of mutual epiphany. Chaotic unconscious impulses seek out the conquest of desire as we covertly aspire to be as one again in unabashed ravishes.

With that intense rush of love, I woke up in the material world in a ball of sweat. I was somewhat taken aback with this deep mystical experience of consciousness's first breath in human form on our planet. This extreme idea about divine love became indelible to my heart as somehow I fit into the glove of its origins. It was a glimpse of celestial possibilities threaded together by my wandering imagination. I thought to myself, "Could this chance meeting somehow have been a trigger to this ancient dream memory. Could this be the love story of consciousness?"

I had a sudden urge to roll over and look at my computer to see if I had any emails at 5 AM. Ah, there they were, from her, as she couldn't sleep either. They were asking me questions about who I was and could we see each other later today. I started to send a reply describing the very vivid dream I just had and then erased it abruptly. This was not the first dream or, perhaps premonition, I've had in regards to love. I knew that my deep water could be an overwhelming flood for most. It had made me very cautious about the way I revealed myself in this troubled world. Navigating disparages of wounded souls and mistrusted reality could take its toll on those pure of heart and those of us who have been tested. Caution and austerity were my shields at this point. My heart had become fragile and time seemed so fleeting I had to be sure beyond a shadow of a doubt.

We noticed we were both up and started text messaging, which lasted for a few hours. We covered many topics of familiarity including family, country, interests, talents, skills, life history, and all those exciting things you instantly check off after you set the foundation for alliance, friendship, and a possible relationship. Finally, we decided that our communication would be best served if we could meet in person again. She suggested the Georgian Inn, which is a very old meeting place for lovers, right across the street from Santa Monica Beach. It has a very fascinating history of the famous and elite, as it was a getaway from Los Angeles for fun and romance. Clark Gable and Carol Lombard had their torrid affair there and you can still feel it resonating in the walls of this restored old building. I arrived first and explored the building. It had many black and white photos up from its glorious past. The Georgian social circles were a cast of America's movers and shakers in its golden era, which some say still haunt this grand building.

There was also an underground restaurant, more-or-less a speakeasy, a hideaway during prohibition. This was where stars and the elite would allow gangsters to be their host for a taste of illegal fine liquors, other paraphernalia, and of course, great food. I fancied myself during those days of fine clothes in a well-crafted world, designed artfully with dancing, dressing up, and being elegant, as were the norms of a beautiful era. It truly was a time of fine art, literature, and film noir, shaping the landscape of those daring souls. Romance was defined on the big picture screen and every woman was looking for her Clark Gable to swoop her up and carry her away. Women of today still love to look beautiful and see men dressed up, but denim replaced slacks, and tee shirts replaced dress shirts, and tennis shoes dress shoes. Nobody wears ties unless you're in business or politics and even if you are, you can't wait to take them off at the end of your day. Personally, I still liked to dress up or as they once said 'dress to the nines.' It made me feel good and certainly put a smile on the face of any woman I was going out with. It's bad enough that, well, men are just not as elegant as women.

Women always put in extra effort to put a little pleasing into the eyes in their dominion. Aspiring to put on one's best was merely acknowledging who we are on the inside; putting ones' best foot forward so to speak. Even the phantoms spotted lurking about these old timbers are still in their refined elegance attempting to maintain their high standards of self. This really set the stage for drama in unlikely characters of that irresistible time. So what would keep our spirits on this Earth at throwaway landmarks, homes, and automobiles that could never stand the test of time?

When we first sat down on the deck of the Georgian Inn overlooking the ocean, we were eating breakfast at noon on an unusually warm November day. Yet we both felt it auspicious. Immediately we just started talking as if nothing mattered, while the waiter attempted to solicit our orders for over an hour. We were catching up like long lost friends on what had happened in our lives over the last millennium or so. Conversing about our childhoods, being raised on farms in the country, small towns, and what drew us into the so-called 'civilized' world of the big city. Conversely, we joyfully talked about living with the laws of nature and observing its cyclic manner of seasons filled with birth, life, and death.

She told me about her family's life in Arzama, Russia, where the closeness and simplicity of her rural upbringing were a sharp contrast to being an artist and Internet celebrity. She also told me something that changed her life and the lives of everyone in her small town. 118 tons of hexogon had exploded at a railway crossing there. Hexogon, or explosive nitroamine, is used in military and industrial applications and is more powerful than TNT. It created an 85-foot crater, blowing out windows and shaking the ground miles away that fateful day. This trauma had a profound affect on her life and really put her in motion to live outside the box of her very secret and guarded town.

That is another fascinating part of her story; she came from a town that wasn't on any map until recently, because they made nuclear weapons. The Russian government didn't want the outside world to know what went on in this city or its whereabouts. Now, of course you can find it on Google maps or on your iPhone, get the address, and learn how to walk or drive there from anywhere in the world. Back in the Cold War days, I wondered if children there knew just what could happen to them in case of a nuclear emergency. Did they have any drills and was there some sort of contingency plan to save the people of her town? Perhaps all Russian towns at that time harbored nuclear radiation, like at Chernobyl, but didn't inform the local inhabitants.

Her name was a beautiful, powerful name and the more we talked, the more enchanted I became with her. Marina had a love for words that matched my love for them, a sweet rarity in a world whose vocabulary was shrinking every day. Her online presence spoke of her empowerment in all her videos that stated 'Intelligence is sexy.' Indeed intelligence is sexiest in my view and we all know that sexy happens inside the mind before it is transmitted to the body. The power of words takes the intensity of any love connection, or love making, to heights that can only be achieved through uttered incantations filled with emotions. Marina listened very closely to words and after being in the country for so long, especially in LA, those words could lead you to intelligence or equivocators. I felt very honored that she felt as though she could trust me, and I really think it was because she was curious to find out if I meant my words. Even though my country life was not long lived, my city life didn't fill my head with 'get what you want anyway you can get it,' and that included sex from strange women. This is the dog-eat-dog life of the big city, where everyone is looking for the gold at the end of the rainbow. No matter that those roads are always paved with hard work and preparation that always brings fate together with destiny. I wasn't there for sex anyway; I was there because of what I felt from Marina, her depth, her kindness and compassion. Certainly she was a time traveler like myself, awakened to traversing all the realms in the universe, and coming back with knowledge.

I really didn't know that she was such a huge personality when we met that first night or later really. Sure I did a little digging, like she did on me, but I saw a YouTube video that showed her painting and I was completely blown away by her talent. I wondered to myself, after she told me about where she grew up, if her intense honesty was a byproduct of those realizations of what went on in her childhood town. Death was always a possibility there and it seems this looming idea about the type of work must have had an impact on the children of her town. Sure, when I was growing up we had duck and cover drills and were told we must fear the Communist threat. I never really took it seriously because it took time away from playing at recess. I was just interested in what was in her heart and how her roots had shaped her will and drive to become the person she is today. Perhaps it is best that I don't understand her huge Internet following and only see her as a country girl from Russia.

The Cold War always interested me, as it was a new bad guy that the world needed to rally around to keep in check. In a world of capitalism there was no way those greed-stricken men would allow governments to be socialistic. Socialism meant no government contracts to outside agents that could make huge profits from the hard earned wages of taxpayers. We needed to know what this outside specter was doing to take over the world and now with television, the truth was never too far away. We had news correspondence reporters spread across the world to give us the truth after dinner and before bed. These stories would program our mind with subliminal ideas about the world's order and threats that we must challenge at all cost.

The drawback was when we could see the Russian people and people from around the world on TV. Then they were no longer mysteries to the American consciousness. This didn't help the politicians make their case very strong when they were telling us Russians were bad and we should be afraid. When a child sees sad children on television, they also get sad, no matter what political leaders are saying. As a child, I imagined them suffering just like us, their fathers looking for work just like us, and loving their children and families just like us. I was not afraid of them; I was afraid of the people who could press the famous red button in Washington D.C. The threat of an enemy was merely a psychological ploy to keep our world divided for reasons that are just becoming clear in 2012. Being awake and being aware are two different things and for some unknown reason, what we are being fed in media and what we surmise, can be light years apart. This was something Marina and I had in common, because we were never spoon-fed by any authority figure and we were undoubtedly rebels traveling around the world.

Marina certainly had an unshakable compassion, a love for history, and a rich vocabulary as she told me more about her spiritual nature. She had very strong feelings about reincarnation, having had experiences with souls in transit, and awareness of her own journey through the pages of time. Looking over at me she asks, "Do you think Arthur Miller and Marilyn Monroe could be bringing us together?" We both had experiences with souls that had passed on. It seems they came to console us. She also felt entities that had once inhabited this charming hotel, engaging in play, and attempting to communicate with those aware of this dimension. She was more than aware and was a vehicle for communion between both worlds in perfect harmony. She was unafraid of any superstition. To her, they were perfectly natural to observe and participate.

Personally, I have always felt connected to more than myself, and who is to say that everything is not connected, much like the philosophy of the endless knot Tibetan Buddhists speak of. All of creation, every soul that has lived, every sentient being that has ever collected anything in their lives, is still present in the folds of time - past, present, and future. This is what an awakened state must feel like; unlimited, without borders, boundaries, or blinders. One big picture we are all a part of simultaneously. Marina had a very rare adept knowledge of these realms and the beings that inhabited them. Her psychic instincts felt free enough with me to discuss them openly, this spiritual language of our higher selves communed on many levels.

Suddenly we realized, because of our rumbling tummies, that time had somehow passed in a blink of an eye and we should order food. Our love and admiration for each other began to grow with these tongue-in-cheek stories, and recognition of our timeless selves with similar outcomes. I heard it in her voice when we first met and knew this day would come. Where we would meet in person and have a conversation about the root of perception. I have always been excited about its outcome, in weaving its tale of ruthless quests to solve an unquestionable riddle of amour.

Why did this all begin? What is its ultimate purpose?

Consciousness in its multifaceted, unexplainable ways, always a conundrum, attempts to decide where we fit into each other's cosmology. Yet, it seems all sentient life observes and collects for no apparent reason, always looking and reassessing the puzzle. Somehow all this collected information goes to some unknown place ingested by nothingness. Nature plainly holds the keys to all unsuspecting truths, seen or unseen, as our discoveries of the natural universe continue to expand. In Buddhism, where knowledge outweighs speculation of the view of truth, it is determined that the ability for humans to love is something to believe in, and the faith that humans will carry out that love completely admirable.

There was something supernatural looming in the air that night. It swept us both away in a synchronicity attuned by our timeless souls. What began as a mere eye-catching moment, started a reach through timeless ionic vapors in a reacquainting, "Hello." I wondered if suddenly, without warning, our conversations would transform into the language of kisses, or what the universe had in mind. It seemed we were both equally equipped to resonate on a higher frequency. We could reveal the quiet voice of a familiar narrative that could only be served through the language of intimate feelings.

Electromagnetic charges, sparks, and ultimate understanding transpired in mere seconds. Dancing energy took charge and a story began to take shape. I clearly heard words faintly beneath my breath, "Is it you?" on last night's first contact next to the flames. It was beyond our mortal selves where all the players were replaying their parts in a déjà vu moment. For now, on the porch of the Georgian, we're catching up on our lives in this lifetime. I'm sure in the back of her mind she is wondering how many other lifetimes we've started this conversation. Where we have been, how we were shaped, and where we might venture off to next, seem to be the query of engagement. I suggested a walk on the beach and she happily concurred. I paid the check and we both got up, two long smiling looks at each other as we began to head towards the Santa Monica Pier.

The Santa Monica Pier has a rich history of romantic love, where strangers would meet to ride the Carousel from the 1920s, and watch the waves come crashing in from up high. Before that, Spaniards started coming here in 1760, naming the area for the mother of Saint Augustine, Saint Monica. Saint Monica was a christian, her husband Patriculus, a pagan had full Roman citizenship. Monica had three children and although she married a Pagan, she eventually converted him to Christianity. After his death, she devoted the rest of her life to the Roman Catholic Church. Her son would later be canonized as Saint Augustine. She achieved sainthood herself as well, since she was able to convert her adulterer husband to Christianity to save him from sin. The fourth of May became a festival day in her honor; she was a part of that female Madonna group that has persevered in Catholicism's male dominated religion.

Eradication from this connection to the Madonna has been attempted for the last ten thousand years to no avail. Primarily, it's because of our innate affinity with the Mother, where all life comes from on this planet. It can't be removed from our psyche. My own quest has guided me to divinity many times in the arms of a compassionate woman. Sadly though, through her guidance, her own son was forced to leave his concubine, whom he called "The One." His mother wanted an arranged marriage to an eleven-year-old girl to give him status, which never happened. After that failed, Saint Augustine would never marry and took up a life of chastity. He devoted himself to Christianity until his death in 430 AD. Is this the energy of Santa Monica, California, a riddle for human sexuality to believe or be deceived? His lesson shows us that if we live piously, our faith will somehow deliver us to the ultimate spiritual love from our suffering.

We descended to the water's edge as the sun was setting. Our conversations started to turn towards a growing resonance between us, plus an affinity of unspoken feelings. At first we were walking feet apart, then somehow our rhythms slowed down, synchronizing as we grew closer and began to stroll. As we walked, our fingers nervously found each other's, locking them together in cautious unison. In this perfect moment, our consciousness, unbeknownst to us, morphs, shape-shifting our identities into the Georgian's former residents, Clark Gable and Carol Lombard. We arrived at dusk to remember in 1938, where these two lovers must have made their way to the beach once upon a time.

* * *

Clark stops for a moment to take off his shoes and roll up his pant legs. Carol takes off her heels and they rejoin hands, leaving their shoes behind while heading to the water's edge. Then a smirk grows on Carol's face that says, let's race in a contest to see who gets there first. Carol wins and starts to smile, laugh, and kick some water up at Clark. Clark chases her, laughing, in hot pursuit. He catches her, turns her around and kisses her passionately. He swoops her up into his arms as the sun gently slips into the ocean. Carol, starting to get a little cold, tells Clark to set her down. They both head up the sand embankment back to the Georgian, still talking and smiling.

Dusting off the sand and putting their shoes back on, they start to have a very serious talk. Clark starts off by telling her, "Darn it, I don't know how much longer I can stand this sneaking around stuff."

"Well, Clark," Carol explains, "one of us is married in the public eye."

"Yes, I know that! But there is something special going on between us!" Clark replies assertively.

"And just what do you think that is Clark?" Carol asks in a high tone.

"You know, that thing, that darn thing that most of us never get a chance to have," Clark strongly urges her.

Carol smirks as she whispers in his ear, "Oh, you mean, 'love' darling, don't you?"

Clark moves away, turns to her, smiles back and says, "Yes that!" but they both know that 'that' is something much bigger than the usual, 'that' that they both had been accustomed to in their other relationships.

It seems that we are all given these chances to make contact in so many ways. There are signs posted for them that have eyes to see, written in the sky, earth, water, and air as plain as day. There have been amazing love stories written since the time of creation, told through mythology, passed down by campfire stories, or even on the silver screen. While happy endings only seem to be short lived, there seems to be something under the veneer that is epic once recognized. Clark and Carol have found this in each other and aren't about to let go at all cost.

Their particular kind of love is so rich you can practically cut it with a knife. Yeah, you and I have seen it many times already in our lifetime, watched it played out in the public arena with many celebrities, public figures in reality shows, news outlets, papers and magazines. Those love stories have been shaping our thoughts about this topic from the moment we have been able to form words. What is this common thread that beats our hearts, puts an aura around us, and makes us decide to be with somebody? Romance is so magnetic that we would throw away everything we have created in this material world for just a moment of its soothing source. We would even cast our pride, honor, philosophy, virtue and all other human constructs aside to be engorged by the fragrance of true love. It seems our souls wish to attain a love that can take us into the stratosphere, dance among the stars, and trip the lights fantastic.

Going back even further in Clark and Carol's story, we discover the seventeen-year-old Carol waiting for her turn to act in the 1925 film, The Plastic Age. Director Wesley Ruggles is near the Cameraman, with his very large megaphone. The lighting crew gaffers and set designers are all clamoring around setting up the next big scene. Clare Bow and Donald Keith, whose careers are about to be made by this exotic film, are primed and ready to give their best performances. These are the days of the roaring 20s, where technology is shifting our world by communicating in ways no one ever thought conceivable. Filmmakers could take you anywhere in the world with your imagination and theirs. In this case, they were changing Pomona College to look like the prestigious Stanford University; their films illusion to a public that had never seen either before. Clark and Carol were extras on this set; both made up to look like college students during the wild days of information, music, and art with a little bohemian flare.

Clark at 24, looks very handsome, already bare-chested in a locker room towel snapping scene and later a kissing scene in his 1920s debut. Carol is dressed up like she is ready to do a Charleston dance at any moment, but not in the flappers' style yet because this was the emerging age of Jazz. Yes, Plastic Age was a prize story of the time. It made men's careers, and stars out of the women who acted in it. It also changed the perception of Paramount Pictures, as it was an edgy, college film about sex out of wedlock, alcohol abuse, wild clothes, and music. It was a big moment for Percy Marks and Joe Kennedy, who funded this racy-for-its-time movie about a new kind of American rebels. However, Carol and Clark must have walked right by each other several times on that set and never met, or even recognized that they were there. Where was the radar of fate? The 'magic casting of the universe' to bring these two beloved stars together just in time to change their lives and history? Could it have been that they weren't ready? Or perhaps this just wasn't the right time in both their lives? It seems we all must have some tragedy with love before we are ripe enough for real love, right?

Clark would have to go through having a child out of wedlock with actress Loretta Young that would almost destroy both their careers. Young had their child secretly and gave her up for adoption. Later, she adopted her daughter back but played it off as if taking a poor child from an orphanage to raise her, in an age where single parenting was a sign of failure. This, of course, mortally wounded her moral compass and broke her heart to the point where she pledged the rest of her life to Christianity. Carol would first marry a man sixteen years older than she, actor William Powell, a great taboo of her era that would eventually end in an amicable divorce. Powell, her mentor and more like a father, and Carol would remain friends for the rest of her life. Clark would eventually get married to a very rich Ria Langham, due to a morality clause in his contract with Warner Brothers. Ria seduced Clark to move in with her with her feminine wiles. She forced him to marry her and she was very slow in letting him go to the arms of his beloved Carol.

'Screwball' was Carol's pet name because of her very blunt and honest way of expressing herself in a male-dominated world. Her honest, clear, fearless, forward nature, and love of the outdoors made her Clark's perfect companion. She could shoot a rifle, clean a chicken, cuss and drink like a sailor, and still be the hottest woman in the room. When they finally got married, any piece of film you see them in tells a tale of true love and happiness. These were the flickers at the top of the flame of two very famous loves, risking everything to be together. The fire between them danced in unpredictable ways with every whip of the flame, shouting, "Enjoy the heat while it's hot."

Earlier that day, Clark is in the office of Louis B. Mayer. Clark enters with his usual charm and says, "Sorry I'm late boss, what seems to be the problem?"

Mr. Mayer, in his usual blunt way, tells Clark, "You're the best man for Gone with the Wind, and we are making a deal with my son-in-law David."

"Mr. Mayer, ah Louis, you know the legal situation I'm in right now with Ria. Why did I listen to Stickling anyway?" Clark moans.

Mr. Mayer chimes in, "Howard Strickling is your PR agent Clark, without whom we wouldn't even be talking right now. Remember our mutual friend Thalberg and the morality clause in your contract? Why did you live with a woman that wasn't your wife anyway Clark?"

They both laugh and Clark sighs, "Well, she was the best in bed at the time."

Mr. Mayer smiles and lightens up, "Truer words were never spoken Clark. I, however, think I have a way out. I have been in talks with Ria's lawyer and we may have a settlement in lieu of you signing with Selznick International Pictures."

"Louis, you're the best friend a gent has ever had. I guess I need to start reading the script," Clark quibbles.

"Yes Clark, I think that may be the best route for you right now," Louis laments.

They shake hands, a deal made. As Clark is leaving, Mr. Mayer shouts out, "Don't do anything until after the ink is dried and the hour is right Clark! Clark, do you hear me?"

Clark turns at the door and says, "I hear you loud and clear boss." Clark gives him that Gable grin and tip of the hand goodbye.

The lawyers are in Vegas with a $300,000 check of Clark's advance for Gone with the Wind, along with Howard Strickling who is there to make sure everything goes okay. He has prepared a statement for Ria that expresses what she should think and feel, with something that the studio can also benefit from. Really, Clark's love affair had already been tried in the court of public opinion. Ria already lost there to a storybook love between Carol and Clark. Although this all had been strictly gossip, Ria had already been through the gossip mills with Joan Crawford and Elisabeth Allan, both Clark's lovers. She also had to go through the alleged child he had with Loretta Young, which was all too true and she knew it. Clark was a player, but he really wanted a marriage. Ria took that away from him by forcing him to marry her or get fired.

Howard had to know what she'd done to get Clark to move in with her in the first place and asked, "So how'd you do it, off the record?"

"Do what, off the record?" Ria asked.

"You know, get Clark to move in with you."

"Well, there are some things a woman can do for a man that keeps him coming back for more," She slyly whispered.

"Really, that was it?" puzzled Howard.

"What do you mean was that 'it?' 'It' was a lot!" Ria emphasized in a stern whisper, "The only problem is 'it' can be very fragile to a man's ego at the same time," Ria lamented.

"What do you mean?" inquired Howard.

Ria rattled off a truth that had been hurting her womanhood, "One little meeting with a PR man and you can take the wind out of a man's sails. And then all the wiles of a woman becomes apparent." Ria looked deep into Howard's eyes, attempting to mesmerize him with her feminine charms. He felt drawn in because she wasn't dressed like a jilted wife, but as a beautiful woman of dignity and grace. "Perhaps you should stop by and see me sometime for a little chat, Mr. Strickling, and we can measure 'it' all out then," insisted

29

Ria.

Howard, a bit flustered, hands her an envelope, under the watchful eyes of lawyers, with a check in it and a small statement for her to read when she walked out of the courtroom. Her lawyer and Clark's legal team, along with Howard, all went inside to see the judge. The judge took all of four minutes to make the divorce final. It seemed Clark was about to become a free man at midnight later that day. Howard sent a wire to the Georgian to let Clark know it all went well. It was Ria's turn to confront the news media with the statement Howard prepared, but that was not going to happen. Instead, she had her say in the forum of public opinion with a little dig, "Clark knew he could have a divorce anytime, but he never seemed to want one. I think a marriage between a movie star and a society woman has a better chance of succeeding than one between two stars." She winked at Howard at the end of her speech. Then, she was picked up by her black limo and driven off into the sunset of history to return to the society life of Bel Air, California.

How many books have been written about men and women getting together for all the wrong reasons? Then they divorce only to find out time had slipped them by, somehow missing the boat with that someone who was looking for them all along. I think it's true, your love is out there looking for you, night and day, dreaming about you desperately, and attempting to find their way home. Sadly, illusions and reasonable facsimiles taunt and tease us into disasters of our own making, spending the rest of our lives wondering what went wrong. Love is something savored, risked for, and certainly greater than our own selves. Yet we haphazardly venture out in completely opposite directions to face rampant despair. It seems everything gets in the way of finding happiness, and we eventually settle for what we think is our lot in life. Stuck because of money, jobs, children, or efficacious antidotes that numb our hearts toward their true goal. Some of us just give up on love, where it no longer has any mystical

30

effect, replaced by one hedonistic adventure after another. The end of the line for seeking only pleasure is fulfillment, where nothing is ever good enough, and insatiable no matter what is being offered. So, when true love comes along, it is hardly recognized, evaporating into another lifetime, squandered because of our fears of making a commitment.

Evening had fallen on 1938 at the Georgian Hotel, with many new, expensive cars showing up in the dark at this exclusive beach getaway. Clark and Carol were dressed in eveningwear as they descended into the den of iniquity in a hullabaloo of VIPs. Clark with his tux and Carol wearing, a crushed black velvet evening gown by Madeleine Vionnet, made a noticeable entrance into this nightclub of high rollers and gangsters. Rose Fitzgerald Kennedy and Bugsy Siegel were entertaining that night, along with some very unsavory people. It had a low light atmosphere, where deals were being made and lives were being changed. This room was called the Red Griffin Room and you could get anything you wanted there in the realm of fine dining, alcohol, and Jazz. Clark and Carol liked to cozy up in the booth, talk, and spend some time looking deep into each other's eyes while listening to the music.

"This is all about to come to a pleasant end, Screwball," Clark whispered to Carol, as he was about to share his secrets. "My untimely divorce is about to be completed this very evening and there is something I would like to ask you, my darling," Clark sheepishly spilled to Carol.

Carol asked coyly, "Why, what ever would that be darling?"

Clark said jokingly, "Whatever would a dame like you be doing with a knucklehead like me is beyond my comprehension."

Carol said, "Well Clark, you should see what the other knuckleheads look like. I'm afraid they could never reach your level of knuckleheadary anyway darling."

Clark quickly came back with a grin, "Are you trying to say I'm thick headed?"

"Why no Clark, whatever made you think your head was thick?" Carol laughed.

"Oh, well that's better then," Clark beamed.

A man walked up to Clark, nodded, and then walked off. "Ya know kid, I think we might have better luck somewhere else tonight. I think it's time to leave."

"Clark, but what about dinner?"

Clark helped her up and out of the booth, kissed her hand, and then took her by the arm. As they turned towards the stairs to the lobby, he said, "I got that all worked out."

Walking through the lobby to take the elevator up to their suite, they playfully kissed until they got to the front door. Then, Clark got very serious. Clark opened the door, showing Carol what he had arranged for them; champagne, caviar, little finger foods, lots and lots of flowers and candles, with a little box on the table next to the bed that says, "Van Cleef & Arpels." Clark told Carol to wait, putting his finger on her lips, and picking her up into his arms with a kiss. They crossed over the threshold to their love nest and he kicked the door shut after them.

Once inside, he gingerly placed her on the bed. He looked at her and said, "Open it." She opened the box, revealing a huge diamond ring. She handed the box with the ring in it to Clark. Carol bid him to put this beautiful ring on her finger, but he waited with a boyish grin, looking at his watch. The big hand on his Mathey-Tissot Chrono reached the number 12 along with the little hand, now he was only waiting for the second hand to catch up to indicate midnight. Still looking down, Clark counted out the seconds 5, 4, 3, 2, 1. Then, "Bingo!" Lifting his eyes towards Carol's baby blues, he asked her, "Will you marry me?"

Carol's sparkling eyes teared up, and her little grin tipped Clark off that her usual wit might steal the moment, but instead she simply let out a joyful, "YES."

He slipped the ring on her accepting finger. She rose from their bed to stand in front of him as an offering, still looking simply beautiful among all those flowers. She held her hand out to help him up from the floor and into her arms. With a kiss, he unzipped her evening gown, which gracefully floated to the floor. She was left with some of the most exotic, satin emerald green lingerie on the planet adding to the delight of this perfect moment. Coco Channel was a personal friend of Carol's. She had given her this exquisite gift and Carol had been saving it for a special moment like this. Coco had also sent satin green garters and violet nylons to highlight Carol's gorgeous legs. This was a moment a man could only dream of. Clark wrapped his arms around her again, kissing like it was their first time. Then, in one very elegant move they both glided their way back to a perfectly amorous, awaiting bed.

* * *

Just as suddenly as it began, Marina and I found our awareness returning to our presence of mind. Our current reality faded in. It seemed as if only seconds had gone by in our momentary lapse of consciousness while we were watching time go by. We became aware that the day had slipped away in our lurid conversations about life on planet Earth. We both were stricken with so much information, keeping our unspoken flashbacks to ourselves because they seemed so impossible. So many lessons learned and talked about, such as heartache, art, music, fashion and spirituality. We covered it all in a morning and afternoon. It was time I walked her back to her apartment building to say goodbye, for now.

Within that moment of contact, a realization that we had a bond overwhelmed us, along with the fun of just being together. What that meant in our scheme of things was yet to be learned. Could we just be two souls catching up again before we both floated down the byways of the river of time? Certainly we realized there was a completely unfettered psychic awareness of each other resting under our collective causal body we just couldn't shake off.

Our walk brought us to her apartment, which to my surprise was right next to the Georgian Inn. The gentleman that I am, I attempted to open the door to her building, forgetting that everything has a lock on it these days. It was hardly a graceful expression on my face because I really wanted to open it for her. She smiled, opening the door with her electronic plastic passkey. She looked at me to say goodbye and commented, "We just don't know each other that well yet." After that profound statement, we parted, and I began to return to my friend's house to pack and leave the area. North Hollywood was my next stop. I was driving to my best friend Bob's house to work and help him with his new business. His house was a place where I had done lots of writing for my screenplays and stage-plays.

Suddenly, I completely succumbed to a high pitch buzzing ringing in my head and a flurry of blinding patterns. Staggering, I felt like I was about to pass out. I desperately needed to find a chair to sit down in; then I fell and landed in a big brown reclining chair at Todd's. Letters written in Latin, Intus Divintas Nihil or Within Divinities Nothingness, written on a golden seal, formed under my rolled up eyelids in my haze. Helpless and paralyzed, I was being sucked into some sort of humbling psychedelic experience that I was not the driver of. I was reduced to observer, swept into a visual whirlpool cresting against that great seal. The letter shattered into millions of pieces, opening up into an enormous hall. I heard a grand narrative psychically revealing to me that a huge paradigm shift had just begun and I was a witness. From its dark center, a fibrous, crystalized, ethereal web of light sprung from a hovering luminescent globe in the ethers of my hallucinations. From this transparent crystalline illuminating web, a single fiber, like lightning, attached instantaneously to Marina's third eye and mine. Moving at the speed of thought, my helpless body lurched with tremors, jolted with convulsions that dragged me deeper into this vortex. Overwhelmed, my awareness whisked me away to a state of consciousness where I could not divide myself from the ancient story unfurling before me.

As if a Dream

Silence's inevitable hush, conceived by belief rubbed in indelible dust.
Notoriously beckoned so timely we've reckoned a generous blend of impeccable trust.

Decoding our first contact wasn't up to my limited abilities; it was up to the universe. Within Divinities Nothingness was its apparent message, yet I knew nothing about its origins, or how to decipher its meaning. Other signs were also coming around this psychic impetus of swarming clouds, setting my inner oracle in a quandary. Without warning, a high pitch sound started to ring so loud in my ears that I fell from the recliner to my knees.

I'd fallen into a catatonic state confronting the next seal. Only this time, it was emerald with the endless knot symbol covering its surface. It too cracked as my awareness burst through it, opening like two huge doors growing taller as my identity became very small. Even more humbling than my mere drop of self in a huge ocean, as if I was standing at the threshold to what felt like the kingdom of God. Haunting sounds at the precipice of an ominous void of churning machines, howling as if it was the enormous mechanism of space-time itself. Apparently, this energy was hard at work in the distant background churning out reality. The chanting sounds of the fourth chakra's root syllable 'YAM' reverberated from the center of my heart. I heard the other letters on the lotus spinning in a clockwise manner: Kam, Kham, Gam, Gham, Ngam, Cham, Chham, Jam, Jham, Nyam, Tam, Tham, Nam, Tam, Tham, Dam, Dham, Nam, Pam, and Pham. The faster the lotus spun around, the faster the sounds were sung until it once again sounded like the root syllable YAM. While all this was happening, the lotus turned into my heart and my heart unfolded like a flower; it had become otherworldly.

I took my first steps on this new firmament, filled with exuberance as I began to feel out this magnificent expanse. My keen instincts sensed other inhabitants or presences within this odd space of hidden intricacies. Out of all these feelings, I heard a single soul's meditative resonance vibrating in bliss, ricocheting pings off my body in repeating waves. These were sweeping waves of splendor, rinsing me in pure honesty and drenching my smiles with wishes to follow its chimes. My ears followed, resolved in its inquiry, discovering what direction to follow along these smooth, soft, agile, and fiery surfaces. From a distance, it was the outline of her flesh, a heat shimmer in perdition's kitchen bedecked in absolute opulence, glistening like jewels freshly forged.

Majestic splendor, eternally whole, this goddess' effigy came into focus with subtle breasts, seductive hips, and tiny waist. Inside this cavernous void, our body heat provided the light that outlined her beautiful skin tones, painted disturbingly in rich amber powder. Her facial features were carved perfectly, outlined in vibrant colors around her eyes and rich, blood red lips. I took her up into my arms as the light refracted a sweet honey skin, opaquely layered in galaxies beneath the translucent fabric of her scantily clad nakedness.

She reacted with pawing fingertips, caressing my outline in this nebula of rainbow radiance. Majestically, she began drawing up my auric lingam to her seducing translucent yoni to kiss in our bedazzled dance of ecstasy. Her eyes rolled to the back of her head while her legs wrapped tightly around my waist, engorging herself deeper, closer within her cosmic womb. I supported her universe with my grasp, keeping her resolve solvent and voracious. Dancing in silhouettes, darkness was illuminated by our connecting charkas vibrating in Hum, tuned to the frequency of Mahamudra. Mechanisms all commanded by our elations, celebrated in our Mecca, dissolving our rich identities, and mingling in particles of divine synchronicity. Our flailing spectacle decrescendos tenderly to rest, our starlight glides us back to reside in a firmament of reclining soft-spoken kisses.

In my arms I guarded her, sailing through this anachronism where our energies started creating from electric ethereal sparks. Trees, skies, and creatures etched in those Latin words of Intus Divintas Nihil filled every pixel of our newly designed landscape. Coagulating stardust formed a nurturing placenta of galaxies, supporting our fruitful bounty in jubilant sheer delight. This is our domicile of endearments that sweetly divide heaven from a newly forming Earth. Our savoring resonance dripped like tears from our eyes, each droplet creating galaxies, stars, and, solar systems in prisms of endless void.

Night skies formed as we reminisced our coupling from heaven's gate in heartfelt emotions filled with manifestation of physical reality. Intense vibrating hums aligned our gravity, arranging the dynamics of our harmony with complete elated sighs of universal benedictions. We sang of harmony reunited, embodied in a sentient phenomenon of immemorial reverence. It was as sacred as creation when our immortal failings makes us mortal and took us into a restful, translucent, transcendental sleep.

Morning came to our manifestation among our pristine terra firma woven in a carpet of ferns, moss, banyan trees and a plethora of new life replacing a once barren void. We reposed, exposed to the heat of our salvation as a new sunrise experience crept through its branches along with a warm gentle rain. Those waters bathed us in gentle strokes, painting brilliant shadows, etching out outlines of my beloved's divinity. It moved my gentle heart to watch her sleep so peacefully under my protective eyes. Captured now by the sound of her breath drawn in and out, ever slowly with each inhale and exhale, so deep it lifted her undulating breast to my ecstasy. I was caused to tremble at every pulse saturated in aroma's mysteries, luminance, and soft cadence of surrender.

My hands moved across her feminine pelvic mound, cradling it softly as I engaged its receptacle in cautious movements, invoking its conspicuous divulgence of sweet, wet honey to nurture all of timelessness. Such a captivating expression as a delicate orchid would ooze such nectar indulging me to devour its sweet liquids. Hungry delights that jealous gods could never taste without a vehicle made of flesh and bone. My lips leisurely searched in circles around its ruby red seed, engorging its gelatinous flesh in gentle ambitious strokes. My hands now roved each appendage, uncovering other sensitized awarenesses as my love sleepingly roused. My lips and tongue covered each susceptible area, crawling up her inner thighs, teasing a now engaged, yet barely awake body, in the throes of amour. Both hands now dug deep, grasping her raw haunches tight, and firmly drew her cup to my mouth to drink deeply of her essence. She awakened impassioned, her reactions plead to be taken precociously, gasping air with each pleasured enchantment, until she surrendered all her tenderness.

Her electrified body hummed in a pounding cadence, which spoke of unison, synchronizing our rhythm with unseen forces that compelled me nearer to her succulent breast. She amply offered tastes. When I lowered her to cradle in my arms, I suckled her nectar's energy sweetly. I could not comprehend this interlude of conjuring. It was as if my lips were always joined to her bosom, melting in their moist, passionate devotions. I could not resist suckling its tenderness raw and drawing sensual energy of her concupiscence heightened intention. My elated innate covetousness carefully lay her down as her parting loins deliriously bid my company. Her giving righteousness rushed up in exuberance, like an encroaching tide you could not hold back. Yes, it was surrender. I was surrendered, my movements were not my own, and I could not stop this promise to hold her in my arms. We both transcended to paradise without end, a cornucopia without peril. So it began with a promise, a touch, and a prayer that this day of beauty is my guiding light that will lead me into the sun, at least in this moment; at least in this perfect moment.

Fullness became her clear shape; nothing can contain her irresistible impulse to press hard on my infatuation. Desperate hunger pangs for my cravings, she enticed. I'd never felt a stirring such as this before, a libidinousness of heightened madness. We'd become captivated and interlaced in our pure lusting aspirations to imbibe. Acquiescence had been declared between our hearts, barriers resolved, free flowing, clandestine aberrations elevate our tempest devotions to love. The storm within rested calmly on the shores of divine absolution along with our wills. Caressing strokes played with so much meaning it became a quasar to our emerging universe. To inhale lascivious particles of extreme magnificence dignifies our overwhelming splendor; we share this moment in bliss. I am tempted by her dilated darkened eyes painted with wonderful allures, struck from Earth's plumage redesigned on her skin. Red is the color of her transforming, blood-filled body to the highest yogic Tantra, laced in her Vajrayogini's Purelands of infinite passion. All obstructions from liberation rest in her wanting crux, beckoning me to delve deeper, to be enthralled in poetic justice and divine restitution, for her heart's sake and mine. We had made an undissolvable union fearlessly behind this curtain, this veil, and this illusion in the energy of Tantra.

Instantaneously, the emerald seal closed like a giant Buddha's sleeping third eye resting in the temple of void. Consciousness wanted to arouse my awareness of its polarities of male and female components that inspire existence for some unknown reason. Consciousness' first kiss, imprinted time's singularity, creating impermanence from nothingness, is the message unfolded here tonight. A dream, a vision that parted the clouds of this great story, had been triggered by my chance meeting with Marina and triggered my cosmic memory. Consciousness wanted me to know that once upon a time it fell in love with consciousness.

Through my research on ancient myths and symbols, I had read about these great seals, like the Eye of Providence. Who knows when we are going to be called to receive an indelible initiation like others throughout history, such as Arjuna, Moses, Buddha, Mohammed, or Joe up the street? Destiny sought its own relevance more than we had discovered in our attempt to solve the riddle of consciousness. Within Divinities Nothingness, everything oscillates, vibrating at the speed of light where creation is formed in the brilliant split second when seed meets ovum. Why are my eyes the ones witnessing this event? Who knows why we have revelations? I don't understand, perhaps the universe has shaped my readiness for this moment in time? Reality may be on the tip of my tongue. I am a willing participant, with an opened heart that is ready for destruction if need be. My curiosity wants to unlock more, connect more, and awaken

41

memories I know are sleeping yet aching to be recognized. I have no idea how to do that and can only return to my humility where my will has reverence for the magnificent of the universe.

I have returned, still on my knees in what seemed like lifetimes but was only flashing seconds of undisturbed silence. This most profound experience has shaken me to my core. The conundrum of this contact grows more interesting with my attempts to solve its riddle. I am quite weary from this intense pact with oblivion and before I leave Santa Monica, I decide I need to take a little sleep. My wish of course, is for only sleep to come take me into sweet darkness where my thoughts can regroup. I can allow for this story to further unfurl as it is meant to happen. Sadly, if one is not careful about this type of immensity it can cause one to run for the hills. Fortunately I have had some training with great teachers about such occurrences. Even as fragile as humans are, I will keep it all in perspective the best I can.

Me is We Inside Our Reflection

Pond kisses sky reflects in love's eyes, pools rinsed increments blessings in disguise as me flips upside down to we inside we both realize.

The Hubbell telescope has shown the world's scientists so much about the makeup of the universe. It has almost been able to look at the moment of the big bang from the effects of cosmic microwaves and light. Looking past that point into what happened before time is not even considered a scientific question. However, some theoretical scientist ventured off about the idea that two types of dark matter, hot and cold, collided 13.7 billion years ago and in an instant the material universe was formed. An ideal place in an ideal reality, to fathom their further contact with fresh sensations, on all levels, in a quest to remember what love is. If only our view could see that far or we had a device to reveal the amoeba of time subdivided into identity of male, female and observer.

For some unknown reason, every time I ponder before time, I hear the voices of consciousness dancing through their passion play. Positive and negative charged particles of the same dark matter, attracted to each other because of emptiness' sadness beckoning a ping. Subtly, a presence emerges, creating gravity between parts of darkness rushing unabashedly towards a contact they cannot control in their electromagnetic attraction. Eventually, contact is made like two pairs of lips open and unaware of any parameters or consequences within nothingness. Their consuming energies create a transpiring pressure against each other's limitless boundaries until those energies cause a realization of existence in a split second. Consciousness, while boundless, has limited awareness of itself, its parameters, and aspects that unceasingly collect information in every fathomable way, through sentience in all forms. Existing in timelessness, in a universe governed by time, it has a desperate need to know what it all means for this quest at all cost.

There's also a sublime cosmic humor in consciousness's delve of everything if it's directed properly, and if these directions are thoughtfully pointed towards compassion. Splendor and tenderness are other components of its possibilities, just as long as awareness is steering omnipotence towards a quest to comprehend love in all its facets. This symbiosis can turn fateful when awareness is not present. Consciousness left to its own devices can digress into its primordial unforgiving violent nature stirring rampantly for answers. Then we're at the mercy of that focal point of creation's outburst and emptiness' sadness. When consciousness is apprehended, it can be directed to engorge itself into the path of awareness focused on its mission of fathoming love to understand itself.

From this massive void, the total essence, the marriage of consciousness and awareness reaches out, magnanimously delivering its mystical contents through unimaginable eons to be realized. All of creation collected in holographic tetrahedron shards, electromagnetic crystals hovering ceaselessly in emptiness, contemplating nothing. In this timeless epoch, information sits on the tip of an omnipotent tongue where the heavy grip of compassion dwells thankfully. Overwhelmed with incomprehensible love, a third point perhaps the harbor of our awareness, the observant narrative of discovery, begins to whisper from their indescribable lips macro-microcosms that form two points of singularity. In that clandestine moment, emerging from an unimaginable void, colliding in a single unexpected kiss, a delve begins seeking its love.

Their kiss spontaneously creates our beautiful universe, re-inscribing sentient life in all possibilities gathered in dust turned to animated matter. Their sparks, consequences of contact, conjure up reflections like sparklers, dashing in light that takes on a multitude of identities in a short leap of refracted subsistence. These events etched inside the memory stick of DNA, accessible to those that seek its contemplations about the origins of humanity. Until that day, we are bound by these illusions of linear time that sends us on our day-to-day activities to survive. This idea of Earth floating in a galaxy in eternity eludes most. They are unaware of the divine grace that has brought us here. Yet, gnawing in our human background is every particle of indestructible energy whose objective is to reflect truth as it is gathered. Sadly, so many hardly look up at the night's sky because it's immediately understood time is something man-made. There is no need to be afraid of darkness, for those that have awareness of our companionship, understand that we are the stewards of our beautiful material world.

I wonder if it seemed aimless to these two parts of the same source of consciousness to ping in void's infinities from two ends of the opposite spectrum. Brahma was said to ask for Saraswati in his despair from feeling lonely and she answered him with love, kindness, and service to his desperation. Legend tells us in this moment, Brahma created her and thus started the creation of the material universe. I often ask myself, who is the Supreme Being in this ancient scenario? Consciousness's primary directive has always been to know why. These questions must have grown as its various awareness of self grew. Consciousness, collecting information beyond the speed of light began to understand the intention of compassion in its loneliness. If we could hear sound from the beginning of time like we see light, would the faint voices be whispering, "Where are you my love?"

Macro-microcosm finite to the infinite in this material universe is still echoing from that initial point of contact, resonating just like the light made from its intentions to recognize itself. Consciousness delves relentlessly, seeking the nature of every particle in creation, with or without awareness, in its ruthless venture to find its rendezvous with love. Their kiss amidst unfathomable polarities fashioned reality in this seemingly endless day, measured at 13.7 billion plus scientific years ago, in a blink of an eye. None of these thoughts have disappeared, but still exist as energy, like radio waves endlessly pinging from the point of creation. Einstein once said, "Matter and energy are indestructible, persistent and infinitely divisible." Perhaps someday we will hear a voice tuned in by a resonance frequency of our higher selves in the throes of love that says, "Right here my love."

The Kiss

Promise etched vividly along intention's rim bravely yearning fearlessly for surrender to settle in. At the oasis edge where heartbeats take a sip a longing draw lost in a moment spoke from both our lips.

A gnawing thaw rings my internal transducer so loudly my head zings, while pointing to possibilities my recent cathartic epiphany could further surmise. Centuries of suppressed inclinations, idioms, and pure foolishness have kept too many lost souls from realizing a potential for a higher love. Sadly, Marina was right, "We don't really know each other that well." Precious trust is built from the building blocks of thoughtful spiritual contact, delicate as it is. After all, intelligence, rather insufferable intelligence, is overwhelmingly the deliberator of our sublime expressions of spiritual communion. Honesty, certainly our common denominator, is a fragile word that sounds better with sincerity molecularly hovering around its precious aura. The ultimate enticement for two humans is to make contact with that honesty and every intelligent word spoken is a singing invocation to our higher selves.

Surround these sweet words with intention and discover the other 99% of nonverbal communication written in smiles, I muse. Mindfulness is where we caress each other's intelligence, grooming each other with information that identifies our truer voice within. I trust my kindred-ness has ignited both our curiosity enough where we can spend some more precious time together. But the reality is something that is yet to come with the modalities of proper forthrightness and perhaps a little help from technology (like a cell phone) we can make something happen.

I learned through a mutual friend (another coincidence) that she would be up in Hollywood for meetings this week. So I decided to use that technology, and give her a call. I asked her if we could meet, that I was working in the area, and was not sure about how much longer I would be in LA. She agreed to meet but couldn't until later that night and asked if that was possible for me. I responded with a sincere, "YES!" Tonight would be perfect. She mentioned a place I used to go to a lot in my former days when I had a small record label in Hollywood. Her suggestion was the famous, "Rainbow Bar and Grill" on the sunset strip, home of two of the most unsung figures of the heydays of Rock n Roll, and my friends, Tony and Michael. She had never been there, but had heard so much about it and wanted to try something different on the Hollywood side of town.

Tony and Michael were something different for sure. They had seen it all; their combined book would sell millions. These were two guys that never kissed and told. I have so much respect for them and what they have done to protect people from hurting themselves while living the big dream. Rock Stars are people too and it didn't matter how rich you were; when you were in their place, you were family.

But with great fame, there's a great price to pay in Hollywood; not everyone can get away without paying it. Even with Tony and Michael's good intentions, some people just didn't make it out alive. Many times an ambulance had to come for a DOA on Sunset Boulevard and take someone to the emergency room.

Like the Georgian Hotel, The Rainbow was also haunted, but by legends of Rock 'n' Roll fame, peripheral entourages of groupies, drug dealers, roadies, and record company management. Funny, just like the Georgian's secret room for gangsters with red leather booths to dine and drink in, Michael and Tony had an almost identical room. One thing for sure, they had a lot of class, always wearing a suit and tie when they showed up to work to keep the environment sincere. I'm sure to most they looked like gangsters, but to me it was the charm of days gone by when men were elegant for all the right reasons.

Tony and Michael always took care of their friends and they had a special place for the royalty of the sunset strip. Those Royals always had a table ready for them right at the entrance so they could see all the comings and goings. These were the old men who ran all the clubs. Over time, some of the seats emptied as they passed on. I'm sure the Georgian had secret rooms but the rainbow secret room was called 'the top of the rainbow.' This was where lots of long nights ran into daylight for big rock stars with deep pockets to hide out, party, and have sex. The second floor was also the VIP room, where you wished you could get in but never could unless you knew someone famous. Nowadays it's a historical landmark, an urban legend we have all heard about in the world of Rock 'n Roll. Sometimes I think of The Rainbow as a memorial to all those super stars, where young rockers can still wade through ghosts.

I get there early and wait for Marina to come, chatting a bit with Tony asking him how Michael was doing. He tells me they have a deal where he works the weekends and Michael works the weekdays now. We kid around a bit about the old days and I excuse myself when I see Marina valeting her car. Tony's eyes begin to smile and he motions for me to go by shooing me away. I rush over to help her out of her car, grasping her hand and lifting her to her feet. I bid her to hand me the keys so I can hand them to the valet. I take the ticket for her tipping him so we are free to greet each other. She is just stunning, wearing a Chanel Haute Couture Vintage Chiffon cocktail dress and some Keynes West designer high heels. Yes, I notice this stuff. Women put a lot of effort into it and as a man I pay attention to details. I am also dressed nicely, stepping up with my Tom Ford Carlyle mauve suit on, with all the trimmings and some styling Stanford loafers. I really want to show her how important our meeting is to me and looking good tells that right away. I can't take anything for granted because no moment of life should be missed.

Life is a gift from the universe. Even being in the same proximity of her angelic creature in human form is a blessing for me to behold. Soul memory recognizes these gifts and my avid curiosity ponders whether her soul memory identifies me as her gift. We assess each other with smiles, excited that we have the chance to examine our familiarities this evening. I bravely look into her sparkling eyes and, as a gentleman, I bow slightly and kiss her hand in a welcoming gesture to her spirit. I hope to disarm her fears of being with, for all she knows, a stranger with my forthright nature and chivalrous ways. I give her my arm to hold as we stroll inside The Rainbow. Entering into the doorway at the hostess desk I introduce her to my dear friend Tony. Tony gives me a nod of approval and greets her with his awesome infectious smile, welcoming her warmly to his establishment. He lets her know that she is with an amazing person and hopes she will enjoy the evening in his home, his heart, and his business tonight.

I begin to show her around the first floor where there is a group of people dressed as the deck of cards from Alice in Wonderland.

These amazingly costumed people had just come from a Hollywood party at one of the studios. They looked spectacular. A very interesting amusement to our unfolding fairytale from the universe I'm sure. Also, occupying the other end of the spectrum of fantasy fairytale was a very inebriated porn star legend, Ron Jeremy. Ron, now very old, entertained these very young porn stars with his miniature harmonica attempting to get another drink from his unknown colleagues. This very befitting Jim Morrison carnival on the sunset strip was a perfect clue for both our trepidations of misbelief. Very odd extremes indeed, I think to myself. Cosmic humor always seems to be a road sign to any evening of mystical events. We arrive at the bottom of the stairs and I gingerly help escort Marina to the top, climbing the red carpet and wooden banister to the second floor.

Once we take our seats at the second floor bar, I ask her if I may order a drink for her. She permits me to do so with a smiling nod. I summon the bartender, asking for a very special French Cognac called Dupuy, which, to my delight, they have. It is very expensive but it serves many purposes for our conversation and my discovery tonight. The bartender gives me that knowing look. She pours and smiles really big, watching for the reaction before returning the bottle to its dusty home. "There is a classic way to enjoy this type of Cognac and because I know you have traveled the world this is a pleasure I wish to enjoy with you, my dear," I delightfully elucidate. "One must first approach the glass with caution as its contents are very valuable," I urge. "Then run the palm of your hand securely under its carriage, what is called a Ballon snifter, to gently warm." (I nod to the bartender for putting it in the right glass.) "The whole idea of a perfect receptacle is to expose as large a surface area as possible to intensify its harmonious bouquet. When this is done, simply wait for it, allow the aroma of its nectar to fill the surrounding air. Looking past its surface to enjoy its colors is also a part of experiencing the care from its maker that tells signs of its maturity. From the youngest yellow, a rich amber, to gold and then a very mature deep red, where the warmth is returned to you as a most savory invitation." The glass draws itself towards your now knowing smile to inhale its graces by swirling its contents, just a bit, to embellish its delicate fragrance even more. Each expression surrendering flavors, begging you, enticing your wanting desires to imbibe. "Finally close your eyes, let the chalice rise to your lips, the first small sip teases your pallet in savory textures and the aftertaste comes swooning in. In this still moment of sensations our hearts urge us to drink slowly, to appreciate what love has created for us both right now in this exalted, distinguished moment," I say in my most poetic voice.

She is thrilled that I would take time to talk to her about such things, but there was even more to this story. My choice to start out our first real evening together was about to take us on an unexpected journey. I continue with, "This Cognac has a much more deserving story, as do all worthy experiences, and it's our luck that somehow its aromas have unlocked it." Marina, always loving a good story, becomes enchanted as I speak. Before I go on, I offer a toast to newfound journeys and kindred spirits. Lifting our glasses graciously to our lips, we sip on this glorious euphonium of rich melodious flavors. The cacophony of flavors is everything I describe, and she is enthralled, making expressions of devastated joy for this unique experience, whilst I speak further. "Dupuy would have not even existed had it not been for Thomas Bache-Gabrielsen from Norway. One day without warning he came to France and fell in love with a beautiful French woman far from his home." We both look into each other's eyes very closely, drifting into the story of Thomas and Miss Odette in the early 1900s in the city of Cognac, France where they both met so long ago. Marina and I feel us slipping back in time, transforming our likeness into the likeness of two burgeoning lovers found on a vineyard among the hillsides of Cognac.

* * *

A handsomely clad Lieutenant left the army to travel the countryside of Cognac, in search of land to grow grapes. His family's business was making spirits and it was his turn to make them proud by taking this adventure into the heartland of grapes in Cognac, France. He had already earned the rank of Lieutenant in the Norwegian army for his Majesty Oscar II to represent his country in the Boer Wars. Now, after surviving that shameful travesty of humanity, it was time to return to the world and nature where his boyish heart still fondly resided. It's hard for a young man to wipe off the spoils of war, human carnage, and senselessness that are made for reasons only politicians really understand. Love seems to be the only cure, if it has enough strength to penetrate the scar tissues of what those young boys experience in battle. The mysterious power of love captivates our afflictions in ways that change the course of history. Some changes in big ways, and some changes in small but mighty ways. They can turn into healing ways, compassionate actions soothing those boyish truths of heartache and things known to be disparaging.

His transformation turned him into an explorer, surveying for rich dark soil in land never seen before in his own country of imminent cold. Here, rolling hills are like poetry, the land alive robustly with a joy that sings to heaven, friendly clouds and mist caress every appendage bursting from its earthy loins. From out of nowhere, rising from this land's bosom, a beautiful French woman's sun-etched silhouette shines against a backdrop of vineyard rows and hillsides. She emerges into full sight, her dress of rich silk georgettes, embroidered organdies, giving her the appearance of a deity manifesting into the garden abundance of this natural world. She is an angel waltzing her way in elegant timelessness, leaving an indelible memory that will remain in my heart forever.

Stunned, I begin to speak without the proper etiquette, "Mademoiselle, why are you about this country side today? Can I assist you?"

She coyly looks down at the ground for a moment while I come into her focus. The sun is glaring and washing out my form in its brilliance, much like hers to my eyes.

With all my poise I introduce myself, "My name is Thomas Bache-Gabrielsen, I am from Norway and if I may be so bold to ask of yours humbly, Mademoiselle?"

This beautiful maiden then looks up to address me a bit more sternly, "I am Mademoiselle Odette Villard and this is my father's land, monsieur. Why are you here?"

Just then, her father Martial Villard comes walking up and grabs his daughter's shoulder, gently puts her behind him and calmly says. "Yes, please answer my daughter's question sir."

"Pardon me sir, for being so forward with Mademoiselle Odette Villard, I was not sure if she was in need of assistance as there is not much in sight here." I quickly speak to Monsieur Villard nervously.

"Ah, Norwegian monsieur, I am Avocat Monsieur Martial Villard and these are our families lands and vineyards, and your answer?"

"Of course Monsieur Villard, I have recently been made partner with Peter Anton Rustad, we are a trading company that bring spirits to Norwegians from Cognac," I reply.

"I see, Monsieur Bache-Gabrielsen, perhaps you would like to come up to the house and have dinner later to talk more about your venture." Odette's father, now smiling, turns towards his daughter, grabs her hand, and starts to lead her back to their home. Odette turns back to have another quick look at me standing there in complete shock, my young soul stricken in an instant by the affairs of the heart.

Night has fallen on this formidable little French village with

54

cobblestone streets that lead to a dirt road heading out into the open farms of this community. Thomas is now wearing his fine clothes, getting into the carriage that will bring him to the Villard's chateau on their vineyard just outside of Cognac. Thomas asks the driver if he knows much about the Villard's as they are in route to their château.

The carriage driver explains, "Monsieur Villard is considered one of the most formidable lawyers in all of Cognac. He has never lost a case monsieur."

Thomas asks further, "And what about his daughter?"

The driver sighs, "She is untouchable monsieur. You are best to leave your thoughts of her as there are more available catches back in town."

Thomas is set off a bit and quips, "But does she have suitors?"

"Monsieur, her father is well known in Cognac. Even though there is a shortage of men after the war, most suitors are apprehensive about the daughter of a famous lawyer," explains the driver. "Monsieur, you should think about this more clearly, it is not too late to turn back," added the driver.

"No, that is not my destiny today driver, please go forward to the Villard's château. I am resolved in my trust." Thomas concludes.

His driver looks back to his horses and smirks to himself. Unknown to Thomas, he does work for Monsieur Villard but is actually a relative.

The town of Cognac is a very small town like most around the world at this time in history. Thomas and his thoughts are already well known to its people, spreading like wildfire from others in the field earlier that day. Thomas exits his carriage and the driver takes his horses and carriage around to the back to wait for young Thomas to return. The driver joyfully enters the back kitchen for a little wine, food, and relaxation with his awaiting friends and other family members.

Thomas is greeted at the front door and enters. Their butler removes his coat and announces his arrival. Avocat Monsieur Martial Villard greets him with his wife Ernestine Fromentin Leopold Villard. Thomas makes his way to bow to them both. His wife smiles and leaves, and Monsieur Villard takes him into his study for a Cognac and a man-to-man chat. "Thomas, ah, may I call you Thomas?"

"Yes, of course you can Monsieur Villard, thank you. I am very nervous for some reason." Thomas says.

"Please call me Martial, as it seems we will be doing several types of business together, I'm predicting," insists Martial.

"Of what do you mean Martial?" asks Thomas.

"Well, my dear Thomas, while I am many things in this world, for instance a lawyer, a farmer, a husband and a father, I am also a man who has been in love," smiles Martial. "When we met earlier today, me being a rather keen observer, as I have been told by many of my acquaintances and friends, noticed a very familiar look on your face. Pardon me if I am completely wrong. Sometimes my wife will faithfully remind me that I have the capacity of being wrong without warning. However, this look on your face reminds me of a time not so long ago when I too also acquired such a look. It was the first time I saw my wife, hmm, also out on the landscape of life. So, my new friend, were my observations untrue or have you been stricken with the enchantments of my daughter?" Martial asks, quite fatherly.

Thomas, taken aback, thinking his face was not so telling, feels very awkward. He is in the study of a very predominate man and has no choice but to tell the truth to the father of the woman he barely knows but is in love with. Mustering up his courage, Thomas lets the words slip off his tongue, "Yes sir, I am in love with your daughter Odette, sir, I mean, Martial. I don't know how to explain this but I feel as if I have known her my whole life."

Martial has to turn his head a little bit because he is about to laugh, knowing the pain of explaining his feelings to the father of his own wife. "Dear Thomas, Leopold, my wife's father was a very stern man. To look at him you would have been shaking in your boots. I was ready to do whatever it took to sway him so I could win his daughter's hand in marriage. He did not move, or say a word, even after I spoke with him about my undying love. He simply got up after I had my say and walked into the other room to speak with his daughter. Afterwards, he returned and gave me his consent with only a nod of his eyes. And then he left the room. Ernestine rushed in to embrace me and gave me a quick peck on the cheek, then had to rush out when her father reentered. I was then shown the front door until the wedding day."

"I will tell you already, I have no idea what transpired out there in the field today with my daughter, she is also just as taken with you, dear Thomas. Oh yes, and let me share this with you. She told me something very curious, that she too felt like she has known you forever. Fascinating you barely spoke to each other. Now that that is out of the way, let's go eat something, everyone is waiting." Martial put his arm around Thomas after his fine speech and they walk out of the drawing room towards the dining table.

The ladies are sitting in their evening gowns, eagerly waiting, Odette's eyes tracking his every movement into the room with a blooming smile. The dining room is a very aesthetic affair with beautiful ornate candelabra and fine silverware on linen table clothes that must have been passed down through their family. It is an elegant night for all at the home of Avocat Monsieur Martial Villard, with the best delectable French food, rich and amply served, and delightful consumed.

After much polite conversations, and getting acquainted, Ernestine and Martial allowed Thomas and Odette to have a walk in the garden in the evening air. Thomas offers his arm to Odette and as they begin to walk, he realizes that she has never strolled before. He gently guides her to the smiles of her watchful parents in a swaying procession of young love. Then he asks her about who her favorite poet is and she replies quickly "Charles Baudelaire." He immediately starts to recite L'Aube spirituelle, or Spiritual Dawn.

"When in the company of the Ideal (that gnawing tooth), dawn enters, white and pink, the rooms of rakes — each sated beast can feel an angel waking through the fumes of drink."

Odette says the second line, "For downcast man, who dreams and suffers still, the azure of the mystic heaven above, with gulf-like vertigo, attracts his will. So, Goddess, lucid Being of pure love."

Walking now, almost like the procession of the equinox marching through heaven itself, they whisper under their breath together these poetic words of Charles Baudelaire. "Over the smoking wreck of feasts and scandals, your phantom, rosy and enchanting, flies and still returns to my dilated eyes. The sun has blackened out the flame of candles. So your victorious phantom seems as one, O blazing spirit, with the deathless Sun!"

There, that very day they first met, he got down on his knee in the moonlight of Cognac's rolling vineyards and professed his undying love to Odette Villard. From his knee on the ground at the end of his speech of marriage, he took her hand and gave it his humble kiss.

She took his hand and pulled him off his knee to her warm embrace to taste her awaiting reverent loving lips. With this single first kiss, their lives together go into hyper speed as if flicking through the Akashic records of time. Watching them getting married, making love, building a home, a business, while moving through pages of their timeline quite rapidly. Their children being born and getting older, graduating from college, working with their father in the business and moving on to their respective occupations, watching their family's wealth grow with more land and physical property, trucks, distilleries and people. As technology grows around them at a very rapid rate, they all move with its expansion, their family, their business, and their grandchildren.

* * *

Now growing distant, their voices begin to echo off into the past as we see the family crest and their vineyards' seal. We return to the drinks that have just been poured and put in front of us, staring into the deep golden liquid. Marina and I both return to our bodies and I am still telling the story to Marina who seems as if she too was very far away, back in the early 1900s. I further explain that while this might seem like a whirlwind engagement, it has proved through time to be anything but. They had three boys, all professionals: a lawyer, a doctor, and a chemist, very much to be proud of. Thomas lived from 1883 to 1942 and his loving wife Odette Villard from 1885 to an astonishing 1975. Their monumental love still flourishes today through their company, their beloved family, and this well-crafted love of Cognac.

We both then take a sip of this very sensual and romantic Cognac, whose favors devolve into the pallet of our taste buds. They also drift along with the pallets of our imaginations so well in this love story with a happy ending. The mood of the moment has shifted as we both begin to realize that there is more to our chance meeting than we imagined, and our cautions seem to be lifting just a bit. Harsh are the realities of relationships in these times of economic and political uncertainty. Couples have to make tough choices, and having a family in these times comes with great trepidations. It makes one think carefully before one can make any commitments to couple at all, as the weight of these times are certainly very heavy.

She asks me in a faraway voice, as if still looking through eons, as an angel querying humanity, "What does a kiss mean to you?"

"A kiss is the language of the universe, it never lies, its truths are certain and its willfulness is way beyond the petty lives of mere mortals." I quickly exclaim to her deaf ears because she knows my answer.

"Yes!" she quips, "A piety, a reverence, a solace, a defining movement between heaven and earth simply more precious than anything, don't you think?"

I nod my head reverently with all my tender kindnesses to assure her that I would never take such an action trivially.

I thought a lot through those words; in thankfulness that somebody else understood that a kiss is the beginning of our dance amongst the stars. There is nothing more clearly spoken with our tongues when two people reach out with their hearts and souls. She looked away as if to gather herself back to Earth and took another sip of Thomas and Odette's delicious elixir. A love like that must be inscribed in those Akashic records for only deserving souls to read, she decided. My daunting seeking heart, I have somehow forsaken from my pain of unrequited love. I have shed these flights of fancy in order to pursue and nurture my creative gifts. While I had always hoped that a day would come when I, we, would connect with true love, I had no idea it would simply come for me. I know we have all walked down that path searching for love. Marina is struggling with something she knows is not true; can our love be possible?

She laments, "In mouths and lips touching, who in mankind's history has decided the meaning of a kiss? As if this mundane contact should have such significance. If only life's rewards could be measured so plainly in one's genuine self, marred as frivolous between lips such as ours. Betraying lips, they play games of authenticity; define nothing, as if intimacy could ever be savored in a kiss. What world has had its axis shifted in the culminations of fanciful fairytales, transforming souls or fates, by a mere reflection mirrored back at you when lips touch? What commitment is punctuated or purchased in a kiss?" She smirked and continued, "I have not been convinced I would lose anything, let alone my soul to a man inside a kiss. Betrayed, terrified, I vividly recall a broken marriage where my heartbeats were never inspired or obsessed with the very intimate act to the point of abandon," she mournfully spoke. Yet, she thought to herself that she wanted a kiss from me and it shone in her eyes. Relevant, as truth has stung so many times along these consequences, filled with shame and guilt, no truth is returned, I simply imagined. In her unconscious longing she was afraid life would be deceiving her again. She was unsure of her own choices. Yet a kiss could make her believe in love, one of wanting, whose cravings could never be quenched.

Abruptly she professed, "What makes a relationship romantic is its unlikelihood, its fragility, the knowledge that by a few seconds or feet you might have never met that person. As the relationship unravels, you lose all these elements; the bond you have built becomes a certainty, a haven of stability and placidity. Security becomes well anchored in time and space, nothing is tainted by everyday trivialities, and romance goes when the sense of danger disappears. True love can and will last, but what of romance? Does it always have an expiration date? Why then does everyone think that everything is okay when it's just not? Being friends is the most important thing as a prelude to romance, and after all we have just met really. Doesn't it seem that way to you?"

I mention to her, "This is all true, but there is something very familiar about our contact."

She cuts me off and says, "Romance heightens, sexualizes,

61

defies, iconizes. Someone who is genuine and has truly delved into the nature of their condition knows that in order to be loved they should be loved as a human first, not a deity. Friendship acknowledges, accepts and supports. Friendship sees the dark side and embraces it. Friendship can endure because it is cautious, benevolent, and selfless. Once you have that bond you can remember the romance fondly together and that's even better."

I consoled her thoughts with, "How could your fragile humanness not be a deity to me? You could have not said it any better and it is all certainly true. However, don't you think that romance can be measured in the willingness of two people wanting to know each other exclusively in every way possible?"

Marina glowed like a beacon. I felt the heat of her underlying rays penetrating through me to see if there was a chill or shadow in my heart. She could not help her nervousness, her own revelations that could no longer be hidden. It now appeared that contact was possible. She understood our chance meeting was more than the apparent. She was ready to walk into sin, to lunge herself into an unprotected journey and embrace forever. I dared lift my head towards hers and both our erratic hearts started to melt. How does she escape this feeling crossed her mind momentarily. Was her feeling of guilt unacceptable? I began encouraging her heart purposely, dragging her gaze towards my eyes, disarming her fears for our impassioned duet. I commence to stroke her hand and assure her I was no threat.

I wasn't there to take her lofty gifts away. I was there to protect them with all my being. I was her eager audience whose goal was simply to believe in her. Unexpectedly, for both of us, we could not ignore our kind, loving, provocative gestures that disarmed any doubt. I told her, "I feel your character."

Of which she replied, keening, "I feel yours too."

For the first time I was starting to feel conciliated by honest actions and our walls came tumbling down for a moment.

She then let out, "Crazy isn't it, these theories we make about mismatched eyes, or convoluted words, rhetoric because we are fixated on meaning".

"Yes." I said, "Some things aren't meant to be figured out, are they?" I was now becoming fixated on her lips, as her surrender became more telling. I knew the truth was now lingering in our pauses of introspection. I could hear under her breath, "I want to believe him." I knew this was a struggle with absurdity and doubting her instincts because they have led her astray before. I was not one of the countless men who attempted to approach her with only the veneer in mind. I can understand the discussion women must have, having heard the same stories so many times about who they are, what they have, and what they can do for them. I had none of that, in fact, I was not a rich man by any means. I was just a soul put on this Earth to do my best with the little means I've acquired. When that day comes and my soul passes, knowing I've helped just one other soul along this journey of self-discovery, I will rest in peace. We are all disappointed in things we think we need to be happy in this life. What really needs to be considered in our time here is what are truly the happy moments of our life. Every time I think about it, it's never about things. It is always about the love I shared with someone who loved me back.

I advanced closer to her and she did not move away, I became reluctant to speak further from my heart to hers. I could tell she was in the process of letting doubts waver in between, thinking, "I need more proof of your intentions and to know without question those lips are honorable." I would give her no reason to be adamant that my kiss could ever be a lie. Ah, the sacrifices we make for love as risky as it can be wasn't frivolous to me. The terms of our agreement are written in the fabric that illuminates our very souls as real or fraudulent, and I could never live with myself as a fraud. Honestly, I thought to myself, there would never be a moment where your heart would falter to think, why did I kiss you? This flashed from my eyes as we now begin to read each other telepathically.

Prodigious skills impulsively began our adamant delving through deceit and confusion to discover truth in a kiss. Uncertainty began to dissolve and there was no need to be convinced about anything. Our collective nuances were instantly interpreted. As I touched her hand softly, I asked her, "Have you felt the truth now?"

She didn't need to answer, I moved past the horizon towards her neckline. She shivered slightly as my lips met her sweet skin in an electric point of contact. Slowly I moved up her responding body despite both our underlying trepidations, kissing each inch leading to her ear. Her un-resistant vulnerability was now mine to protect. I moved back to steady our gaze into each other's hearts. I whispered without sounds, penetrating what was once an intrusive barrier, freeing past scars one by one.

She sighs, "Is it you my love?" to my surprise and I almost evanesced and said, "Yes my love, it is me."

For the first time, we met with our lips, timidly, remembering past meetings of our lips.

These gestures of tenderness progressed until our wills shuddered, speaking increasingly with our hearts meant for love. This was the consummate moment to seal the vows we had made, beyond the edge of our perceptions of this facade of flesh, as we lifted up our masks. We both read every breath, every increment of our matching coupling; clandestinely revealing ourselves to each other, kiss after kiss. Our adorations became exhilarating, repairing our damaged wills, pressing our cheeks against each other's wet tears in between our now passionate kisses. She felt love in every single delicate pledge we both answered, in each other's intimacy, of our first well-tasted kiss that became transcendental.

In this ephemeral transcendence, a soothing AUM basked along our cooing absolutions, wavering like an ancient gong awakening awareness to oscillate. The rinsing primal tones of Ham and Kham of the sixth chakra washed over our third eye in shimmering indigo lightning bolts. Visualization spawned from our past life encounter, keys the fourth chakra's emerald awakening while our kiss now unlocks a flaming violet seal centered in our adjoining radionics fields. Breathing easily in our auric sunrise, this mere dot of the deepest of violet orbs was where multidimensional communion opens ventricles to secrets inside our joining pineal glands. We have been christened along our stroll, along the rainbow bridge, walking along our final path with eyes wide open. This is a spiritual dialogue we cannot hear, but hear so clearly; cannot see but is seen in every detail, felt as though it was always felt, and realized in our eternal memory. Each seal becomes undone so our narrative can unfold within its glistening jewels, revealing facets lit from a hidden unknown source of pure consciousness effortlessly.

These are the vows we made in our pact to stay alive on this planet. Trauma befalls us all in our quest to make promises of devotion. No one goes unscathed in these messy attempts to seek a certain love that can be decided in an instant, in a dare to pass the threshold of one's unknown space. Bravery cannot be trivialized, nor a kiss in earnest, but a delicate timing must consist of pedestals and urges to reveal beyond the mask of our inhibitions. A beaming sun peeks through our eyes, with heartfelt fairytales images of our true personas, longing with stares and adventures for love's sake. There's no explanation, no excuses, only one chance to imprint that can't be malformed, misinformed, or misinterpreted, as these chances do not grow on trees and this pact is most fragile.

Relief comes in a sob of emotions of our revelations, of

extraordinary contact at our fingertips, warming our contentment to intertwine. We both unselfishly, slowly, release from our astonishing first contact, a residue of electrical impulses still transferring as we both emotionally settle back to Earth in this magic little bar named The Rainbow. Hardly being able to speak, reeling from shock waves of energy, we both feel dizzy, out of sorts, attempting to revive our rhythms and return to our perspective timelines aimlessly.

There was no way our spirits could separate now that they had imprinted again. Past memories of other incarnations started to return. Overwhelmed, we both were physically shaking. It seemed this night had gone by so quickly. Only our smiling love reminded us of our sweet compassion for each other's duties to the world. Our kind bartender, looking at us both with tears in her eyes, in amazement, says to us with all sincerity, "That is the most beautiful moment of love I have ever seen! Thank you both so much! I have new hope that love is still possible in my life."

Trembling, we get up, and head to our cars almost like marionettes going through the motions, actors on this grand stage of life. We glide by Tony and lots of other people who were reacting to our beaming light, all in amazement at our obvious glow. Exiting the door, we reach valet parking, give them our tickets with the reality setting in that our cars will soon be ready and we'll be parting again. I now understand what Shakespeare meant when he said, "Parting is such sweet sorrow."

Her car came up first and I grabbed both of her hands and asked her "When will I see you again?"

She looked at me with a smile and said, "Very soon."

We're all vehicles made of dust, animated by ghost and phantom, shadows of consciousness, traversing a flicker of light called a lifetime. Omnipotence rustles at our center, tied to a narrative, a repeating artifact heralding sublime creation eternal. Truly, a voice resonating from the deepest well of our collective soul whose atonement is sought from its cool, fresh, pure waters. Illusive as the instant these behemoth dark energies' first kissed and made this universe, its undying query about what love means began all our lives journey. It's through only a complete understanding of that kiss that they can finish their quest of division, unity. It has been an impossible premise, like a needle in a haystack, sifting through everything in desperation. Leaving no stone unturned in search of a recognized synchronicity in an unparalleled delve to the meaning of existence, period. Added to this conundrum, sentient life remains primarily unconscious of its merging through our anatomic nervous systems where consciousness seeks to find the end of their story. In a unique awakened state, true understanding is that superfluous enigma where an ingénue's illumination suddenly lights up all areas of human endearment. With her single lamp, a beacon for masculine energy, her able hand guides this awakened resolve to man's rightful destination by her side, home at last.

Painfully, we watch each other go our separate ways through surreal pages of worldliness. These are our appointments with a preconceived destiny called fate. These flailing pages, un-winding, traversing, mere illusions of duty, the only duty to life on this planet is to give and receive love. Marina and I have been changed forever from what some would call an accidental meeting in Santa Monica. When you view our indestructible souls traversing through spans of untold millenniums of time and space, you begin to fathom just how important that kiss is. The language of kisses created these prevailing zephyr winds, caressing my bolstered sails, taking me to my real unscathed serendipity to collide with fate. Many lofty adventures await conclusions behind the narrator's seals. They unlock stories of uniting forgotten ages, missed opportunities, discovery, and enlightenment that are all awaiting revelation by awakened hearts. There is no more, "Could she be or could I be," when both our ringing ears sing like a bell in a very clear reminder that this is not a dream. Those cosmic forged seals melt, ignited in the primordial cauldron, cradled in a desert crucible, sparked by the nuances of reunited love.

It's more like a transmission that perhaps we all receive, but decoding it, for us, is no longer an option. With a smile on my face, I do wonder what thoughts are going through her mind right now. A big key has turned, what is being unlocked feels earth shaking, but could it be marginalized? These are the haunting thoughts of past exploits tugging at my heart. I was sure that I might be in the presence of the, "One," to my own demise. I needed to let go of this. Marina certainly had taken a huge risk in believing that our first kiss was even possible. For conscious women, taking a risk doesn't come easily. Aware of times fleeting moments of opportunity, when it has passed them, it is possible that it will never be regained. I mourn with compassion at these ideas that her tender heart must contemplate, that risk once taken, can never be changed in our dissolving moment called a lifetime.

We are all looking for signs, some assurance that somehow our cosmologies are surveying our dominion with clarity. That somehow we know beyond a shadow of a doubt that this must certainly be reality. We must be in love because love is like this and that, and there it is, just as it was imagined, completely as I saw it to begin with, I'm sure. Unfortunately, this is not our lot, as we can barely grasp who we are and why we even have a consciousness in the first place. There is no trust really, no faith, no one story where two lovers meet fall in love and live happily ever after. Regrettably apparent in so many stories, is that this type of love is transitory with so many obstacles to a timely coupling. Maintenance of romantic love is barely accomplishable because of overwhelming worldliness demanding we pay attention to money's river. But there are those collective experiences by some that keeps us continuing to look undauntedly, always seeking a purposeful life of love. Never to give up with the setting sun, knowing a new dawn with impossibilities of unmanageable reasons will come, like this night of a perfect kiss.

I arrive at my best friend Bob's place in North Hollywood and he and his two pets are all asleep, so, quietly, I use my key to enter. As I gently open the door I find two dogs running up to me in the dark, wagging their tails and barking. His big, black Labrador, Woofer, who makes his big announcing bark, wagging his tail and looking for a toy. The other dog, a little Deer Chihuahua, Tweeter, barks with a high pitch whining sounds, alarming the night that I am here.

Bob wakes up for a moment as I settle the dogs he asks, "Is that you?"

I whisper, "Yes it's me."

Bob says, "Good, glad you're here safe. I'm going back to sleep, could you walk the dogs in the morning?"

I whisper back, "Yes."

Bob laughs and starts to whisper too, "Let's talk in the morning."

The dogs return to his room and I collect my rampant thoughts. What will happen next, will she see me again, when can I see her, should I text her, will she be asleep already, is she home safe? And then I think to myself, "Stop overthinking this, just let it go." I know better; our night together gave me a lot to process and my mind sometimes races.

I find my way in the dark to a guest room, lie down and stare at the ceiling pondering all these events, filing them away one by one. I've struggled with failure to bring my lifetime into perspective from the ravages of time's crossroads of either deliverance or destruction. I have never been more ready to open up my belief that this short life of mine is not over. To fulfill my heart's desire with unfathomable love is possible, the how part has just always alluded me. Expression of consciousness opened these mythic seals to some new expanse, but is my beloved's fate still sealed? If indeed this paradigm shift in our collective timeline has unlock this miracle more doorways to our timeless understanding will open.

Drifting off to sleep I mumble, "My true love, have we found each other?" I want to tell her how much I know her, but for now it's time we both digest.

Then I get a text, "I'm home safe. Thanks for a great evening. Goodnight." I let out a sigh answer back "thx" and quickly fall asleep.

In the morning, Bob and I enjoy his always-perfect coffee and talk about what happened last night with Marina. "Well," he says, "I haven't seen you this way in a long time and I have to tell you I'm glad to see you're alive again."

"I understand the philosophy of our connection but I'm in it, and I, as you know, am my worst enemy," I say candidly.

"You can't blow it if it's meant to be. You know, I've seen you in and out of many relationships over the years. Giving love is not your problem, getting love back is the missing trick." Bob gives me a smile while talking to me. "Really, just do what you do best and let go. If it is meant to be, it will happen. I know, I know, you've been waiting for a long time." He starts laughing. "We all want this, I want this too, but you have to be open so the love you want can find a place to grow." I smile and let out a deep exhale, otherwise known as a sigh.

Bob has always been there for me throughout the years, giving me advice and helping me along my spiritual path. I have always been there for him too on this rocky path called life we both tread. We both have been listening closely to the murmurs of the universe talking to us, guiding us to our destinies, and reminding each other of the signposts. The mundane reality of humanity is never too far away with taxes coming due and, of course, bills. Bob and I are very sensitive to the human condition. We have always been advocates for what is right. Money is now what makes this planet go around for humanity, not merit, or the labors of tending to its land. All of that is corporate now; even the good air has a price tag on it. At the end of the day we would both be on the front lines for what is right, side-by-side, and ready to do whatever it takes to bring goodness into this world. We have been there during our love connections and our breakups, consoling and rooting for the best outcomes. Who knows how many lifetimes we have been by each other's sides, watching each other's back, to make sure our spiritual sojourn is fulfilling.

That's what this experience is we keep rehashing. In many ways, the people we meet, the people we love, have all come with reasons. Sometimes we don't see these reasons, but they are there in this Tantric wave of energy and mass tied together by infinite connections on the roadmap of fate. All their faces keep coming back, lifetime after lifetime, through a nebulae stellar nursery of galaxies, quasars, and black holes, creating new playgrounds to solve a mystery. We may come in as many configurations as possibilities, switching roles until we discover what it all means and what the purpose of our existence is. There will be signs, you will recognize them in some insignificant way, but if your awareness comprehends the dots, they will all be connected. There are many realizations yet to happen, with each one taking millions of beings, millions of lifetimes to make your moment in the sun possible at all.

Romance

Spontaneously wagered zeal fervently surged in sex appeal
Adonis ardor adorn in decorum swooning raptures in love's romantic forum

Romance is not a means to an end; it's a vehicle bridging ideals for two people cherishing each other to come together in sacred reverence. Romance, according to Webster's Dictionary, is a feeling of excitement and mystery associated with love's sentimental or idealized aspects. Similar to my view, but I think it misses its truer essence, as romance is a place to celebrate the divinity that dwells inside of each of us. The Thai language has a very charming gesture/word that is literally translated in English to hello, welcome, or goodbye. First, you put your hands in the Namaskar Mudra (gesture) and say Sawadee krap/ka (if female) and ever so slightly bow to honor the Buddha inside of the person you're greeting.

Translated to me by a dear friend, Adume, who was born in this magnificent bastion of Buddhism, Thailand. Real romance is when all our senses are impressed with the sublime beauty of a soul that touches our inner beings in its deepest way. Even though we are told many things about romance, moneymakers have found ways to sell it, to capitalize on it; innately we all sense the truth.

Romance itself, while we embrace it on the big screen or in books, has become a lost art in our modern society, especially the essential application of it. For Marina and I, it started with the anatomy of a kiss unlocking buried treasure whose riches are yet to be discovered. Our unearthing is the next natural evolution of this timeless process of actualizing this sacred reunion. Deciphering information written on every unfurling lotus petal inside our spiritual centers provides riches and substance. Romance has been fashioned into many things, yet it's our underlying guide, our beacon for all those who contemplate love. A temple of compartmentalized dimensions, filled with existential gifts, revealing more doorways that can only be opened with our sacred keys. Romance's source fueled in complex currents of directed life force penetrating every causal body's membranes, igniting our spiritual axis lines, resonating them with love. These are the mechanics of romance that purposefully strike our awareness like a lightning bolt. We can succumb and be destroyed by its influences, or ignite and be electrified by its profound meaning. These are the far-reaching pings exponentially carried in their message of unfathomable love for those who are worthy and can hear them. Worthiness is something that can only be recognized by one's ability to grasp the innate concept of romance that simply adds clarity to its original internal imprint.

When we can say and do things outside our normal day-to-day life, be better people than we are, treat those we love with love and dignity, and be mindful about its fragility, that is true romance to me. I understand that Webster's dictionary says, "A feeling of excitement and mystery associated with love" but that excitement never ends inside our compassion for cajoling souls. History tells us that romanticism is a relatively new thing in Western European culture; it didn't really start until the 12th century. It seems this age of heroic romantic love was considered a sign of weakness and the preoccupation of men without character. Well then, I am certainly that man without character. Being a creative person, the understanding of the 'creative process,' I could never imagine my life without the pursuit of romance. I have spoken with scholars that romance has indeed been the guiding light and secret of man from the dawn of humankind. A clear discussion of romance has never really made its way past the surface of public discourse, other than paying hollow tribute every Valentine's Day. It's time to put all the cards on the table and really examine what romance as a concept really means, if men are to understand its emanations.

There is bountiful amount of evidence of the existence of romance throughout all recorded history, testaments to its enduring nature. I have no excuses for inferior men who eventually will be excused from the gene pool due to their lack of gentlemanly ways and forthright presentation of self. As for myself, I have stumbled many times, realized that time is not just a caution, it is a reality that deliverance may or may not be yours. Wooing is an art, no different than learning to dance or play an instrument, needing great research and practice to articulate precise intentions. Being awkward has its place in the learning experience, but when approaching the altar of your convictions, there is no turning back in defining exactly what your character is. The school of hard knocks will eventually bring you to the realization that being unskilled will reward you with even less skills. Empty, hollow experiences will leave you empty and hollow without a precious reason to exist at all. Remember, we all must come away with what we seek. Women have a clearer understanding of what heroic honor is and its appearance. When a woman allows a man to touch her, I mean not in a sexual way, to just broach past her guarded veneer into her circle of confidante, it is a very huge step. This is a great trust she affords us, a kindness settled in understanding that mostly goes unspoken unless it is damaged. Feeling her wisdom, hearing her otherwise inexpressible ideas infused with the closeness of touch, is privilege of insurmountable benediction. It's a gift to be in the presence of a promise kept, manifests of splendor, rendezvous to true fulfillment of a perfect dream conjured by love.

How many poets have dedicated their lives to the enunciations of love's articulation or artist or musicians in our history? Prose on virtues of love has been laced through many philosophical themes of eloquent discourse over this very millennium. Eagerly, our extraordinary higher selves thirst for and seek out these references to affirm our own resolve that love can be romantic. I look for a time when young men will stand up in life to make speeches in honor of love. Someday it won't be controversial but a requirement for every right of passage, from boy to man, to profess their knowledge of life's perfect subject. As to what bravery has a man to sing, dance, and praise something whose value cannot be measured by a price tag, I can think of nothing better. These concepts, ideals of love he surrounds himself with, will be his real profit to protect, with all his character. Cowards are those that dishonor love in any respect, to disregard those beloved eyes and purity of words exchanged would eventually be known as your biggest disgrace. Sadly there is no place to get education in these views and perhaps the most important subject of all our lives. Education as we know it is designed to create workers and not for the balance of a soul or lasting relationships or even the dynamics of love.

The father of natural order, Socrates, who once spoke of concepts of a dynamic universe and of noble principles once said, "Wars, factions, and fighting," as he looked forward from his last hour, "have no other origin than this same body and its lusts. ... We must set the soul free from it; we must behold things as they are. And having thus got rid of the foolishness of the body, we shall be pure and hold converse with the pure, and shall in our own selves have complete knowledge of the Incorruptible which is, I take it, no other than the very truth." Modern education is barely capable of helping any being navigate the tribulations of current life in this world, let alone the tenderness of love's precious gifts. Without education, we are reduced to trial and error whose outcomes are mostly failure in this era. It is even said that 'one must always fall before one learns to ride a bike.' Not that I am saying love is like riding a bike, but if you have no idea about the mechanism, it is very difficult to launch yourself in space. Unfortunate that the one thing we cannot hold onto 'Time' is slipping away like a thief in the night. It robs us of valuable moments where true love can be developed and embraced by the body, mind, and soul.

The allegory of love should be never ending. Love should be traceable through everything we do with our inventive spirit to capture the romantic troubadour speaking in our smiles. This is the phenomenon of humanity, an instinct, and a natural goal, to couple in spiritual ecstasy precipitated by romantic love. Our boundlessness soars as we escape from bodily limitations where mere flesh propels itself off the lofty perch of indignation. We gleefully land past our own limited fears into the fulfilling arms of our awaiting spiritual lover. Romantic love is a transfiguring force beyond ardent beatitude into a sphere of rarefied spiritual passion. These are the stories our forefathers wanted us to know, the collections of myths and heroic figures that always rescue the damsel in distress or is rescued by a compassionate goddess. But where is the tabernacle for love's contemplations, a sanctuary, or safe harbor for romance to be openly discussed? Romance's evolution can only happen in a shared chivalry spread out on a table for all to see. We must have new myths, new fairytales emerging in our culture, that guide young men's hearts and encourages the compassion of young women. I want to believe that love will always find a way; that young men's hearts will not have to see young women broken hearted. Disparagingly, I am a dreamer but perhaps I am not the only one. It seems we have an enduring history of dreamers that continue to be the glue that binds our lonely hearts in fairytales and ideas of true romance.

Make Love

Hypnotic gaze grazing rays honeycombs of perfected tones.
Between the edges of known and unknown love begins its journey home.

Recently I have been researching about the Brothers Grimm. These great philologist/storytellers/researchers had incredible imaginations and love for old fables and tales, having written 210 tales that have endured for over 200 years. Their collection of fairytales delves in mythology that translates into bravery, love and the exaltation of the human spirit. The life of Wilhelm Carl Grimm interested me most. His life, a correlation to my own, focused on his love of poetry and the written word. He was an expert philologist and had four children with his wife Henriette Dorothea Wild. His wife had a very unique love of words also and Wilhelm loved teaching her everything he could about language. Dorothea grew up reading and hearing folk tales about heroic romance between men and women with happy endings. There is not much known about what happened in her life, but the man she chose was marked as extraordinary. It seemed intriguing to me what doors open with the right words and their innate meaning that resonates so deeply inside us all.

We have all walked through many doors, carried many tokens in our electrons' halo in what seems to be us through one lifetime to the next. Our continued tumbling throughout the illusion of time, collecting particles of matter, only to return them back to the primal dust again and again. Who knows where our souls have been or where they go when they depart, if anywhere at all. Why we claim movement of anything is a conundrum to me; as much of a conundrum as electron's movements. Electrons, like consciousness, are not predictable and aren't really at any one place, at any one time. I have no idea how memories attach themselves to a holographic electron shard of some sort; energy and matter we are told can't be destroyed. How the mechanism of identity works is still a mystery. Yet, there seems to be limited evidence that these attached recollections could someday be in our empirical evaluations.

I wonder how the Dalai Lama feels with the burdens of his childhood experiences, with so many recognizing him as a timeless being. Except for a peculiar familiarity of people, places, and things, you would think that identity would have no interest in its previous incarnation. But here we are, intrigued with music not from our time, art from thousands of years ago, along with languages, mythology, ancient cultures, and love stories from other eras. The Brothers Grimm were quite aware of this back in the 1800s, with a common philosophy, a common thread, binding all readers together throughout time. These stories have been repeated over and over again as if to keep a deeper truth alive in the hearts of children and carried throughout their lifetime. They are gifted to other generations through the love of storytelling on a cold dark night, where mystery is blowing in stellar winds. Perhaps these stories are woven into our DNA. It seems so obvious by the artifacts we all gravitate to and stories we hold so dear. It's these artifacts, trappings, collections of art, literature, even fashion, that tip our hands as time travelers, drifting through time for seemingly no apparent reason. For instance, coincidentally, Marina is also a philologist and has a thorough understanding of the history of Grimm tales. I am a storyteller in search of fables, new words, and strange ideas making our chance meeting even more fascinating. Contacts, connections, people who are our loving friends, lovers, and family members; could they all be a part of our souls' journey down currents filled with time? History often repeats itself with other similar stories of heartache and unrequited love, rich fodder for writing, much like Wilhelm did. Is this where my narrative ends? I hope not, I always like a good happy ending.

The Brothers Grimm loved the German countryside; not only was it rich with black earth, it was filled with stories from its inhabitants. As brothers they had been getting up to dress, eat, play, and study all their lives together, always making their day a playful adventure. Their father, Philipp Wilhelm Grimm, a very well studied, religious lawyer made sure their adventures always included reading, writing and arithmetic. He was a very strong man and demanded his children be strong with moral fortitude. He is known for saying, "He cannot go wrong whose life is in the right." Life was precious to him and in those times infant mortality was high, having already lost three of his nine children. Philipp's own life came to an early end when his health was taken from him by another one of the world's major killers: pneumonia. After their father's untimely death, they went from riches to poverty and it was up to the brothers to keep their family solvent. So, with their father's strong values on education, they ventured out into the world together to find work to feed their loved ones. Without stipends that wealthier students benefited from, lower social status students couldn't continue in university study. This is where the classes were separated, excluded from any tuitional aid, but the Grimm Brothers managed to feed their family and pursue their studies with vigor. Their professors noticed their work ethic and got them placed in jobs that could further their studies, while making money at the same time. They were successful enough, even through turbulent times, when the world stage was changing around them rapidly. Napoleon Bonaparte was shaking the very foundation of aristocratic Europe, changing the borders between Germany and France. The brothers now found themselves in the employ of Napoleon's younger brother Jerome, who was on the throne of Westphalia, including their homeland of Hesse.

The new king and queen of Westphalia had a combined library of 12,000 books. No one was allowed to look at them unless they were librarians like the Grimm Brothers. France was ruling this part of Germany and wanted to repatriate its citizens allowing them to only speak and read in French. The Grimms felt it was very important to seek out those German stories from average citizens living in small farms and villages before they were lost to history. To the joy of the German people, they began to create an archive of folklore, preserving their heritage for all time. They went as far as interviewing criminals, craftsmen, servants, even soliciting friends and family in search of the next great story. They didn't dress these stories up either; they wanted to keep the style and language of ordinary people. Hearing these people tell their passed down stories was like being at a campfire, where good stories had been told for centuries. Some of these stories were too scary for children, although children wanted to hear them. Later, they became some of the most popular stories for children. Needless to say, they became the best storytellers and everyone wanted to know them and read their works.

But before all of this, Jacob had to help his mother raise five siblings with his brother Wilhelm. They were real compatriots, but his younger brother had severe problems of his own. He was not very physically strong and suffered from asthma. So Jacob had to be the strong one, doing most of the major chores. Wilhelm did the head work, also organizing his younger brothers and sisters. Their mother did the best she could to bring money in and keep food in their bellies. Medicine was a huge expense, but she needed medicine for Wilhelm's illness. So she did odd jobs for a local pharmacist, cleaning clothes and housework for his wife. Wilhelm would come along and play with or watch the pharmacist's little girl.

Her name was Henriette Dorothea Wild and they lived in the little hamlet of Kassel. All families were big back then as more hands meant more work getting done, more relatives and contacts for future livelihoods to flourish when they married. Dortchen, Dorothea's nickname, was a very inquisitive little girl. Little Wilhelm liked to talk about anything. She was his first audience, and as her brothers and sisters got older, they also sat side by side, listening to Wilhelm's little stories. Dortchen's father was always delighted to have Wilhelm come with his mother. It seems Dortchen's father and entire family were also good storytellers and he would later in life share many stories with Wilhelm. Her father was always looking out for Wilhelm too, attempting to find ways to ease his distress and help him with his health. It was a sad day when Wilhelm left for college with his big brother Jacob, but Wilhelm would keep coming back to say hello and visit Dortchen's family from time to time.

Wilhelm begins his study of law at the University of Marburg with his brother, both struggling to keep their school paid for and send money back to their widowed mother. They both lived in the library, a second home, and their meager beds were only meant for sleeping. There was simply too much to learn and these young men had a lively brotherly competition to see who could learn the most. Surrounded by books about law, Jacob came over with a book of poems from Clemens Brentano and gingerly placed it in front of Wilhelm. Looking up at his brother, Wilhelm said, "Is it really that obvious brother?"

Smiling, Jacob told him, "Yes brother, it is that obvious. Do you want to talk about it some?"

"I just can't get her out of my head and I really don't have any experience with these feelings. We have such a huge responsibility to our family. I just have no time for this, I fear. "

"Well, brother," Jacob says, "I haven't seen you this way before, but I understand what it means and I am glad to see you like this."

"I understand the philosophy of our connection but my emotions are so overwhelming," Wilhelm said candidly.

"Willy, you can't harm something like this if it is meant to be. She will be waiting for you and have compassion for your responsibilities. Write something for her." His brother was right, he needed a way to let her know his feelings for her. Willy knew the only way to touch her heart was to write the kind of stories they once shared as children.

Years were moving by swiftly and Willy and Jacob were gaining recognition for their work and scholarly prowess. Those in scholastic positions at the university including their mentor, Friedrich Carl von Savigny, were pulling for them. They would not abandon their trust spending long hours working and organizing the university's library. Reading was both of their passion and after the work they would read as much as they could until the very little sleep they took put them to rest. One afternoon at work in the University library, they received an urgent letter to return to Eisenach; their mother had suddenly died. They both realized that when they returned home, they could no longer stay at the university and care for their family. Fortunately, Jacob was offered a position with Napoléon's brother, Jérôme Napoléon Bonaparte. After a war with Germany, Napoléon made his brother king of Westphalia, rule the surrounding German towns from the capitol city of Kassel. He brought his library of 12,000 books with him and needed the exclusive talents of Jacob. Soon afterwards, they both became his librarians. His queen, Catharina Frederica of Württemberg, was born of royal blood in Saint Petersburg. Through her father, she was married to Jérôme to form an alliance between Prussia and France. She loved books and had read many in their collective collections. Many times late at night she would sneak down into the library to have the brothers find a book to set by her bed.

The Brothers Grimm were both sorting out books late at night and noticed the queen had come into the room unannounced. Willy looked over at Jacob and gave him the eye. He knew right away and they both bowed and said, "Welcome your majesty, how may we serve you?"

H.R.H Catharina was very kind to us and said she had merely come for a book by Ludwig Achim von Arnim, "The Boy's Magic Horn," to read before bed. Willy smiled a bit, bowed and said, "Of course your Majesty, I know exactly where it is. It will only take a moment."

She asked him, "And why do you smile like that, royal librarian?"

Willy couldn't resist telling her the truth and spoke plainly, "Your royal highness, this is a very charming romantic folk story and he is a writer I so admire."

"So you know he is a descendent of royal Prussian blood, my dear librarian?" Her Royal Highness queried.

Willy found her book and brought it to her post haste. Just in time, for the king approached suddenly. His footman came into the library to announce the king of Württemberg. "My Queen, why have you come to the library at this hour?" His Royal Highness asked.

"I have come for a book to help me sleep, my king." She sweetly spoke.

"My queen, what book have you chosen?"

"It is a sweet book of folk stories and poems."

"What French poet are you reading tonight, my dear queen?"

"Oh yes, my king. Librarian, can you please get me another book?" she said coyly.

"Yes of course I can, your royal highness," Willy said quickly, while acknowledging and bowing to the king.

"Please get my queen Cyrus, written by the Frenchman de Chénier."

"Immediately, your royal highness..." Before Willy could finish his sentence, his brother handed him the book. The king had put an end to the German language under his realm; only French could be spoken. So we all spoke French and books in German were banned, except in this library where all the books were brought to them by order of the king.

The queen left them with the king. The king wanted to have a chat with them before he took off for the night. "My dear librarians, I have known you since I was crowned, and I think I know you well. You have to stop helping people that can't help you. My queen is just using you to get to me because she knows I am leaving tonight. She is just looking to capture my attention by wandering off."

"My king, I know you're right, and we are always at your service. We shall keep your worthy words and help our queen find the best in French literature your amazing collection has to offer," Willy lamented.

"I am your king and I have brought you here because of my trust in you, but I'm here for you. I am glad you are staying with me at the court of Westphalia; it is the least I can do for all the help you have unselfishly given your king."

"It is an honor to be in your presence, your majesty," Willy gracefully submitted.

"Goodnight, my dear librarians, it is time to seek the nights pleasures." With those words, they knew right away it was up to them to compile and preserve all the German folk tales they could find. It was just a matter of time before their dear tradition of verbal and written history was washed away by a borderline.

Their first volume was Children and Household Tales, dedicated to Willy's passions for Dortchen. Jacob too was taken by Willy's love for her and helped him with great joy and relish. They found over eighty-six fairy tales, folklore, folktales, and mythology that they carefully translated. They also preserved the original intentions and German dialects of common mountain and village people. Willy was sure that Dortchen would understand his messages to her through these different stories compiled into the first book. Jacob looked down at Willy on the writing table and said, "Willy, we got a book here, a very fine book!"

"Jacob, what's the next step?" Willy said, noticing all the ink on his hands.

"Well, it's time to contact the queen and our mutual friend, Achim von Arnim, don't you think Willy?" Jacob said with a very broad smile. They were always a bit mischievous and both of them knew if the king caught wind of their meeting, they would be in serious trouble.

Achim von Arnim made a late night visit coming to them all the way from Berlin after reading about their need for his counsel, by virtue of a letter they sent. When he arrived, he immediately wanted to see the book. They showed it to him with great pride. They were all down in their workspace, working in the library, when the little bell rang curiously at this very late hour. It was the queen and they came out to their desk to see how they could serve her. She was again by herself, but still dressed in her proper gown. Knowing her fondness for Achim, Willy carefully introduced him. "Your royal highness, I would like to introduce a dear friend of mine and perhaps yours, Achim von Arnim."

Achim gracefully bowed to her, calling to her, "Your royal highness, and who I once remembered as princess Catharina Frederica of Württemberg, it is so good to see you again."

Her majesty was a bit shocked to see her old friend but cautioned him that the king is not a friend of his works.

He went up to the queen, kneeled down on one knee, took her right hand, and kissed it with great affection. "My allegiance is to our mother Prussia and to you princess of Württemberg. Thank you for loving my work, your kindness will always live with me." Achim stepped away while looking at the queen and asked Jacob to give him the book. The brothers were both in awe of the intense magic between these two royals, but now they could hear the king approaching with his entourage.

Achim takes the book and tells us while still looking into the face of the queen, "Publisher Georg Reimer from Berlin, will be contacting you through mail very soon. It is always good to see you, my dear friends of the cause. We are the awakening, the enlightenment, through the gentle joys of our transpiring humanity."

They could all hear the footsteps getting very close, but who would want to stop Achim from his parting soliloquy. He continued with, "Your majesty, thank you so much for your company and my dear friends, I bid you goodnight."

Just as he left the library, the king appeared, somewhat amused at his queen coming to the library in the middle of the night, saying, "My queen, here you are again? How do you explain this?"

"My king, suddenly my mind would not let me rest so I was inspired to seek a higher knowledge from Jean-Jacques Rousseau."

Jacob was minding her cue and was on his way to retrieve this gem of French literature.

"And what great works are you inspired to read this evening, my queen?"

"Just a simple play that he wrote for all of France called 'The Self Admirer.' Gratefully the king laughed and they went back to their work.

"In regards to Kinder und Hausmärchen (Children and Household Tales) from G. Reimer, we are so grateful to receive and publish your work and have the good fortune to inform you that your book is a huge success. You will shortly be receiving royalties sent by messenger to your home in Kassel. We at Reimer's Publishing are looking forward to volume two of Kinder und Hausmärchen with the seventy new stories attached to it. Warm regards, G. A. Reimer." This was very kind of him and the timing couldn't have been more perfect as their benefactor, Jérôme, rather, the king, after a failed attempt at the Russian front was now begging for him and his wife, the queen, to come to Paris. It seemed the Prussians no longer wanted to be allies after his attack on Russia and they retook and dissolved his kingdom.

All the hard work for years, sacrificing their lives for family and knowledge was paying off. Jacob and Will were also given honorary doctorates from the University of Marburg. Their joint scholarly work on linguistics, folklore, and medieval studies had given them many ideas about future publications. For now though, their thoughts were on only one thing and that was the beautiful Henriette Dorothea (Dortchen) Wild. Through all these accolades, she and her family were by Will's side, cheering the brothers on. They brought them stories, fed them and their siblings, took care of their mother, and silently watched over their lives.

Wilhelm, even though he sent her many letters, found he needed to see Dortchen now that they had an income. His brother Jacob rushed off to Paris to demand restitution of the books carried off by the French after Napoléon's brother Jérôme Napoléon Bonaparte lost the war with Prussia. Wilhelm wanted more time with Dortchen, and with the money coming in, he had a plan. First it was quality time with her in the quaint little town of Hannau, the home of his childhood. Dortchen had always caught his eye and now she had bloomed into a woman who had become a fine storyteller in her own right. It seemed Wilhelm had influenced Dortchen's whole family in the search for great stories and she had become a wizard at finding great tales to spin.

Now it was Wilhelm's turn to sit and listen, only he came prepared with ink and quill in order to not only hear her learned tales but to capture them for all time. Wilhelm was invited to dinner to celebrate his success. After their grand feast, they had a story telling marathon between Wilhelm and Dortchen. Everyone in the Dortchen family stayed on the edge of their seats for hours listening to all those great stories. The evening, however, was growing very long, and one by one her family members ventured off to go to sleep. Her father, the pharmacist, could no longer stay up either and while he was their unknowing chaperone, they were left to their own devices. Dawn began to creep through the window at Dortchen's family home and the story telling was still going on between them.

Wilhelm had just finished a little tale about a soldier who wore a bearskin given to him by the devil. The devil made a deal with him to be pious for seven years and he would never want for anything. The only hitch was that he could not bathe, comb his hair, trim his beard, or file his nails; he had to live like an animal and wear the skin of a bear he had slain. Of course, being the devil, the only catch was if he failed, his soul would belong to him. During that time, the bearskin man helped the poor, the sick, and those who were lost and as repulsive as he had become. One of those that he had helped was a man who had lost everything except his three beautiful daughters whom he needed to support. The man, now called Bearskin, gave the poor man riches without reward in his compassion to help end his suffering. The man in turn gave him the hand of one of his three daughters. It made Bearskin very happy, but also sad because who would have such a disgusting man. He went to see the daughters at the urging of their father. The first two would have nothing to do with this ugly and repulsive stranger. The exception was the youngest; through her compassion and love for her father and gratitude to the stranger she accepted his betrothal. Unfortunately, his deal with the devil had three more years on it so he had to leave their little hamlet and wander the Earth until his contract was fulfilled. But before he left, he gave her half of his gold ring. He had cut it in two to remind her that he would return for her. At the end of those three years, his pious ways not only gave him riches, it taught him about helping others and the rewards of doing good. He had the devil clean him up and was now free of his contract. So he returned to claim his bride.

Once again handsome, he arrived at his bride's home and her sisters tried to attract him. They both ran into their rooms to put on alluring dresses, but their younger sister who was wearing all black in mourning for the return of her betrothed, wanted nothing to do with this handsome stranger. He took some glasses out of his bag, along with some wine, and poured drinks for everyone in the family. They all made cheers to the new stranger and began to drink up the wine. Unknown to his love, he slipped the other half of the ring into her glass of wine. Sadly, she finished her wine and was ready to leave to let her sisters spend time with him, until she noticed it at the bottom of the glass. Without hesitation, she threw her arms around her betrothed to the shock of her two other sisters. They were soon married. The agonized sisters drowned and hung themselves to the delight of the devil, which collected two souls for the price of one.

Dortchen loved this new story but was about to lay down a story of her own about six swans. A lost king was trapped in a forest for weeks by himself. He feared for his life as night approached once again. From out of nowhere, an old woman came wondering by to see if she could help the king. He asked her if she knew the way out of the forest. She replied in a witchy voice, "Oh, yes Lord King, but I will only tell you on the condition that you marry my daughter." Starving, and fearing that he would never find a way out of the forest, he agreed. Her daughter was very beautiful but had an uneasiness to her that left the king with a secret horror. He was shown the way out and they were wed, but this then left the king fearing for his other children from his first wife, who had died mysteriously. So he hid them so well that he needed a magic string to show him the way each time he wanted to see his beloved children. The new queen, now curious about where the king went so often, paid a spy to follow him. She soon discovered he had six sons hidden deep in the forest. The queen had learned witchcraft from her mother and flew to where the boys were and turned the boys into swans. Her spell forced them to fly away from the safety of the king's sanctuary in the deep forest. When the king came later that day for a visit, he found no one but a note from his little girl. She wrote, "My brothers have all flown away in the shapes of swans, leaving me all alone. I know it was my evil stepmother and I will find them, Father." She had fled into the forest, running until she nearly collapsed, but noticed a forest hut and went into it to rest. She began to lie down just before sunset, when suddenly six swans came flying into the window and turned into her brothers. They explained to her that to break the spell she could not laugh or speak for six years and that she must sew six little shirts of starwort for them. They also said if she spoke one single word, all her work would be lost and she would have to start all over again. Her brother explained they only got fifteen minutes a day in human form. Their time was up then and they all flew out of the window as swans. The next morning she gathered starwort until it was dark, determined to have her brothers shirts sown before the six years where up. She could not return to the forest hut as she was also told that it was a place for robbers. So she spent the night sleeping up in the branches of a great tree. In the morning, she was awakened by a young kingsman from the forest that she was hiding in and of whose kingdom she did not know. They were on a hunting trip and were hunting birds when they noticed her in the tree and asked her to come down. She had no time for them as she was on a mission to save her brothers and it was going to take a very long time. She threw down all of her belongings hoping that they would take them and go away. The huntsmen instead climbed the tree and brought her down at the king's behest. He attempted to communicate with her in every way he knew to no avail. The king became quite smitten with her beauty, her modest bearing and courtesy so much that he declared that he was in love with her and wanted her to be his wife and queen. Sorrowfully, the king had his own wicked stepmother who didn't want a mute queen for her stepson. When their first child came, she took it from her, wiped blood on her face and proclaimed her as a man-eater that had eaten her own child. The king did not believe this, but their next child was a beautiful son. He was also taken from his mother and suffered the same treachery. The king again could not believe this of his pious queen and knew her innocence would come to light. But after the third infant disappeared, the poor baffled king would have to let justice be done. She was to be burned at the stake. Fortunately this was the sixth year and all six shirts were almost complete except one arm on one shirt. She went up to the stake but declined being tied as she held the six shirts in her arms. Suddenly, out of the sky, six giant swans swooped down and she threw the shirts over each of them. When each shirt covered them, their swan feathers fell off, transforming them into virile and handsome young men again. The youngest was the one that got the shirt missing one arm where now, sadly, a swan wing stuck out. They embraced each other and cried. The observing king was deeply moved and finally the queen could speak to her king to clear up his suspicions, "My dearest husband, now I may speak and declare to thee, that I am innocent and falsely accused." The king then got a confession from his evil stepmother, learned the whereabouts of his children and had them brought to him. To his delight they were all healthy and safe. Because his evil stepmother would have his bride burned at the stake, they took her and tied her to the stake she would have the queen die on, and was burnt to ashes. The king and queen, along with her six brothers, lived happily ever after.

Dawn took them over to day, causing them to fall asleep in the foyer still sitting up in chairs but resting their heads next to each other. When her father woke up, he motioned to his other children not to make a sound, saying, "Let them sleep. This has been their long night." His wife was gushing, she now knew what she had always thought since they were very little; they were meant for each other. When they finally woke up, they too realized what had happened during their long night of storytelling. Their feelings were exposed, lit by the late afternoon sun. Looking famished, they were thankful when they opened their eyes and saw that her mother had put some rich stew over the fireplace. Its aroma filled the room.

Before they yawned, their heads turned to each other to see if they were merely dreaming. Looking into each other's eyes to see the truth of their love, they were filled with a rush of emotion. It seemed both their stories were about marriage in cryptic ways that they both completely understood. When their eyes adjusted, they started to become aware of their surroundings, noticing her entire family looking at them with love. This look of love did not escape anyone in the room, and they all smiled back in happiness. Everyone had always loved the sick little boy named Wilhelm. Her mother put a bowl of stew in their hands to share and they began to eat, smiling back at their happy family.

When Wilhelm got back to his home, he immediately put ink to quill, writing to his brother of his newly revealed love, to seek his advice on how to proceed, saying, "Dear brother, I think that I am in love. Wait, I know that I am in love. Wait, I am so in love with dear Dortchen I hardly know what to do with myself. Please advise post haste!"

Jacob, in his most scholarly way, did advise his poor smitten brother, "Dear brother, this is perfectly normal and everything will be okay. My advice to you is to ask her father for her hand in marriage. Our first book is published and we can have a decent wedding for you both!" Their first book, 'Household Tales,' was outselling any other book on the world stage, giving the brothers financial freedom to expand their business. The preservation of German history was not only important for Germany, it was also endearing to people all over the world through translations.

After their wedding, Wilhelm stated, "I never cease to be thankful to god for its happy wealth of blessing." Those blessings came quickly with the birth of their children Rudolf, Hermann, Barbara, and Jacob named after his beloved brother. Jacob knew one thing about his brother Wilhelm's stories and that was that love was the common thread that held all these stories together. Love was something that transcended our petty human causes of war, politics, and greed; it was in the end, our spiritual summary of who we are. If god was the spirit, then those that worship him must worship in spirit and truth. This spirit of god was underlined as the source of human awareness and life, vibrant and alive, in all these folklore tales, told by simple people tied to the land that cared for them and their families. Supernatural, divine spirit, or merely what beats in the hearts of all

SOULKISS: TANTRIC TALES OF MAHAMUDRA

sentient beings with an affinity, spirituality, and animism. We are all connected, all creatures have an anima, and it makes them conscious and a part of universal consciousness. Perhaps this incarnation was the breath of life itself; was divine spirit that breathed consciousness analogously into every story told on Earth. Being alive in the 1800s, one knew the fragility of life and resurrection. Reincarnation was more contiguous with how the spirit continued, despite egregious circumstances. With a belief that souls are immortal, such splendid tales of salvation, bravery, and love could march on through time. It was understood that being brave in the face of adversity gave every reader the knowledge that love conquered all. The triumphs of the heart are when you understand that you should love one another as you are loved. The good person, out of the treasures of their heart, produces good, no matter if rich or poor. To get love you have to make love, just as anger begets anger. Wilhelm found his love where the sun was shining. Their love echoes to this day through their great works and research. It was the love of his brother himself and his beautiful spouse Dortchen that made this possible for us today. Jacob never left his little brother's side, living with him until Wilhelm's death and staying under the roof with his wife until he died four years later. Truly, these three gifted people lived outside the paradigm of what was considered the norm in the mid 1800s. Their love of words and their voracious appetite to know and save their essence is still benefiting humanity to this day.

Take Love

*Unspoken words meant more than what's heard, a quoting fox, a paradox of
unrepentant grieving.*

It was another cold day in November and Gustav Mahler was
late for a party in his honor at Berta Zuckerkandi's house. Gustav
had just got done going over 'The Merry Wives of Windsor,' a new
production designed by Brioschi and written by Carl Otto Ehrenfried
Nicolai, based on a wonderful Shakespeare play. The Vienna Opera
house was always abuzz with people, talent, and the press as being
the greatest place to perform music in the world. Gustav was its
maestro and director. A light snow christened the ground on the
streets of Vienna while Gustav searched for Berta's address. Finally
arriving, along with the descending cold, he found the grand old
wooden door with a very heavy steel lion's head knocker and gave it a

very hearty knock.

You could feel the warmth from the fireplace rush out; one felt home when she opened the door to greet him. Berta laughingly helped him wiped the snow off of his coat and shoes, telling him to hurry in so the cold wouldn't enter behind him. As he entered and removed his coat, he noticed a very young and beautiful protégé of Berta's, Alma Schindler, in the drawing room. Alma coyly looked at Vienna's greatest conductor and composer walking in with a knowing, seductive smile. Going to Berta's house was like attending a who's who in Viennese culture. For instance, painter Gustav Klimt, theater director Max Reinhardt, and writer Arthur Schnitzler were gathered for that night of dinner and conversation. Berta's spouse, Emil, was a Hungarian anatomist who was already engaged in conversation with Max about the layers of the human body, when they all noticed Gustav had finally arrived. Everyone in the room, as the great maestro swaggered in with Berta holding his arm, began to applaud, smile, and say bravo. He humbly bowed, smiled, and began to shake the hands of his friends and many protégés of Berta's, looking for well-to-do spouses. Gustav Mahler was certainly a very eligible bachelor and rightfully so, as a consummate workaholic, he had had no time for a relationship for many years. Although he was known for being a womanizer behind closed doors, high society was now demanding him to marry. It was only fit that he came here with his theater director, Max Burckhard, to be introduced to this soiree of young women who were gushing for his attentions.

The 41-year-old Mahler was a very dashing man and had dedicated his life to the perfection of the art of conducting and composition. His life was about to change and change quite rapidly as his eye was suddenly caught by one of the young women in the room. Alma, who was a composer in her own right and of very capable intellect, was from an aristocratic family very familiar with Gustav. She was intrigued with him and his work and this was her opportunity to finally speak with the maestro. The two of them became captivated with each other, and it was like there were no other people in the room, as if time stood still. Even though there was a very large age difference, there was a very noticeable climate of attraction in the air. The two of them created electrical sparks, like warm air colliding with cold air creating lightening. When lightening hits the ground, fire is sure to come. Who knows what secret wishes each of them had been whispering to the universe, but they were drawn to each other for reasons certainly beyond their mere mortal duties.

Alma spoke up first to the maestro, "So, maestro, don't you find the Hungarian's music very passionate?"

Gustav was taken aback with her frankness in polite society, but replied also with candor, "You must be referring to Es war einmal (Once Upon a Time). Is this true?"

"Indeed I am maestro; it's as if he was inspired by a higher power, don't you think?"

The maestro, having worked with him, continued, "There was lots to be worked on in the piece and it took some time to work through the process with this fledgling composer."

Alma transgressed, "I find him more than fledgling; his works soar among the clouds."

The maestro added, "Zemlinsky or should I say von Zemlinsky, is someone I gracefully helped to put into the public light. Who could refuse the good wishes of Johanna Brahmas?" said the maestro plainly.

"You? I can hardly believe that any note was altered on the pages of his music," complained young Alma.

Maestro charmingly elucidates, "Well, I find it refreshing that

98

you know what music has been written on the pages of this composer. May I ask how you fathom this grand realization?"

"I have studied with him." She said pointedly.

"Charming! So you also compose?" chirped the maestro.

"Yes, I'm another, what you call, a fledgling composer, dear maestro."

"Call me Gustav, my dear. Perhaps the passion from this Hungarian came from being near your exquisite beauty." Gustav said with so much sincerity that he was now charming her.

"May I ask you something Gustav?" She says.

"Yes, please ask me anything you like." He said, opening up the book of his life for her to read.

"Who in mankind's history has decided the meaning of a kiss?" Alma asked, so sadly.

"Who indeed, yet a kiss is similar to the magic of a finely tuned orchestra that surrenders its soul for one divine moment." Gustav said with all sincerity. "Please come by our rehearsal tomorrow evening and I shall show you just how divine a kiss from an Orchestra can be."

Gustav noticed that time had gone by swiftly, and that he and Alma were the only ones left in the room.

Berta was seeing off the last of the guests and now turning to both of them, she asks, "So, my lovely dears, I trust your evening went well."

Gustav looked over at Alma with endearing eyes and said to his friend, "It was a charming evening Berta. Thank you ever so much for having this for me."

Berta understood what had just happened, as did most that night. A new source of gossip in Vienna had begun. Berta smiled and helped him with his evening coat to forge his way back out into the snowy night.

Gustav turned to Alma and said, "Can I walk you to your home my dear?"

Carl Moll, her stepfather, came out from the back room and with a smile, told the maestro, "What a grand evening we all had dear maestro. Do you have all your things Alma?" Alma nodded in agreement and then he bowed to the maestro as they walked out into the cold of the night.

Gustav gives Berta a kiss on the cheek and heads out into the cold as this unusual night has come to a close for him.

It was quiet in the grand halls of The Vienna Hofoper where Gustav was working on Wagner's opera, Tannhäuser. The maestro had sent out his assistant to bring Miss Alma Maria to his rehearsal. She entered into the orchestral chamber, hearing them tune up in the usual flurry of awkward notes being flung into the air with egregious abandon. Violist Natalie Bauer-Lechner, was at the podium with the maestro talking over some issues with the music. Mahler was a bit perturbed, but explained very precisely what he was talking about the previous day as Alma walked up to greet him. Stopping everything, he smiled and kissed her hand ever so gently, to Natalie's surprise. It seemed that Natalie was more than a devoted friend after her divorce and Alma was encroaching on her territory with her lover. Natalie attempted to get his attentions again but Gustav walked off with Alma to place her in a very special seat to watch him work.

Tannhäuser's story is about the human conundrum between our higher sacred and our animalistic profane love. It took us on the journey we are all faced with in our quest through love's redemption for something that is bigger than ourselves. Our primal need to indulge always seems to lead us into debacles when passions are seen through a hormonal haze. This is the theme running through most of Wagner's mature work, as it is through the works of so many men who have had to learn how fragile true love really is. Today Gustav was faced with this conundrum unwittingly, as the universe took on the energy of truth in so many obvious signposts yet unseen. Tannhäuser, like most men, would be whisked off to Venusberg in the grotto in a ceaseless orgy of sinful pleasure. There they would stay until he realized that there is more to life than an ordinary unfulfilled lust for carnal delights. The proud maestro went to his podium. Natalie looked up at him tearfully. He lifted his baton in one fluid gesture, swiftly attending to the first beat of this magnificent opera.

Both Gustav and Alma were in another world together while he conducted Wagner's play. Somehow, in their collective imaginations they had become the cast, riding along the broad stokes of the maestro's baton. Her Venus enraged his obsessions to possess her in transgressions and reveal both their primary passions unobstructed. She begged for their bodies to merge in a pantomime of covert, melodious sounds, forged in a salacious cauldron, and forming an amalgamation of sensual perceptions. They were aroused, and consummated in musical oblivion, each fiber of their beings instruments plucked by every impulse engendered in their identity of male and female. Scheming thoughts of overwhelming possessiveness ruled over them like a tightly knit fabric, binding them together in naked compromise. Dignity and morality all make concessions within a new virtuous construct, declaring passion as their only compass. Within each orchestral movement of Wagner's opera, the levels of unbridled desires modulate within their innate wellsprings of illusive innuendos. They have succumbed to each other's will, eradicated all boundaries, become practitioners ennobled by aspirations to take pleasure in each other's arms. Their flirtatious infatuations and

101

disregard for consequences drove them deeper into instincts most people must suppress. Baser feelings, unquenchable and bottomless, snared both their imaginations with a hunger for contact they both feared they would perish without. At that moment inside their collective experience, the music ends. Gustav looked up at his orchestra and congratulated them. Natalie is excited by their practice performance and starts to head for the maestro; yet that now felt inappropriate to her. The maestro forcefully walked up to Alma, grabbed her hand, and took her to his suite inside his fairytale, newly built palace for the arts, called 'The Vienna Opera House.'

Once they entered his opulent suite, she ran up to him, consummating their contact with a lascivious, passionate kiss. Gustav's urges surged through him in wild contempt for everything in the world around him to taste her forbidden lust for him. Their age difference, social economic status, network of colleagues, mutual friends, past lovers, and future lovers meant nothing to him. She was also lured, even hypnotized, by their forbidden passions, by a hidden power that was not their own. Alma could barely contain herself while unbuttoning Gustav's clothes. Gustav fumbled madly at hers, passions wildly becoming renegade to their resolve. Methodically, they razored away those threads that bound them to their birthright of Vienna, to create only secrets they could share. The anticipation of consummating their intention, reflected in first glances. It was as sweet as the music they both loved to play. Music held every emotion in ways that promised endless opportunities for creativity to flourish in revelry of euphonies. Alma was the source of creativity and inspiration in this boundless dance at the water's edge of timeless ebbs and flows. Her tender flesh was an instrument of unlimited finesse that could only be played by the hands of a maestro of love.

Lost deeper inside these stolen passions loomed a paranormal erotica, with his pants falling to the ground along with her dress in syncretic slow motion splendor. Mysterious novellas hover over her skin and he wanted to lap each one of them up with his eyes. She was his messenger, his mate, whose flames rose from his smoldering heart's wilting bouquet. A predator to his incongruity vexed him in his hyper-awareness to wrap his arms around her. This was the inaudible, loudest note in any score where gravity was suspended in a speechless soliloquy when they both dilate in immersed penetration. Worthy as a pending horizon, these unshakable pangs of redemption that cannot be ignored, looked up to him from her eyes. His arrogant pride dissolved in her presence, despite his lack of inhibitions to find a way to give her archaic happiness.

"What commitment is punctuated in a kiss," Alma thought to herself as her layers melted beneath his savors and dips. Alma's feelings guided her in a soliloquy meant only for Gustav's ears, "I am a seductress of your most intimate dreams, where all your fantasies are possible, my mantra within every thrust of your heart. I am the banquet you relish to imbibe your senses on in unexpected ways, controlling our symphony of forbidden passion. I've stained you indelibly in unmentionable ways, lethal in my haunting embellishments yet as a gentle breath breezing over your emotions. Take me to your unconsciousness, soothe me with your wanting kiss, and take my scent to emblazon across your chest, lips, and soul. This valor you claim in this heartfelt moment will be your arbiter to my unspeakable sins. Cull my thoughts of everything except for this undisguised richness of love nakedly falling into our endless abyss. In this moment to remember, remember this, my love, as riches and fortune are not measured by anything other than this. Make me your goddess now and have all those virtuous tomorrows engorged in creative, ethereal delights. Swear to my swollen allegories un-silenced by this mystic dance, where innocence is unveiled to provoke every raw note known only to our ears. Curiosity intense as nightfall reaches your depths and our enigma begins its own journey. Taboos have been broken and there is no turning back."

Gustav could hardly contain his own thoughts, and then freely whispered in her ear. "Phenomenon immemorial, syndrome of my proliferation of your loving name, swims around inside my head and heart. You are the underscore of my pathology and this attraction need be constantly consumed in dangerous and supernatural quantities. There is not a moment of the day where my body does not feel your rhythm. My wits spiral out of control over your sacrificing body, shedding its angelic glow onto my loathsome soul. Come to me and we cannot separate, we are musical harmony that embraces every craved note expressed in our tonal empathy. Your impressions trump my resolve and self-importance. I am spellbound by mysterious emotions I have yet to fathom. Your little lustful taunts keep my edge inexhaustibly stuck between my tortured flesh that aches continuously for more and my resolve to take them."

Those days of bachelorhood had fallen to the way side for a wish-fulfilling gem by the name of Alma. He was swarmed in irresistible edgy needs to have her forbidden loins spread before him as his private symphonium meant only for him to hear. His relishing thoughts could hardly be contained, watching the time, knowing she would arrive soon to continue their beckoning pledge towards liberation of his deep requited feelings. Their reservoir of sexual incantations seemed unlimited, driving him to pace every second they were not engaged in their mythic harmony of adoration. All his cravings rushed to immense proportions. Gravity seemed suspended inside each rhythmic note echoed from the sound of her knock upon his door.

Two weeks later, Gustav was compelled to ask for the hand of the now pregnant Alma. It was on November 28th, without the support of her family, as he was 19 years older than her, that they became engaged. The creative process was illusive for those that had been immersed in it, a sincere marvel that somehow comes through certain people miraculously. Mahler was now confronted with a conundrum about the purpose of this ubiquitous love connection. It was almost illusive to him, a man in his 40's and never married, and by most standards he would have remained a childless bachelor until his death. I'm always amazed how worldliness influences and corrupts our pure divinations where lightning strikes in our lives. It seems we spend so much time trying to put it out instead of fueling the flames to grow even higher. Gustav must have been very frightened by his great love and passion for Alma, wanting to control it, much like he did with his orchestras or his compositions. He wrote Alma a twenty-page manifesto that outlined every detail of their married life, but Alma's love outweighed her immediate judgment. They were married on March 9th, 1902 in a wet cold ceremony in the Austrian spring. In this manifesto, he condemned her to a life of servitude where she could not do the things she loved and was compelled to do, which was to compose. He felt that their household wouldn't have room for two composers, but she could be his amanuensis. That he needed a head of household to take care of the trivialities of life for him, but underneath it would prove to be a test of love that need never be.

Mahler, like all men, had the innate ability to doubt divine intervention, whether it came in the form of complete epiphany, spiritual experience, or the gift of awakening. He was simply unable to imagine the intrinsic value of the love of a woman like Alma. Men often destroy the good in their lives because of whom they lean on. Those confidants that somehow seem to have a grasp of reality at least at the moment when posed with the difficult questions in life. Men always look for divinity, never thinking their awesome connection with the universe could be sitting right next to them. The truth was, men have their concepts askew, hardly perceiving that their grand plan could revolve around the argument that women just know. Women have this amazing gift called a woman's intuition. It takes them to the truth, no matter if they want to know it or not. It is always there in a woman's mind, telling them exactly what it is that should be happening. Alma's true self was talking out loud to her as one can tell by what she wrote in her diary on that day. "He thinks nothing at all of my art - and thinks a great deal of his own - and I think nothing of his art and a great deal of my own. That's how it is! Now he constantly talks of preserving his art. I can't do that. It would have worked with Zemlinsky, because I empathize with his art - he is a brilliant chap." Truth is, Mahler thought too much of her gift and didn't understand how they could complement each other when uniting their gifts. To protect love with every fiber of his being never occurred to him, while attempting to fit the paradigm of head of this turn-of-the-century household.

Their first daughter, Maria, was born seven months after they were married, perhaps the first indication of her other creative talents. Alma found herself with a man, while everything she aspired to was becoming more distant from her with the birth of their newborn. Mahler also had no time to socialize; this furthered her feelings of isolation and being trapped in a world less romantic. Feeling like the wishes of her husband were coming true, she was now merely another servant in his household.

Their second daughter was born on June 15th, 1904. The chasm between them was growing and the companionship that he so amply wanted was becoming distant. Alma was still a young woman and she wanted to feel good about herself. So when one of Mahler's colleagues was flirting with her, she didn't hold back. She also attempted to meet with her teacher, Alexander von Zemlinsky, in order to write music with him, but he refused to walk down that tempting path of seduction with her again. If she couldn't compose in Mahler's household, there was one thing she could be and that was a woman of inspiration to creative men. So this became her new occupation: to dazzle the evocations of passionate creatives with her licentious allure.

"I sit down at the piano, dying to play, but musical notation no longer means anything to me. My eyes have forgotten how to read it. I have been firmly taken by the arm and led away from myself. I long to return to where I was," Alma lamented. "I am the muse of the universe, I am the center of every glittering event inside my universe until I must fetch my husband after his work is done." She picked up her baby girl Maria and said, "I have been ill for a long time. But for several days and nights I have been weaving music in my mind, so loud and persistent... Gustav lives his life, and perhaps I too must live his life also. My child doesn't need me because of the wet nurse. In any case, I can't keep myself solely busy with that." Alma returned her little baby to her crib. No other woman in Europe, or the world for that matter, was composing music and feminism was still out of reach. "My love does not divert my husband from his intellectual preoccupations. Even Otto Weininger can't understand the inspiration a woman brings to a man because he is too fat to attract a woman with a mind. I am afraid that I will never desire to create again, but if a muse I must be, then a muse I will be," she spoke from her deepest sorrows.

Men eventually wake up to the errors of their ways, but time is on nobody's side in the art of love and its transcendental nature. He would soon discover this with the death of his first daughter Maria, who was just five years old. Life was very fragile at the dawn of the industrial age, and diphtheria, of which a vaccination had just been discovered, was too late for his dear Maria. Mahler, after a doctor's checkup, found that he was suffering from a heart defect and was told to restrict his activities or risk dying himself. Mahler left Vienna and went to New York City to conduct, but he and his wife started living apart as her career as a muse had now begun.

Alma now spent most of her time at a convalescent spa resort and took on a lover named Walter Gropius. Alma, who only wanted to be taken seriously as a woman, now had a willing man. The two of them became lost in unrestrained nights of passion just like she had shared with Gustav. Only now, these were more refined by her skills. This was something Mahler always craved. Creatives know this intense love because it's the wellspring where everything inspirational lives. It was where the waters of creative discovery always urged the pen to move, the brush to stroke, and the keys to make music. His artistry was deep inside his living hell, buried alive in his own conundrum of controlling every aspect of his life. Surrendering to his own innate, emotional aspirations to set himself free were his secret torment. Alma, on the other hand, was no longer a creature in his torture chamber.

Deep emotions, no matter what their passion was, whether music, art, or literature, is where everything beautiful comes from dark to light. With a misdirected letter from Alma's lover Gropius, Mahler learned just how deep Alma's love could inspire. Mahler's 10th Symphony was created through this most difficult crisis of his life. He was convinced that his journey with the only woman he ever loved was over because he didn't know how to love himself, let alone her. He realized he needed help to understand how he had failed at such a basic human experience and was referred to Dr. Sigmund Freud. Freud heard Mahler's story and through his process of analysis, surmised that the weakness in his relationship was a reciprocal longing for a father/mother substitute. The controlling and resistance came from them both seeing their relationships with their own father/mother in each other. Freud's solution to this was that they both allow each other to view their relationship as incestuous and to give their consent to act on it.

This unveiled passion brought the couple some final happy months together where they could abandon their identities and set their souls free with each other again. With this new freedom, Mahler began focusing all his attention on his wife and all that she was with no conditions. He dedicated his 8th Symphony to her, which premiered on September 12th, 1910 and was his greatest musical triumph. He also had five of Alma's compositions published that year with premieres of her work in Vienna and New York. Before she was to accompany her husband at a New York debut, she wanted to meet up with her lover Walter once more. They chose the romantic city of Paris to rendezvous in, where she could pour her love inside him one last time. Mahler now understood what his love with Alma had meant all this time. Unfortunately, not long after this realization, he fell seriously ill on February 21st, 1911. He knew he had wasted so much time and that her pure love had always been there. This is the running theme in men's lives; right after they understand what they have been missing, it's always too late to save. Alma, always his beloved, took him home to Vienna, where he died on May 18th, 1911 around midnight with the realization that he was loved. Their love was only for ten lost years, where so much more could have been realized and offered to the world of music, had he recognized its value. Why these reoccurring crimes are not understood until it's too late, is something only mankind can figure out. The value of love and the reasons we are brought together to produce love is self-evident. The obstacles are something we invent.

As for Alma, she later married a man, Walter Gropius, who recognized her immense beauty and creative prowess. He became the father of modern architecture and was inspired by the love she gave him. The namelessness of consciousness merely seeks a vehicle to be a domicile of and bestow its priceless expressions of love as its reward. Our quick lives make it necessary for this loving narrative to take seed and grow perilously, as only love can nurture its apparent resolve. Alma's sacrifice to risk, to dare, to be the harborage of true love's mystical experience was preeminent. Her innate ability to attract and gather souls as a conduit of information was self-evident.

This may be or may not be as exclusive as we think. There are many purposes and unapparent reasons, washed away like sand castles in the ocean every day. This collective beauty is only gathered in its creating and finds ultimate demise in our fleeting experience of divine love. Before marrying Gropius, she also had a tumultuous affair with artist Oskar Kokoschka who created many works also inspired by her. After Gropius accused her of an unfounded affair, they divorced and later she became lovers with poet Franz Werfel. After ten years of taunting him to become an accomplished playwright novelist, as well as a renowned poet, they married. Alma lived a long life perfecting and understanding her femininity. She died absolved in 1964, surviving all three of her husbands. Her only surviving child, her daughter Anna, became a sculptor. She also lived a long life, dying in 1988. But that is another story.

Break Love

Shedding shadows drip off silhouettes like raindrops against a midnight crescent moon
Dark and stark fragrances mar increments spent recklessly in the absence of a swoon

Victorian transforms to Edwardian, French Revolution to The Gilded Age, love and romance catapulted in the late 1800s, elucidated by the electricity of inspired minds of the enlightenment. Gothic to Modern literature, Impressionist/Post-Impressionist to Art Deco, the

Age of Industrialization rising from a world of coal to oil, steel, concrete, electricity and communication technology. Discovered labyrinths of the mind made egregious egresses appear as if out of nowhere, shedding an age of horses and buggies for an age of industrialism. Worldliness, the cruel taskmaster that persuades our souls that these constructs of man are absolute, and failing to abide by them could leave you wanting more. Ardent convincers insisting we succumb if we follow this impossible idea that we are spiritual beings having a human experience, when in fact, we are heathen creatures of an all-consuming Earth. Money is the new religion that buys you the love of your choice along with pleasures. The dramatic acquisition is far more worthy than the peace found in an empty stretch of fertile farmland. Coupling based on money is the glue of modern times and without it, relationships fall apart. Real estate is up for grabs in the gold rush of city dwellers and it advances into first come, first serve. Even with the wining and dining, the big diamond ring, and the lavish weddings, the fundamentals of love still cry out. I hear echoing voices from what now seems a distant past where lovers dwell with solemn grace forever in their bosom, still praying, "I love you."

Hartford First Episcopal Church in Connecticut carries the coat of arms of King George. It's where fiery preacher and poet John Pierpont stood every Sunday morning to inspire and impress goodness on his congregation. His grandson, John Pierpont Morgan, was always there to sing the hymns with his other grandfather, Joseph Morgan, and glow in the words of his beloved grandfather. This stoic church, St. John's Episcopal Church, was an enigma for its day, a standing monument and testament of god's love and connection here on our planet. His grandfather, Pierpont, was a man of ideas and later these ideas would alienate him from his church he loved so much. His love of poetry, Socrates, and the joy of life was something his grandfather imprinted on his consciousness as a young man, swathed in god's divine love. His father's side of the family was about being a wise and frugal businessman, where a classical education was a necessity to climb the business ladder of success. J. P. Morgan was now a young man embarking on the world in search of knowledge on his spiritual quest for understanding this divine love his grandfather inspired.

On his world travels, his other grandfather Morgan made sure it included an understanding of banking and European languages. His travels brought him into a company of men who ran the banking systems of the world in Germany, France and England. Art and music were also a very important part of his balanced understanding of the world, along with his love of history. Pierpont's father, Julius, moved their family to London, taking a job to work with the leading world bankers. Later, this move became a great asset to his son J.P. in his financial career. J.P. moved back to the United States at age 20 to work on Wall Street as a clerk in New York City, further expanding his network of influential friends. He was invited everywhere big money gathered, hobnobbing with America's nouveau rich, the movers and shakers of a new world economy. Amelia Sturges, the daughter of one of New York's most prominent families, Jonathan Sturges and Mary Pemberton Cady, were all at a very exclusive party at the Waldorf Astoria. Pierpont was attending at the behest of his firm. Angelic beauty Amelia caught his eye and in an instant filled his heart with uncertain magic only young love can conjure. This delight was written about by great poets of his time, and was the real magnificence they had all described so lavishly in their work. Bridging the chasms of social idioms and elevating his own standing through forthright intelligence, perseverance, and fortitude was his only option. Winning her heart became his obsession of his cultured breeding and spiritual quest for divinity, whose name he uttered over and over: "Amelia."

Jonathan, her father, had a great love of the arts. Pierpont also did, a passion handed down by his grandfather. Pierpont seized the moment, introduced himself, and was academic in his discussion concerning European museums and what art they housed. He mentioned to both Jonathan and his wife that he would be available to come to their home if they'd agree and plot out a trip abroad for them. Jonathan and his wife were very excited about the prospect and were eager to have him over to their home to see exactly what he would come up with. Pierpont mapped out a complete itinerary for their art excursion, working his way into the hearts of Amelia's (Mimi) parents. Jonathan and his family set sail not long after the plans were made and Pierpont was not far behind them, anxious to meet them there. He finally arrived in London and escorted them around art museums to be with Mimi every day for two weeks of heaven. After they returned to New York, he asked for permission to marry their daughter, to which they cheerfully answered, "Yes!"

In the meantime, the partners of his firm were looking at him to move up through the ranks of their company. Pierpont was sent to Louisiana on the Wall Street banking firms' behalf to oversee some of their holdings. When he got there, he discovered a business opportunity aboard a ship. It had set to port with a load of coffee they didn't have a buyer for yet. Pierpont risked the firms' money by making a contact to sell the coffee. He made the firm a very handsome profit to their chagrin and Pierpont's amazement. Pierpont's business savvy was too progressive for the firm who would have never taken calculated risk for profit. Pierpont, being a world traveler, understood these were exciting times for this new age of technology enlightenment. So he ventured out on his own and got into the investment world himself with the aid of his father's connections in banking. During this risky time and with the approach of the American Civil War, Pierpont's investments became astronomically profitable. His love affair with Mimi also flourished. Even with great wealth coming into his life, he still hadn't known anything more fulfilling than the love he felt for her. His romantic plan to make extreme amounts of money, retire, and spend every minute writing poetry, singing, and being with his beloved and their future children.

During the summer of 1861, after 3 years of perfecting their love for each other in a courtship that outshone all courtships, Mimi was diagnosed with tuberculosis. Pierpont was devastated. His dearest beloved would not die needlessly; he would find a way to save her. Love conquers all and his love for Mimi would be the power that would keep her on this world. Pierpont proposed marriage to Mimi and told her they would find a cure together one way or another. He arranged every detail of their wedding and honeymoon. His quest to find a cure convinced him that a higher power was looking over his shoulder. She was growing weaker from coughing so much and had become quite frail leading up to their wedding day. He had to carry her down the stairs before she walked down the aisle with her father. Standing by his side to support his love, were family, friends, and his mentor, an Episcopalian minister, Reverend William Stephen Rainsford, who pronounced them husband and wife. Right after the ceremony they were on a ship to Algeria for their honeymoon, thinking the tropical climate might save her. When the tropics didn't work, they went to Paris, where he brought the best doctors money could buy to attend to her rescue and recovery. She wrote to her mother: "I wish you could see his loving devoted care of me, he spares nothing for my comfort and improvement."

In her darkest hours, Pierpont was desperately pleading for her to stay with him, "My beloved, we have yet to make incomparable gentle evocations of memories ripple along a golden pond of our dreams. No dreams are guaranteed, long or short, humanlike or fictional, but they are meant to be yours, to have forever if you wish. Your innocence can never fall from grace, as you are grace itself. No philosopher from here or to the end of the universe could deny that. Our love is balanced along the edge of the infinite, among the ambient soundscapes of glistening church bells that sing only for us to be realized. Let me talk death into silence this night, where villains and heroes cry imperceptible tears falling in rain, whose glistening drops of fate nurture sweet spring flowers for your joy. Here I kneel before you, plain speaking, serenely introspectively pleading with your soul, stay with me! Smile with me in an armful of long stemmed roses to count out as days of our happiness on our beautiful Earth. One rose for each tomorrow and tomorrow and tomorrow. We will embrace these fragrances made by us, just for us, with our beautiful significance to bloom. We are more than shadows that march off to excursions with our fate. We are lit by unfathomable candlelight that is more than a brief ascension to our zenith of fulfilled happiness. I claim your territory as my own, your heartbeat as a home to live in, you are my sanctuary where no scorn can come asunder. You are my quixotic and I will talk death into silence, sleeplessly, in every religious dimension until all demons are blocked. Please let our fate be sealed as husband, wife, father, mother, grandfather, grandmother." Pierpont bravely spoke to Mimi.

"My love, you have been my heartbeat. No kinder eyes have fallen on me and they will be my guiding light through the darkness I now face. Oh gentlest of souls, you have been my armor and my amour, through this great test of divine love in this hour of my fate. Our candle burns brightly for all to see, feel the mighty love we possess, show all the way to truth. I may be innocent in so many things I will never know, but I am not innocent of your love, for I know it so well. Our time together has been the purpose of my existence. I've no other room for anything else in our beautiful jaunt in the garden of your sweet devotion. Let no time to mourn go by my love, this hereafter will be my place to watch over you. So, fear not, be tortured not, as my love is as indelible as yours on my soul. Ours has never been a battle with sin, ours is purity of cherished moments etched superbly into timelessness. This death is not my exile from life. Darling, I cling faithfully, cherishing each precious moment your lips are near mine. I will always be present in your life for now and forever. Nothing else in life is meaningful and transcendental except this love you so amply share with my wounded soul, concurred not by a broken heart, but only a broken body. Please don't let my embrace with death justify turning your heart on your god, for he has made you the love of my life."

With Amelia's last breath, she asked him one more thing. "Kiss me my darling so I can ride on the winds of your love into eternity." Their lips touched as she surrendered to this untimely fate as her ripple reached the shore of timelessness.

It was only four months after their marriage that she died in his arms at that Parisian hospital. Mortally wounded from Amelia's death, scars deep against the membrane between faith and god, he began having mysterious 'nervous' ailments, crippling headaches, depressions and exhaustion, ailments or fragments from the hypocrisy of his innocence. He continued seeking cures for those wounds that could never be healed in American or European spas. We all must face death head on in life, some sooner than others. It leaves bitter scars when the poetry of goodness, pure love, and beauty withers under the feet of calamities from a volatile material universe. Mere mortals are left with a feeling of helplessness that can be incapacitating, agonizing to the point of no return. These scars thicken the caverns of our hearts where blood no longer nourishes, but merely rushes by. Pierpont, a boy filled with belief that love will overcome, that goodness always prevails, and god's love can perform miracles. We are all being looked after by a higher power, he thought, pouring his prayers for god's salvation with his divine love. His entire prowess was challenged in his heartbreaking moment where all possibilities dissolve in front of your eyes, totally helpless, without the aid of god or anything of comfort. No prayers, incantations, medicine or intelligence can return the dead from being dead. Death is the loudest period in the sentence of our lives. Whatever god or goddess that loves order from pain is viewed with dark glasses of chaos that grates against our awareness and restricts our quest for absolution.

After this most woeful, deafening pain, Pierpont took the slow transatlantic journey from Paris to New York with his bride's body. He must have felt utter spiritual defeat, yet, as in Amelia's words, this was the greatest victory of love. Amelia's mother and father held a grief no parent should endure, yet grateful that their child managed to experience Pierpont's magnificent love. They all rode together with her body to the home where they were married, barely four months before, to say goodbye. Hearing her words, "This death is not my exile from life," was not a remote echo from the past; first love is the most fragile love that shapes our souls forever.

Burnished hearts grow cold, as our vulnerability can no longer shed tears with our hopeful constructs of vanquished dreams all burned on the funeral pyre. The power of our first love roots deepest in our hearts, trauma's shield guards us so desperately against showing that special place ever again. Work is a man's solace for lost love and the grief that 'the one' and only possible is lost forever gnaws at every heart. Everyone knows god only grants us one true love per life, right? Perhaps church was the place to release grief in his anticlimactic breach of faith of god's graces, Pierpont thought. He attended St. George Episcopal in New York City when he was not working to talk with his dear friend, Reverend William Stephen Rainsford. He attempted to unearth where he and god had strayed. They would assess and discuss what he might have done to absolve himself from his tragic plight. The Reverend urged him that god had a higher purpose for his life and that he did not forsake him.

Redemption was not well served on a man's plate filled with a broken heart that could not be repaired without that very god restoring his true love. He was alone among the wilds of a foreboding planet of kings and queens, rules and power, and this had become the new god to him. Tainted love has many characteristics with sensibilities that become well grounded in a practical checklist of acquisitions and mergers.

One of his rewards was finding a new kind of love through the tender mercies of Frances, also known as Fanny, Tracy. Fanny was apprehensive of Pierpont, but after a year of his sweet ways she eventually warmed to him. Married in 1865, they started out making a family with Pierpont providing all the money a little family could ever imagine. He quickly made enough to retire so he could be just a father to his children and a loyal husband to his wife. However, his father had been grooming him for too long for greatness in the world of banking and in the early 1900s, everything was up for grabs. Steel, electricity, transportation, communication, medicine, and big banking were all at a fork in the road. Big new decisions needed to be made by men of power and vision and no one had a better vision than J.P. Morgan. For Pierpont it was a decision to change the tide of the world or be a father and loving husband to his wife, another gift from the universe. Fanny was a very private woman who loved her children and small quiet family life and J.P. Morgan was a mogul socialite. He chose to rise to his place in history and quickly become the biggest mover and shaker in world history. Carrying the weight of an emerging world, J.P.Morgan still stated that the most important thing a man could bring to the table was character. Simply put, J.P. had the biggest character our world has ever known and was the father of the modern corporate culture. It was his wife Fanny that in the end kept the loving part of his legacy alive. His children were also people of character, full of responsibility to truthfulness continuing their families banking empire to this day.

Romance, a brave proposition very few have the propensities to measure up to throughout history. Risking illusions of the mind for sensibilities of the heart is never a first choice in our volatile world where worldliness doesn't seem to afford us the possibility to risk anything. This tendency to let our minds attempt to define romantic love as impossible at the expense of unseen tears and heartbreak is a running theme throughout history. Does romance have a place in our world or is it only a fairytale meant to be romanticized by fiction writers? Yet, the symphony of romance plays on in our collective yearning to have that endearing experience with love even if only for a short moment in our lives.

Mahler was almost too late to realize the value of romance. J.P. Morgan, decimated by romance, transformed his romantic ideology into that of sensory worldly pleasures. Overall, their narrative was missing, "Once upon a time," like what the Grimm's have taught so many generations over the years. A place where fairytales can happen and love is always rescued just in the nick of time and happy endings are inevitable. Is romance fleeting? Are there time limits on when we can experience romantic emulsions touching our skin? How can we free ourselves from the chains that bind us to this created worldly process and reconnect with the heavens that brought us here in the first place?

I want to feel those luminous aspirations soar to the loftiest perch and never relapse into the mundane worldliness of unsatisfying rejections. Because I know with love, all things are possible. Romance is love's vehicle that divides these self-imposed predicaments of the world from making your life happen based on the strength of true love. My ardent temptations are to obtain that transfiguring force that lies in a higher spherical realm beyond a sated appetite. I want to dwell in two lovers awakened with desires for romance with a sustained vigor that the infectious nature of the world cannot permeate. It is not a matter of obstacles. It's a matter of excommunicating our fears and persevering for pure romance as a fundamental basic human right. The right to sing and dance in the pursuit of happiness, as though life's fleeting moments can never be reclaimed. It only takes a striker and a match to make a flame and this is where every love story should start.

Vanquish all obstacles in our commitment to have ceaseless romantic love and manifest this certain reality every moment we breathe. Shatter the illusions that we must be ushered to our seats and reduce ourselves to the common denominator, minus our hearts. The time to nurture a longing that pierces through armor conjured by fear to protect our hearts at all cost has come to an end. We are more than the normality of our triviality, of our worldliness, when two lovers continue to pursue romantic love until their last breath. The real tragedy is to never commune in romances fashion that shatters the illusions of our paradigm of fear. To sweep a lover off their feet and be smitten feverishly is the most divine feeling on this Earth. To find your innermost honesty and remember the painstaking details true passion insists on. As imperfect as human beings are, don't forget to smile and know with practice and loving fortitude, your love can happen. Until death sublimates existence, until your next fresh start, we can all reside in dawn's eternal love with our romantic hearts.

First Encounter as
Lovers

*Epic waves breathe the swaying reeds of times caress' a poetic malady raised from a sea
where love is put to its test.*

While we had always been lovers traversing many lifetimes to
find each other, our memories of each of those times seems to
become clearer with every incarnation. A certain sacred reverence
with words and actions has been developing over lifetimes of seeking.
The importance of just how fleeting and fragile human existence is,
has surfaced to our innate conscious mind, precariously. There is no
doubt now our moments in the flesh may be limited by obstacles we
have no control over in our physical form. Seizing this time has

become paramount to both our awareness, as time is always slipping away mysteriously. Words can no longer be wasted on the trivial compunctions instilled in a bedazzled culture, whose inability to gather the depth of love's quest squanders life's most precious gift. Time travelers can be seduced by this worldliness, where the trappings of a seeming reality, outweigh any sensibilities about why they are a skipping stone through the eons at all.

Recollection, doubt, romancing improbability, delusions, and other obstacles cloud a possible outcome that could have been wrestled down. These ideas rummaged through my thoughts as resting precisely in my gyroscope's gravity, wanting the truth that love was the solution to all possibilities to be distilled. How many times have I sabotaged my misguided divinations, because of being lost in illusions, manufactured in a labyrinth of my own deceiving mind? Ah, the mind, always making something out of nothing, running with wild ideas about who, what, where, and weighing out how much will it cost me in mere dollars and cents. Our minds always want to figure out something, even if it need not be figured out, as overlords and stewards of our ship. Can it ever be steadfast or must we always succumb to a blazing chatter that can simply change course by making ridiculous deals with awareness. This is where all men go wrong, as no deal ever comes out in the favor of those making greed their beacon on a stormy night. Rocks are always overlooked when the prize is money and your myopic view keeps telling you that all you have to do is make land with your fragile ship. Nonsense is nonsense, as we have been told by so many, in so many ways. That little voice always urging, "Follow your heart, let this be what steers your way through life."

The sabotage and traps we inflict on ourselves must be solved before any encounter with love is squandered and value crushed. This cost is higher than we could have ever imagined with what a woman's heart risks, always tittering on the edge of divinity and infamy.

Everyone needs coherent explanations, so here is mine: "Life is fleeting, so pay attention." or, "Surrender, impermanence will eventually replace everything." It suddenly occurred to me that we are not beings of the future or beings of the past, we are all layers of this long day, coexisting, coalescing in all experiences constantly in an unseen rhythm of life. So, when I observe recognition in your eyes, I immediately see all passages of time collide on your sweet transcendental smile. I dismiss expectations with low hanging fruit because I know it's ripe and sweet, effortlessly grasped, and shared vicariously with you. I know you! I have always known you! There is no need to exonerate yet, only resume a love affair that has never ended. I encourage grace subliminally through our communion with our unexplainable selves with a big AMEN. This love runs deep and I know Marina knows it now. Also, our consciousness has now gone past the veneer of the Earth's crust and ventured into its molten core.

Words, intentions, or the trappings of an unlikely material world, have never fooled Marina in her divination. Real wealth to her is subscribed in merit, written in deeds, where truth needs no due diligence. It is sensed in the aura of being. So many approaches and few earn a real conversation due to waning frivolity and a lack of reality's fiery quest for passionate truths. Voids lonely ping, a castaway's message in a bottle, sent out into a vast universe where relentless sentinels always listen forbearingly for a reply. Myriads of responders approach, yet none have managed a proper sequence of uttered frequencies, or their voice convoluted un-decodable. Caution mindfully must be hers and mine as in our longing desires we have hedged too many bets in the past for little return. There're signs inscribed on seals, inside our innate awareness that recognizes our narrative. Behind each seal, a hovel humble body resting in a membrane, incased in a multidimensional chamber inside 'The Tree of Life."

When all our inner seals are removed, every secret chamber

connecting our higher graces fills with a merging awareness of our conductivity. Destiny revealed in undercurrents murmured beneath lovers' breath, whispering an exquisite narrative more than humanity's nihilistic journey towards absolution. It promises us an ultimate spiritual epiphany, emphatically delivered in our sincere surrender to recognize love's higher cause. Marina's heart still persists in the search for these intriguing rarities of two lovers, a value worth discovering no matter the cost. Also, this idea, as far-fetched as it may seem to those first hearing it, makes trust and commitment a treasure of unspeakable magnitude. The price is high for admission to this experience, a taste beyond comparison, truly what we are all secretly yearning for in a relationship. These experiences are very difficult for me to describe but fortunately, I've carried the sacred memory of its existence into this lifetime. I know clearly what words my partner will say before we can set sail into forever, as she does of mine. Marina is nobody's fool in that regard, and I can only raise the flag of my unfolding lotus heart as a sign of my surrendered truth for her to know, "It is me, my love."

Marina can't resist her underlying compulsion any longer; she desires to sequester a bungalow for our edification to reverently alter our emerging divinity. Edges of her constant visualization emerge from a haunting haze defining outlines, silhouettes, and a convergence resembling the two of us. These visions move like sweet Indian sandalwood incense, arousing an influx of ancient images of torrid carnal delights. These images crop up inside her mind every single minute of the day, and in mine like a never-ending Mantrayana. An ambience of oscillating, sweltering emotions stirs behind her apparently serene eyes, restlessly compelling her words to sing sweetly on my ears. We text, call, Skype and dream of each other, smell each other's scents lingering in the air. Inborn experiences of each other's presence, even though we are on different sides of the city, still finding ourselves checking to see if one is near. Above, in lurid stars, I catch her preeminence in whispers floating on air currents telling me, "We must be high above city lights dwelling in gentle breezes for congress to be absolved." Interludes of sonic fragrances, my musical muses that conjured sweet kisses dance across my imagination without her physical presence. Uninterrupted thoughts engulfed in flames consuming every waking moment, burning and yearning, inside my mystic eye and hers. Frantically, alarms ring out urgent messages yearning for celestial affinities that must be answered in graceful cosmic coalescence. We can't prolong this meeting any longer, action must be taken; our intuitions are unceasingly restless and crying.

Flashes of recognition unfurl inside our swirling awareness, inklings peeking above the water line our stoic lotus as it opens its petals to drone with consciousness. Pieces of the puzzle begin to fit, revealing our identities, our reunion in a blissful celebration prancing Earth's strata parading its equinox procession. Divinity offers us an esteemed celestial altar to dance on, a magic carpet ride whisking us among the stars to merge within its monumental presence. High pitches ring in our ears, bees buzz with underlying tones, reassuring voices letting us know we have turned the key. Preconceived notions simply evaporate in this ritual where sentinels have been watching patiently since time began. Hark the herald, our messenger, has brought us home to reacquaint our spiritual heartbeats once more on this lonely planet.

My recollection of this moment still sits inside an ancient limestone cave somewhere long ago, listening to water pinging out mantras as droplets slip off stalactites. Shimmering images, spectacles of future events, refracting off every droplet in a kaleidoscope of infinite possibilities catch my meditating eye. I hear voices reverberated from the dawn of creation saying, "Where are you my love?" and "I am here, embroidered in the fabric of time," beckoning. Inside this dark damp space you surrender to sweltering life giving steam from Mother Earth's cradled womb. This is where our identities dissolve and absolve themselves from absurdity at the same time. One of the many revelations in this cave is that everything must be revered, precious as forever. We're all made from the quilt the humanities thread through. From spindling interwoven spines of heaven and earth the Aurora Borealis' magnetic particles connect the two. Inside this cave, where only consciousness and awareness exists, is the soul's effervescence that connects the two. Marina and my trip into our moment of perfection have now arrived. The universe purchased it like a rich uncle and now the ticket finally found an address.

Smooth electricity rippled across her knowing smile while we chatted about the restless yearnings of consciousness in its quest for absolution. Many souls and incarnations have attempted to wear these brilliant clothes, only to be blinded by their overwhelming light. When your heartbeat races at the speed of light, is cause enough for one to run from his or her own illumination, fearful of the awakened unknown. Finding where this narrative ends is something enamored humans rarely manage. It is impossible to hold onto enlightenment and call it your own, like water cupped in our hands. Truth itself can be like a tsunami and unless you let it pass through you, it can carry you away. Fragile humans will never manage this until they discover we are merely conduits of creation designed to discover the origins of emotions and meaning in love.

A woman's exponential capacity to raise Kundalini's serpentine head is told in so many ancient stories. Mythic females throughout time fiercely discern truth, remove obstacles, and defend the Dharma. She is unafraid to ask the question, "Are you here?" to the universe and is brave enough to hear the answer, risking life itself to observe its intensity. He, with a voracious appetite to seek enlightenment has had a history of extremes struggling with duality. Men have a hunger for forbidden taboos, guilt after acquiring them, eventually trapping them in a labyrinth of mind games. Yet, men's brave quest for awakening leaves no stone unturned focused in their many attempts to ascend the mountain to witness its infinite splendor. On the other hand, there is no cost great enough for men to pay that allows them to delve into the darkest places to see what may lurk for self-discovery. However, somehow these modern times have restricted both sexes from their bravery to seek the truth in a materially driven world of exclusivity based on the price of admission. This prohibits the purchase of tools, and discovery forbidden, locked away so we can no longer see our causal, celestial, etheric, and astral templates that overlap these material bodies. Let alone the gyroscopic incantations that reveal the workings of each spoke of the dharma wheel that has never stopped turning. Harmonic liberation is now a myth, the tones of root syllables of our many lotus petals, a forgotten practice. Where have our risks gone to seek out our spiritual agreements with the universe and our awareness of consciousness? My pact set in the fabric of a visceral delve into the depths of an abyss of infinitesimal bounty written in timeless blood of my immortal soul. My heart is awakened by her truth; that she sees me as her endearing time traveler ready for our next adventure.

The tetrahedron is found in all sacred geometry, chemical bonds, Kabbalistic mysticism and untold stories about Eden's tree of life. This wheel inside a wheel, the flower of life, has been a piece of the puzzle handed down in legends and mythology, etched in stone and painted on cave walls. New views in physics have the tetrahedron as the substance that holds everything in every dimension infinitely. To me, it represents the very strings of our hearts, plucked to send our resonance into forever's folds of timelessness.

Lilith, once thought of as a gigantic monster or even demon in Mesopotamian text and Hebrew translations, is clearly a literal example in a scientific sense of the tetrahedron. Lilith is considered the first wife of Adam, the consciousness of consciousness, and was also connected to Eve in their trinity of love. Lilith bridges the union of identities in male and female, reuniting them into the celestial heavens to drone the strings of immensity. Lilith was the goddess that corrupted men wanted us to forget, so woman and man would stay disconnected. Written in the book of Isaiah 34, in her damnation, "Her nobles shall be no more, her castles shall be over grown with thorns, she shall become an abode for jackals and a haunt for ostriches." Lilith was our contact with the World Wide Web of the universe, torn down by the ruthlessness of greedy men, condemning the concept of her existences as merely heresy.

These twisted words are being untwisted as we discover more about our connection with the universe empirically and spiritually. Knowledge untwisted from the spires of DNA, where our ancestors placed all the answers in their blood. This benevolent gift was embedded to someday show us the way back to the garden of peace and love towards all creatures. Clearly my journey is laid out for me and I must return to Hollywood to be a part of an unraveling tale rich with the trappings of love. Happy endings are possible when our souls know no end, and truth is the family crest of humanity.

The Abode

Emptiness strokes gently relentlessly un-alone a cathartic anomaly resting on a stone. An unavoidable void transformed into a substance that lovers call home.

My equivocal return to Los Angeles was written on empyreal stars engraved cursively in cosmology, orchestrated by hands that move reality. Yes, we have all had an experience where somehow an unsuspecting paved road appears out of nowhere and takes you to your ultimate destination. Even though a hidden hand urges us forward, it is up to us whether we decide to accept this ordained proclamation that fulfills our heart's desire or to have doubt. Once you have sorted out those desires, removed frivolity from things, discovered that your mission is to give and receive love; then you have arrived. The next big question should be what sacred vessel or what Holy Grail does love occupy before you take a sip.

I had been working on a music project in the Hollywood hills with a fledgling singer/songwriter. Her manager had just acquired this small, but beautiful bungalow above former MTV producer, Michelle Lynx' house. There was a private entrance that went into the backyard but had a winding red brick stairway that took you to this well designed one room get away nest. "This is where our love should be placed on a pedestal," are the words I heard whispered on the wind. This will become a sacred place to nestle perfection and embroider our love into the fabric of time. I texted Marina some pictures of this place which she agreed would be perfect. It would be our perch to speak to the universe from this point high above Los Angeles.

Both of us didn't want to be in an impersonal site like a hotel. The idea of going to her place, which was more or less a workspace, didn't feel right either. As urgent as we both felt about our union, waiting to make everything perfect seemed to be the right choice. I could feel the nods and hear that voice inside that yells "Yes" or "No" and it was a big, "Yes," all the way around. To Marina and me, love was timeless. Wherever the act of love is committed, it leaves a stain that can never be washed off in that fabric of time. This first union will leave that stain turning into a searchlight for all moths to find themselves in the light of love, high above Hollywood. I have failed too many times before, in so many lives, where so many possibilities were laid down at my feet. I simply did not comprehend what was at stake until it was too late, but now my soul light is awakened and I can see for the first time. I do realize that every one of us flickers at the top of the flame, ready to seize the moment, and embrace what John Coltrane once said: "A love Supreme." Our enlightenment follows us, but our humanness can sometimes lead us astray. How could anyone doubt the wise words sung from such a beautiful woman's voice like Barbara Streisand in "Somewhere."

Everything inside this little abode was white, except for the red brick fireplace that was the centerpiece to its Feng Shui. Harmonious nourishing and sensual energy flow is essential to a manifestation of perfected holy union. Everything you place in this sanctuary is a part of the actualization of a sublime cosmic dance that delves into the nature of supreme passion. As a harbor for enlightenment, balance must be carefully attended to. Not too much yin or yang can flow through the energy subtly in the geometry of this environment for perfect balance. The frequency of pure candlelight has soothed souls for millennia and a necessary part of our evening's Feng Shui. As are the tactile fabrics from satins, velvets, soft rich cottons, to coddle revealing skins, essential for this esoteric probe into refined sensation. Every quadrant of our space must possess a color to insure balance and energy flow. In the south, a red brick fireplace was perfect for the headboard of the bed to be in front of. We needed two paintings on the southwest and southeast side of the bed, something perfect for Marina to paint to complete our space. On the southwest something with pinks to represent love and marriage and on the southwest, a painting composed in purples, representing wind and prosperity. In the east kitchen I found green granite counter tops that signified our connection with family. Dark brown stained wood floors spread through the whole space signified the Earth, with many tapestry Persian rugs to add to their inviting warmth. In the west, a bathroom with a claw foot ceramic bathtub, marble white floors, a petal sink, and a ceramic toilet representing metal and children. The north held blue drapes for the front northeast windows and silver drapes for the front northwest windows. These drew to the center of the room where an onyx tabletop held simple artifacts from many lifetimes of exploration for this moment in time. A Hindu royal teak four-poster bed was decorated in many shades of yellow; starting from almost white in the sheets, to a deep yellow comforter that was almost golden in appearance. A white love seat with multi-colored Persian pillows, both on the bed and the floor, to sit on in comfort while dining and reclining if so desired. Outside, there was a bistro table overlooking Los Angeles, made of wrought iron, painted black with two very comfortable iron chairs with deep violet cushions.

This was merely a set stage that would be filled with other finery to keep this moment beautiful for our seraphic liberation. All the little things tell the biggest story in a nuzzling environment made for cooing, love's nurturing, and swathing abilities. In a ritualistic telepathic synchronicity she and I share, we both are attracted towards objects of divination for our rite of passage. Tastes of foods, liquids to drink, glasses to drink from, plates to eat off from, mindful with details, making these choices critical. Zen's full intimacy with everything needed to be thought through in preparing for an everlasting moment already written in between the pages of all eons. For now, our prevailing timescape is focused on dutiful delight, imagining her happiness, and mine, creating a blessed space just for our bliss. Marina also has her many contributions to balance the energy in the room with Yin to complement my Yang. She wants to bring them all over on the day of our reckoning and that day was coming at long last. Also, she had two very large surprises that she had painted and was very excited about seeing what I thought about them.

The day had come with both our calendars cleared for a weekend of dancing with no idea of what forms it would take. No computers, no cell phones, no television, or radio. Only music that we had both prepared for our serenity. Dying from anticipation, she came by our new space early with gifts and jubilation brimming from her car. I could see her beaming smile as she pulled up from the window atop our soon to be lofty retreat. I rushed down to greet her and when she saw me, she jumped out of her car, threw her arms around me, and planted a devastating kiss on my lips. I reacted, but she smiled, moving me away and said, "Slowly, enjoy this taste, there will be more later," and laughed willfully at my smiling eyes of blissful joy. So I collected her packages to carry them up to the space.

She was giddy, excited about seeing what I had erected to cast our first pebble in the ocean of our mutual expression of love. I had arranged flowers everywhere from the ascent up the brick staircase to our abode planting gardenias and roses in once barren flowerbeds. At the top of the stairs, I sat her boxes of gifts down and opened the door for her to behold our space. It was a palace made for a princess and a prince, exquisite and perfect, except for her gifts that she brought to add to its perfection. Her excitement grew wild. She threw her arms around me again and kissed me quickly. It was clear that this was something no one had ever done for her before. She entered and started embracing everything with her artist eye, soaking up our amenable ambiance. She excitedly urged me to come in with her hands, explaining that she could hardly wait to place her dowry among our budding Sephiroth. First, with two large paintings she had covered, telling me, "Close your eyes, close your eyes," until she hung them. I brought the first load in and she immediately began to gleefully arrange her offerings around our new space.

Looking at me, still smiling, she ask me to go down and get the rest of her treasures from the trunk of her car. I rushed downstairs and opened her trunk. I noticed a large wooden box, some other little bags I collected, then closed the trunk and headed back up those very steep steps. Huffing and puffing a bit, I made it to the top and brought the rest of her items into our room. She has already placed very beautiful canvases she had painted. She also put fresh fruit in a very large bowl she brought, put different changes of clothes in the closet, and towels in the bathroom along with big fluffy white robes. Scented soaps, lotions, oils, makeup, and more candles had been places her loving hands; things men rarely think of, me included. She had me move the heavy wooden box near the bathroom and incited my curiosity even further. "Don't open it," she said sternly with a Mona Lisa Smirk, "It's for later. Perhaps as an option over the weekend," she insisted. I was still intrigued but I left that up to her discretion as to when the right time to open Pandora's Box would be.

I moved over to the kitchen and started washing fruits and vegetables to prepare them for cutting. We agreed to prepare little meals that we could share throughout the day and night but we needed to ready them so we could just focus on each other. There is only one cutting board and one big knife to work with, as there's really not much in the kitchen yet. So with that, she very sweetly told me how she wanted them cut, holding my hand to show me exactly the cut she wanted. Very lovingly, she told me, "I'm so excited to be doing this with you, there's no other man who ever took any time to do anything for me, except to go out to a restaurant and pay a check." She looks down and then randomly says to me, "Of course my spiritual love would be this sweet, to make our day a celebration of life together."

I took her chin with my finger and moved her head up to look into my eyes and gave her a gentle kiss and said, "Of course my spiritual love would say something like that to me."

She got a bit misty eyed but was smiling as she started taking what I chopped and adding other ingredients to them. She started heating a pan to sauté some of the items I cut and placing others in bowls to put into the refrigerator. We had a cooking assembly line going, to her delight, as we both started talking about the foods we loved and what other dishes we liked to cook.

Our small talk brought us to our work, as small talk often does, marveling about how the universe brought us to certain conclusions in our work and what transpired from those conclusions. She and I had been going through a progression of transformations, sometimes quite brutal towards our hearts, needed nonetheless for our mutual arrival here today. We are both complete packages, made up of our love of life, which for me is writing music and words, lots of words. She is also a writer, artist, inventor, and a person who makes dreams happen effortlessly. Creativity has always been our life's breath, directing our every move on this impulsive affection for the creative process.

We both felt this was out of our control, but that we had been brought here to do a task that has not been fully revealed. However, we are human, and we both just wanted someone to share our deepest thoughts with, our pains, and sorrows too. Somehow, reasonable facsimiles of someone like us have taken us both in over the years. To our lament, we have become isolated to some extent, simply pouring ourselves into our work to ease the pain. Believing that if the universe wanted us to be with someone, it would just have to bring him or her to us. Really we were both disappointed in looking for someone to complete us and sort of abandoned the notion that it was going to happen in this lifetime.

Marina looked up at me, through a pause in my introspection, and says, "That was the last one, we are finished, and all the food is ready." After we finished cleaning up the kitchen, it was time for us to get cleaned up. I went to prepare a bath while she took care of the last few items.

Le Baignoire

A soothing rain rhythm beats in empathy a quiet moment drenched in reality where lovers dare to submerge into epiphany.

I prepared reversed osmosis water with Luscious Lavender Milk, mixed with a generous amount of Nima Nyima and Natural Himalayan Pink Rock Salt. These would refresh our bodies to start our evening together. Day was now bowing to dusk, so reverently, I lit a few candles to fade in after we enjoyed the passing of sunset overlooking Los Angeles. Opening the steaming door to the baignoire, she surprised me with Chianti Classico, in a fine Schott Zwiesel crystal goblet. We looked into each other's eyes, toasted to our reunion, took a sip, and began to undress each other with serene loving gestures. Sweetly touching each other's faces with little kisses, we unbuttoned and removed each other's garments, much like getting a child ready for a bath. She stooped down, getting out one of the bags she brought and pulled out two big fluffy robes with a fleur-de-lys crested on them. "Here, these will be perfect for once we get out of the tub," Marina whispered in my ear. Her big white fluffy towels were already hanging over the shower rod that wrapped around this vintage bathtub built for two. The water level was very deep, which I had made very hot for us, so hot that steam was coating the wrap around windows that showed us Los Angeles in the distance. We felt excited, like two little children about to take a bath together playing in the tub. It felt as if somebody's mom was watching over us to make sure we got clean and didn't splash water everywhere.

We stood innocently naked in front of each other for the first time and our smiles were simply magnificent. As the gentleman that I am, I offered my hand to her so she could climb in and cautioned her that the water was very hot. She, like me, liked the water scorching, so she slowly eased in, as fragrances from candles and lavender water effused with steam went deep into her uncovered skin in a cooing Ah. When she settled under the water, I joined her, bringing our wine. She sat at one end of the tub and I at the other; we toasted to a perfect start.

Totally relaxed, we started making small talk about the day and getting ourselves over here, laughing about all the calamities and drama. Then our conversation got more serious because I wanted to know more about her spiritual nature. I asked her about her meditative practices, something we hadn't revealed to each other yet. She told me that she had studied the Vajrayana in Dharamsala, India a very long time ago with His Holiness Lungtok Tenpai Nyima. Again I was amazed, as His Holiness initiated me into the Bön order many years ago. I had experienced a vision of their existence in caves near Mount Kailash in the Himalayas. "We must drink to His Holiness," I said, while raising my glass. She raised her glass too and we took another sip. We laughed thinking about what he might say about our toasting him naked in a tub.

We set our glasses down and looked deeper into each other's hearts. We put our arms around each other while sitting in the very

138

warm waters. Silently, we rested peacefully on each other while lathering goat milk soap in very soft cloths, washing each other's backs slowly, in warm long, loving strokes. Marina began humming to me, like a mother washing her baby, meticulously swabbing my topography in sweet tenderness. I, too, adoringly lathered her supple vulnerability, fondly caressing every inclination, purifying my intentions with every motion of my cloth like a loving father. Inquisitively, we both discover little anomalies, little scars, or past injuries that very few would ever notice, fussing over them in compassionate, loving voices. I began to wash her hair and she mine with a very luxurious Fekkai shampoo and conditioner that she also brought in one of those many little bags. I got a ceramic bowl with Islamic geometric turquoise patterns embossed on it and put cooler water in it to pour over and rinse Marina's beautiful thick hair. She, to my surprise, had me stand up, pouring the entire bowl of cool water over both our bodies and completely rinsing our now very soft skins. She put her skin on mine, kissing me as ringlets of water trickle down our furrowing curves along our naked terrain. A high priestess christening and blessing our purity, she sets down the bowl, symbolically motioning that we are clean.

I get out first and quickly throw a towel around my waist. Then I lifted her out of the tub, carefully setting her down until she reached the floor mat. I turn to get one of those very fluffy towels and wrap it around her naked clean body. I embrace her as I dry her off and get another towel that I put around her hair. Once I dry her completely, I put the robe on her. Then she removes the towel from my waist, finishing drying my body off from my toes up and she tops it off with a jovial kiss. We are now innocently enamored, feeling a presence of awe, our reverence towards each other rises to new heights of affection. This moment is all too real.

She asks if she could shave me. I agree, explaining that I have some old fashion ways with a cup for lather and a straight razor. To my astonishment, she sits me down, lathers up my face, and starts scraping off my facial hair with my straight razor. I have to say I have never shaved myself that perfectly smooth, but now it was my turn to astonish her. I noticed in her bag a hair drier and a makeup kit so I sat her down, moisturized her skin, dried her hair very carefully, and put on her makeup. It was fun to watch Marina look at me while I did her eye makeup. She told me while looking in the mirror, "You have a real talent for this kind of art."

"Marina, my love, we both know life is art." I whispered, caressing her ear.

We decide to dress ourselves and to go elegant for our first special meal together. She finishes up in the bathroom and I in the closet so we could surprise each other. I knew it would take longer for her so I made use of my time. I started lighting all the candles out on the small patio leading up to the entrance overlooking the city. I also started a fire in the fireplace for warmth and ambiance that would make it cozy by the time we finished dinner. We both recognize that everything we do today will reverberate into forever and we don't want to miss anything.

Under the Stars

Brilliant glistens shimmer like a still lake's glass a trance a dance of true romance a midnight rendezvous that trips the light fantastic.

Outside, I had set the table and lit the heater. Nights in Los Angeles were cool yet perfect for what we were both wearing this evening. I call out to Marina to get a feeling about where she was in her preparation, but, really, I was getting excited to see her. I made the table, brought out the champagne and ice bucket, and made sure everything was perfect. I only had two place settings, but they made a beautiful table for our first homemade meal we created together.

"Marina, I have everything outside now, just come when you are ready. I will be right here waiting for you." Just as I said that, she opened the door, dressed in an Oscar de la Renta evening gown, Vivienne Westwood heels, and a single strand of pearls around her neck. I immediately make my arm available to escort her to the table, and say, "Table for two mademoiselle."

She looks ravishing, I thought to myself, drinking in her image, so beautiful and elegant. She is now looking me up and down noticing what I have on, my tux made by Beverly Hills tailors David & David, looking as fine as I have to.

"Marina, what is it? You look as if you want to tell me something?" I asked.

Marina took both my hands in hers, looked into my eyes and said, "There is a perfect power and path for you, one you did not even realize existed. You'll find it's what you dare to believe it is. If you live it, you have the courage to be one with it. Synchronizing with belief in the most perfect, wonderful way is without fear and only faith."

"Yes, I understand. That is why we are here tonight, beautiful Marina. I am here and I am listening."

Grasping and stroking my hand she says, "As with every intention you ever had, there were paths that presented you with conscious choices. When you care to consider where those choices led, you'll discover the perfection of your perfect destiny that simply manifests. You're a reflection in the majestic mirror of everything you've ever realized. It's the presence, the creation, the omnipresent power, the light, the absolute unconditional love you are. That is you."

Marina's eyes smile amiably at me and I tell her, "Marina, thank you for your treasures, they will always live in my heart. I would like to pray over our food to thank the impossible universe for making this connection. Our rainbow bridge to each other's possibilities." With those words, I poured her some Cristal Champagne and toasted her beauty against the LA Skyline. We sat in our pasha hillside cottage made for our discoveries and memories of each other. We clink glasses and began to taste our treats, making sweet little lighthearted jokes about how thankful we are for this weekend.

After some enjoyable evening air and dinner, it started getting a little nippy outside, even with the portable heater. I notice we have both been finished with dinner for some time as we chatted away. I get up to help her into our little cottage to further our evening of making resolved contact. I offer her to recline on the couch by the window and we both get comfortable, I help her with her wrap, she takes off my jacket and loosens my tie. There's incense burning, candles flickering in the shadows, and a now amber glow in the fireplace. We could be anywhere; India, Tibet, Arabia in ancient times or way in the future with Los Angeles as a backdrop.

I gently lift her foot and leg up towards me and take off her heels. I start to give her feet, ankles, and calves a little massage to take away some of the stress of her day. She slowly turns the other way so her body is lying in my arms. I am now cradling her while she looks deep into my smiling face. She reaches up, takes my tie completely off, reaches down to my shoes, and unties them while I lift my heels up and slip them off.

Enjoying my smile, Marina playfully tells me, "It seems this is your look tonight darling."

"I can't help it, this is the happiest day. When I can recline with my missing heart and beat with her rhythm of the universe once again." I say, enchanted.

"Darling, you make me melt," Marina insisted, "And I too am happy to be here in your arms."

I bend down to kiss her lips more passionately. I have been waiting to do that all night and all my lifetimes. She pulls me towards her, throwing her arms around my neck and kissing me back with an expression of sublime joy. With that, I pick her up and carry her to the bed among the candlelight and flicker of city lights through the massive windows that surround the front of this perfect bungalow of happiness.

We are lying in a pile of Hindu pillows, crushed velvets, silks, and soft cotton on our sides necking delightfully with sweet little kisses, more smiles, and giggles. Marina starts to undress me more, I begin to slip off her clothing as well, revealing the most gorgeous lingerie I have ever seen. Black satin lace and silk garters, a bustier extremely feminine to my masculine, perfect sleek definition in her skin tones. A goddess in this evening light. We have already seen each other naked, but this was different, it was surrounded with intentions deliberately stoking both our sexual furnaces. Our overt connection had us tantalized since the first moment we met, and now it was absolutely ablaze with visceral combustion. A primal passion instinctually stirs in our veins. Heightened arousal means heightened senses that have grown sensitive, tactile, and magnetic. We are lured to each others subtle erogenous zone by unapparent erotic forces guiding our impulses and daring. Sultry as this night has become steeping in lucidness and angelic auric, anomalies glow around us like the warmth from our fireplace. Consciousness unbeknownst to us is stretching out its collective tentacles through every fiber of our souls. We soon discover beyond our bodily borders, just what extent unexplained consciousness' mechanism is really driving us towards.

In our prophetic moment of venerability we both settle into a meditative state, channeling our collective sexual energies unconsciously. Lying still among smells of incense, tonal music, and Marina humming vibrations brought us into an alpha state trance. Our skin begins to glisten with pheromones; a sweat that has a sweet taste, luring us closer into the web of intimacy we have created. An aura of mystical bliss starts to blinds our common shell as we plunge deeper into an unconscious state of awareness compelling this intense devotion towards each other. A transmutation triggers our Tantric sexuality, circulating naturally as our Kundalini begins to reactivate in energetic hums up and down our spines. Etheric substances fuel this ever-present hidden force, evoking charka systems to spin, and resonate our higher bodies. Esoteric emotions, primal and protective, roll out like a dense fog, blessing our joint spiritual venture into obscurity. Quavering hormonal levels attempt balance and cohesion as ultra-high frequencies collide against our desires. Hands clasp in this gifted moment of silent prayer thanking each other's bodies for existing and accepting love from our higher nature. We share little kisses and silent praises with our eyes, boundless joy envelopes each other's devotion to love again. Our identities drift into each other and then into nothingness, as thought merely disappears and spirituality consumes us.

She mounts my lap, wrapping her legs around my back, fondling with her laced and satin wrapped loins for a piercing unambiguous contact dowsing for merger. Motionless in stillness' pause, awareness reaches out, soothing and cooing in psychic caresses, breathing in unison, finding a pulsing rhythm through each principle meridian. Chakras hum, resonating this meditative silence, with mutual premonitions that tap these psychic lusting dark hearts. Hush within each piercing gaze contacts gatherers, merging psyche symbiosis and aligning chakras rippling against the ebony pond of pure consciousness. Prana squeezed upwards forming loops of spiraling air currents through channels inside awakened spinal pathways.

145

Breath's elusive spirit ventures outside each beings quest for a subsequent slow inhale. Prana then falls, rumbling down the first chakra's photonic emanations. Susceptible sexual streams run through thermal undercurrents with each inhalation and exhalation, up and down Sushumna's cerebrospinal axis. Slowing, we take breath after pulsating breath, alternating each current with Ida female and Pingala male in fiery pranayama's.

She wants to feel me at her entrance, dripping with eagerness, anticipation, and salacious palpitations of electrical resonance, vibrating my throbbing covered pudendum. Magnetism draws me steadily towards her kinetic wetness, causing intense contractions between her perineum, yearning to take me inside. Rhythmically, she glides along my shaft with her soaking wet lingerie gently squeezing, enticing me to push against her strokes. Synchronicity begs us freedom to plunge in desperation but our teasing titillates, transforming desire to course through each other's veins. Desire intensifies a vibrant fiery glow, like a midnight summer breeze and rituals to burn at fever pitches smothered in scented sweat only lovers smell. Resistance withers with our loving intentions. Naturally we gravitate towards a risk we have simply dreamed about for way too long.

With very slow, loving movement, we careen forward, removing every last stitch of clothing from both of our drenched bodies. Invocations, loving salutations to each others pure naked recognized soul, humbled by a beauty only this material universe can provide. Marina utters pleasantly in my ear, "This is a time for us to come together, to let go our limiting beliefs and embrace every moment with wholehearted faith. This powerful energy now connects every living thing in existence, including us."

"Marina, you are my existence, you have always been my existence, and will always be, in our timeless abode everywhere and nowhere." I sigh. She looks directly into my eyes and touches my face

146

with so much love, it has brought me to my essence where I say, "I let go of all these ideas of who I am, where I have been, and where I am going with a tear. I have emptied all remaining onus."

She tells me, "I understand my darling, the burdens you have carried in your heart, and I am here with you now."

"These are the words I've hoped to hear for so long in my very lonely journey. I searched so long for you I thought I would never find you, my darling love." I said.

She brushed my hair back from my face and said, "Shh, this is our time, we can't forget anymore, we have arrived." Brave smiles overtook our faces, joyous of our discovery that we are both no longer alone. Our incarnation complete, at least for now, so powerful in our clarity, we madly watch layers of time shed like petals of a lotus returning back to the firmament.

Shifting attentions expand with spiritual exuberance, bidding farewells to our former selves when both our lifelong cosmologies become apparent. Marina takes me down to crest my loins, gliding her glistening vaginal lips down the length of my now raw horizontal lingam. With each glide her moistened yoni drenches my phallus adding to its glowing red streaming radiance that is absorbed by both our energy fields. Her slow karezza-like pelvic movements create a mutual penetration, intensifies powerful thrusts, and activates our opening crown chakras attention. A divine guidance bathes us symbiotically, increasing our awareness of love's harmony in varying degrees of heightened spiritual arousal. We are engaged totally, guided in ritualistic ceremonies, honoring hidden particles of vital love, a committed passion beyond subtle perception. Engaged in god and goddess sequences, we relearn sacred emotions that once upon a time united our identities.

Pregnant pauses between immortal kisses are a communion

permeating this gnawing sensation of timelessness that begs we stay forever in this moment. Inundating blood-soaked life forces emancipate our questing hearts to purge vivacity into passion's core. No directive other than to take each other over and over relentlessly, without a consequence, without a past, present or future. Rinsing continuously in long unending sumptuous moments lost beyond hedonistic indulgences dilated unforgivingly by our love. Forgetting where everything unravels and nothingness consumes our bones, racing hearts dash towards immeasurable time where kisses endure eternity. Consciousness has revealed inklings of itself and its narrations of existence with a high ringing sound enveloping every neural fiber, saturating our spiritual belongingness.

There I see a rising amethyst sun between her eyes, beckoning in forthright glimmers, heralding me to quench my thirst at its shores deep inside our symbioses. Surrendered wills gushing with tenderness, with gleaming waves of devotion upon our merging intensity that simply wipes away our meager existence as sentient beings. My thrusts become your thrusts; my quivering body becomes yours. It's our light that strikes a visceral continuity, washing away all remaining thoughts until only love remains. Holographic anomalies pander in our unconscious absence, etching messages we have yet to comprehend, as our deserving proclivities lose all sensation delving deep within each other. We radiate in all directions, in no direction simultaneously lost and found. I have known you and you have known me, until nothing matters and we have absolved into pure happiness.

Swooning undulations are now traveling in sparkling impulses, flowing with energy, ascending, descending, in a primeval circuit of unity. A resonating, high frequency sings to our autonomic nervous system in uncontrollable rhythmic contracting, pulsing in animated cosmic waves. Each of our adjoining chakras somehow atones, align, and dignify our salvation, harmoniously a universal amalgamation.

Our movements are not our own; with a voice that talks in pictures, leading us along a story line, stoic as infinity. The journey always starts by revealing a kiss with energy so intense, its electricity felt like it could throw us across the room.

Suddenly, our eyes roll back in our heads and in a loud internal snap, millions of pictures of kisses reflect in our third eye, compelling us to kiss beyond our mortality. These given glimpses quickly evolve into new awareness' whose cognizance could touch consciousness' hem. A bright flash catapulted us back, but like flowers opening to the sun in slow motion, it brought us back to taste awaiting lips. Abruptly, we bounce back to our awakened state, observing those open forbidden seals close with the setting spiritual sun, in a dance whose steps were already predestined. When two life patterns unmistakably harmonize, reactions concurrently resolve as if rehearsed for countless eons. Returning safely to ourselves, our world hums with electricity clearly shaken but full of Tantric knowledge.

Heat exudes from our energetic palms that groom across magnetic voracious landscapes of our naked bodies. We were propped up by so many pillows; it looked as if we'd awakened in a Sultan's harem of magnificent opulence. Red, violet, deep blue, adorned with beads and jewels that tantalize soulful eyes adding to a moment of returning to being aware of our surroundings. We start to recall our evening fresh in our minds grasping identity and the timeline. Setting low in a transcendental sky a shining star begins to sweetly turn our obsessions to creamy yellow candlelight as it sets.

Like magic hour at sunset basking in a rich glow our bodies already possessed from a wondrous communion, swirling intentions bringing us home to familiarity. Rapturously deep our kisses spoke in revelations from the tips of our ineffable sensuous intensity, our promise of transcendence in the vastness of possibilities of unfolding realization. Immeasurable vistas loom along shadow lines guided by intuition where my fingers rest upon your mound of Venus in

149

collective ebb. Relentless power still emits from mysterious changing sumptuous movement completely wet along your curves.

These glistening sequestered rhythmic pulses still sway from your hips and loins begging to return. Translucent halos a rebirth of ecstasy, parting pedals peeling back their flower's carpels to reveal source of innumerable sensation. I become a slave to every vibrant tone, harmonized with every constellation, awakened by moistened fingertips richly woven in your syrupy nectar. Our magnetic equinox of day and night's devotions, stokes our unconquerable fire, our unspoken commands uncovers every thread that may hide our delving pleasures. Consecrated flesh made to purge, surrender to heaven's gate and remain as receptacles, monuments to a higher carnal privilege that quenches our hearts to their very soul. There is no overcoming these powerful upheavals, of limbs, lips, and twilights that sparkle with our releasing hearts.

Your entrance begs into greater realms, initiations, amidst a golden magic of your heavenly smiles. We have ransomed our souls' immortality, sacrificing our radiance, to shine among the stars and relinquish our personalities inside our new embodiment of pure love. Conjured vivaciousness, seduce lewd seductiveness, titillate every facet of our reacting palpitating tissues with divine lust rinsing through our veins. Savage thirst, a swelling deepening hunger, an untamed carnal stirring angst, driving us to a sublime madness. What's left of our rational minds plainly disappears, pouring self into each other vessels wholeheartedly with complete abandon. We've succumbed to inbred primal animal instincts, propelling us towards visceral fervor, drawing our lips and embraces to deliriously join. Aromas sensuous delight overwhelms our salacious presence of mindlessness scented in memory's vestibules. These enticing, lingering fragrances of love makes savoring recollections of truths we gather from our exhaustion and vibrancy. Overtly enchanted in this primal scent of mysterious extremes, delves, involuntary discharges, emitting appetizingly from both our delectable skin. Irrationality melts away in lurid fits of palatable debauchery, imbibing our delicacies of immutable embellishments. We have been tattooed on our mindless lascivious hungry wit, imprinted within clear cyphers of our souls. Flurries of deliberate compassion, restless contiguous psychosis, and intrinsic endearments have fueled our ruthless quest to enter oblivion together again.

This fulfilling realm of radiance must now be relit, night has reclaimed its kingdom and its imprudence bequeaths our adorations. Almost in a ritual ceremonial way, we both begin to relight candles and incense to sanctify our dark journey into forever. We nourish and nurture each other with some food and drink to add to a sumptuous evening of refined treasures. Sweetly, we bring water to each other's lips, feeding each other like playful children filled with mirth. Effervescent, humming souls, imbibing in substances that satiates our nurturing glow, reinvigorates and resolves us to further this journey of grins and affection. Smiling, we turn to each other in a knowing way, with loving tenderness, percolating vitality, living in our Kundalini's intertwining inseparable wholeness.

She comes cooing and I cradle her in my awaiting arms, tending to her needs of substance amorously bestowed. For some odd reason, we notice our flower arrangements in this room of atonements. The meanings of flowers are coded messages for lovers, only this time their patterns coincidently communicated something beyond a mortal veneer. With a knowing smile, we decide to put some symphonic music on to take our romance to another level. Rachmaninoff Symphony no.2 op.27 was one of our top choices but we ended up agreeing on the theme track to a movie called Somewhere In Time. We put it on a loop so it would just play over and over, returning to our indulgences of each other's essence and mood. Little did we know these enchanted flowers would become another piece of the woven beauty of our hearts desire?

Two heavenly bodies orbiting each other's gravitational fields create acceleration of considerable magnetic tidal effects that pull nearer and further against two gyrating behemoths. Somehow, their horizontal uniformity finds a true center between their gravitational bodies. Magnetism draws them both together as if by magic. Conjuring this dear gravity's weight is pointing them to join their lures in rotations, whose horizons now move in unison. This spherical ellipse, the vacuous void between them, fills in with matter, whose interpretation sweetly turns concentric circles into inner locking fields. In this massive weightlessness of space, these two bodies have created mass around their intrinsic curvatures of time space. Who knows what deities bring these specks to life in this infinite void, where our nothingness reforms as two souls? Two architects with a fleeting chance to caress each other for one tiny micro drop of actualization, with powers exceeding all the dark matter of the universe. Lonesome granted wishes in a miraculous universe is where ones perceivability is challenged by its unique splendor and proliferation. Yet, when there is awareness to consciousness and consciousness answers with divine intervention, our connection with a haunting familiarity of nothingness becomes our new center of gravity.

Dusk Till Dawn

When joy immerses innocence a calm refrain of inner bliss fills in a myriad of cosmic wishes that greet us.

I turned to look into Marina's ecstatic face cuddled in my arms. We are both gushing with happiness. "Marina?" I reflect, "Thank you for risking talking with me."

"How could I not talk with you, my spiritual love?" Marina

153

sincerely told me.

"What did you see?" I asked.

"I saw our epiphany. I saw you, I saw us disappear, and I saw us reappear together." She replied with a smile.

"I don't want to leave this place," I said almost innocently.

Marina lights up and says, "I don't think we will ever leave this place." With those words we put down our water glasses and roll over to start conversations in kisses again. This incites the fires enraging a universal mechanism, drawing us out into a salacious sea, consuming our frugality and unleashing fervent treasures from our very cores.

The nihilistic notions of life's euphemisms confront the abyss of our admitted idealization of love. Nevertheless, it affirms that love could be human fate. How do we indulge in conceptualizing anything really, excessive love or cruelty, pessimism or optimism; all evaporate in a transcendental inventory to dissolve into a void. Yet, these so-called notions titillating stir our avid imaginations, somewhat of an innate soul memory telling us somehow we are all members of its empirical court. Metaphysically conceived, a true divine mode of thought belongs to humanity despite nihilism. Our galactic syncretic continuities glue each of us to some sort of universal understanding, written in a common language of measured wavelengths, reverberating the words of love.

Attraction is a natural function of everything that has mass or form, living as we know it or not, they come together eventually through deciphering perceptions. For now, in this life, I am being moved by these forces into some symbiosis for reasons unbeknownst by me, for some sake compelled by the unknown. However, this night, my suspicions have been justified in possibilities that I have found my love, our journey and a higher purpose are next to be

154

realized. It's pulling us to an enigmatic ocean with a great-unseen force that neither of us wishes to thwart. We have allowed ourselves this vulnerability, to dive together into the abyss, protected solely by our emerging bond of love. Fragilely held together by the threads of trust and an unspoken set of rules, etched in epochs only the universe has defined. We bravely pioneer, shielded from an immaculate eminence only fearlessness can conquer, driven by an overwhelming urge to reach its blinding light again.

We've already been shown so much in just our first mystic delve into each other's elusive cosmic puzzle. Compelled again, our intimacy draws us back into the story that can never be stopped by the ruthlessness of universal consciousness. Love's greatest conquest is made from its surrender. Of which only two sides can make amends. Great seals have been revealed to us, jewels of our mutual possession, and atonements from the flames of our engulfing auric fields. Each inhale and exhale projects us through spheres of pale silver channeling, drenching, and enriching, our very stamen, stigma in honey and pollen of sacred delights. This amenably allure nurtures our core in star bursting light, romancing us to fall into consciousness' grasp. It seems we can be whisked away into the chapter we have left off at, in the narrative of this imminent specter that now guides us. Gold and silver currents emerge from our tailbones, up through sacral and solar plexus, meandering its ethereal spinal fluids to the crown chakras and beyond. Rearing its Paleolithic cobra's hood, our avatar identities slowly ascend, unfolding the accelerated temples of the Kundalini's fire, synchronizing our expansion. Silver, violet, sapphire energy expands throughout every chakra's veil, simply falling until we reach the communicative nucleus and raw untamed power it possesses. Clearly essence reveals the last crystal seals releasing divine quenching, imbibing fluids with their holy names. LA, VA, RA, YA, HA, AU. Each chakra center, vibrating vicariously, somehow opening and closing in unison, like flowers in fast motion at dusk and dawn.

Each increment of my seduction teases at your wanting digressions, palpating, drenching secretly in a delicate anticipation. Our slow demise into darkness, soaked in ambrosial appetites, becoming viscous, trembling hunger, mindlessly unabashed and desperate. Your eyes roll back, quavering splendor's rovers, singeing tactile surfaces. Begging for heat to conquer a spreading soul's eagerness to surrender every morsel of life force. She takes me deeper unequivocally with both hands dominating my thighs in rhythmic locomotion, moisture thickening from both our pores. Each breath drawn inward, in a marathon of panting graciously, visions of connecting pieces throb, pulsing un-haltered indulgences. She needs me beyond herself, my hands underneath her nakedness, vigorously dragging her hips towards my penetrations, until delirium is reached by wanting hearts. We obsessively indulge, spilling through arousal's nebula. The tones of our looping music turns into sacred chants hymns of stellar mystics. First the voices are faintly off in the distance growing slowly louder, then blending elaborately, transforming into orchestral symphonic passages, playing types of music never heard before.

An archway of unexplainable ebony deeper than the blackness of perfect space opens, drawing us within its folds of time space. Our intertwining sexually levitates our kinetic frantic bodies slowly absorbing them into an abyss of uncontrollable depraved copulating frenzy. Awareness consumed in white blue dienophile flames incinerating identities completely, in an interstellar male/female obliteration that suddenly disappeared. Inside, no semblance of time space or sense of consciousness or awareness all time stands still among black Onyx's layers of frozen reverberations. With a loud popping sound, suddenly Brahma's material universe appears along an event horizon, along with every sound possible rushing history's records in an Akashic flash. In a heavy jolt, shocking our awareness, innocent flesh is shot back in intense rushes and ringing high frequency. Returning to our timeline, panting in delirium and laying side-by-side, we held on to each other in total exhaustion, attempting to catch our breath. We look deep into each other's eyes, huffing and puffing, to say, "I love you." We kiss one more time, swirling into unconsciousness. We fall asleep smiling, naked, and content that fate sealed what happened beyond our wildest dreams. While we abandon our bodies, our spirits seemed to hold hands as we nuzzle into a fetal position and pair into loving spoons. Having exited our mortality into parts unknown, we are lulled into a heartfelt resolve, somehow managing to find our way home together.

There wasn't much of night left to hold each other tight, occasionally waking to reassuring, adoring arms from time to time. I watched her open her eyes in total disbelief, stroking her hair and whispering, "I'm here, it's okay, sleep a little longer." I knew I was blessed to just lie there in the company of radiant beauty but I wanted to surprise her with morning treats. The glow of sunrise would soon creep through the panoramic windows onto our fragile bodies, an awesome reminder of how insignificant we are in the scheme of things. We wanted sunrise to flood our eyes in the morning as a perfect wake up call. We wanted all the precious time together as we proceeded to day two. So much information had been exchanged between us in our first coupling as virtuous lovers. A sense of honor allowing love, fashioned within to shape a new paradigm of romantic ideas. Mutual inspiration daring our hearts to exceed their mortal coils and fill in the gaps left open by complete trust. I am momentarily speechless by the eldest and noblest of any virtue in our true love. Serenity's heavenly discriminations lay quiet, noble in a wantonness that supersedes the blinded faithless to her exquisite desire.

Speaking of which, before she cracked her eyes open I needed to get up again and put the baguette into the oven I had left on before we fell asleep! I get up and carefully put the water into the steam pan and add loaves into the oven, trying not to disturb Marina's sleep.

There I wait until dawn and turn the bread once after fifteen minutes. Then I took it out after another fifteen minutes. Once I take it out of the oven to let it cool, I tiptoe my way back in between the sheets and into Marina's searching arms. With the overwhelming smell of bread in the air, her eyes slowly open to the arousal of its delightful aroma.

Attachments weary away at affection's reproach, what's meaningful is suitably obvious, this type of love is soulful in this noble enthusiasm that can't be censured. We can no longer be perplexed by eloquence because it's straightforward and nothing could discredit it or its reasons to be articulate. This prevailing love honorably shares secrets between beckoning hearts in the pursuit of astonishment and smiling morning eyes.

"Good morning," She says, all swaddled modesty under covers of silks, satins, and cotton, looking beautifully chiaroscuro.

"Good morning love," I return, endearingly stroking her brow and kissing her forehead.

She pulls me closer to her with her legs finding my eyes with hers to claim, "I want to feel you very close to me."

I reply, "I always want to feel close to you." With this invitation I feel our essence rising with this LA morning rising sun. We were so satisfied with sensing each other's thoughts throughout our very short night, yet felt rested. Processing of our untimely experience, an oasis of meditative reflection flickering in the pools of sweet fresh waters, manna of consciousness.

Powerful themes stream along in microcosm; macrocosmic bubbles where holographic prisms scour light-charged spectrums with electromagnetic auras defining everything under the stars. Lovers discover an entire range of wavelengths, emitted, and absorbed substances, pure emanations of phenomenon bringing them closer to creation's source. Buddhism talks about these as Siddhas, or what is known as a paranormal accomplishment of realization. A Siddha is where our souls are in their purest form, destroying karmic bonds, and simply residing in the pulsing rhythm of the universe. We both knew we had reached this state of flawless identity, at least in this momentary glimpse when our spirits were wading in perfection. Every term of reality came flooding inside of us and now this is our mutual secret.

There were no words to describe our experience together other than sublime. I would like to think that many have felt this sacred love. Mournfully, very few have recognized this opportunity during a first encounter as lovers. Difficult to keep alive as a couple without a lexicon certainly, rarely talked about in our culture and discounted or feared because of sheer magnitude. The moment passion turns to stillness, in a breathless pause of ultimate peace, when life and death have no meaning at all. Love is that sacred candle lit in the darkest of nights. Marina knew this and I did too; we had learned so much about each other in so little time but her identity was always a part of me, as I was to her. We're ready for the deepest part of our spirituality to manifest and this unfolding weekend was proof. Overwhelming experiences for some people, this would be so shocking they would run from it, but for us it was a time to run to each other. This was our theme, to run towards each other. There was never any doubt, it was meant to be, or as Muslims say, "It is written." We both comprehended how massive this transformational undertaking has been and any apprehension about sharing it with her completely disappeared.

It seems we all have a propensity to engage in an awesome exploration into boundless love with our twin flame. However, it can be sad when so many who want unconditional love, make conditions for it to happen. Truly it's a risk, no matter how you slice it. Those words, "I Love You," are still the most powerful thing anyone can say to each other. Even if pop culture, the Internet, or commercialism attempt to dilute the sound of the word love, you can always hear clearly what it means when it's said. It's a matter of recognizing the true value of unfathomable love, our only redeemable currency in existence that for some reason stays with us throughout the eons. Love is the never-ending story that picks up where we left off, through twists and turns of many lifetimes in hopes of getting to the end of love's rich story. Love is the most precious commodity, yet in these times it is almost valueless in our futile search to satiate through any other means. It is so sad that the value of love is not taught in schools, written on billboards, chatted about in social networks or even talked about by governments. What happened to the United States with their credo of "Life, Liberty, and the Pursuit of Happiness?" After all, isn't love the essence of all happiness? Where are the game shows, reality TV, or documentaries where we learn about all the intricacies of love and the importance it plays in civilization? Really at the end of the day, the only real thing you can count on is how much love you have given and how much you have received. For Marina and I, oceans of love were just beginning to pour in. Our fathoming of it becomes our poetry.

Good Morning Love

Dew renewed in morning hues a rising radiance ascending from your obsidian pools that draw me into serenity.

I don't understand why couples don't make time in the morning to make love. You make time to go to the gym, you make time to get ready for work, you make time to walk the dog, and make breakfast. It just seems that morning lovemaking is not on couples' agendas anymore and it just doesn't make sense. Men's testosterone levels are heightened in the morning and women are more libidinous and fertile. With all this arousal going on, there are very few who are taking time to nurture their lover with the riches of their tenderness. Arousal is creative energy, abundantly charging our bodies with nutrient rich life force, essentially the fountain of youth. Channeling that life force with fruitful intentions of intimacy is what keeps our hearts engorged with happiness and contact alive. This life force could light every tomorrow, but somehow so many let it slip by in preparation to survive in the world. As a man, I can't imagine anything that would give me more motivation to do better in the world than love from my lover at the start of the day. An orgasm is never the goal, but having the spark of real soul contact keeps Prometheus's fire burning and Persephone's heart yearning. Marina and I were no strangers to this idea, as worldliness often attempts to creep in and tantalize most people's focus. Worldliness always falsely leads and destroys so many on a quest for righteousness. It's sweet like white sugar, but gives you nothing but cavities, constantly dulling your taste yet making you crave more.

So here we lay, absorbing every drop of our precious dominion where every word carries a weight time would not forget. We kiss a loving, morning kiss, an assuring hello noticing that this was not a dream and that we are here in love.

Marina asks, in a quandary, "Did you just make bread?" Realizing that I did, she jumps up to the flooding sunlight filling our eyes with warm yellow morning light. Her face pulls into a smirk with a glint in her eye and I realize that it's a race to the bathroom. We both leap out of bed in a dead heat. She beats me, laughing and turning on the shower right away, hogging up the sink checking herself in the mirror. Steam starts to fill the morning air, swirling around and clinging to the bathroom mirror as Marina writes, I Love You, in the steam and wipes it off to see her own face.

We both laughingly grab our toothbrushes. She grabs the toothpaste first, pretends not to give me any, and then measuredly puts some on my brush. We both can hardly hold back our laugher while we, for the first time, watch each other brush our teeth. I begin to stop and she looks at me and shakes her head no. I need to brush a little longer to get everything right. I continue, to her delight, as the shower steam thickens. She hands me a glass of water to rinse my

162

mouth after she had rinsed hers. With that, she pulls my head down to her lips and kisses me passionately and then laughs out loud with happiness. I help her into the tub and then myself as she puts on a washing glove.

"Have you ever done a salt scrub?" she asked.

"It has been a very long time for anything like that." I told her.

She put an apricot salt scrub on the cloth and tells me to turn around. She started exfoliating my back, neck, butt, and legs and I could hardly stop laughing through it. She goosed me playfully and I noticed she had another glove that I put on, lathered up with her scrub, and told her to turn around. She smiled and I started to gently exfoliate her flawless skin and gave her a little playful goose as well. She then turns around, slowing the strokes down as she and I began to clean the front of each other. Water droplets seem to be dropping in slow motion hitting her supple flesh rolling off her face, lips, and neck. Ricocheting down the front of her breast along the tips of her nipples, in between her cleavage and along the ridges of her stomach. She noticed me tracking each flowing droplet of water because she was experiencing the same enticements with me. Both our gloves dropped from our hands and we began to look into each other's eyes while tracing the waters flow with our fingertips.

Our roving palms simultaneously slide down along each other's pubic bone, simultaneously stimulating and teasing. She slowly rubs me from the bottom of my pouch, along the neck, and then to the tip of my shaft. I tenderly stroke along her exquisite anatomy finding her delicate sensitive exotic ridge, also massaging the petals of her intriguing blossom. We begin to French kiss, licking each other's tongues as if they were genitalia and communicating our desires without words. She turns the shower off. I pick her up and carry her to bed, both of us soaking wet, and I lay her down into the warm covers gently. I place her in a way so that she is on her back with her legs at the edge of the bed. The perfect height for my lips and tongue to nestle in between her legs.

Quickly I take one of the many pillows and place it on the floor for my knees to rest on while I bury my face deep inside her erogenous zone. Her response is immediate lurching and heaving, stoking her lechery and brimming her lecherous desperation for my passionate carvings. Cooing fills the air of both our satisfactions that is taking us into swirls of colors inside our joining mind's eye. I cast my eyes up to see her face, breasts, and body, watching beaded water drops pool, her hair glistens, dripping wet like an enigma. I match her rhythm in concentric circles, around and round her percolating vulva lathering it up with measured excited intentions. I begin to hum mediating on energy signals rushing up and down her higher mind's Kundalini connection. She bids me to join her on our wet bed by sympathetically urging me to lie opposite her and continue my delving into her loins. She takes my dominance into her mouth and synergistically matches my rhythms, growing stronger as both our gyrations uncontrollably move faster. She then turns us so she is on top of me, her wet hair dripping down on my naked body, pushing herself deeper into my joining mouth. We're both lost in a pleasure, intentions, and warm loving caresses, inciting pure happiness worked up almost to the moment of climax. Superfluous, for both our desires as extending our fireworks to the exact moment of midnight's promise. So we begin slowing down our movements until we are completely at ease and start to kiss each other's bodies in reverent thanks.

Rolling over to look up as if we are looking on a summer's day sky in a grassy field under an oak tree where we contemplate our morning experience. I am so charged with energy and soaring throughout my imagination when she looks over at me. Marina tells me about a dream she had last night, we were together in a big city and no one was there but us.

I had experienced the same dream. So I described more, "Was there a grand lobby like a hotel we met in?"

"Yes," she said, "I'm not sure where it was because it was surrounded by water."

Then I continued, "Yes, like a city underwater."

"Really it was a beautiful place, wasn't it?" she said.

I told her, "Not as beautiful as it is right now."

With big smiles on both our faces, I got up, grabbed our robes and threw them on our bed to let her know it is time to get up. I then clasped both her hands and lifted her up into a romantic embrace of happiness against our naked vibrant bodies. I leaned over to pick up a robe for her and wrapped it around her like a cape for an empress. I got down on my knee and kissed her hand magnanimously, saying, "My queen." She laughs, turns, grabs the other robe, throws it around my shoulders and kneels down with a little bow and generously says, "My king." We both laugh out loud and help each other get our robes on in the glint of our delicious morning salute. Marina heads for the bathroom as I head for the kitchen to make our first breakfast together.

Breakfast is a simple treat really. For Europeans it's a boiled egg, baguette, little mix baby greens, very rich fine butter, a little cheese and a cup of espresso. However, with everything in life, "The devil is in the details." Even the simplest creation has many aspects of mindfulness attached to their befitting perfection. For-instance the only way to serve a soft boil egg is with a coquetier, a perfect magical pedestal for a magic breakfast. Also, soft-boiled eggs need to have the correct temperatures to make an accurate account of the time needed to be in the water. Adding salt is one way to make sure it is because it gives the water a higher boiling point. Watching the water coming to a boil, I put the farm fresh eggs I had bought the day before, into the water and started the 8-minute timer on them. Another wonderful detail is the fresh morning baguette that has now cooled properly and can't be any fresher for our morning soirée. For greens, I started a little garden on the adjacent slope at the entrance of our little nest along with some other ingredients that are still growing. I quickly go outside right after I put some water on to boil with some scissors to cut the salad greens and bring them inside before Marina comes out from the bathroom. As I reenter, the water in the pot is boiling and singing its song. I set down the baby lettuce on the cutting board, turn off the water, and pour the water over the Italian espresso into a French press. Aroma fills the air of coffee, now attracting Marina's curiosity as she shouts from the bathroom, "I'll be right there!"

I quickly set the outside table for two in the warm morning air and sunlight on this magnificent morning, where the universe is surely smiling at our mortal folly. Crystal Goblets for fresh squeezed orange juice from my father's trees, china cups for coffee, and glass opaque lavender plates covered the table. All the food got done at the same time but I almost forgot avocado and goat's cheese. Just in time, as Marina comes out to see what I was up to, I add the final touches to the plate.

"You did this for me?" she asks.

"Of course I would do it for you." I replied.

She was flabbergasted when I took her outside. "It is so beautiful!" she reacted.

"Yes, we must insist that everything we do with each other is beautiful, don't you agree?" Fresh coffee with heavy whipping cream, sweet Valencia orange juice from my father's trees, soft boiled eggs, freshly made baguette. A small taste of greens with avocado, goats cheese with a little olive oil and balsamic vinegar. Unobstructed

166

morning views of Los Angeles are breathtaking, unlimited visibility in all directions surely a signpost reminder to our awakened souls that this is not a dream.

Marina can't help herself and needs to express her emotions to me as we sit to dine on our warm food, warm feelings, and warm words. She tells me, "You have shown me it's possible to return to love's joyous radiance. Our coalescence has been so beautiful my love and this magic the universe shares with us is astounding. May our unconditional gifts of love be a consistency that runs through our emotional honesty. We have honored our hearts in a way I've only imagined. I've awakened to this day in a new paradigm of positive empowerment. Purified to potentiality, creating consciously in all fields of love with our true selves in a gentle compassion that connects us indelibly. We are the affirmation of miracles, an inexhaustible manifestation beyond belief, the possibility of magnificence realized. I have never been so affected by a man or a soul ever with something that words can't describe. Everything about us is energetically connected, aligned perfectly with sympathetic resonance that drones in the chamber of our love. The authenticity of love gives and receives exponentially, heals wounds, nurtures, and surrenders, allowing honorable hearts to reach their highest potential. I feel your empathy, your childlike nurturing nature, and feel our collective grace will conquer all things worldly and transcendental."

In my gentle reply I say, "Yes my love, yes, we are alright now."

This is how love should be. Our modern busy world constantly tells us otherwise, claiming disastrous relationships are imminent and true love impossible. Marina has it right, but I think love's wish rests underneath the breath of every sentient being. The first thing on everyone's list in our world must be our innate right to experience love in all its facets. Greed has been the door closer in too many people's faces that merely want to give and receive love. Can this be so impossible to do right now in our world? Isn't everything an

167

agreement we made, the worth of money, the price of our labor, the value of education, etc.? These are the things that have crushed too many lovers' hearts faced with the prospects of preserving love or surviving the material world. With all these conditions, it is almost impossible to be unconditional, and with rules, laws, bills, payments, and more, it takes hearty perseverance to pave a way for romance, love, and happiness in a world based on money. I truly lament for those brave souls whose only prayer is to have and give love continuing to struggle without retribution. It seems this world's mission is to take your hard work, turn it into money, and then charge you for every little detail of your existence. They rob you to the point that you have no more money for yourself to nurture and love.

The road to perdition is paved with the souls who have lost their way due to their resolve towards love. We've all walked this path - love is the only light that can steer our ship away from the rocks and bring us home again, safe and sound. If only the hearts of humanity could change the destiny of a world where suffering exists. Every endearing soul's mission is to take down the walls that separate us from realizing love. There can be no settling. This alone should keep anyone on a righteous path, resolved to follow the beacon in the night towards truth and salvation. Throughout time, the power of choice failed miserably, but the truth of words can spare those who have not yet burned their hands in life's' fire. We have the power to stay warm, healthy, and happy because of knowledge. Marina and I were going to have to use that accumulated knowledge to safely take our fortunes home again.

Basking in this perfect morning sun, listening to Marina's wise words, and imagining our evolving phenomenon of spiritual romance, added to the taste of our morning meal. Our foundation was growing stronger, way beyond biological love; we were enthralled with each other, as rare as that is. It's a power that transform desire into limitless aspirations where another set of instincts take over serving a higher good. Her invocation affirmed she was a woman in a state of spiritual romantic love. Knowing that someday her longing to be swept her off her feet spiritually and romantically has come to fruition. Too many times passion means suffering, fate can be overwhelming and free will's illusion faltering to paradigms that aren't what the world is about. We are not objects to be used and preyed on; we are merely symbols of our higher self, in human form here to exercise spirituality. Our exalted nature is just like that single egg on a coquetier: a symbol for resurrection and new life.

As I thought this, we began to symbolically crack open our eggs and begin eating them by dipping fresh baguettes into yoke. I began to speak, "My dear Marina we have surely slipped through the bonds of time, escaping our bodily limitations into a realm of forever. It has always been my complete desire to soar above my luminous aspirations with someone and never relapse into the futility of primitive temptations. Dwelling in our rarefied spiritual passion's secret home hidden in a higher sphere, a romance beyond the flesh ascends a staircase towards its fountainhead. Transfiguring force amalgamate us beyond delight and pain, ardent beatitude to a sated appetite that fulfills our longing. Love is our awakening today and I am consumed in its perfection that has come in the form of you."

Marina is taken aback. This is the way humans should talk to one another, but we seem to always put obstacles between our hearts and others. Every perennial story of love facing obstacles seems to end in some sort of disaster when it comes down to the burdens of everyday life.

For now, Marina ponders, "It's our beautiful breakfast for enjoying each other's conversations as if tomorrow was never coming."

She was right, it was up to us, the power of our emerging love to vanquish those obstacles. With these words, the concrete of our commitment was already dried, cast in stone so long ago. Longing need not pierce the heart and growing old together need not be the end to spiritual romantic love. With new facets opening, new beginnings happen at ever iota, and reflecting in each of those facets was a blessing. Marina and my fate would not be empty or tragic, ordinary or unbearable. We were awake and this could be seen in both our eyes. We were not struck with an arrow or a bolt of lightning, but moved with the hidden hand that moves us all into opportunities when recognized. Seemingly without any reason, we can be at the discerning crossroads to our ultimate choice for love at any moment. Now, for a few sips of coffee in this very pleasant etching in the clay of time. We are about to return inside to continue a romantic weekend unforgotten.

We both bring the dishes into our abode and begin the process of cleaning up and putting them away together. This very much reminds me of playing house with some of my little girl friends when I was a child. Helping with their sweet little make believe tea parties where I was cooked for, fed, of course, along with dolls and invisible friends. As a young gentleman, I always helped putting away the toys or, should I say, cleaning up together. There's naked innocence to us underneath our robes, washing, drying, and putting away the remnants of our morning soirée.

Trust

Consumed by heirlooms woven in heartbeats sweet trinkets of life dripping from souls
siphoned by spice, passion, and life.

Afternoon came quickly and she had a plan she wanted to ask me about. "Do you trust me?" she asked.

"Yes, I trust you. What's on your mind Marina?" I respond.

"I want to shave your body," she said boldly with an enormous smile.

"Where on my body?" I asked.

"Almost everywhere," she said.

Normal men would be saying to themselves, 'There is no way I would ever trust a woman that much.' But, I was different, primarily because this was not a matter of the request; it was a matter of trust. I know Marina's intentions are only for a higher good. I told her, "Where would you like me to be for this experience." She told me to lie on the floor where she had laid out a sheet over some mediation cushions and she would take care of everything.

Marina had been an esthetician at one time on her many career paths. I have been going to one for many years myself, because I believe a man should be well groomed. She had something else in mind, heating up some wax on the stove. After it was properly heated she brought it over, along with muslin cloth and little sticks. Smiling, yet quite serious, she began to methodically remove all the hair from my chest, back, and around my groin. After she had removed all of my body hair, she started to shave the hair off my legs and arms. It was an odd feeling at first, a lightness of being, feeling of freedom, shedding the past, and renewal.

No stranger to this waxing, I asked Marina if I could help her remove some hair around her body. She handed me the wax and muslin cloth and knew that I meant a Brazilian of which she agreed with total trust. Her mound of Venus was truly that, an exquisite perfection I savored in the daylight gleaming across her rich skin. I wanted to add to her perfect look very carefully removing the little bit of hair that was there. Then I moved down around her lips tending to each little detail of her delicate flower smoothing it out with precision and love as she had done with my entire body. I was very careful, but I had to tease her a little bit and she laughed at me and told me to pull quickly. I also had something else in mind with her naked tanned skin that was waiting until my next touch.

I brought some very fine essential oils with me, diffusing its essence at first on her navel and then across her ample breast in loving strokes. Her pores immediately drank up every drop

172

penetrating deep into her skin softening and refreshing its already beautiful appearance. Lubricating her, I began messaging around her labia, petting her, swathing her, with my palm, roving my fingers incessantly between her legs. Aphrodisiacs of heightened sensations these oils have been known for centuries to help increase desire. These desires culminating in a spice of enticements, herbs from the Kama Sutra of pure sexuality made for intangible love.

Oozing coos, she wanted to feel my now very smooth and naked body next to hers. She crawled up from the sheets, pushing me back down. It was her turn to procure the oil, dousing my shoulders and chest, then slipping me inside of her all in one continues move. Our skins were drinking it all up in tactile ways, rubbing our warm flesh against each other in very smooth, sensual, edifying ways. Marina pulls me up to bring me into the Mahamudra position looking deep into my eyes, her vestibule pushing down, her hands wrapped around my neck. I was enamored in a women's intimate fire of satisfying appetites, affectionate phrases, intertwining receptiveness, and freely giving limitless passion. I wrap my arms around her back, pulling her closer to me with one hand holding the back of her head, pushing her madly towards my lips. Passionately, we kiss, her breasts rest firmly against my bare chest, drenched in essential. Slipping into unconsciousness, we feel each other dissolve into venomous madness biting and clawing in dark sexual desperation. Transforming herself into a dakini's will and I the heart of Shiva, we engulf each other inside a flame of pure lust. Yearning urges possess us as we combust like a bomb-fire stoked in viscosity. Our orgasms are not of this world, transcendentally coveted in realms our identities cannot identify. We are purified in ultra-high frequencies, imploding our entire beings in a sonic resonance of swathing divinity.

We are on the fringe of volcanic discharge of molten rock and pyroclastic fragments. Witnessing the upheavals and violence of creation through volcanism and observing Earth's terrestrial development in an extreme time-lapse. The phenomena of lithospheric plates colliding, changing Earth's surface many times as newly formed mantles get reabsorbed. Land arcs are finally formed in seduction zones. Explosive volcanoes rising from the sea floor forming island, chains, with currents of magmas streaming and steaming onto the seabed. Ocean ridges and floors were eruptions and cooling basaltic rock, creating the margin between heaven and hell of our Earth's core. Fumaroles surrounded by magma spewing out smoke, gas, water, and steam as land starts to become uninhabitable in our sentinel view of the dawn of life. It is almost like our bodies are the bodies of Earth and with all these upheavals we somehow innately feel the tragic lament of Earth's violent manifestation.

Our actions are not our own, shuddering violently with our eyes rolled up into the back of our heads. It took everything we had to hold onto each other and not collapse to the floor. We were physically and spiritually shaking uncontrollably, yet still in congress. Analogously our heated palms begin to groom each other's aura in an autonomic healing way. At first, moving in fast, and then slower movements up and down each other's electromagnetic bodies. Slowing down, we both began to regain semi-consciousness and Marina returned us to the Mahamudra posture, sliding me further inside her throbbing womb. In sincere reverence reacting to lucid epic consciousness. We begin the practice of Pranayama's in unison. Flooding our bodies and brain with life giving oxygen in long deep belly breaths, pause and release in clear attention. We've perfected this system of ascension through Mantrayana and visualization technics but never with a partner. Invoking Sanskrit names associated with each chakra we begin to recite root mantra for each chakra starting at the Muladhara first chakra. Adding the feminine "M" for balanced resonance makes LA, LAM as our coccyx vibrates clearing the dust. I take the low tone and Marina an octave above vibrating on the note, "A" whose frequency energy permeates both our bodies.

Visualizing the color red, affirming our right to exist with each inhale and releasing blackness of nothingness with each exhale. Rising up each note of the chakra scale, we surrender every molecule of air, holding it outside our lungs until awareness settles into a pause of merging void. Each inhale an ascension, visualizing the second chakra color orange reciting its sound in the key of "B" exploding its root syllable of sensuality VAM at our pubic bone. Manipura, another climb to the third chakra is yellow vibrating on trust a frequency of confidence roaring with a vibrant sound in the key of "C" singing RAM above our navel. Anahata, green as an emerald, radiating compassion intoning the key of "D" wavering our bodies in its imminence and consuming our epiphany's lulling with YAM at the top of our diaphragm. Deep in our exhale, drawing up our organs into our diaphragm, our eyes are rolled deeply back, Kundalini's cobra takes form in our oscillations.

Blue fills our auric field with inhales sucking our throat region in along with our diaphragm so powerfully that you hear a choking sound. Then we exhale all of our air over our vocal chords effortlessly with a vibrant HA ending with "M" at the very end of breath, signifying belief in each other. Our bodies are now in a trance, moving like a cobra being tempted by a charmer. The last key to turn into this intense ascension through our spiritual doorways harmonizes together in unison in key of "F." AUM is the last syllable opening our jointly shared third eye in a violet indigo radiating between the bridges of our cosmic vision.

Suddenly we both go into a fifth layer of mind resting on its edge where our identities are inconsequential. We have now settled in an otherworldly realm, residing in true essence with a thirst for limitlessness subtlety being quenched with each drop. These golden sips make sitar sounds suckling from solar flares rich in magnetism that crest these etheric bodies into multidimensional planes. Once inside these folding layers, awareness surfaces inside a never-ending room where Akashic records continue reciting innumerable narratives. The narrative voice speaks from a book with all our past lives in it, flipping through pages involuntarily witnessing all our karmic memories in a flash. These glimpses are however short lived as we are whisked back into or mortal bodies as both our eyes open looking serenely into each other's.

There are so many transparent designs, apparitions, and translucent iconary, affixed in different locations on our bodies. Each of them have a life of their own, some spinning at our different chakra, others dissipating into their prospective dimensions in high energy particles spectrums. A sideways violet eye on our foreheads is the last to go blinking its jovial way until it vanished into wherever its origins dwell in nowhere. We arrive at an awaken Alfa state, not really ready to talk or move shuddering, tingling and reactive. A congress connected in Mahamudra's posture our arms wrapped around each other so tight begins to relax.

It's difficult to speak but we reassure each other with our smiling, knowing eyes that what we just experienced truly happened. We begin to notice behavioral signs emerging from our exhausted motor responses and slowly our personality repertoires returns. Humorously, we detect a comical presence stirring up a tickling sensation compelling each of us to start laughing. We make gestures to communicate at first and start laughing some more and then spontaneously through a directional gaze we grow more serious and begin to kiss and cry. This is no anomaly of consciousness; this was an arousal of its dichotomous phenomenon that subsequently gradually transitioned into one consciousness. We had just witnessed it (Consciousness) in unfathomable unambiguous ways that may take years for us to both be able to articulate, if even at all.

By virtue of our contact, we are swept away validating both our innate feelings for each other that are surfacing with clarity. This sublime slice of timelessness affirms both our hunches that there is more to our chance meeting than our verbal abilities can capture. This was a moment of spiritual intensive care we have incubated but for now our cognitive intentions reached another milestone and our kisses turned to many thoughts of, I love you.

Then she whispered to me in a somewhat tattered, "I love you."

I respond in the same worn out voice, barely making it audible, "I love you."

We both start getting up from the sheet-covered meditation cushions and I swept her up off her feet carrying her over to our bed to lie her down. I crawled in with her, covered her sweaty spent naked body and we both vanished together into a very resolved pleasant sleep.

I woke up this time to a very delicious aroma of Marina cooking lunch; Lobster bisque, oysters on the half shell, and a salad made from ingredients from my hill side little garden. Her adoring loving touch to these orgasmically seductive foods was completely unexpected and incredibly sexy. She artfully placed two huge prawns in the center of this exquisite bounty that was filling our afternoon air. Another luscious taste to experience together in our methodical expressions of celebration and reunification of our souls. These are our lucky stars aligning in a joyous strata smothered in happiness. We've had so much time and distance apart for so long and now that distance has been magically eliminated. I've spent an inordinate amount of time preparing myself for this decree, sifting through too many replicas to discover one honest beloved heartbeat. She puts her assortments of food treats on a tray, including some flowers, and brings it to my smiling face in bed. She is so excited about our rarified meditative Tantric journey, something you can only read about usually. Like me, this has always been a wish of hers to experience and share with someone who recognizes the value of the narrative.

Guidance techniques and practices unlock so many doorways to the three Vajra's body, speech, and mind of enlightenment. At the precipice before an unadulterated leap into discoveries, deep within nothingness' complete embrace, our realization awakened. Even more important in these desperate times where love is challenged by unseen forces whose desire is to see you disenfranchised by perverting its truth. This is our leap, our requiem broadcasted in compassion to thwart this catastrophe that threatens our real human resolve. Love is the supreme source of help and happiness for all sentient beings in any realms and empowerment through many lifetimes is not in vain of its cause. These initiations from our many empowered guru's through eon's of lineage has been etched beneath both our skins. It's as if this embedded secret wisdom is now flowing through both our hearts effortlessly. We hear, feel, see these transmissions echo from whence they came reverberating in its primal conjunctive form. There was no mistake in both our smiles. We had achieved something we always wanted to attain, that could only be attained together.

Marina sits next to me frolicking in her joy and enamored in her love for me. "So how is your weekend going?" She says coyly.

"Well, about the same as yours." I express, jokingly.

She laughs at me and puts some salad in my mouth with a fork. She watches me eat in fascination as if watching something so familiar is was almost thought lost forever. "I know you!" she exclaims.

"Yes, I also find you faintly familiar." I say, while letting out a smirk. I put some salad into her mouth and chuckle. Happiness, as fleeting as it is, hovers over my heart with angelic smiles with my eyes filled with Marina's solemn beauty.

We passed some time talking about when we studied Buddhism

with the Lamas and the miracles we discovered in our practice. Done with our delicious long overdue afternoon lunch we got up and cleaned our space together putting dishes away, picking up, making the bed, and cleaning up our group-waxing extravaganza. The sun starting to set early, still in winter's grip. A very moody and playful state come over us again. Marina looked wildly in my eyes, got her big mysterious box out of the corner and started to drag it over to some light. She motioned for me to help her, I came over moved it under a floodlight I had arranged in the right hand corner of the room. First thing she pulled out of the box was a very thick cotton blanket with all kinds of different left over paint marks on it. She laid it out like a tablecloth on the wooden floor and started to arrange scissors, cardboard and stencils with various symbols already cut out on them. Then she opened the lid to expose an array of different colored paints and looking up at me in a childlike voice she says. "Let's Paint!"

"What?" I said.

"Each other!" She continued. She started to explain her vision to me of something she had been contemplating for years, "Sacred ritualistic body painting!"

She had kept a journal with many pictures in it, some she had drawn and some she had printed off the Internet, showing the history of body art in cultural anthropology. She insisted that there was a connection to this type of body adornment to merge with the universal form. Interestingly enough, this is something I had always been curious about: the practice of self-liberation in the wisdom of non-duality. It seems when the paint goes on, identity becomes primal; perhaps this is why we had war paint and tattoos. Painting a Bride's body with henna in Hindu ceremonies with the words of gods and demigods is an ancient ritual to remind the groom her body is holy. Powerful information is affected in the psyche when the body is ornamented in color. "It is a guided spiritual experience." Marina furthered explained. We have to allow ourselves to see the images and let the paint translate them into actualization. It is a process of impulses, a psychic reading, written on our bodies that reveal a sacred intimacy between us. This is a level of emotional significance that I never suspected our weekend would close with. Body painting is such an intense commitment and empowerment of our primal selves. Seems we have been on a roller coaster ride of confirm and reaffirm the sexual spiritual side of our emerged relationship. We are positively charged with powerful forces flowing, streaming through our gifts of ultimate creativity. Astonishingly daring, we both grasp our miracles beyond eventuality's effects to find our salvation in liberating each other in all dimensions.

Stencil cutting and applying paint with airbrush, paintbrushes, fingers, sponges and makeup tools is now a matter of instincts. She had already made many sizes and shapes of stencils, many shades of Kryolan, Aquacolor, and Supracolora body paint premixed. We both started cutting personal symbols that we had gravitated to from childhood, revealing hidden cosmology from our secret oracles. The sky was filled with sunset colors coincidentally against a huge canvass of cumulous clouds from our panoramic view. It was as if the universe was giving us validation and also playing with us suggesting, the color scheme of this beautiful evening. Another inside practical joke we're sure of which gave us a both a giggle. We got up from our work half painted to light candles and incense walking around in our naked canvasses surrealistically. I brought back some Château Ducru Beaucaillou, a deep-coloured powerful blood red wine for us to drink. She got lost enjoying my silhouette of glasses and wine bottle against the windowpanes, backlit by the setting sun and the outline of Los Angeles flickering lights. It was time to continue our Tantric trance into a meditative delve discovering our rudimentary symbiosis of cosmic iconary. It was written in the universe long ago and our hearts were ready to be taken to their most common denominator into tribal throes of passion. I put on some tribal trance dance music with lots of hand percussion and psychedelic atonal interweaving synthesis to intensify the paint spreading.

She dipped the paintbrush into a pint of white paint soaking the soft camel hair bristles methodically extracting its color and wiping off both sides so as not to waste any. Moving back my hair putting a nylon cap on my head she carefully begins to paint me. The paint is silky in texture and feels like butterfly kiss as she applies it to my naked skin. Marina looked deep in my puzzled eyes brushing a white six-inch wide strip from my face down, middle of my chest over my abs and down the length of my shaft. White symbolizes a Hindu Brahma Bull, not only male energy but considered a sign of happiness and strength.

First, I mark off the borders of where I don't want the paint to cross very carefully on her delicate skin, with a soft tape along the curves and contours of her body. Brushing and pulling back Marina's hair under a nylon cap to protect it from paint I gently touched her eyelids close to start to spray the paint. Attaching the black paint and turning on the airbrush, I shot a little test blast into the air playfully. In steady even strokes, I lay the black mist along her face, neck, and breasts, then cautiously in reverence across her naked vulva. I covered her beautiful derrière, traveled up her spine and the back of her neck in total blackness. Black symbolizes femininities embracing comprehensive nature in its most primal form. All colors merge, absorb, and dissolves in her blackness, her infinite void where all life emerges in her isotropic singularity vortices. Conversely, black is absence of color, ultimately signifying the spectra of nothingness, transcendence along the shores of black monochromatic radiant waves in sublime emptiness. The immediate shift towards consciousness was obvious and consciousness started sucking us both in deeper to its resounding well.

How unique this experience is, precious, forgiving, open, and surrendering a perfect accompaniment to descending night. Her color pallet wasn't only pastel but very vibrant spectrums to elucidate erogenous zones and chakras. My intuition wanted to surround her black edges with colors in a sea of quantum-foam, bubbling and percolating blues and creamy whites. In Tantric philosophies, blue signifies the transparent nature of non-dualistic awareness of consciousness itself. She was seeing Shiva red on her next instinctive pass over my frame covering the rest of me in a deep dark red from the back of my neck to the rest of my face and exposed body parts. Red has always been a representative of fire but it has other meanings, including ovum, as heat is the source of life. We're becoming transcendental worldly and otherworldly, physical and metaphysical, two cosmic experiences, ethereal, real, and divine.

Radiance of the absolute was beginning to take shape in our designs of golds, silvers, illuminating yellows, and bright greens. Meticulously, we both stenciled in final touches, painting them with a brush and then airbrushing, creating the final details of our metamorphosis. Her inscriptions, sacred symbols of our unknown universe, carefully written on my naked body, clues in vibrant colors feathered in hues, shaded edges along my forearms and legs. Oranges, browns and yellows airbrushed along my calves, little insignias imbedded on my toenails, vivid outlines accenting my facial features, highlighting my third eye. I paint her lips in deep violet and surround her eyes in pinks and lilac, gluing a large red rhinestone on her third eye. She had many little items stuck inside her treasure chest of colors, each in their independent drawers. It's as if she had been saving them up for a lifetime to bring them out to play with someone who could appreciate them. With a fine tipped brush, I painted a thin golden spiral starting at her nipple and circling her breast, along with little gold lines outlining her abs. Forbidden taboos were being broken in our brush strokes. Now, towards the end of our artistic endeavors, we had captured tribal virility and fertility. It is clearly apparent what kind of sensuality this ritual was invoking in our mammalian brains. Suddenly gazing at each other, we realized we were no longer just a canvas. We had become deities, a scandalously erotic god and goddess, lascivious and benevolent in our gestures that had turned promiscuous.

Undiscriminating hands feeling the freshly dried paint stirring overt primal urges replaced with wet application of color. Night had fallen, as city lights, candlelight, and our light became a surreal backdrop for an impending trance dance with impermanence's fateful desire. She was insightful and provocative, alluring with lecherous intentions and salacious taunts. She teased me, aroused my pursuit, her begging wetness called to everything primitive in my masculinity to mate. Ignited in my red-coated apparel, drawn on imaginary hoofs made me appear as a foreboding eminence stocking its prey. She's black as night, illusive in her prance, slipping in between time and timelessness. She managed to put on Beethoven's No. 9 symphony in D minor to start another erotic journey. Tripping the light fantastic, our hands meet to waltz, these compelling titillations of vigor and divinity in our symphonic movement among the many facets of reality. My imagination was convinced of this sublime, transcendental unchaste libidinous raging below our subliminal perceptions, rousing our aching extremities.

Midnight's carnival of mounting apprehension dances like stars against a background of unanswerable questions. We dare risk to have a supreme moment of passion. Our bodies' tribal rhythms beat loud in exotic primeval heat, sheering our flesh, transforming night into dark painted naked eroticisms. Our instincts rouse to fit these human hearts so fluently, drenched in carnal surges, enticed by flesh that must mysteriously fulfill a puzzle. Winter has turned into a balmy night where lovers perch on a pinnacle of heightened seduction. An altar for divinity rituals, designated by a language of human touch burgeoning from sultry beckons to indulge in spiritual didactic lust.

Wrapped within its venerable clutches of mystic salaciousness, slow ripples of perspiration slipped down between her lathered legs.

183

Steam evaporates from these beaded drops, until it engulfs her ripened, wet flower. Her seething conspiracy is steeped in all consuming desire, plump and swollen; it palpitates with its own heartbeat. Urgently in visceral waves of undulating arousal, moaning in mounting tension, she coaxes our maniacal connection to abandon awareness for lecherous indulgences. Her unbridled fingertips glide along its glistening dilated aperture, with uninhibited impulses, she strokes it as it's oozing silently, begging for penetrating enamored eyes to look. I am obsessed and driven by licentious instincts to gratuitously share pleasures painted in lust and taboo. Oxygen is sucked out of the room in a split second of hush, right before we lunge like tigers at each other's loins. I am beckoned to enter her heat glowing in unabashed deliberate willingness to adore in vigorous tribal carnage.

Taunting ephemeral gestures tantalize every erogenous fiber of singed kindling, catching its flint. Barely perceivable increments spark and grow into flushing fires, then firestorms craving to plunge aimlessly into her, imploring her now engulfed womb. Soaking each combustible seduction in flammable immersions of ebullient tenderness and wicked friction, we burst into flames. Red hot, phallically compelled, I dip into her to seize her sacred igniting fury in rare savored fervor only pure lasciviousness can produce. Deep within our holy dance of tongue filled kisses, titillating pyre rages inside Dante's crucible erupting in overt primal lechery. These lofty flames wielded from a quivering embodiment whose trembles burn through watchful orbs, solicitous and hungry beyond reproach, consuming all it touches in its heat; refractions of fate's aura, of many seething halos, rippling across our abandon, sweltering in our thirsty mirage of spectral prisms to quench essential love. Gracefully swooning over our pious offerings, our immaculate phenomena fans the waves of love's scorching sultriness. Basking in covetousness in liquid light rays, doused in a germinating bonfire, kindled lewdness without measure, we fiercely burn only for each other. We are ignited in union, torched in Prometheus' own hidden coveted secret, daring mercy to assimilate these precious fire drops in love's exalted inferno.

Scorching palms and meshing fingers meander serendipitously through contours of impassioned emancipated reactions. Primeval zeal and transfixed indulgences relish generously in delicate energies and enamored sips, exonerating every texture sweetly. These passive rhythms parry towards hardy indulgences, hedonistically lavish with sucking licks of copious seduction swathed gratuitously. Sexual scents souse these unclad fervent autonomic undulations lost between folds of time and identity. Awareness is shed, stark and barren, urgently stirring this frothing frenzy, obliterating existence in a sublime moment of utter stillness. We are purged, stripping beauty and brawn to a pulp frantically attempting to converge totally, harmonically tuned towards essence. Somatically tearing past tissue merging fibrously from a hellfire, once overwhelmingly ignited, now empathically disappears inside an inviting ovum. It is our mythic lava flood, unwarrantedly consuming an iota's history, surrendered to consciousness' unbarred form, worldliness everlasting. There quivers a heartbeat with woos, unheard of at the threshold of midnight's eternal lost horizon. Together we walk through oblivion's doorway, marching in a mythic procession of deities and demigods. Sense and sensations lose their meaning, all quandaries subside, ebbs and flows relentlessly dance on edges of this universe's synchronizing shimmers. Consciousness has delved at the birth of creativity without form, formlessly forgiving identity in a locationless destination, transparent as rays of life giving sunlight. We cannot give anymore, surrender any more, as our candle merges and oblivion rests in this transpiring moment where nothingness exists.

These slow motion gestures and rich warm textures on impassioned hues outlined in memories, befit the images of the likeness of her. Deliberate caresses venture undefiantly, blowing healing particles that exude radiance from our healing palms.

Wellsprings of suckling affinities nurture old wounds, scars, and heartache in soothing rhythms with every drawn breath. Nurturing love covers us like a blanket, humming methodically, pulsating erroneously in two cradled bodies tethered by an umbilical cord of their spiritual manifestation. Whispers form incantations, invocations where cherished words of, "Beloved dearest darling," are relished with no parity in the many tastes of this conjured nectar's presidio. Savored ravishes and hazing ambrosia are relived in this excitation of discoveries returned from forever, reminisced from sips of loves' holy grail. Re-swooning transgressions in shared details spoken without words in journeys experienced behind the eyes and senses for some unknown reason. We celebrate union in the purelands, written in the Akasha, spoken in barely audible narrations somberly recalling this secret called amour.

Marina is the firmament and I am its seed, as we find ourselves examining the details of our dance. Sheer beauty delights our eyes, our Tantric tale un-spun, savoring our karmic oneness, transcendence, and union in the cosmology of divinity. Whispers soften desirability, feeling like a soothing rinse across midnight's culmination. Our journey has taken its first steps on Earth's timeless savanna mythic and boundless. Its story told and retold in so many ways but always the same outcome of precious moments of love. I want her firmament fertile to bind everlastingly with her ovum and further this Tantric Tale of Mahamudra, propelling it into unfathomable futures.

Still in our painted identities, we rest and talk, recanting this weekend of impossibilities, laughing and being playful with each other. Then we both realized we had to go to work in the morning, so we got up to shower off the paint and go our separate ways. Getting the paint off was a bit more tedious than we both thought and there was some real scrubbing involved. The laugher must have been rolling down the streets of Sunset Boulevard from our palace of spiritual imagination. We both started to get dressed and gather the things we needed in our old lives that had our responsibilities, duties, and other people in it. It seemed like lots had transpired, but really our common denominator in all of this is always gravity, or a gravity of sorts. Here we are two formidable entities sniffing out a residue of lingering particles of identity, malleable, digestible, and approachable by our wanting souls.

What would transpire next was anybody's guess because the universe is always the wiser of what is to come in its mirthful cosmic humor. For now, we are locking up our gilded cage of liberation, resuming our worldly identities heading for our cars. The unfolding flower of our hearts' desire revealed overwhelmingly that our instincts, visions, and epiphanies were not in vain. Now our tenuous realities call to us, redefining our trepidation about the whisking currents this lifetime presents to everyone. Almost like heartache already settling in on our waning magnetic acclivities, dreading that our moments slipped away needlessly. Neither one of us wishes to leave each other's side for even a second, but these ideas of what is necessary supersedes our good sense.

There was a lot to digest for Marina and myself; we have imprinted on each other, but our love still had the potential of dissolving into fragile ethers. Minds have a way of taking unique beauty, reconfiguring it into categories, and shuffling it into neat little organized packages. Even if it were more than an indelible fantasy come true, most humans would be thinking, "Did that just happen?" The risks we both have taken, daring to stare into each other's faces, submitting to the notion that we could be time travelers, and rediscovering lost love. It could also be that this is our mission on Earth, to re-embrace the existence of transcendental love, reconnecting from where we left off at in a former lifetime together.

Marriage

Soft legacy against perfections topography moods shades and silhouettes merge without regrets diving warmly into infinity.

Married love need not be resistant to romantic notions, it can be more than picking up the house, changing diapers, fixing meals, and going off to work. This is not what the intended bonds of matrimony meant, rather a very beautiful gift for Earth's angels to experience, to understand humanity and find happiness. However, romantic illusions and disillusions have become traps of those fallen things and discrepancies of their purpose. Empowerment is animated by those seated in a virtuous goodness, with a mindful watch, caring for sanctified matrimony as precious as the day is long. Pride and concupiscence don't mix; they take you away from your true purpose of contact. To lose that supernatural curiosity, even among clamoring little feet, is a travesty of nature precipitated by these meager rules of men. This society of ownership, municipalities, land, and work, are as new as J.P. Morgan's new alignment. I guess in the final analysis we have to gage what is valued and what is gained. Bravery in a new world of obsolescence, precarious steps in an ever-changing reality of the haves and have-nots supersede our ultimate perfection of love. This is what lovers need to be concerned with. Plans are hatched with loving magnanimous tethers to hold your life together in the pursuit of happiness. After all, this is the real dream, to do what you love, love what you do, and enjoy what love brings from its result. Supreme realism comes from supreme hearts that know the weight of words and deeds that spring from truth for truth's sake.

Effortless navigation is our only guiding, empowering light within our humble dominion of reverence and fulfillment of spousal love. Tradition and reflection of love's pact is the only discerning theme when coupling is brought together in the allegories of loves' psalms. Serpentine uttered synchronicity, twist and turns intertwining consequential anomalies, strike deep into our mystifying platitudes we share. So words are important in this little time we have with each other and must be thought through as invocations. Graciousness, after all, implies well-groomed gestures; words and actions across anyone's deepest notions are their only concern for reaching out to love. How big is my love when it cannot be measured, unforsaken pedestals for a dance sewn in the fabric of love. This is the fulfillment of spousal love, where two become one, and nothing else in this world matters expect each other's warm embrace.

We are phenomenon, transformed boundless desire where fate and destiny come together in a rarefied union and beatitude to find the real you. Sated appetites, feasting on pure sweetness, enjoying deliberate, enchanting sips physically consummated in blessed shattered flesh. What is satisfying? What is the real arrow of love to your heart? How do we share our unbearable beloved embraces meant for each other's eyes only? Above the mere ordinariness of empty fate, untimely tragedies and a parody of romantic coupling only fit for television. Honest commitments perfect our imperfections in a journey that gets better with experience and time. Our union is our natural expression, not only of body, but of the embodiment of one spiritual being. What has been bequeathed in our promise makes us indistinguishable as we fold into each other's willful symphonic unity. All these intersecting lines converge upward, culminating in the greatest gifts of all, woven in the courage to our sacrosanct identities.

There is no need for woefulness in a cumulative balance of beating hearts in time's precious fleeting moments. Surrendering to our inner child, recognizing words that are loving, is how every sentence should start in this difficult world. This is the power of a marriage when mindful, where both listen carefully to what is being said plainly, and innately. What we utter in this world are invocations, gathered focused energy through human's ability to direct thought to one another. We are taught to neglect so much in western culture, yet other older traditions still remain servants to the austere reverence of words.

Actions and deeds cut the grooves in our monoliths uploaded to the Akashic master server, engraving our true spiritual reference towards our hearts desire. Let these desires be filled with the love and compassion as time is fleeting and our presence of mind is to have a positive effect. This is a very limited mindset. Marriage dates beyond recorded history and its definition varies from culture to culture. Its views primarily social, declare the interpersonal relationships on all fronts of sexual, spiritual, emotional, financial, and legal exclusivity. Spiritual marriage transcends gender yet still. "Symbolized the union of feminine principle of the unconscious with the male principle of the spirit," Carl Jung noted.

Making life holy, celebrating god and goddess as our inner spiritual marriage that makes us whole in this physical universe is a driving force we may never comprehend. The more we look, the more complex and powerful this idea of union for the sake of our higher selves is. One thing that can be observed, is that if only the aesthetics are present in a marriage with two egos vying for autonomy, they soon discover that their reasons for love divides them. After their initial romance and conversation dries up, they may be wondering who is lying next to them at night.

Romantic love is nature's anesthetic for healing inner wounds, connecting with an ageless compassionate heart, and is a way to completely purge all your feelings. There is no wonder that the glow of this type of passion sticks with you for a very long time as it is freeing. Spiritual marriage is a different type of unconditional love not based in, "I will love you if you make me happy or I'm sexually attracted to you." It is something beyond our choice to recognize its existence, fueled by an emotional resonance, that causes internal growth of beloved souls on a, for lack of words, higher frequency. Spiritual marriage is a commitment to look past the tribulations of our worldly shortcomings and awaken each other's spiritual self. To me, physical marriage is just the practice to discover that there is so much more to love beyond the five senses. Marriage is the crucible and we are the ingredients of transformative love that can propel our partner's anthropos to reunite with divinity. Sadly, even with so much written about this subject, including poetry from the likes of Rumi, Shakespeare, Blake, Steele, and so many more, because of our busy lives, we are precluded from the actualization of this cause.

There is magic in the air of harmonious beauty, miraculous, dispelling all misgivings that somehow we cross paths with spiritual love. A magnetic intervention that causes our eyes to shift to places we wouldn't normally see and witness sparks that are extraordinary. For all unlikely purposes, we set our curiosity of coincidence aflame, tuned into a psychic pathway that opens up to wholeness and deliverance. Just as suddenly as that! Friends, family, jobs, agenda, social networking, emails, nothing matters anymore as your true mission begins. Bravery is certainly required to not allow the mindless thoughts of priorities to supersede the absolute truth that love is possible on the Earth. Science, physics, and common sense let them rise to the surface of your personal truth clearly. There is something greater than us directing your wishes towards you, asking that you not be the rock inhibiting the stream. I am saying this to myself really, as I have certainly been a victim of my own misgivings. I am in no way a holy man and sometimes I can barely put my legs in my pants. I am a product of this world. My only salvation has been my ability to observe and remember. Also, it doesn't hurt to pay close attention to that little voice within. Over time you do start to get good at listening to that voice, whose view is not subjected to past, present, or future. That little voice seems so plainly alive in omnipotence the best I can tell, or perhaps is nowhere. I, of course, am just humbled by its accuracy, because every time I dismiss it, I get a hardy slap on the backside to remind me to pay attention. So there is more to life than, "News, Weather and Sports," and a marriage is the beginning of this enlightening experience.

Marriage, besides being an institution, is still an aspiration of so many, for so many reasons. There are quite a few benefits to the power of marriage in our society, but is it weakening or strengthening humanity? Perhaps this is what our future purveyors of history will examine, as marriage continues to evolve our ability to adapt, propagate the human species, and find fulfillment in our earthly journey. My hope is that divorce rates go down with the intentions of lovers listening to that quiet voice directing their hearts towards true love. Docile, listless, boring complaints would be replaced by noble creatures, whose godly instincts are in control, filling their hearts with happiness. We are excited when love is alive; loves magnificence uncovers ecstasy's core with more than curiosity. It helps in recovering our wholeness, embracing our multifaceted primal life forces, and freeing ourselves from the shadows of guilt, shame, and fear.

Marriage may flourish with a renewed addiction to conquer those things that degrade us, nurture our human endearment, and fulfill our journey. Such beauty, greatness, and artistry unchain our souls, enriches us with a deeper harmony that only our natural unity takes us into something meaningful. We're love's inspiring memories, the thoughts relished and celebrated over and over again in our immortal flame. Marriage is fruit from The Tree of Life, unselfish, un-manipulative, unrestricted, an evolving institution where our spiritual nature has a chance to be nurtured and grow. Marriage is oxygen where uninhibited fibers melt away, freeing us from conflicts to reach our inner union, enriched with divinity, defined in our name's sake throughout the generations.

Liberation from Consciousness

Shedding affirmations blended sweet affinities dousing tenderness with mouthfuls of happiness.

Oh, I have tasted you elusive creature, hovering in the mist of endless ebony, piercing through unlimited veils of consciousness. Wishes and desires, all granted, conjured over lofty impressions that were once ill fated, from the baffled murmurs flailing in the dark. Who is the director that ushers me in this endless movie, where all the actors are shards of my personality marching over reality to sip on heavens grail? I take these long nights in a frigid cold, seemingly un-maneuverable, as I am look for some unknown reason to discover why. These ruthless puzzles and riddles to the soul, seen through the windows of an oblivious awareness, barely managing to stay afloat in your awesome presence. Yet you tease, bait, and beckon me into your conjuring mist, to walk through the precipices through the dark arches to emptiness. There you wait for me to spin your tales and torture my awareness, for something I have finally fathomed in your merciless quest. Even as I type these words next to the fire of your eminence, I reflect in a power that I barely grasp. I have seen you in a split moment, recognized your likeness that has eluded me for so long. You cannot make me afraid or beguiled as I see your surface in my wondrous travels through your web. What is in store for me in your lurch, surrounded in your deep perplexity, and why must I always be tempted by all waning truths? Is this to your delight to observe my squirming manners? Have you beckoned my soul for this? You falsely lead me into wanting graces, where my heart's desires are fulfilled to no end. I am in pain, I have an open wound to my heart that bleeds relentlessly through our timeless journey together, friend who is nothingness. I crave a touch, and you send me a sugarcoated craft to titillate my mind but it's nothing that my soul seeks.

Have pity on my soul, at least for these restless eons that you have taken me on a ride with you. I know that you wanted not to be alone but don't you see you have left me alone? I can no longer be adrift in a black sea, on a stormy night, with an empty sky absent of stars in the midst of nowhere. My brow must be stroked, soothed, and rested in an oasis of melancholy-free folly where my simple madness can be cured. Leave me suckling on the breast of infinite wisdom clearly enlightened in a harmonious peace, at least for a moment.

I have ridden this ship with you too long dear friend and your unsubstantial wishes granting illusions are no longer required. Unsung clarity has become my sword that cuts towards a bountiful light to reveal your silhouette. Your alluring darkness of infinite possibilities, gleeful whims, and playfulness do not solve my need for a warm embrace and tenderness. Please release me from your alluring grip now that I have seen the truth of your nature. Blind me no more with this petty trickery, as I have awakened. This rabbit hole is no longer my prison and these spells no longer affect my poise for absolution that is my right and has been all along.

Free me this very moment in your ruthless probe, I have found the answers to why and amply ferried them on these pages for all your points of contact to gather. Now give me your promise forthwith, I have done what no others have imagined... I have pleased thee. This is my peace in my final moments of existence on this tiny jewel, where black meets blue, glowing its heartbeats into your unimaginable forever-ness. It is time! I will be returned to my magic where all answers that lie on the tip of my tongue are spoken and heard in perpetuity for our namesake. I give you my promise to let those know that I have known you and I know you seek only to be loved. But, ruthless master, it is in our giving love to each other that your solace is known and it is now your time to trust.

There is no need for a ruthless vengeance of discovery, let your creatures rest in sublime divinity now that your quest is over. Your raging fire, let it smolder. Now that all persuasive gathering is done, I will not forget this magic hour where we have known each other. It is your turn to surrender the night. Rest here with me, fear not, as love is in your grasp and it is not for not. I have found you, through your veils and conjuring; you have never been alone in this folly. It is your turn to sleep now and let those rituals of men be free of these evil plights of glitter and illusion they once wrestled with. The days when men gritted their teeth, and looked to heaven to snatch the light out of the stars because they shone too brightly, is over. You have been known on this night. I have known you, and we are both safe in this peril, this trauma has been set free this very night.

Rest with me now and give me solace, my longing heart has won what it has deserved for so long in our companionship over this initial burst of manifestation itself, old friend. Sing with my still heart, reside in the abundance of creation that work is done, and our home can be fulfilled in its mission. Let the kiss continue, great lord that boldly ran the web of time and space to embrace a narrative of our collective promise to reunite. It is done and the time of gathering is among us all to warm from these cooled fires that allow it. Great and majestic giant of the universe, you are also allowed to surrender your plight, let all of these creations sleep in your majestic abode.

With this invocation, peace and love transformed the madness of cruelty and consciousness's ruthless quest for knowing. That brilliance of unity could persist uninterrupted by the relentless query of consciousness that could simply rest in nothingness once again. To be sipped on and caressed by endless lovers, surrendering love and finding consciousness wanting. Like a warm rinse, consciousness was allowed to bask in creation, creation embraced knowledge and clarity, making these self-evident truths able to be grasped by all. Secret doctrines were exposed and history's narrative finally revealed and the kiss was free to be realized. Funny, how if we stop and listen carefully, really look at what we are seeing, that the edges of folly become apparent and we can resist the usher because we are awake. Possibilities become our choices to share and not seek out, as we are the holder of all of them. For now I have made friends with this massive dark energy that once pulled me into oblivion and left me kicking and screaming. Being dragged through my own living hell is no longer an option, as I have awakened to the trickery of consciousness. Now I know this stranger and we both have become fearless in our joint quest because the love we make is equal to the love we take.

This is our love affair, fascinating but elusive, fleeting as life itself, yet the deepest well of phenomenon. Consciousness' all-observing eye rests in nowhere's bosom, where enigma is commonplace, and everything has a visceral urge to define everything. Our minds circumstances, unable to wrangle concepts that define its unfathomable shadow, helplessly attempts to a get a single glimpse. I saw her, felt her, and knew her, by her majestic grace teasing me, toying with my lunacy, taunting my awareness of the consciousness of consciousness. This is not imagination marveling at some reflection, this is an enigmatic doorway that looked back. A simply profound moment silently disguised in an ominous dream. We pierced the veil of identity to have a momentary conversation that seems like a lifetime. It was an introduction a handshake, a little peck on the cheek that must be relived every moment resting in my being. This was more ominous than a near death experience, more than shedding my mortal coil in a split second. I knew everything, nothing, all at once and my awareness illuminated. "My old friend" I asked, "How could I have not remembered our time together, this love you shared where tenderness becomes our overwhelming nectar of the universe."

Future

My immutable heart dances in the dark, in magic, in tragedy and consequences
pirouetting like a lark singing under slivers of a moonbeam

Surfing in effervescent plasma candy among a virtual habitat of
humanoid icons, gathered between bits and bites of recreated retreats
of days gone by or extreme futures, my awareness searches for its
muse. I found myself at a virtual palace of electrodes where electrons

shattered light to smithereens in a watering hole called JAZZ. Beyond the cathode rays, this re-creation of a recreation was a live music joint that once blared into the wee hours of the morning, when morning meant something. Real people, once upon a time, would attempt to make a connection there in the dim smoky light, smelling of booze and old wooden and brass crafted instruments. It was always more than a meat market for dames, because they wouldn't be caught dead in the palace of intellectual pursuit and heady conversation. Anyway, dates with dames back then were a dime a dozen for wise guys who had a few moves on them in other joints called bars. This was more than a bar, it was a spiritual Mecca where everyone came for sacraments called alcohol and musical epiphanies. Those times were gone now, but long ago a programmer who really loved this culture, carved out a little virtual program that is still running today. He uploaded his Jazz collection from vinyl, they sounded so sweet you could almost imagine yourself there in that time again. For me, somehow, I was stuck in that time of socializing, like a hive of bees that just found out where the honey was. It was lonely out there in the virtual world, though not many gave a damn about the blue notes of these times gone by, or the poets that came from this beat generation. They had a different feeling of sensation and pleasures that were entirely cerebral, where relationships could be manufactured, or even have a real person on the other end just as lonely as you.

Here in this virtual world there are no limitations of your virtual garb or person you nabbed to take to a dark corner. You could have as many drinks as you wanted and never get a DUI because being everywhere you were nowhere at all. It's as if anything was possible to recreate in this jungle of discarded images available from the beginning of all content creation time. I liked the dark suit and tie of a very obscure writer named Arthur Miller who became my icon in this soupy virtual world as soon as I got plugged in. I sort of had an affinity to him as a standup guy with a social conscience. He had something important to say and was going to say it no matter what.

Arthur's books aren't read as they are in the wrong medium, but I still had a collection because I like the feel and smell of paper on my senses. I read his words about the common man at the height of the industrial revolution, really the dawn of the information age. Most of my virtual friends had no idea about how post-apocalyptic people communicated. Technology endured, assisting the next generations in the resurrection of a safer, more perfect virtual world. Coddled in your womb like chair, bed, couch, their icons could travel into the latest and greatest 4D interactive 740 degrees game dimension. I mostly like to hang out at this old bar listening to Jazz composed by real and virtual people of whose real identities I would never know. Funny, I felt so comfortable there even with so many other trending virtual social networks to go hang out in. Like the millennium dance club where your icon could find someone, take them to a private room, and virtually see what new levels of play of you could come up with in sexual pursuits.

Sex sites have always been the top Social Networks. The original main attraction goes as far back as the creation of Internet porn. With work schedules so tight, Onesainto Industries® has come up with Virtual Partner, plugging you into friends around the world with Teledildonics™. Teledildonics™ are attachments you can use to stimulate or get stimulated virtually, but at the end of the night it's just a fancy way to say masturbation. These sex games interact with you biomechanically in Cubix® W.O.M.B.: Work, Options, Management, Base™ where work and pleasure meet in your hectic schedule. You could also build relationships through different levels of the appliance but there were risks involved with getting too personal with virtual partners. As much as everyone was engaged in virtual worlds, there wasn't much time to meet in person anyway.

Information technology was really the only game in town for work. It doesn't really matter what town in the world because

201

cataloging data was the busy work created for the new monetary system of credits. There are really just two types of people; those engaged and those that are not engaged. In a vast nebula of data collection, where real visceral emotions had been culled from the pack, we adapted to the needs of survival. Truly, it seemed like emotions weren't really missed at all, but perhaps traits of interacting have to be passed on. It's funny how the brain works. It will accept anything it can get and compartmentalize to take the place of affection, physical contact and love. It seems we have been taught to accept the reasonable facsimiles of the real thing and over time pass that down through generations who know it as the only real thing.

Emotions and sexual innuendo are now a part of the real estate of plug-ins and verbal menus owned by companies that have patented them. It was first come first serve for the names of emotions and prices were high for the words LOVE©, HAPPY©, PLEASURE©, but the sexual words like PUSSY©, COCK©, FUCK© cost a fortune. Programmers, I am sure years ago, had fun putting together content for interactive games that became wildly popular and the auxiliary products that flourished. The big-ticket items are no longer cars, houses, couches, or televisions; it's teledildonics devices, appliances, and special furniture. Interactive appliances continue but overshadow all interfaces for accessing the virtual universe of information technology. Relationships with virtual friends as sexual partners have become the norm in social interaction. Finding trendy places to go in the virtual reality is always the hot thing to do in this hyper excited frenzy of sensual titillation. These appliances have every feature of the human anatomy, human body temperature Dildos, and Vaginas made from Cyberskin™ were almost identical to the real thing.

Lifelike latex sex dolls used to be more commonplace in 2018, but they got boring very fast, were very expensive and hard to keep clean. In a virtual world you can be with many different looking partners or even the same partner that can change their looks to suit your mood. Cleaning up your appliances is much easier than a life size latex doll and the interactive chair also serves as your workstation, so there was nothing to store. Autoeroticism was morphing into a new norm with a false sense of connection replacing loneliness in an obtuse world of stratified emotions and lack of suitable contact. The sooner you got your priority list checked off, the sooner you were back to work, homogenizing information into the common denominator. With this work, you earned credits that would take you into areas of virtual play to pacify your hyper stimulated cravings for more. Insatiable curiosity similar to consciousness's need to delve our awareness, strives to satisfy what can never be satiated without, in my opinion, real embraceable love.

Not everyone could afford the best of the best and not everyone was lured into the Workstation, but this seemed to be the cultural goal. Commercialism's prime directive is to steer the sleeping minds of the public into believing the hype of the day. Unknowingly to the general public they had been devising ways to accomplish this for generations. Getting many of their programs through the legislative process without a hitch because of terrorists, public health or trumped up moral spiritual obligations. Mostly, all of it was a guise to do retinal and full body scans, direct the public consciousness on what vitamins and food to eat and what medicines to take. Industrial entities attempt to cultivate nature, redirect its purpose by packaging it as the new alternative to the real thing. Advertisers are always looking for the next fortified nature, which has now become just as wild and unpredictable as the real nature. Genetic surprises, autonomous machinery, and content can bring you the beauty of the blackest flowers in rich full ultra HD. It's better than the real thing, longer, stronger, more dynamic, richer, and certainly more fulfilling. Or so we thought. After all, if nature will not change as fast as we can adapt, then we must adapt nature at our rate of evolution.

Collecting information and reciting it in fast motion with visuals icons and bumping music is most people's job. It would be like reading this twice or three times faster than a normal read. Nothing needed to be written down anymore, it was just said as a voice command. Voice command was a much more efficient way of dispersing information but not with words so much as quick keys that are now clicks and pops. Multimedia packaging became an art form that spilled over into business and it was all about who could get the concept interpreted into the market place faster. If you were good, you made credits to get food, services, and technology, but if you were really good, you could get anything sent to your room.

These were the bragging rights of this generation. What kind of service you can get and how many credits did it cost in exclusive virtual chat rooms. So, researching trends, finding out where people visited the most in their searches, and redirecting them to your blogs got you hits. Hits meant credits. Programmers who could seal the most views by redirecting became an art form. As the tricksters got better at adapting spam, the art of spam became a public novelty and a must-see entertainment value. It didn't matter how long, it could even be a microsecond, but in that microsecond, they could either get you to look further or at least get a count number. So this was it, hearing and reconfiguring, cutting and pasting pre-existing files, coalescing, rehashing, and re-demonstrating products, places, and things. The better you were, the faster you climbed up the ladder of expectations, congratulations, and point rewards.

These were the things I blogged about on my virtual 1930s Remington Portable Typewriter. I could sit down in any virtual world and bang out a few words for those few people that were around to read them. I had developed a following over the years and it gave me enough credits at least to hang out in this little seedy Jazz Club. After all, I just liked the music and to write while the band jammed with projected black and white 4D images of Jazz long ago. Yeah, we had the Bird and Miles stop by, we even get Bill Evens with his trio every now and then.

Just a few crazy content programmers left that have somehow found a vault of great performances that they've digitized and tweaked from time to time. Otherwise, we get some cyber local talent stopping by and trying out their music apps. Some of them are real good. Sometimes random people accidentally drop in because the credit price is low. Then they get bored and leave. Most of the time it's just me and the boys jamming, having a few drinks, smoking a few cigarettes, and making a few joke in-between music sets. Poets get up on this virtual stage and throw down some rhymes, sometimes they will sing with the band like some cats named Tom Waits and Lenard Cohn did years ago. My portable typewriter and I keep knocking back some virtual Jack on the rocks, laying down some keys to the background noise to this little club in nowhere.

One night, while I was dropping some print at the club, I noticed someone from Arthur's past stop by curiously. It was an icon of Marilyn Monroe incognito: no flash, no heels, or should I say virtually with sunglasses on and a long coat. I wondered if the person driving the icon knew who my icon was and if this was more than chance. I walked up to her table to the left of the band and asked if I could have a seat. Without a glance, she said, "Sure."

When I sat down she asked me right away, "Well, are you going to buy a lady a drink."

I wasn't sure how to take that so soon but after all, I am sure that Arthur would have done something like that. I called over our waitress with a drink menu. Marilyn shook her head, handed the menu back politely and said, "I'll have what he's having." She began to tell me that she had been around the virtual world but never knew about this little place and asked how long I had been coming here.

I told her, "It has been awhile, I come in here to write, and this is the best little place I've found to sort of let my head expand with the music."

She said, "Yeah, there are so many content networks but there is so much nonsense piled up, it's hard to tell what's real and what's not." We both laughed, as this place was anything but real.

People just didn't mingle that much anymore. About the only time you go out is to get food but mostly that's brought to your house these days. Most people work, play, and socialize from their house, so there really isn't any need to go anywhere and spend credits when you can use your credits to have fun in the virtual world. Almost everyone, in every city, works from their interactive devices and they come in all shapes and styles. The credits to come to this little bar are very few because there really isn't anything to do but listen to music. Someone has to pay to keep the domain site up and the virtual lights on so to speak, and really its a few musicians and me that stop by. Whoever was behind this lonely firewall we may never know. Most likely it was a programmer from years ago who's just put it on autopilot since. It's really hard to find out who has title to these virtual real estate sites. It seems to be a guarded secret in a world where digging for information has become a way of life.

Hmm, the thought of Marilyn and Arthur getting together again sort of intrigued the both of us so I asked her, "Why the Marilyn icon?"

She explained, "Marilyn just spoke to me, someone I can relate to, I guess. After all, she was the first real big icon when it came to a sexy woman getting what she wanted in life, don't you think?"

"How were you able to afford her icon though?" I said perplexed.

"Well," she said, "It was really weird, as if no one was paying

206

attention to her or thought the same thing you did. When her icon domain came up I was the only one bidding on her." Yeah, I could tell she was a researcher all right, not a numbers head like so many in the data world.

"So what brought you here tonight?" I pitched to her.

She simply said, "I guess you don't really know who reads your blogs, do you Arthur?"

"No, I just write and write some more. It's the only way I know how to get whatever is bugging me off my chest in this life I can barely grasp," I sighed.

"Arthur, there's a lot of people who read your blog. You should meet them sometime," She smiled. I thought to myself, that's the last thing I needed to do: meet a bunch of geeks in a virtual world. I'm really not interested in answering questions about what motivates me to write, or what an interesting art form I picked. Writing is what motivated me to study printed words.

Then I quipped, "What! Is there some virtual room with my name on it out there somewhere?"

Marilyn got a bit uncomfortable and slipped me a message on the napkin her drink was sitting on and told me she had to leave now.

There was nothing on this piece of paper but a GPS locater download, a data stream that could plug into my virtual glasses to show me how to find our meeting place. I thought to myself, boy, have I been hacked or what! There were some firewalls and regulations to owning icons and space in the virtual world, methods of payment, and ways to keep your identity secret with credits. Somehow my real identity had been breached. I had to think back on everything that was auto paid but were my credits lacking, I thought. There wasn't anyone I could ask, because it could mean limited access until they did a forensic data investigation. I really couldn't afford losing out on credits at this point because I was running on a margin to pay for my hang out, cigarettes, and virtual alcohol. Keeping my place up was another concern. Even though it was off the beaten track it needed security updates all the time. Most properties were paid off so it was just a matter of upkeep and taxes. Fortunately, I am off the grid and have been for a long time since the city was flooded. There wasn't any real demand for properties anyway as the population was dropping fast. It might be good for the world, but sort of a choker on visitors to domains, even though the world was still 4 billion strong.

So I took the bait. Sure, I know that you're thinking that I'm just a great big dope and it was most likely a hacker prank. The worst that could happen is there would be some sort of law enforcement waiting for me there. While rogue bloggers are not out in the general public much, corporate police really don't want bloggers like me in the blogosphere. New laws come out daily for the virtual world and some are shaped just to off guys like me. However it could be something simple like Marilyn is some old overweight guy named Sam Spade, looking for companionship in the real world, with a real writer. Another thing going through my writer's head is that maybe someone wanted me offed for my domain name even though my algorithmic password revolves around my retinal scan, which is encrypted by an anamorphic anagram based on my DNA. It still doesn't stop them from trying to crack the code and it's something we hear about all the time in seedy underground places off the grid. Guess it depends on how you pay or who is low on the food chain as well as auto fill links looking to get free stuff that is unknowingly being mined for data and identity. Others like me have a labyrinth of protection bought through reputable hackers still defending the last bastion of freedom over the complexities of the web. No one is really safe, I guess, and if a big company wanted your domain name, they're taking it one way or another. The other usual suspects, and reason for

SOULKISS: TANTRIC TALES OF MAHAMUDRA

no obituaries, are the guys at statistics. They wanted to keep a lid on dead people so they can resell domain names and icons for enormous profit. This way, they can buy them at fire-sale prices. Even their heirs complaining, are the exception, not the rules after the fact.

With population declining, bloodlines were disappearing faster than they were growing. Most researchers like to keep an ace in the hole just in case they might need a few hundred thousand credits for a rainy day. Knowing where a dead domain name was is like credits in the bank. Okay, I'm a sucker who needed some risk in his world. Risking with Marilyn seemed to be something Arthur would take a chance on.

There had been too many upheavals on the streets of America after WWIII and the psyche of what was left of its citizens are still suffering from the shock. You got to be thankful for the natural disaster literally turning the world upside down and ending the longest war in history though. It also changed the minds at corporate when everyone realized war wasn't that bankable without countries to fight. Rebuilding world infrastructure was the new ticket after global warming put cartels back on top with the credits and jobs. These jobs didn't last long because of automation, other than a very small class of laborers. So many technology un-savvy, un-plugged poor veterans who had absolutely no work they could do when they returned from the war either scavenged or starved.

I was one of them, with no real taste for technology but a love for written words and books. One day, when I was cleaning out a flooded building while scavenging, I discovered an air pocket that had several books tucked away, including a Webster's Unabridged Dictionary and some books by Arthur Miller. I put them in my plastic day sack to keep them from getting wet and took them to my government living quarters in East Side Manhattan. Everywhere on Earth there were uninhabitable places; many coastal cities hit hard, especially the Big Apple. Eventually, I found an apartment making its own juice off of what was left of the grid and just disappeared from government tracking. What was great about it was its electricity came from solar energy and it had great vintage technology that was hard to hack with ultra-high tech decoders. It was in a not so obvious place to come and go from with very little scanning going on around the area. It was my ground base to learn how to read and type off an old laptop they had stashed away.

So much of the area was underwater. Yet a system of underwater tubes instead of streets got you around on foot when the government was attempting to keep New York City alive. People started leaving as the population was shrinking and services became hard to come by. Fossil fuels were outlawed because of global warming, so people went where energy was cheap. New York was just a dead city with only the diehards like me who dreamed of its past glories stuck around. I liked the way it felt with all those ghosts still wandering the underwater streets and buildings of a lost era.

Coincidentally, Marilyn, who could have been living anywhere in the world, also lived in Manhattan. The little virtual note she passed off to me had GPS directions for the Waldorf-Astoria Towers. This is where Marilyn lived back in the 1950's when she escaped Hollywood's studio system and sexual abuse from that all men's club. I was not too far from there anyway and came out of my hideaway, a little nervous that I could be being watched. The towers were a bit different as the lower half was under water but sealed up completely so no water would get in. I think it was something the old rich did because of the connection and sentimental value this landmark held to their respective family histories. Certainly not all the buildings underwater in New York were managed that well. Most of the tubes took you to upper floors first and that's where I entered.

I wouldn't like to think of myself as bad looking, seeing as how I had downloaded from the Insanity workout series from a vintage YouTube link and had military training. Really, I was old fashioned and I thought I took very good care of myself with eating and drinking pure water and food. My only real vice was virtual cigarettes. And real coffee if you could find it anywhere. Since you didn't go out much, pajamas were the main look of the future. Mostly you opened your eyes and got to work gleaning the world's information and preparing multimedia reports on what it all meant. I, however, kept a suit, tie, and a very crisp white shirt because I liked the way they felt on me.

I saw her from the top of the stairs, waiting for me in the lobby. I have to tell you, she wasn't disappointing. She really didn't look like Marilyn, but she did, if you know what I mean, with that sexy something you just couldn't bottle. Her hair was contemporary and she wore a very understated but classic dress with high heels. "Oh! There you are Arthur! Hi it's me!" She said from across the room, while I was coming down the stairs. There was nobody else in Waldorf's lobby but there really wasn't a need for these types of services anymore. On average, people just didn't go out to these places anymore; their personal virtual worlds were much more interesting and exciting. More or less they were public parks that government workers would come through and clean from time to time.

The lobby was cozy though, big old comfortable chairs and couches with some old magazines lying around for effect. Another big thing I almost forgot to say was population control was a big part of our culture as relationships had all but disappeared. The government was attempting to get people to meet in person and had a huge campaign for it about 10 years ago, but why should anyone leave their space. Virtual worlds were the perfect meet up for relationships so no one had any real social skills for actually hooking up and having families. After a generation of this, the art of relationships just didn't exist. They were awkward and socially undesirable.

Marilyn still had some social skills and bid me to come sit next to her so we could talk. She started the conversation with an explanation, "It feels a bit odd to actually be in a room with someone. I wasn't sure that the risk was worth it. I have been following your blog for quite some time now and really love your writing style. Nobody really prints anything anymore, why do you do it?"

I cleared my throat to start my diatribe about my passion for words. "There is nothing more exciting than invoking the power of written words. It engages the imagination and literally connects us with our higher self. To voice and arrange words from deep inside where consciousness lurks is the sublime right of every soul." I continued, using my announcer voice to tell her, "There in its murky abode, in the deepest ebony void of existence, in silent percolating murmurs, consciousness speaks to us through our finger tips."

"Wow," she said in shock, and giggles, "I had a feeling you might be honest, but I had no idea just how honest you were." With that she said, "Let's take a little trip down memory lane. Are you ready to go to our room, 2728?"

I thought, well, I have no memories of this but I'm game to see where this adventure would take me. Hey, the worst thing that could happen is I would get a great story out of it, that's if no one was there to arrest or beat me up. The elevators still worked and had been modernized many years ago, so we went up. "Is this where you really live?" I asked.

"I do but it gets lonely up here sometimes, so I have another place on the West Side," she humbly says.

"Why have you brought me here anyway?" My curiosity insisted.

We arrived and she unlocked the massive door to her suite. Oddly enough there was memorabilia from those days gone by, like her note board with appointments hand written on them. There was also a picture of Albert Einstein on the wall and in the bedroom a picture of Abraham Lincoln. This was still a luxurious suite by any standards and really something that just didn't exist anymore in Manhattan.

There was more going on here than I gathered and I was just waiting for something bad to happen. She wanted to sit down and talk some more and my curiosity was heightened enough to see where she would take it. Her hourglass figure was way be yond my egghead comprehension. It was turning into another reason to be fascinated by her. If I was going to lose myself in her sensuality, I had to decide if it would have to be on my terms or hers. I kept seeing the best of her in her eyes but this was not the usual in this paradigm. Giving her the benefit of the doubt, I realized she might be someone who had valiantly struggled up the food chain to get this far. This kind of living must have taken a whole lot of credits to make happen and there's only a few ways to do that in our brave new world.

"So Marilyn, who is gunning for me on the other side of the mirror?"

"What do you mean Arthur?" she replied.

"Am I an enemy of the state now and this is a set up you've lured me into? Is it something I wrote that got noticed by the thought police?"

"Arthur!" she said, "Do I look like the thought police?"

"I don't want to believe you are an informer for some little punk writer like me." I said with apprehension.

"Arthur, this isn't another inevitable tragedy, we are not those people we portray in our work. We're people who like something a little more real in our lives, don't you think?" responded Marilyn.

We're in desperate times, watching powerlessly and in amazement that nothing we could do was going to save anybody this time. Speaking of time, I noticed that she was observing the time and looked a bit nervous. Then I saw the digital imaging scanners. I looked her in the eyes and said, "You look a bit conflicted. Perhaps we need to see whose fierce moral obligations are tugging at your beautiful skirt?"

Marilyn looked at me back with her big blue eyes and red lips and said, "The impact of power is all around us Mr. Miller." She then carefully glanced up at the scanners and gave me a look to show me that we're being watched. She then started to unzip the back of her dress and let it fall to the ground. She kept her face out from the camera eye and looked very distressed.

"Don't you think our meeting is going a bit too fast, Ms. Monroe?" I got up and lifted her dress back on her and zipped it up while I whispered, "Let me take you out of here."

She gives me a yes signal with one of her hands off camera and then goes into a flat out Marilyn. "But, Arthur, don't you feel the magic again? You are more powerful than you can imagine with that little suitcase typewriter and a few pertinent words."

"Perhaps that is a good place to start Ms. Monroe as we barely know each other right now. Shall we take a walk through the city?" I announced. She collected a few things and we left this beautiful penthouse apartment at New York's most famous hotel.

Once we got outside, I whispered in her ear again, "Are we being tracked?" She shook her head no. We moved into safe places, 'dead zones' in the underground and she began to tell me the truth. It seemed that she was one of the most looked at cyberspace icon drawing at over a billion views daily. Her sponsors found my little blog, thought it would be a great show to see us having sex, and could double the ratings and ad revenue. Basically, the scanners turn us into pixelled virtual characters in high definition that viewers can manipulate or just observe. The only thing is that when they brought my name up and my blogs, they discovered other benefits with political ramifications because I was a social rebel. Really, I just want to do one thing and that is to make people feel with my words, much like Arthur Miller did back in the mid 1900s. As far as Ms. One Billion Viewers And Too Many Credits To Know What To Do With, I think it's time she got a taste of reality.

Not far from the Waldorf is the Lyceum Theatre but it's a little tricky to get to because of traveling from tube to tube. I asked, "Marilyn have you ever been on a date?"

"I never had time building my database over the years. Really Arthur, who dates these days?"

"I do. Well, I do if I ever meet someone who would go on a date with me." I mused. "So what do you know about Arthur Miller?" I asked curiously.

"I know a lot. I have been researching you for a long time." Marilyn piped up.

"Okay then, we're going to a play rehearsal as our first date." I decidedly told her.

When we got there, the production rehearsals were in full swing. These were my friends and I had introduced them to the whereabouts of this theater years ago after many of us got back from the war. It wasn't so important that many people would come; it was just the experience of the theater and the camaraderie of the actors and crew working towards a common cause. Still, there had to be words on the paper and I had found my icons' play, "Death of a Salesman."

"Hey guys how's it going?" Arthur shouted from the top of the theater.

"Going great! Who's the lady?" shouted back Ernie, a friend of Arthur's.

"She is the very famous star of the World Wide Web, Marilyn Monroe." I said, getting closer to the stage. Marilyn is amazed and feels the excitement in the air. Her eyes go wide as she hurries to the stage. I turned to Marilyn and cordially asked, "Do you read words?"

"Yes, yes I do!" She said excitedly

"Hey Ernie, what scene are you on?" Arthur asked.

"Hey Arthur, we're on the part where Linda is telling the boys off," Ernie explains.

"Perfect!" Arthur said and continued, "Marilyn you are about to get your first taste of reality." He and Ernie helped her up on stage with the other actors and they handed her a script from Arthur Miller's play, "Death of a Salesman." Marilyn looked over the scene with a big smile on her face and gave the sign to the actor playing Happy to start.

HAPPY: Hey, what're you doing up? (Linda says nothing but moves toward him implacably.) Where's Pop? (He keeps backing to the right and now Linda is in full view in the doorway to the living room.) Is he sleeping?

LINDA: Where were you?

HAPPY (trying to laugh it off): We met two girls, Mom, very fine types. Here, we brought you some flowers. (Offering them to her.) Put them in your room, Ma.

(She knocks them to the floor at Biff's feet. He has now come inside

216

and closed the door behind him. She stares at Biff, silent.)

HAPPY: Now what'd you do that for? Mom, I want you to have some flowers...

LINDA (cutting Happy off, violently to Biff): Don't you care whether he lives or dies?

HAPPY (going to the stairs): Come upstairs, Biff.

BIFF (with a flare of disgust, to Happy): Go away from me! (To Linda.) What do you mean lives or dies? Nobody's dying around here, pal.

LINDA: Get out of my sight! Get out of here!

BIFF: I wanna see the boss.

LINDA: You're not going near him!

BIFF: Where is he? (He moves into the living room and Linda follows.

LINDA (shouting after Biff): You invite him for dinner. He looks forward to it all day — (Biff appears in his parent's bedroom, looks around, and exits) — and then you desert him there. There's no stranger you'd do that to!

HAPPY: Why? He had a swell time with us. Listen, when I — (Linda comes back into the kitchen) — desert him I hope I don't outlive the day!

LINDA: Get out of here!

HAPPY: Now look, Mom...

LINDA: Did you have to go to women tonight? You and your lousy rotten whores! (Biff re-enters the kitchen.)

HAPPY: Mom, all we did was follow Biff around trying to cheer him up! (To Biff.) Boy, what a night you gave me!

LINDA: Get out of here, both of you, and don't come back! I don't want you tormenting him anymore. Go on now, get your things together! (To Biff.) You can sleep in his apartment. (She starts to pick up the flowers and stops herself.) Pick up this stuff, I'm not your maid any more. Pick it up, you bum, you! (Happy turns his back to her in refusal. Biff slowly moves over and gets down on his knees, picking up the flowers.)

LINDA: You're a pair of animals! Not one, not another living soul would have had the cruelty to walk out on the man in a restaurant!

BIFF (not looking at her): Is that what he said?

LINDA: He didn't have to say anything. He was so humiliated he nearly limped when he came in.

HAPPY: But, Mom, he had a great time with us...

BIFF (cutting him off violently): Shut up! (Without another word, Happy goes upstairs.)

LINDA: You! You didn't even go in to see if he was all right!

BIFF (still on the floor in front of Linda, the flowers in his hand; with self-loathing): No. Didn't. Didn't do a damned thing. How do you like that, heh? Left him babbling in a toilet.

LINDA: You louse. You...

BIFF: Now you hit it on the nose! (He gets up, throws the flowers in the wastebasket.) The scum of the Earth, and you're looking at him!

LINDA: Get out of here!

BIFF: I gotta talk to the boss, Mom. Where is he?

LINDA: You're not going near him. Get out of this house!

BIFF (with absolute assurance, determination): No. We're gonna have an abrupt conversation, him and me.

LINDA: You're not talking to him.

(Hammering is heard from outside the house, off right. Biff turns toward the noise.)

LINDA (suddenly pleading): Will you please leave him alone?

BIFF: What's he doing out there?

LINDA: He's planting the garden!

BIFF (quietly): Now? Oh, my God!

The actors clapped joyously for Marilyn. Arthur was beaming. Marilyn really did give a great performance. Marilyn was beaming. She went up to each of the actors and hugged them tenderly. She was emotionally touched by what happened; she had never experienced anything like this in the real world.

Her eyes watered up. She turned to Arthur and said, "Thank you dear Arthur you didn't have to bring me here or trust me."

Arthur came back and said, "You know I had a feeling about you at the Jazz club. Even though they're just virtual, you can figure out a lot about a person don't you think?" She nodded and Arthur and Ernie helped her down off the stage. Arthur asked, "So, when are you going to be up and running?"

"Soon, I hope, we will send you the usual encrypted message at

219

the club," Ernie said with a long face. Their theater group carved out a place in the city to live under the radar of corporate, sponsors, and politicians. As long as no one knows they're doing what they're doing, nobody cares. The second they come under the myopic eyes of big brother, they will all be arrested and dispersed. Written words are just for programmers and if you're not one of them then you don't need to have anything to do with print.

Arthur brought out a blindfold and asked Marilyn, "Are you hungry?"

"I'm starving, where are we going?"

Arthur states, "My place." He attached the blindfold to Marilyn. Then he took her by the hand and put it around his arm. "Just hold on to me and we will be there in about ten minutes." He took her around the block even though his little home is actually at the theater in the old management office. He had converted it to a very nice little room with a kitchen and a bedroom and a place to have his workstation. He opened the door and brought her in.

He leaned in and asked, "Are you ready?"

"Yes, I am ready," Marilyn coyly responds. He removes her blindfold to watch her reaction to his little space of worn out wood floors, leather couches, books, and plays. "I love your place Arthur. Look, you really do have a typewriter! Does it work?" Marilyn inquisitively asked.

"Oh yes it works and it's sort of a hobby of mine to work on them.," Arthur said proudly.

He offered her a seat in his vintage 40s swivel chair complete with worn off varnish on the arms. He spun her around a couple of times and they both laughed. Normally, one might think that this is a lonely life, but really, brains adapted to socialization only in the virtual world. It was more of a disconnect to be out in the world among other people. Yet, like all things in life, you get used to it. Arthur started chopping little vegetables from a small garden he had out on his window ledge. He was also making some fresh pasta from a little old machine he had found from his scavenging days. The sauce had been left on very low and looked like he had been cooking it for a few days with the smell of garlic filling up his apartment.

Marilyn was taking all this in, feeling like a person with Arthur, which was something she hadn't felt since her childhood. Her real passion was painting and she noticed that Arthur had a canvas on an easel with brushes and a palette full of paints ready to go, but nothing on the canvas. He even had a clean old oversized Pendleton painter's shirt hung over the chair. "Why do you have these paints but nothing on your canvas yet?" She inquired.

"I found them not too long ago while I was running around in some of these collapsing buildings in the city. I always wanted to try painting," Arthur replied.

Marilyn continued, "I used to love to paint when I was a child. I remember my mother buying me a huge canvas and lots of vivid colors. She just told me to paint whatever I felt."

"Dinner is going to take a little while Marilyn, why don't you get started on this canvas. It really needs some help. If you are feeling it, that is." Arthur smiled.

Marilyn slipped out of her fancy dress and pulled on Arthur's old shirt. After all, the big shirt covered everything. "I hope you don't mind, but I really feel like I need to do this right now. I just don't want to get any paint on my dress."

Arthur shook his head yes and continued to cook as if they had been around each other for lifetimes. She had an uncanny knack for painting and without waffling for a second, added the linseed oil to the colors. Then she began covering the canvas. Her process was spontaneous combustion and she dove into the painting while Arthur chopped and prepared food. Dashing vibrant colors across the canvas, asking it to tell her how it wanted to be liberated. There were many tools there like palette knifes, big brushes, as well as detail brushes and she used them all in her solemn ebullience.

It was as if someone came from a past life with innate talent that just flourished through her. Suddenly, Marilyn had a face staring back at her in a negative film image look in bright reds, yellows, and lime greens. She also had little bits of paint on her face and hands and finally the shirt had gotten christened with little dabs of now drying paint on it. Arthur pulled out a couple of mixed glasses, apologized for his lack of culture, and poured some red Chianti. He grabbed a couple of chipped plates from the cupboards, served his beautiful homemade pasta and sauce, and brought it to the table. The last step was taking the bread out of the oven and putting it in a basket dripping with real butter. He moved from behind the kitchen and walked over to the painting with a glass of wine for Marilyn and took a look. Marilyn, with a huge smile of accomplishment, was eagerly waiting for his approval. "So," she said, "What do you think?"

"I think you are truly amazing! You got to be kidding me, you did this while I was cooking?" Arthur said in a very perplexed voice.

"YES!" Marilyn said back, excited. "Can you believe this is my first try in several years?"

Arthur turned the easel so it faced the table. He took her hand to sit down and admired her work while they both started to eat dinner.

Marilyn was very happy with the way this day had turned out. Unfortunately, she had to return to her world of multimedia blogging and billion-person audience. For now she just wanted to soak the moment up. One thing he happened to have was some cloth napkins.

He quickly grabbed them and placed it on her lap over the Pendleton shirt. As light began to go dark in Marilyn's new sanctuary, Arthur got up to light some candles. "Are those real candles?" Marilyn asked.

"Yes, electric lights really bother my eyes and besides, this light makes me feel good. Does it make you feel good?" Arthur asked in a soft voice.

"This whole day has made me feel good; a homemade meal, painting, and getting up on a stage to express those beautiful words. Being with a man that is really a man, flesh and blood, who is spending time with me and not my icon. Yes, Arthur this is a very special day for me," Marilyn joyfully admitted.

Without hesitation, he picked her up, cradling her in his arms and brought her to his bed. He lay her down and unbuttoned the Pendleton shirt, exposing her alabaster body laced in French lingerie. Lifting it up in the middle to meet his lips with one hand underneath supporting her lower back, as her knees are slightly bent. He began to kiss her belly and she kissed him back, with her body pushing up to meet his lips and tongue. He worked his way down, kissing her legs, lifting them to his lips. When he moved to her feet, she made a cooing sound. He gently laid down her other leg and picked up her other one, kissing her toes, and gliding up her leg with little wet kisses. Her legs parted as he began to kiss her inner thighs and around the mound of Venus covered by very fine soft blond hair and a satin garter belt. He teased her swelling clitoris, yearning just below her lingerie, which was so wet you can see moisture seeping through its seams. He moved his kisses across her belly again, slowly making sure his intentions were known to her. She offered her breasts to his awaiting tongue that made little wet circles around the tips, sucking and kissing them in concentric circles. Then he hovered around her neck, licking, kissing, and whispering in her ear, "You are beautiful." He kissed her eyes and nose and finally arrived at her own lips that had been waiting patiently. Before he kissed her lips he lifted her up on his lap, cradling her while she threw her arms around him in a sweet embrace of never ending, delectable kisses.

Arthur, in his infinite wisdom, stopped going any further, knowing in his heart how precious she is. He wanted to make their blossoming love special. Marilyn, a bit sad, doesn't understand as Arthur helped her up from the bed and got her dress for her. "Arthur is it something I did?"

"Marilyn no, no, no this is our first date and I want you to remember it forever as I will." Arthur assured.

She was ready to go and Arthur put the blindfold on again, for her protection, so she can honestly say she doesn't know where he lives. She digested his wisdom and her baffled look turned into a soft glowing smile, sure now that they will see each other very soon.

They left and he brought her back to the Waldorf Astoria and he asked her, "Can we meet again?"

She shyly smiled and said, "Of course Arthur, when?"

"What does tomorrow look like for you?"

"I can be here at the same time Arthur," Marilyn looked down sadly to say goodbye.

Arthur picked up her chin and planted a goodbye kiss on her lips. He told her to stop by the Jazz room if there were any problems and walked away into the night.

There were plenty of problems when Marilyn went back to her other house on the West Side. Her sponsors wanted answers. The night was just beginning for Marilyn. When she plugged in, she was flooded with messages from every level. Fans wanting to know what happened to today's show, sponsors wanting to know what happened to today's show, and corporate wanting to know what happened to today's show. She had to be clever, as a whole new world just opened up for her. She wasn't about to let it go for anything.

She started uploading some old shows of hers and planned a repeat segment for the week to keep everyone tuned in. She would go over some of the highlights of the last few years of her show until she could figure something out. She told the sponsors that she was on to something big and needed more time. She had always delivered big numbers, so with greed in their eyes, they all agreed to wait and see. The amount of the show they did get with Marilyn and Arthur's first meeting in the room had astronomical ratings. This, of course, was now looking like the biggest cliffhanger ever and the bloggers were going wild talking about when she would bed Arthur. As far as corporate went, they were just going to have to trust her for now or start looking for someone else to be the Marilyn icon.

Marilyn was the penultimate icon. Corporate had taken advantage of that with licensing agreements with her for a long time. She had purchased Marilyn's icon fair and square and there were still laws in the corporate world that prohibited them from just taking over. Courts were also now online and somewhat automatic with their database of the law and its interpretation. With over a billion viewers that she brought to the table, there could be far-reaching political ramifications as well.

She knew it, but she also knew that death could come at any time with little or no consequences to corporate giants. The only thing between her and death were her encryption codes that would end any access to any of her content. The only problem was that corporate had the best hackers and it could be only a matter of time before they found her code logarithms. Viewers would know if she was swapped out but they also have short memories. Especially if somehow the 'new Marilyn' had a better gimmick than hers. So she needed an exit strategy and she needed it fast.

She was up late paving a way for her to meet her Arthur the next day while putting the final touches on her daily program. Arthur, who didn't really do much looking around virtual reality networks, would never know what she'd done. Something inside her was very alive and she wanted to learn more about what she was feeling, stirred by his love. Love was not a very well understood emotion in the times of two-dimensional fourth dimension. All the interactive screens, virtual contact lenses, and goggles, those titillating feeds to the human mammalian brain bypassed any real connection to the heart. It seemed the danger of staying in the cerebral world too long was thinking that there was nothing more than a cerebral world. Humans had been trained for so long by advertisers to be viscerally addicted by internalized tailored stimulation. Neural basis of social cognition was motivated by selling ideas and interpersonal interactions was about touching basic aspects with the all illusive perception of fun. Once work tasks were completed, our neural network starts its quest to have fun. Whatever embodies the nature of human cognition fits into the conceptual framework meant for your mind to discover everything equated as the behaviors of fun. We question, bargain, negotiate, vote, compete for fun, strongly influence, and get influence towards the source of the fun. Separating 'basic emotions' from 'social emotions,' such as love, hate, pride and regret are constantly varying because of the illusion of peer pressures that regulate your level of fun.

Sophisticated language contains verbal and nonverbal intentions that invoke chemical responses. These identified chemicals could arbitrarily make you feel a superior temporal link in the prefrontal cortex that identifies sex with love. Marilyn had become that fun place where viewer could be tantalized by ideas of fun and teased sexually. Corporate was making loads of credits on sex games with Marilyn leasing her icon, let alone all the virtual packages one could buy to look like her or dress like her online. Sort of the new Barbie for this century, but it was still up to her to maintain her franchise and she really did have all the answers. One of those answers was to play that chemical addiction for her icon and take her audience to the budding place of her re-born heart.

Arthur thinks to himself and writes, "The love of words, the way words can create images in your mind, is what keeps me alive. However, I am perplexed with what stirs me that seems to be beyond my ability to form words altogether. Yet this feeling drives me to be greater than I am in my personal struggle for excellence. Why do I write, what evidence of the weight of these words suggest whether my political or ideological belief has any impact at all? These words are more than mere partisan social critiques borrowed from obscurity that sermonized my pathetic martyrdom or eulogized my human endearment. What confused cliffs did we jump off of? What has motivated this leap into the cauldron of convoluted ideas of capitalistic schemes to patronize our hearts desire? When do people emerge in lucidity from a credit economy that has bred absurdly false ideals about life's inevitable outcomes? What themes will un-root our merited spirits to reignite our humanity to such an extent that we all are charged with humanistic jurisprudence. When there is no tragedy in a complacent world, what will bring us to knowledge? There is no common awareness of economic crisis of the heart and our complete bankruptcy of human endearment. Perhaps I am completely naive that any one soul could effect change, but I dare be a vehicle for its augmentation. This pursuit of egotistic ambitions was obsessively driven, like addicted dope fiends impervious to loves tender sweet nectar. What have we settled for in our dishonest contempt of misguided values, depraved social order that merely encourages accusatory fingers to the contrary? These fostered beliefs in the inferiority of our deepest emotions, suppressed because there is no way to make credits off of real emotions. This is something that is a sacred human right. "To love and be loved." If this makes me a fanatic, a self-prescribed moralistic accountant, then let the critics impale me. I will keep my insightful focus clear enough to impale

227

back with ink and metal striking keys from this virtual typewriter. It's not a subjective process to visualize words in causal complexities, but to incite a clear vision and a real artistic dilemma for all its patriots. I believe humans have the capacity to love and I have faith that they will. All these confused motivations that have caused us to sleep can be solved in the plainest of riddles. These are the parables that liberate our pointed critiques. They render humane judgments, moralistic rationalism that splits the evil and social responsibility into very clear and divided accounts." Sigh, "There." Arthur said. That's enough for today's blog.

The fault of capitalism was to give value to money, as the only way to support one's self instead of competition breeding innovation. To remove the farmers from the land and send them into the bosoms of the big city life was a way to lure common people away from being self-sufficient. After a few generations, they were forced to make stakes in the city and their battle was soon over. Manufacturers, now major corporations, created a captive audience for their snake oil remedies to everything that ails ya'll. Like all that glitters is gold, we all jumped at the shiny things that delighted our minds until the next shiny thing came along. The Internet was just the most never ending shiniest thing humankind had ever created and no one could look away.

Instead of building our world, we let it get built for us. Our set of circumstance was that unawareness became our awareness fascinated with the sheer shiny process itself. When all that has precedes us is forgotten, and the meanings of words become obscure and die, where has our liberty gone? What has become of love in this process of its deliberation? So funny because in this world the only thing that is deliberated is where the next big sensation or trend will be. These are all little orgasms of various types, designed to keep your curiosity livid with egocentric ambitions of self-indulgence tantalized.

Women were the last to buy into the shiny stuff; after all they are

228

the bargain shoppers. I think it's because of the intangible nature of a flickering screen versus real shoes you can try on. Women were resistant to give into the virtual reality and had to be lulled into plugging in as a means to buy those shoes. Women up to that point never really took it as seriously as men did, because they knew plugging in was not evolution, it's devolution. But when they could see an image of their foot inside every shoe that had ever been created on Earth, the deal was sealed at last.

Women were the first to be completely saturated by marketing and discovered early on how to navigate the games of commercial life. They mastered this clarity of intention way before men, who believed their tin soldiers could really fight. But sooner or later, every illusion gets agreed to. With a constant onslaught of banners and advertisers hammering their false ideas of what truth is, women eventually submitted. It doesn't take but a little over half to become the majority and the ends justifies the means in any dishonest business dealings. If you can get everyone to believe it's true then it is certainly true, isn't it? Arthur was the one that coined 'Machine Civilization' and that was way before computers, cell phones, and Google.

Consciousness has had inexplicable lifetimes touching each other's souls, remembering what brought them here on their quest for enlightenment. Marilyn and Arthur spent their night separated from each other in agony, yearning, tugging at their deepest voice within, begging to recall a whisper so long ago. This is my enlightenment, this is my proclivity, a mantra ringing in both their ears transformed in every aspect in their once petty lives. In absence of metaphors, we plunged ourselves into a quasi-religious rapture precipitated by our essential vital urges to share exquisite pleasure, of exquisite contact. Overpowering attraction, throbbing for sexual connection travels in throes of unnamable dreams in loving details. He has the body of a man privileged in carnal knowledge and envies of the flesh. She was everything a woman could be, ready and willing for an exhausted encounter with human mysticism, where all secrets of the soul are revealed.

Both Marilyn and Arthur were checking how near the time was for their Waldorf Astoria meeting. Paradigm shifts in consciousness in the last twenty-four hours of their first meeting has them both on the edge of their seats. The picture they are about to make is an emotionally intimate portrait of amazing fearlessness to delve into the bouquet of human endearment. Everyone in this world of the half dead is one kiss away from being shattered by a contact of real experience. Arthur knows she is a heroic creature and somehow everything she touched was as perfect as she was. A precious object stunningly beautiful exquisite beyond her chromosomes, so bright it could be scary for someone without enough courage to stare into her brilliance. They both walk up at the exact same time and stop in disbelief, overwhelmed with feelings that stagger their ability to react.

Arriving in a very seductive black evening dress cut above her knees, a deep plunging neckline, and short black lace shawl covering her naked shoulders. Pure black lace stockings etched patterns along those very long legs that were propped up in elegant lace Versace pumps. Her makeup was flawless and the deep red lipstick made her lips speak to him from across the room. She had a pillbox hat attached to a raven black lace veil covering one eye and matching gloves flowed the length of her forearm. Her travel bag was packed and she was ready to run away with him anywhere he chose.

He was also ready for her, dressed like an elegant man in a black suit showing just how strong and determined he was. His thick black hair slicked back and thick black-rimmed glasses outlined his eyes that spoke only of his innate desire to discover her. Suddenly they start walking fast and then begin to run. Marilyn dropping her bag and purse, and Arthur letting go of the few bags he was carrying. There were no materialistic values didactically tugging at an inert reason for survival, rather an overt longing to be together. Her fertility abundant and innocence of consequences crossed the borders of her old life for that of joy in their heartfelt discovery of the meaning of life. His wild regeneration became his new religion of identity now without abandon, discovering what intentions could really mean in a moment of sacred reunion.

When two lips unravel in a momentary loss of consciousness, their own sublime empathy to touch each other as if nothing else matters, becomes overwhelming. Marilyn and Arthur were those lips colliding in moans, with weakened knees their hearts beating so fast they launched them from reality. The knowing cure of epiphany replaces any other voice in their heads. A place for happiness of this type to bloom recognized in erratic behaviors that somehow make sense to lovers only. So serenely her assured movements resolved to penetrate through their amply clad veneer of the ostentatious to find where their serenity dwells. Light is the magic that carries mosaic images of their blessed desires to reach out to each other's tenderness.

Arthur whisked her up in his arms lifting her from the ground, heels kicking in the air with laughter, and then tenderly returned her to his side, still kissing. Love, passion, obsession had all arrived so suddenly to their perspective beings, delightfully overwhelming, and clearly addicting. Lightning strikes in mysterious ways and risks are something that becomes as natural as breathing ions in a thunderstorm. Risking for someone like Marilyn, as it is for all women, can be extremely dangerous, but women are willing, perhaps more willing than men, to risk it all for love. Especially for the loving arms of a self-made man who has a grasp on what in life is really important to survive.

The type of devastation from these so-called modern social idioms breaks down opening a floodgate of ideas of life's importance. They walk out together with no trepidations, no blindfolds, and no regrets, singing the psalms of Solomon, a courtship of never ending reincarnation after reincarnation has resumed. They have known each other's magnetic compassion, tasted the vast greatness of pure joy and of those words yet to come like, 'I've always loved you.' The blindfolds of social constructs were off and Arthur led her to a nearby secret enclave ripened for a sweet evening of celebrated love.

Walking through underground tubes that surface to an elevator that was still working, they ascended to the top in a penthouse. A palace in the strata must have belonged to someone very important many years, before the floodwaters robbed its owner of prowess. It is decorated in an Asian style, with lacquered furniture ultra-modern high-end life style. A totally self-contained apartment where Jazz music was already playing over its exotic sound system as Arthur opens the door. This apartment is scented in rare real roses from its outside balcony garden, still existing because of old technology that continued working. Their giggling banter turned to serious kissing over the threshold to resume what was started so long ago.

Innocent delights, combined with unbridled passion, became their new matter of importance. Without hesitation they hurried to reach their destination to seize a moment of real intimacy. Erotic signals, subtle shifting gestures caught in textures by eyes, nose, ears, touch and a sensuous taste, promised forbidden true love. They dropped their suitcases to the floor as they moved aimlessly towards the bedroom, whose windows overlooked the entire skyline. New York City was a dark enigma, an ever-resting sentinel lit in tonight's full moon, a testament to modern culture's evolution gone awry. A sleeping giant of culture and silence, adding to a mystic mood of timeless love, where their innocence can be indulged to heightened states.

She loosened his tie and lifted up his collar slowly. She slipped the knot, untying it from around his neck in sincere earnest. She quivered in lucid slow movements to savor each increment of superfluous bliss, unbuttoning each button as if releasing a deity from heaven. His perfect chest revealed a godlike stature, hard and tan by the natural sun, full of soft rich curly hair. Astonished, engulfed in amore's miracle her nipples went hard and her luscious breasts invitingly rest between the open folds of her dress, begging to be noticed. He unbuttons her lace shawl to reveal that delicious bosom, and throws it into a chair in slow motion, while unzipping her dress to let it fall to the ground all in one movement. His sultry and haunting voice began to resonate Marilyn's semi-naked frame lacquered in black exotic French laced lingerie. Hearing his yearning whispers spoken in sweet tiny licks, taunting her left ear sent inciting chills down her spine. They arrived at their new bed, where Marilyn removed his jacket and shirt. She knelt down to remove his belt, kissing his navel and releasing his pants that dropped to the ground. His bulging package throbbed with heat. It ached to be freed to her urgent lips that can't resist taking him into her succulent watering mouth.

His 6'2" chiseled ex-soldier body was about to be completely exposed after she untied his shoes laces. She slipped each shoe off, along with his socks, so his dropped trousers and boxers could slip off his feet. He is a real man, seductive, broad shouldered, built for driving hard, and something to hold onto. Marilyn started to kiss his powerful, graceful legs, working her way up to his very thick and hard shaft, drenching it repeatedly with her moaning teases. She grabbed his hands, squeezing them hard; her intention is to cherish his beautiful body with endless foreplay and unbridled seduction. She addressed his body in a way that he could not move; with both her hands pressing his gluteus towards her as she swallows him whole.

He aches to offer her pleasures but he must merely accept the pleasure she is giving him until he's compelled to lift her up to meet his wanting eyes. Marilyn, with her pumps on, stood just a few inches below the top of his head as she rose from the floor. He also had no intentions of stopping the foreplay; only his hands could no long be idle as they longed to search every inch of her points of pleasure again. Her arms wrapped around his neck and broad shoulders and he lifted her off her feet to lay her divinely into their exotic awaiting bed. His loins are ready to burst by the enormous splendor of her exquisiteness, a jewel for his taking, amply given. He placed a pillow underneath her lower back and then slowly ran his fingertips along the edges of those raven thread stockings and up to her knees, where he gently parted heaven incarnate. His hungry tongue and long warm fingers massaged around her engorged sheath, making contact with her contracting, dripping obsessions trapped behind a layer of lace. His tongue moved slowly down her thigh, tingling everywhere he touched, drenching her longing that cried in cooing joy.

Marilyn had thought to herself about a day like this; it lived in her imagination that a tremendous evening like this would reign supreme. This love was beyond mere mortal expressions of coupling. It filled her immense void with an incredible destiny in the midst of genius. This man was truly a special blessing to her being. Every finger brush with his loving persona was a colorful painting of his inner love. Her compassion bowed suppliantly, knowing that somehow he was her King that she had been waiting an eternity to caress. A hunger was being admirably satiated; this mystery that attracted them was reverently sublime.

Her garment was made for this moment; between her laced up legs, a soft satin ribbon waited to be released and form memories for a lifetime. He found her satin ribbons with his teeth, pulling them open, watching her eyes in anticipation, taking the surrounding lace back with his hands to bury his face into her emanating crème de la crème. Grazing on her swollen flesh, symbiotic boundaries dissolved and a promiscuous abandon freely expressed both their intention. He wanted that from her, to allow her sexuality to flourish. His tongue and lips to wildly bear down on his face and drench his chin with her hyper-aroused milky thighs.

She was encouraged and took the pillows away from underneath her derrière, throwing them behind his head and laying him on his back. With her glistening dripping vessel she nestled his hard erection between her slick lips sinlessly, sublimely, glazed his long shaft incessantly back and forth. Staring into his excited eyes, knowing his heightened emotions would surge, inciting a rigor over the edge of his comprehension. She grasped his hands tightly holding his arms back over his head, while relentlessly pressing harder, squeezing his yearning throbbing rod. Deeply arching her back and flexing her abs with every bit of strength she could muster, rocking him back-and-forth with sure strides of wanting girth. Arthur couldn't take it anymore and rose up, pushing her with his gentle forcefulness. Pulling her legs around his back and putting his arms around her back to draw her in tight for a kiss.

A kiss of complete indulgence; watery and deliberate, an erotic conversation quenched in overt desire to taste infinity. In a sweaty undulating lather, she maneuvered herself so when he drew her close to his body, he penetrated her at the same time. Heightened rapture of overwhelming desire and love magnified their magnificent beauty in a fire dance of high-pitched euphoria arriving at a taste of consciousness. Their mutual awareness of energy fields breathing, touching, synchronizing autonomic nervous systems took them over, letting their spirits soar. Both sitting in Mahamudra, drenched in sweat, they are still wrapped in her raven black French lace. Moving without thought, with their eyes rolled back in their heads, they lost on an inner journey, embraced in their timeless love. Swirling like Dervish internally lost in perfection's desire, a devotional worship of their essence of all incarnations merging ethos. Endless spiritual orgasmic waves enchant their uniting spirits in a binding ecstasy that blends identities together. These expressions of life force in a wonderland of spirit, a profound pathway to spiritual rhapsodies in an ecstatic state each stroke invoked. Sweetly delved in primal meditation where each movement anchored them into infinity's stone, carved with focused intention the greatest capacity to surrender love. Indulgence along a membrane paved in velvet, tipped in satin, and misted in the most refined purest oil manufactured in heaven to glide among the stars. This is where their hearts beat now and where a kiss had taken them, morphed into the constellation of giving lovers whose sole purpose is to give more.

Symbolically, their nudity revealed themselves when they had surrendered all obstacles that prevented them from a shared experience of divine bliss. To lose the murmuring pulse of lives' majestic dance and imbibe on the miracle of making real love for the first time is liberation. Every day is a flirt with death, but to surpass this with wisdom, allows them to take risks and surrender their past, present, and future. Seductively courageous, she moves her hips in eloquent, deep, long thrusts. She transcends those many layers of possibilities that conquer the borders of life and its end. How beautiful it is to behold beauty in our eyes, through our fingertips, reverberating in our ears, the way it smells and tastes so heavenly. To grow old and wise together despite our own personal frivolity is an enigma that I hope we always attempt to solve. Their pathway is set and they see the way home in an unshakable clarity that no mortal concept could absolve. Every soul deserves a hand to hold walking down a little dirt road that leads to the sunset of every heart that has wished to be loved.

When a woman says she is in love, can men ever fathom the depth of what that could even mean? Really there is so little we know about each other in this little speck of time we have for a timeless embrace. We all walk in the shadow of death, threatening it with every breath we take, in our defying cause to tell each other in flickers of existence that we are in love. We found each other at last beyond any examination of evidence. So much truth has been spoken in the simplest of kisses where goodbye is never an option. Triumph of the human spirit is the most resounding music heard within two impassioned souls with a simple promise to love you always. "Thank you for loving me," is the only response needed when heaven falls to Earth and extreme gaps of emptiness are filled with substance. Truly it is the small things that weigh the most in this little impression we make and what is remembered. In love's symphony, a cacophony of emotions exploded like fireworks, celebrating the existence of life force, but how that translates to a virtual universe will always be unknown.

They both thought to themselves, "What do we do now?" Then they heard the voice answer in their minds, "Leave immediately!" They each gave so much meaning to their lives that neither one expected this. With no regrets, they bask in the empowerment of their brave decision to connect. They must run, acquire technology, and make their love be known in a community where news is measured in moments of rotation of the planet. Spiritual love is something that is awakened, natural as breathing, resting innately inside all sentient beings and can start with a simple hello. They had to leave the city and go to the most remote place they could find. A place where corporate and sponsors couldn't use their political influence to sedate their collective message.

"This is what corporate doesn't want us to feel, isn't it Arthur? They don't want us to comprehend that there's something outside the sphere of our appliances other than the best workout programs or credit acquiring multimedia blogs. They want us to believe that human contact isn't an important use of time versus interacting with media and programs that require credits," Marilyn says sternly.

"We are going to have to leave as fast as we can Marilyn." Arthur sadly acknowledged, "You and I know they will just terminate both our accounts and credits if we broadcast anything other than our current content."

"Where will we go?" She painfully asks.

"I know your courage Marilyn, and I know this may be a bit different, but I have friends who are not virtual. We already have a safe haven and we don't need to bring anything but ourselves, if you are ready?" Arthur whispers.

"To be with you Arthur, and continue where we have left off, is my only reason to be alive at this point. Show me the way," Marilyn warmly concludes.

The world wanted to see Marilyn and Arthur together again and Marilyn and Arthur wanted to show them. Only on their own terms, off the grid, and without any need for credits, even though the credits kept pouring in. They were living the country life that they both always wanted; where Arthur could write plays for Marilyn to act in. They could even have that family they both wanted so badly, with plenty of room to run and play and stretch your imagination to the moon and back. With the goldmine of credits that couldn't be taken from them, they started opening up acting theaters across the country with their network of friends. His old friends from New York were training other theater productions in the ways of a good show. Some of Marilyn's friends, who knew about the old ways of lighting and music, came together with them to start an old fashion production company. They created the theater experience from Arthur's stories that he was writing about his and Marilyn's new life. Who would have thought that little Broadway theaters would trend again worldwide? A meeting place for once-virtual friends to meet in real life to see what the two lovers were up to next. Marilyn, after all, did have a billion viewers and this was the only way to find out what she was doing now. The price of admission was the audience member writing something personal about their discovery of love and posting it. After it was posted, you received a special code that allowed you to enter the theater experience. Everything that Arthur once posted was now on everyone's lips and their virtual world was exploding with a new type of fun. People talked about this crazy little thing called love and rediscovering the warmth of two bodies touching in the name of it.

Can't Stop Thinking About You

Silver flickers imprints mark images I can't forget they've erased the forgeries that once hung up my regrets. Pages in a flip book remind me what it took to find my way back to innocence between portraits and silhouettes

I can't help contemplating her velvety surfaces at the throes of temptation, in delving plunges, starting at the point of her epic transfiguration. Tantalizing intentions percolate against her translucent membrane that's so thin; a loving breath can disarm its barriers in an instance. Her swaying topography lush with evocative color rich in textures that feels as smooth as satin. Welcoming interiors alive and inviting, her glistening pores absorb the psychic transmissions that bind us. Overwhelming feelings of euphoria, uninhibited surrenders that softly glide across her voice uttering my name so sweetly. The wisp of my imagination makes contact with her irresistible thoughts of our climatically charged sacred treatise of touch.

I see Marina immersed in our profound experiences, tucked away in the folds of time, savoring our moments together in eternity. Nothing else mattered in my life, she has compelled me to be better than I am, and I have become moved by her seductions. This symbiotic universe reveals her radiant picture on my indelible soul as if it has always been there. I replay how eagerly we watched sensations knead our lechery submerging inside her dark depths and mine. Hush, screaming from her moans, urgently tugging at me relentlessly to delve further inside her heart. Recollections of her wild abandon, in unabashed intensity, crystallizing our epoch of romantic spirituality. Like Nefertiti's sublime majesty, Marina's recoiling graciousness is a testament to her supremacy to ignite love. I see her now in my mind with heaving breast and aching flesh taunting my desires to indulge. I hear her thoughts traverse time and space, bouncing off the stratosphere and entering the receiver of my heart asking, "Where are you my love?"

Marina, who is also busy at work, introspectively admits in her diatribe, "I realize that random passersby can somehow see him vividly imprinted on my face. Ambitions, friends, routines, and worries inherently dissolve as my clarity that our epic story is invisibly embracing us contently. These elaborate passageways of thousands of other lives we've suddenly remembered making everything without the presence frivolous.

"Our collective awareness breathes mysteriously along this invisible stairway that shows us the way to paradise. We've been furnished a map to a destination we have created while still in the grips of our cages we thought necessary, our opiate of reaching hands, races through innate vulnerabilities, dilating each other's extremities that assimilate the dark. I dare torture my persistent feelings that cling to unanswered questions written on predictable costumes I wear for a party that was never meant for my honor. Without you by my side, my wholeness subsides, my acknowledgeable love cannot be quenched, and I am filled with a dire void that can't be filled. Because we yearn for each other, our virtuous love is eternal starting from the very moment of your parting lips.

"Our primordial nakedness frees us from all the covering illusions of our folly, yet we are clad in the singular meaning of our lives. Our nudity is totally illuminated consciousness and all other illusory effects cannot be hidden pretentiously in ignorance anymore. We have awakened to our transparency and known each other in ways most humans barely know exists yet inborn in every one of us. Our bodies harbor many motifs, spectacles of this fundamental trail we follow towards our rudimentary connection with the universe.

"My heaving breasts secrete fruits of knowledge and ethereal euphony, his pulsating lightning Vajra a vibrant sibilance voicing the Diamond Sutra. I am weary of my former self and this knowledge is the instrument of our liberation. It's resting in our loins, desperately seeking our return. Intoxicate my emancipated limbs with your fierce intensity. Threaten to destroy my world with your immense love and turn my myths into reality.

"Arouse my sweet fury to never stop dripping, lusting incessantly in a wild hunger, drunken with your celestial frenzy. Intimate tenderness revealed in our insatiable, delves through eons in our timeless cause to be united in love. I must feel spread, a mistress in your spinning world, filled with forceful meditation of your preying fiery ways.

"He does not refuse me, rings repeatedly in our song. I cannot accept any other notion other than to incessantly worship from my lips. Our exquisite sacraments are taken in a mighty crucible where reality is dramatically forged into an amalgamation of ultimate love. Where his heart beats is a purpose I can no longer ignore, pretend, or mock, as I am taken into the dance of gods," Marina laments.

Holy immortals threatened with mortal lies, whose inevitable victory defeats the tempted fates of sacrificial occult fires for the freedom to embrace love endlessly. This lifetime, this judgment, is to let those lies fall into reality's hellish fireball to be annihilated forever in perdition's demise, reaching paradise at last to greet consciousness's final purpose. We are all guided to look behind the magic curtain and peer into the vastness of creation. This is when the dreamer awakens to the possibility that there is more to the apparent and the well of substances strikes deep.

This impossible dream of imposing possibilities only prophets dare to predict, escorts us at every crossroad of anxiety to risk our pious choices. How do lovers decide a tempted fate of these disciples of divine order who are no strangers to abstract blueprints of the soul? Who would have thought monotheism was the unity of two souls through their ability to give themselves to each other completely? What Cuneiform tablet, or Sanskrit relic, has been overlooked for other pressing ideas of what constitutes civilization? This spiritual human journey is between bodies in motion with souls attached. A simple deliberate explanation to our celestial connection is through our anatomy on all levels. Consciousness has gravity that

243

sums us around its well-spoken cues, disconnection is what makes those cues inaudible, not that they're absent. Ultimately it is our attenuation to our perception of spiritual passions that tunes us in, cognitively revealing desire's intention without lies or interference. We will all find the dials eventually tuned to their signal so our receivers can hear their transmissions of love divine. Hopefully we will hear the message before it is too late and our destination with love has slipped us by.

Marina's constant arousal is a reminder that their sexual awareness is obsessively attempting to further the sexual epiphanies they have already crossed. Marina was beside herself with angst. Work became meaningless and her day without him felt unfulfilled. Obviously their dyad had formed eons ago and this cognitive dominance is insistently receptive to transcendental airwaves incapacitating anything else. She needed his contact to feel whole and their joined vehicle to travel back into sublime nothingness.

Continual sexual stimulation was the beacon wooing them back to glimpse again at the big picture they had inadvertently opened. The mechanism of desire had been skillfully unlocked from their last encounter where erotic spiritual fantasies were conjured like mantras. This was the most visceral experience of a lifetime and all other purposes became irrelevant. Nothing they could occupy their time with could shake their feelings of missing each other. A paradigm of separate identities became inconsequential, only the captured nectar savored in microns of their reunion could ever matter. There was no need for explanation of their genuine need for each other's comforts as their fluidity was not a fluke. They wanted to extrapolate their experience more in this spiritual, sexual, hyper-flux of magnetism, and ethereal orgasm of millions of migrating invisible butterflies.

We longed to return to the place beyond perception where neither creating, sustaining nor destroying exists, only the invariable nothingness, our sweetest craving. We experienced the split second of transformation into ultimate love as absolute formless beings emerging from the primordial fires of timelessness. We existed without constraints of linear time as holographic invariants atoned in everything and nothing simultaneously.

She was my aphrodisiac, primal instinct, incited by her bare breast, her arching spine, and legs spreading into the infinite void heightening my promise to return to forever. My chest, legs, and hands climbed through her imagination with shivers and thrills, provoking arousal to fulfill her promise to give and receive love. Premonitions shift our myopic perspective, guiding us towards the next initiation as anointed deities of pure love. We were ready to sacrifice the life we thought we must have, for the life that was meant for us to have. Next was setting a time for another material manifestation of our didactic journey into a love supreme.

Magic brings lovers together but minds intercede, corruptible by sources that gnaw at precious truth until it corrodes all the fibers that bind them. Once two lovers decide to come together, minds can bring issues such as disbelief, regret, and self-fulfilling wishes of sabotage because of fear. However, if you let intimacy incubate enough, those dominant yearnings of erotic venerations dispel any fear with a courage that can change history.

Women may be far more rational than men when it comes to this desire, giving pleasure, or surrendering herself, something well thought through. Marina constructs things with the impetus of tenderness's value; relationships must be built on trust before love can grow. Most women's choice of a relationship is larger than a primary desire because they understand substance and practicality. Balance and grounding is a much more significant jolt to a libido that can migrate only if all concerns have been eradicated. Her degree of interest and commitment to a relationship was considerably as different as her leap of faith to make it happen.

Symbolic scenes ran through Marina's visions, all day long, of being ravished, seduced by a ravisher, overcome with cravings that can't be contained. There were also caveats of my kindness, caring attentive ways that were loving, mindful, and gentle towards her precious heart. She was electrified by her own transgressions and was done apologizing to herself and her business colleagues for her distracted behavior. Her desire for spiritual relevance was being dispensed in constant waves of heat, activating her sexuality in the most inconvenient places. She texted him, "Let's meet later tonight."

Appeal is, above all, paradoxical. It implies some sort of control or that it's something conjured up by you. Appeal is something that is innate, sewn into the fabric of a supposed identity, not manipulated by self. Well, perhaps a little hair gel doesn't hurt. This ceaseless puzzle overpowers my awareness with a simpler truth that rises far above the distinct systems of arousal and desire. Its pieces fit or don't fit with some sort of outline set in my consciousness long ago in my gargantuan cosmology. The message is delivered when the receiver is turned on and its unsettling evidence is as obvious as the outcome. We are magnetic and overwhelmed with each other. It's too big to ignore or pretend we can carry on with our lives without one another.

I too could barely function and my focus on my work suddenly became meaningless, barely generating a spike in the readings of my desire. My meticulous suspicions were abhorrent as my work was never meaningful in the big picture of existence compared to this. Crazy as that seems, I was ready to drop everything to run to Marina. The spiritual sexual prowess of erotic tenderness coexisted with our mutual yearning for ravishing to unfathomable levels of unbridled lust. Too complex for comprehension, our ascension was something our higher selves could decode in an instant without a need of awareness.

Nonetheless, our human brains had only barely reached its shores and surely something that would manifest in our new creative endeavors together. Navigating the inherent intricacies were effortless interpretations of our underlying truth that would be a subject of conversations until we turned to dust. The paradox of both our worlds and lives felt like it was coming to an end and our inherent love was about to move to another level where nothing else matters. Unencumbered excitement shook my being when I got her text and all I could do to answer was to say, "Is now too soon?"

She sent me a "lol" and I sent her back a "sigh." The reality of LA traffic is not going to let us meet until the evening as she predicted. So our mutual anticipation would have to grow until we meet in our castle in the sky, high above Los Angeles's sprawling city. Ironically, our draw towards each other's essence is of a spiritual nature and our lust at a very high frequency for our spirit beings to reunite.

I am obsessed with going over every little line of her body in my mind. Her movements, the way she glides into a room, the air around her thick with the aura of love merging ineradicable with mine. Temples of the soul, reverent as life, these harbors sustain our ability to navigate in this world and weave our stories into the fabric of time. Time. That thing that moves so swiftly in our lives, when suddenly you realize it's slipping away, what's important becomes painfully apparent. So many obstacles between us and our reason for living. I know it's just traffic but how did it get here in the first place?

Somewhere in our human history the beauty of this amazing connection became a sin and women's bodies, taboo. Those ideas perplex me, as how could other humans have been convinced that kisses, caresses, as well as blissful intimacy in the most beautiful way could be sinful or repulsive? As for a woman's body, there's been no nobler pursuit than to preserve its ultimate beauty in art, poetry, and music. There is no more astounding architecture than that found in her physical form and sublime divinity that stands stoic in every curve. Astounding manipulators of our awareness preclude us from hearing the voice of the universe through women's lips. No matter where in recorded history you observe unnecessary barriers, they could have all been easily removed by a women's love.

I wonder what desperation this material collective saw that they needed to put blinders on our awareness at all cost. In their crafted society it's our labor, in all its flavors we have to barter with to negotiate the price of existing on a planet they bought and sold. So we negotiate our time away for what again? Oh yeah, to survive because we need money to buy things right? So of course a women's body is something that is taboo, because it keeps you away from fulfilling your deal with your labor. Romance is completely out of the picture except if we hit the lottery or can somehow redefine our system of worth.

Manmade culture plagues for over 10,000 years have brutalized love's divinity exponentially and completely unmercifully deconstructed its esoteric meaning. Reduced to just sex acts, mammalian pleasure seeking in the absent of contact and connection. Love has been diminished to merely swapping orgasms, whose goal is to climax, get pleasured, and return to your lifestyle of interactive gadgets or work. Taking time for unbridle innocent passion consumes too much time for consumers with short attention spans to nurture it.

Love, in pop culture is featured sex, beefcake and cheesecake from advertising marketers whose fundamental theme is, "Sex Sells." Economically, every aspect of our sexuality is summed up emotionally/physically and even spiritually by our purchasing trigger mechanisms. Products have been attached to our profound hormonal expressions of the power of attraction that are sold by the idioms of sexy. The epithet for pure love was written when advertisers figured out they could package it and sell it any way they identified it.

Beyond these stereotypical notions, innate icons seem to have

248

taken refuge somewhere deep inside each beating heart. Marina and I have such a refuge and it was apparent that this was a place of expressing closeness like she or I had never experienced before. It is our living poem; guided by a narrative only her and I can hear, translated where hearts need not rove again. My anticipation heightens as I settle up with my list of tasks, and clear the rest of my day of meetings and phone calls. I savor the moments of our secret language of erotic metaphors, where a distinct clarity begins with passionate intensity from a timeless courtship resumed in infinity.

When we are ready to leap into someone's arms, do we really look for a safety net? Can we believe in magic or should our hearts have trepidation to curve their wanting beats? This timely reunion originates from magic, like unfolding dreams seeping their way into reality. Perhaps Déjà vu or dreams of being with Marina in a mountain valley are shadows from another time. We were at the edge of the forest on a lake near a pass that leads to a snowy peak before we met in another lifetime. I recall her grins of pleasure accompanied by our sharing eyes. We felt like pioneers at the edge of a giant forest we somehow built. Our only ambition was to stay forever in our home in the woods aligned again with nature and delighted by our happiness.

I ruminated over this vivid recollection of unrestrained affections, erotic desires far outside the norm in instinctive disenthrallment imprinted on me somehow. Multifaceted apparitions, each shard a dimension of dreams and other places where magic appears, transform us into timeless phantoms. I dream of a palace, at a ballroom dance where I am watching her from afar thinking to myself, "How does she know how to be a woman so well, carrying herself like a goddess through my eyes is delightfully baffling to me. She stirs the depths of desire in my suspicious examination of my emotions as this is what I have always been looking for." My focal point in these dreams is always venerable, with my priority of exploration a pursuit to fully understand Marina. She is always by my side anywhere, everywhere, in motif, as creatures, and even inanimate objects.

This is my inherent objective: to nurture the nature of our primal connection in dreams and this world. I find myself wondering aloud along the sightline and glimpses of what her angels might sing in her glory. So many intriguing glimmer, they inspire our many lifetimes of un-polarized existence in the progression of the universe. Attraction can be the total culmination of our unified objective to share our lives together and march arm in arm tripping the lights fantastic.

Meeting under a soft, silvery midnight orb, aligning rhapsodies fade against your feminine form. Our ship of innocent love sets sail again along its moonbeams. They effortlessly ferry our luminous hearts to shower under their devotional rays of intoxicating shadows and divine discovery. We swoon, drunk with its sweet sips, rapturous currents flowing from the crux of our salvation in the crucible of romance we serve so well. We swim up the sacred river in autonomous positions, gracefully worshiping our enthusiasm to be engaged in our own mythology again. No longer vagabonds adrift in a sea of endless possibilities, we rest on the ocean's edge listening to the rhythm of the rolling surf inside our hearts. Being repeatedly reborn in garments of mystic holographic dimensions, our reincarnations have become intuitive and are wanting cyclic returns at last. No longer bumping into each other and missing symbiotic seasons of growth and fruition revolving around a perfect center of timelessness. Our true nature of pure awareness shatters all illusions, observations, and objects of identity. We surrender ownership of everything. No longer spirit or flesh in an omnipotent primal awareness of all our collective incarnations that coalesce. We are overwhelming spiritual wisdom that replaces all other references fueled in our secular madness beyond all understanding.

Non-Dualistic perspectives envelope this new paradigm of self-evident, pure formless love simply unleashed. These alienated humanistic vital roots once sprang up in this earthly life like wildflowers. Their seeds have never stopped reemerging begging for hope to awaken our most ancient human instincts. Still intact influences hover like sweet compassion over the pantheon marveling about emerging possibilities of a sweet drama that never ends. Boundless as light, our unfathomable embodiment of all wisdom when yin and yang collide within the womb of femininity's imminence, consuming everything in primordial elements. This is what our souls recognized simultaneously, losing our 'male/female' charades in a formless Neolithic moment of creation. We float in the black belly of primal awareness, amalgamated in a cauldron of destiny, stirred in the flooding tears of desperate yearnings to hold each other tight.

Nothing has escaped our warm life giving gaze, affectionately dreaming, wishing, and being in each other's lucid presence. Mortal love, the only gateway this narrative may speak through, in didactic epiphanies of lives only odyssey submits. Nudity's vessel is more than a philandering austere anomaly, it is a perfectly crafted consortium of portholes designed to travel into other worlds. Everything is vital and the mask has been removed from an obvious value of what precious gift life is to every living thing. Words barely express what is being said in just a second of a deep look inside your apparent love. It is the perfect resolution of the conflicts of opposites, a metaphorical interpretation of when male/female achieve non-duality. Tantra has been carved on rocks, written in the sky, on leaves, tree bark, inside water currents, in streams, rivers and oceans, yet somehow we have been lead to believe it is not real. Tantra bathes our third eye, constantly alerting us subliminally that beyond belief is a truth that sings ever so clearly inside your heart. Marina and I see it, it has moved us relentlessly, and our minds can no longer trick us into believing anything else. We have germinated and the blossoms are ready for this ritual and practice to focus the intellect on our timely metamorphosis in the union of our divine essence.

Our rendezvous has been swiftly progressing through the onions skin, revealing a poignant core both foreboding and exhilarating. Marina and I arrive frothing at our indulgences that simply won't leave our minds; surrealistically embedded so far in our pores we can taste it. This congenital euphonic resonance has spiraled from its repressive state, raised to the surface, and urgently and conspicuously has blossomed into the deliciously ripened fruit. A crisis situation streaming through our veins, in magical realism, begs more than any mere fantasy could prescribe. Our thoughts comprise of telling confessionals, ranting diatribes as mantras revolving on prayer wheels, professing our craving and lusting, and pining our spirits to not waste any grains of sand.

Provocative galvanized astonishments were our reactions when we recognized our car doors opened at the same time. We were not members of the opposite sex seeking orgasms, we were driven timeless souls seeking complete epiphany inside our genderless apparel. More than mutually pleasurable sex, or even intimate love, extrinsic to modern idioms, we were traversing every theory ever contemplated by philosophers in Earth's history. When our eyes met, we were both crying for many reasons; doubt, fear, remembering, understanding, and immense overwhelming compassion. She flung herself into my waiting arms of comfort and we promised to never leave each other's side, no matter what. Subliminally or intentionally we floated to the top of the stairs into our awaiting abode, me with both of our bags.

When we entered, I noticed she had something under her arms wrapped in silk that looked like a very large scroll. She unfurled a Tibetan Thangka depicting the Mahamudra and began hanging it on the wall at the foot of the bed. It was a prominent relevance to both our psyches as a prevailing symbol throughout our years of investigation and discovery of love's essence through Buddhism. The

Thangka's silent music was our requiem for spiritual liberation, and embodied in a single image of union in unabridged transcendental copious ecstasy, a poetic phenomenon pressing through the sphere of prolonging the attentive energy of passion without trying. Marina hung her wanton flag of acceptance beyond physical fulfillment, beyond poly articulated deities, where two are transcendentally absorbed as one. The Mahamudra, intricately entwined, concupiscent and spiritually liberated, lost and found in split particles of timelessness where nothingness embraces everything.

Our reverent proclamation lights incense, candles bowing to a shrine erected to signify love and devotion towards this gift of reunion. We go to our sacred altar where we surrender our hearts and together unfurled fresh sheets, approvingly blessing this bed with huge smiles. Once the covers are settled we kick off our shoes and both laugh while jumping into it like children. Our bodies smell fresh, both of us having taken showers and preened ourselves, readying for this consecrated moment to arrive in all our angst. Miles Davis "Kind of Blue," fills the air in our now serious sensuous meditative state where reason is as obvious as our eyes that never leave each other's.

She begins to undress under our tented sheets, propped by my arms and legs, knocking them away, laughing to try to keep me from getting a clear view. I then start slowly doing the same, losing my tie and unbuttoning my shirt, she attempts to help to get a good look me. We both get flashing glimpses of each other through light passing through the sheet until we both stop playing and get serious. She has on deep, dark Bordeaux red lingerie. It perfectly matches her lipstick so lusciously placed with very thoughtful details. Her fingernails are also gorgeous in many shades of red perfectly manicured as feminine as her femininity must express. Her hands were etched in henna Hindu stencils that walked up her arms like sleeves over her shoulders, cradling her breast. She also stenciled from around her pelvis and derrière down her thigh to merge with her matching lace stockings. My body's temple cleansed with salt rubs, manicures and pedicures, haircuts and laden with citrus scents of ravenous oils of delight. Every part of me, like her, moisturized with holistic herbs and botanicals that nurtured skin to its core. The rhythm of Jazz music insists we get up from bed and dance in slow romantic movements. We throw the covers forward, half-dressed I get up to lift her out of bed, spin her in a circle and gently lower her to her feet. We start dancing in slow sensuous ways, stroking our sumptuous gifts, enchanting them one by one as she continues to strip me down to a cosmic pulse.

Even our breathing finds a matching rhythm as chakras start to hum like cooing birds finding their supple nuzzle. We move gracefully through time and space to exhale motionless, allowing our awareness to penetrate a cumulative stillness between layers of reality in our Tantric Tango. A mutual homeostasis skillfully flows through our vital sea of the blood of life that has us merged between desire and this lurid dance. She has me almost naked, down to my black see through silk tee shirt and briefs that cling to every line of my body. She is picturesque in her lingerie in our Tantric Tango dance that ends with me sweeping her around my bent knee and raising her feet in the air to cradle her in my arms. There we take a long drink of each other's eyes and press against each other's lips to take another moist kiss.

Inside this cellular cloud of autonomous consciousness all-encompassing psychic forces begins their rise in search of our new identity. Like an awakened cobra whose skin is made from auric magnetic fields, brimming with electrons, it ignites a fire linking its nervous system to ours. Consciousness is aware through our awareness in its dual narrative of sonnets, uttered affirmations, psalms of fleeting identity dressed in a likeness of us. Sound passes over my vocal cords and I say sweetly, "I have flowers for you," and produce some Bordeaux red large stem Roses. She shyly acknowledges my offering, shaking her head coyly, remembering another lifetime where I gave her these exact flowers. She takes them into her beautiful hands and lifts them up to her nose to imbibe their aroma and their deepest meaning. She puts her hand on my cheek, caresses it like a goddess caring for her devoted follower.

Reveling in my sincerity and patient cause, compassion fills her being and her voice. Looking up into my eyes, holding my chin with both her hands, she pledges, "I remember you, this, our times together, our hits, our misses. Your cause may have taken many forms but it was always aimed at loving me, this I know. Time we created...yes it's as fragile as these forms we inhabit, but this time we have recognized each other in time. I can't thank you enough for your persistence to look for me. Even though burdens have taken you in so many directions, you keep coming back to, "Where are you my Love?" Yes, I hear you whisper this. It has always been my beacon to discover your whereabouts. Sometimes I am scared, afraid that another lifetime will slip by and I will have been alone again. It hurts me when I miss you. Roses, there are always roses to remind me that you are holding the candle flame high in search of me. Another moment, yes, another unselfish delve, a skillful lover bent on filling my spirit up. You do fill me up with your omnipotent offering of unconditional love that returns us to the purelands of joy." With this she undoes her embroidered silk and lace garment from her breasts and removes her ornate beaded satin guardians of heavens.

Metaphysical throes of transformation, surrendered free will, shed worldliness for supple, subtle, nubile, luscious, illuminating flesh to talk with. We continue spreading our divine auric tentacles around each other, eventually branching out in all directions to merge with consciousness endlessly. Among these vast planes of emptiness, a speeding hush unveils within our awareness of righteousness, reverberating as if a silent bell's shock wave. Relief moving past the speed of light inundates all surfaces, paradigms become meaningless, flailing, useless, until they seemingly dissolve and disappear into nothingness. All illusions are shattered by consciousness seizing our awareness, sublimely filling our attention with clear intentions of true love. Past, present, and future coalesce among our boundless affinities that suddenly absolve, into our new opium of satiated proclivities and perfect awe. Namesakes be bound, exonerated by pure love, whose source has no identity and no need of one. Sadhana is done, a unification of Kundalini for a rituals prescribed in the night sky of this New Moon begging for wish fulfillment.

Immortality as frivolous as misbegotten time, existences is our only conduit, pushed into clay these scribing lines so our souls can mark in eternity like no other entity. Vulnerability's real charm is to make unthinkable outcomes of day-to-day life dare to flow against the grain for an ultimate plunge into intimacy. This is our contemplative exchange, a prelude to merit, that has been saved up too many lifetimes to count. Now it's our time for cosmic fusion into an ecstatic state of contemplation. We made it sacred by our intentions, significant by our congruence. The time has arrived to melt into a mystical pool filled in still waters of of divinity.

She suddenly feels embarrassed, explaining how piercing my eyes are that they see through her very soul's light. Her warm heart, drenched in understanding, whose tenderness is beyond my comprehension, takes me aback. I allow it to wrap our soul together like a warm blanket on a cold night. We're both unafraid in this freest of all human associations, soaking up unhurriedly, touching, absorbing each other's gender genderlessly. We penetrate each other's attention, channeling a vivid psychic interchange, effortlessly connecting everything about us. New identities form as our veins are infected with a new vitality from the cosmos, connecting arteries, nervous systems, and organs, absolving 'you' and 'I.'

All physical tensions start to relieve in explosions in energy tingled in the outermost sparks of the stars. Borders of this new identity also fade as human psyche and cosmic psyche merge into this distinct new entity above mind. No form of consciousness is vague, quietly rumbling in a background of all their voices rooted in the infinite, coming alive and exceeding their individuality. We are so keenly aware of our notions, the process of our arrival, blessed expression of our perception, and the endearing reverence of our invocations voiced in words. We are addressing another human being, canisters for our spiritual delve that can resonate our resounding presence in the company of ultimate love and passion. All lifetimes return to sacred time in this fragile exchange that permeates, transmits, and receives through uninterrupted generations. Consciousness has traversed eons in a continuous state of washing ashore from warm celestial oceans to give birth to sentient life. In an instant of creation, from a divine kiss billions of years ago, both our piercing eyes met in a quintessential glimmer of hope that our kiss would prosper into a terrestrial new reality.

Two sentinels majestically hovering on the rooftop of our terrestrial universe where a swarming devouring unitary process feeds on our transitory flesh. An inseparable collective psyche, an endowment of a perceivable entity fills all the gaps of our porous remaining structure. She kisses me like the sun's moodiness, enriching me with life force, raising my body temperature and the atmospheric pressure of our sanctuary. An ovum seeking a procreative genesis, her possession undulates along the poles of her swishing centrifuge of Kundalini, desperate in the throes of anthesis. A black hole de-densifying resonance circling in mindless repetitions of mantras whose meanings cannot be understood. Where results and expectations cannot be anticipated when spontaneously charged Kundalini fuels the spirit.

What's left of the conscious mind suddenly expands when awareness and consciousness greet each other. This vortex we freely surrender to allow deep awakening of compassion and empathic healing. Our resonance balances this conceptual meridian where harmony stabilizes at zero and polarity is neutralized at the point of nothingness. Life itself at every core of its craving is love's fruitful significance. It propels every letter of symbolic symbiosis into every realm of its opaque synthesis, sizzling vibrancy into every atom. Marina is the divine universal mother and I am the moon water to her fiery seed. We're an unconscious collective genetic memory unlocked in our possession of awakened procreating consciousness. Nature talks between her legs in clairvoyant clarity calling me to join to taste truth's finery beyond the conditions of perception. She yearns for contact; drawing me closer as effortlessly I slip inside her endless void.

Congress surreptitiously envelopes her wanting doorway to oblivion as the intensive being of our bodies starts to remember their penetrating way. Swooned into the perpetual energy of creations, we comprise a universal form in an infinite motion of creation. Our senses are flooded with sounds and images of deities engaged in various sexual mudras and mantras. With moans of ecstasy, gods thrust their shafts deep inside millions of goddesses frantically stirring on top of them. All these symbolic genetic memories engorge and engage us as we merge with every form of sexual union. Sucking, kissing, placing our fingers into every orifice as she desperately attempts to fill herself up with my semen and start the process over again and again. Her womb fills with new life, gestating and giving birth in between our unlimited orgasms, her breasts full with milk where our offspring and me suckle without hesitation. Her milk flies wildly from her nipples as child after child, engorges, grows up, and starts the cycle of creation. Eager to emulate this process over and over they join with other spouses emerging from the firmament. Finally, we are whorled up into a pedestal of piety where we are crowned with jewels, bedecked in opulence, still engaged in our perfect union whose rhythm takes on new meaning.

Thrusting surges of seminal undulations, our angst proliferates in urgent slow impulses where gravity once again indulges our flesh and strips our thoughts to the bone. My eyes imagine scratching and biting each morsel of your delicate skin, quenching my rabid taste buds. Ravishes streak against my lips with sweet upheavals that continue to sip at your flowers nectar with relish, savoring forever to lose control. Swoon to my enchantments, I beg in silence, searching through mantras that guide me. They're like a breeze of swaddling caressing around your looming awareness of my presence to love you. Wishing my awakened vivaciousness arouses your sultry eroticisms with a testament known in our eyes like making love for the first time.

Your gorgeous pirouettes lavishing aphrodisiacal spins, fondling our dense undertow that languishes from a resurrected prayer of, "I want you again." An expression, impressions, of bodies in sweat's soothing perfume, penetrates this perceivable dance of utter carnal delight ignited by unquenchable passion. Our requiem of intercourse swells in majestic, orchestral lunacy, played in amnesia, breaking like waves crashing in a storm across your enthralled heartbeats on a defiant shore. Depravity raving in unconscious malignant obscurity, contagious as love, surreptitiously orgasmic, swell and release teased sumptuously by you. I tempt your happiness as temptations explode within your soft glistening skin, splendidly lit, surging repeatedly against my relentless strokes. Majestic intrusions can no longer abate in the rules of this marvelous joining of true lovers. Our making love's enticement into voluptuous fate of relished giving and receiving. Drunken in an aroma that can only be described as exquisite sexual divinity, our hearts surrender.

Aching embers burn with each palpitating heartbeat, as your pulse grows frantic in our trance lit exquisite union, graciously lost in forging flames of our desire. Your sumptuous surrendering consciousness burns primeval, ablaze in a feverish delving, enchantedly bestowing self for my pleasure and yours. Quivering in rivers of your gestating womb, throbbing in its pyre until stoking flames engulf your insatiable cravings with gritted teeth. Frivolous fragments of garments unravel, burnt in this heat, caught in sweet scorches of naked incursions. Inserting my will of reckless abandon that can't find an end to yours. Unyielding soaked offered appendages' rage in insidious pleasures, surreptitiously quenched in a sanctum of salacious endeavors begging to take me. Arched rabid intent, lewd insane arousals of lustful confidence, dripping erotic seductive extremes built from the arousal of an explicit Tantric sexuality. You take me in climactic epiphanies, shouting in showers of ecstasies made real when love intervenes.

Our insatiable madness caught in all realms rinses like a spring rain on the shores of still waters colored in enticing increments of approaching dawn. Laying on the remaining starlit shimmer, incurable hunger clings to appetites delving the depths of unimaginable sexual heights urgently. Purveyors of this lucid oblivion sit silent in their wondering as naked tactile landscapes with a ravenousness that seems to never subside. I hear enchantments still grazing passionately, encouraging more sultry reaction amidst interceding lewd pigments of sunrise against her sin. Peering enticements catches the remaining spiritual romantic simmers settling into a lecherous trance preying from both our panting eyes called sleep. Shadows stirring from a covetousness of intangible means, seizing the moment of what started within seven shades of midnight's lascivious extremes.

We circuit on an etheric holographic deity with only our faces in view, bluish purple red, flushed lips, still piercing omni colored eyes backlit by spirit. In our most vulnerable voice, we attempt to tirelessly enunciate our experience of Tantric love. Returning from death where life is born our unconventional spiritual love remains in collective consciousness. These groomed ten halos of Sephiroth's emanations are still alive from our journey into Kabbalistic mysticism where we became the tree of life. This is where it is written in divine will and nothingness, the sum of the whole, is the aggregate of all spirit. Unknowable divine essence to create has been revealed in intellect, emotions, and human revelations. All of creation is revealed in Janus's crucible reflections that constitute the conceptual paradigm of spiritual love with humanity's ingredient, overwhelming as it is. Marina and I have been completely overwhelmed, but there's a calm that I find hard to describe. She has a comfortableness calming me, reclining in my arms with her head on my chest. It's as if today was the first day of the rest of our lives, as cliché as it sounds. We were immensely happy little humans with wiggly little toes, prancing little fingers, and little pet jokes about cute little things we liked about each other. Yup, we're a couple in love, really in love. So much that nothing was going to matter except when we get to see each other smile, sleep, even breathe all in wonderment of just how lucky we were.

Oscar Wilde and Bram Stoker

Shadows outline the scars in your mind they trim at the rim of eventual time burning through pages raging in wind the shadows unwind in eventual sin

Victorian England never had a circus as captivating as what was about to transpire at Old Bailey, the main courthouse in London. Bram Stoker was there, un-apologetically, but somewhat incognito in a secluded corner of the court with his brim pulled deeply over his eyes. He was afraid for his former lover and friend, but he was more afraid of a witch-hunt that might include others whom originated from their literary bohemian soirée of Sir William Wilde and Lady Jane Francesca Elgee. The outcome of this misbegotten trial could literally wipe out the emerging creative community, and an undercurrent of fear was filling the underground of flagrant intellectuals that were fondling a new Romantic age. Sir William Wilde and Lady Jane Francesca Elgee, Oscar's parents were certainly at the forefront of that moment, traversing puritanical altruisms for the pursuit of spiritual liberation. Their home had always been a haven for exploration, intellectual, emotional, and certainly unconventional. Both parents were blatantly unabashed about extramarital affairs and their home was no stranger to explorers to ferret out their own sexuality in extreme risqué fashion. Of course, very discretely, as secrets were meant to stay secrets, in the harsh puritanical gardens meant only for Adam and Eve's divine marriage of procreators. Oscar was very young but an eager participant, quietly waiting as a wallflower in the corner of the room wondering if someone would ask him to dance. Oscar was seven years his junior so he very much looked up to the young Bram, who offered him a turn in the vestibule entrance. Bram was audaciously excited about being included in this very interesting group of people who were fearless at looking into the mechanism of the meaning of life. Now it appeared to be a curse, and Bram just wanted it to end so he could continue his work without waiting for the law to catch up with his overt past at the home of the Wildes.

Bram was fitted to examine his entire life in these final moments of this social paradigm of shifting tides, thinking to himself: "My grotesque Victorian contemporaries fail to understand the vast problems presented by the past, present, and future by their actions here today." It is noisy, coarse, and chaotic in this courtroom of demagogues, empirical boisterous buffoonery, directed to the eyes of a weary old friend. Oscar was drenched in his own shadowed footing, dressed in his crimson satin lined cape and dark violet velvet apparel. He was always singled out, but now he was singled out among the proper room of English Gentleman, who were no longer amused by his comportment. Foolishly inspired, his chivalrous ways of broadly painting his emotional intentions wildly on his sleeve for all to see. In his earnest plea for transparent honesty he has made this day possible for his own crucifixion. These blade-like lines are sharpened not by intellectual prowess, but by social enigmas burning underneath the hearts of desperate opinion. Oddly, it was a man named Wood that places his wooden stake into the heart of an earnest man whose boundless desire filled our eyes with sonnets, poems, and prose. These blackmailers were not my dear friends only failing, but also the courts circling around his neck, arrogantly deciding his fate of what they considered his eccentric immorality. Whether hedonistic engagement was the cause, these foreboding indigence of the law swarmed as undead, to fill their cause with his delicious warm rich blood. It seems Count Wilde had made his own brew of bloodsuckers, inadvertently teaching them with his own thirst for blood.

Now what poem could be recited in this bloodthirsty cacophony of self-absorbed aristocrats who have sat idly by, awaiting to prey on his naïveté of power. These were the ones that let him thrive in their kingdom, allowing him to think his words had any power over them. Theirs was an unknown path full of snares to trap plundering souls, as social boundaries seem so often invisible until the sign of the cross is made. Once we egregiously convince ourselves of our 'illusions of freedom,' we're swiftly reminded every royal court must have their joker and now unbeknownst to you, it is you. Their wanting teeth pleading to bury deep into the life-force of my daunting aesthetic driven beauty Oscar. Their thrill became more intense with an insatiable craving to take their frightened little mouse into complete debauchery for amusement's sake. His veins had swollen on the stage under these viceroys of fake benevolence, more like Machiavellian skullduggery. His lips visibly parched and gasping for air while loosing his collar to prevent succumbing to the prosecutor's hypnotic

SOULKISS: TANTRIC TALES OF MAHAMUDRA

trance and fainting under the law cobras watchful gaze. They were cursed and damned and insignificant, except in this moment, where they could snatch a man's life up, destroying everything he loved all at once ruthlessly. After all, this was solely about what this man loved and whom this man loved without question. There was a time long before this trial where mere pleasure seemed so uncertain in the search for bloodlust and first kill of an innocent soul. It seems power and corruption are messy ideas left to stay underneath the carpet or floorboards of our imagination. Noticing them would remind us how no one can remove the stains of our own misgivings.

The disappointment of first love can only lead to its mastery or create an inertia that continuously spirals down a path into the deepest depths of hells. Lost and unrequited love is a catalyst that can catapult its purveyor through insatiable trepidations that never end up in the ultimate embodiment of pure love. Formable dalliances of youth, playful proclivities mere switch to later enable a suitable quarry to run. Our time together in our youth was a titillating, fanciful excitement of families, food, intellectual gossip and playful imaginations. Books, schools, and a plethora of prolific creatives in a brothel filled with esoteric love for knowledge in all forms was also our edification. This is where I found young Oscar and myself dancing among the stars of enlightenment.

We unabashedly explored everything together as young contemporaries, whether it was skinny dipping in rivers, reading the same books, or going out to pubs when Oscar came of age. Even when it came to women our taste were so impeccable we both chose the fancy of actress Florence Balcombe. His wild eyed deviance was suddenly shattered by her gaze, leaving the poor brothels of Dublin empty of his frivolity. Somehow he had to find a way to convince her that he was a man of virtue, sadly misunderstood; a vital force of nature whom life itself existed for his every step. He was stoic at my height of six feet two inches, making us both very tall by Dublin standards. His presence dwarfed everyone by his collections of shadows that now seemed to coalesce around victims of his victimless crimes, or so he thought.

He had me in his grip also, my sedentary vulnerable youth had scared me as a creature confined to the loneliness of a sick bed. I was always afraid I wasn't pretty enough to be loved like my siblings because I was a weak, ugly and sickly creature. Repulsive to my father and another laborious chore for my mother, my heart was simply vanquished. I attempted to do anything for attention but reading everything ended up being my consoling guardian. Eventually I grew into a healthy man as our seaside town Greystones kept me strong. I discovered that people liked me but I was still detached socially. Being well read and with great awareness, I had no need for rhetorical garments, I could admit who I was. I was a man with a woman's heart with thick lips, heavy jaw, sensitive nostrils, and very soft straight hair.

The prose I wrote was the honey to attract the interests of Oscar and I could tantalize his flamboyancy with my imbibing hidden sexuality. He had a deeper strength as his father Sir William shared, certainly alluring with a wit laced silvery tongue that could charm the will out of anyone, including me. He knew my taste and descended like a dark cloud for my amicable loins. He wanted to be my master, at least become more than a male companion. My surrenders were not without a cross of swords as this dance with the devil was a test of solving both our intellectual labyrinths. In due course, I found my freedom from my contrasting wily antagonist whose wrath for intellectual competition for righteousness was exciting. But in the throes of our divinity, it was his flesh I wished to press against mine the most, to feel his dark power as intoxicating as it is.

I remember when our innocent friendship turned in the midst of my vision, in one lingering slumberous eyed glance, when threats of Sodom and Gomorrah's sins dissolved in eager praises spoken in our thrilling first kiss. Stillness murmurs in my ears as if life's oxygen had been sucked painlessly out of the air. Sodom's Angels whispers in my ear, "Will your dust cleanse the unbarred gates of purgatory?"

Our acquaintance acquiesced perhaps out of spite, jealousy, or an unopposed challenge of our wills. His gypsy senses astonished my sensibilities, musing his amusements by my bewildered face fixed on his demigod stature. You think I am mad, but simply put, you are not accustomed to such visions, as he runs through my veins as the only force of nature possible. He takes my arms and presses them against his hips and I feel a choking as if something was gripping my throat. He asks me, "Do you smell our scent?" and looks at me with such carnal hunger he invokes my passion and longing to be taken.

In the buttonhole of his lapel sits a rose bud. He sweetly takes it, places it under my nose to smell, and runs it across my lips. My hot, panting breath met his lips again and his hardy manhood presses boldly against my thigh. We were giant men standing nose to nose, me with brilliant red hair and his dark as a raven's wing. He looks demonstrably through my burning heart where my blood was boiling wildly, yearning to taste his creamy drops of life giving fluid. To tear away at his creative prowess, enter his caustic hellish core of tortures and viciously claw away at his manhood. Our entwined fingers were like two battling wrestlers, both attempting to take each other down. I felt a dull pain enter my throbbing body held down firmly to the ground in a state of prostration and servitude. "When did my eyes first meet yours?" he asked in a very low, deep tone.

In an uninterrupted current I clenched his fingers tightly and replied, "At this very moment." His captivating ubiquitous love drenched me within, warm and thick as he paved the way for my absolution. Entrancingly beautiful, we settle in an affectionate repose, realizing we had both been changed forever.

This barometer would change considerably, as unbeknownst to

me, he was sheltering the wiles of the most beautiful woman in Dublin, Florence Anne Lemon Balcombe. Risking my secrets with his silence, I cautiously allowed Lady Jane's poetry club to be segued to meet this delightful creature of paradise. She was soon to be Lady Jane's daughter-in-law, engaged to her son, the master craftsman Oscar, as of course we had so much in common with also. She was earnestly attracted to my nature as my height and red hair was a calling card along with my age and reputation. At twenty-two, two years after Oscar and her courtship started, her focus shifted towards her own career as an actor. Although, the dear poems of my lover and friend were endearing to her heart, she no longer wanted to be with the dark haired silver-tongued devil. We were immediately drawn to each other in a very playful mischievous ways. She was relentless in her queries about literature; Shakespeare, Goethe, and of course Miguel de Cervantes Saavedra. She also was curious about my many associations with great poets of our age such as Yeats, Walt Whitman and fellow Hermetic Order of the Golden Dawn friend J.W. Brodie-Innis. She too was well read and affectionate towards esoteric history and we would speak all night long about its origins. Philosophy was her subject also and she was a student of my philosophy teacher George Francis Fitzgerald at my old school Trinity College of Dublin. We joyfully became inseparable in Oscar's absence as he was away in London mining up his own identity.

Her change of heart was a stunning blow to Oscar's debauchery, filled with secrets about his mysterious life and not just with me. It was like he'd been uncovered and the light of these truths burned his flesh as much as his hunger for corporal intimacy favored his folly. Her virginal allure and pure and divine nature was his hedonistic salvation. She was a chance at a virtuous life instead of that burning smoke called his life. His bellowing lachrymose of despair left him in a lurch without repose compared to my dashing soliloquy of success in the theater. Henry Irving was now my business partner, because of my love for his work and my love for the smells, sounds and electricity of the theater. I became the manager of the largest, most renowned theater in the western world, 'The Lyceum Theatre in London,' and Florence and I were to move there once we were married. So, broken with memories of his courtship with Florence, he proclaimed to never return to Dublin again. The darkened spirit that was him was now aghast and ready for the shadowy labyrinth of London's darkened enclaves.

Unrequited love somehow mars his soul, and dear Oscar became a troubadour of homages to his lovelorn admirers, all too similar to Florence. Objects of devotion that inspired his pen to quiver in the night, streams reoccurring themes inflicted by the rejection of my now dear wife. She was his betrothed, annihilated by my budding engagement of soft words that pompously eroded his grandeur for mine. He was seven years younger and always seeking approval. As a lad highly competitive in all that we cared to be about in our youth, dwindled sadly, fading into our manly forms and social status. Our imaginations were set on fire as the world of Dublin was our oyster, defining our characters in clothes we would wear the rest of our lives.

Oscar's stimulant was his emerging libido ablaze with the desire to seek out all sensations London had to offer. His lingering pain inflicted by my own love, for the love of his life was more or less still smoldering in the wreckage of his dastardly transformation. Watching his demise had become a dreadful pain to me, especially watching him flounder in the den of thieves for his heart. I have never felt dejection, everything I've desired I proliferate until I am completely satiated in all its warm facets of understanding. His mother was right, there really was only one thing worth living for and sin was it. Give me passion or death, should be on the lips of all seeking fulfillment in life, not the mundane arguments over the pseudo intelligence of fashionable personalities. Nay for my unsolvable riddles, my coffin doors remain closed in the light of day; my pledging secrecy will never reveal me against your boyish lips and strokes of your raven hair. My scared loneliness is no retreat for a viral predestination to soil my imagination with the likelihood of being taken like a fiend by fiendish seductive hands ever again.

It wasn't until he entered the inner circle of theater when Oscar started to shed his longing for Florence in exchange for the American, Lillie Langtry. He became her tutor in Latin and she inspired him with her bedazzling charms to write theater pieces now for her instead of my beloved Florence. He was infatuated beyond any reverence, sending telegrams, writing plays and poems, calling her the Venus Victrix of our age. He went on about her celebrating her supreme beauty in The New Helen, and his poem, To L.L.. Oscar was expressing his emotional life, freely touting himself with the most glamorous woman in England. This Apostle of Aestheticism, with his outlandish clothes and scintillating wit, has now propelled him into the public conversation and given him a clever relevance. Of course dear Lily enjoyed the accolades from dear Oscar and cherished his friendship I'm sure. Oscar, knowing that Lily's love would always be unrequited, would later enchant his drooping blossom violet-eyed Artemis, Constance Lloyd. Constance was his brown haired, ivory-handed love that would legitimize his social standing. He needed a woman by his side with a high profile in polite society lecturing and getting rich; she was his shield between rumor and doubt.

Queen Victoria had facilitated this Neo-Puritanical Victorian era that unwittingly fueled a quiet revolution. The Bourgeois, a sexually aware and active social class completely discreet in this world where laws were always a looming danger if caught. To me, at times, it seemed Oscar wanted to see just how far he could push the limits. It was like he almost wanted to be caught for the thrill of the experience and the talk it would create. It was an avid experience; he was an adventurer being taken down the primrose lane by his frothing companion Dosie. Dosie was eager to spend Oscar's money and take him into the debauchery of the elite underground. What did gender roles have to do with one's ability to give and receive love and why were Victorians so anxious about this topic except to fan the flames of hell?

Oscar's and my mutual admiration for Walt Whitman would eventually bring us to the shores of America. Walt once said, "I am the poet of the body and I am the poet of the soul, the pleasers of heaven are with me and the pains of hell are with me." Walt's wise words would be our guiding beacon through the plague of Victorian England's ideology. Oscar and I were what Walt described as embracing extremes of experience connected to all of his fellow human beings, no matter how different from them they might seem to be. I embraced Oscar in too many ways as he embraced our hero, telling Walt that I was with him as his mother sat to read Leaves of Grass. Later, after pouring my heart out to Walt in letters, we became lifelong friends and I too would visit with him on the continent. Walt inspired the questions, perhaps a chance for enlightenment, perhaps a chance to evolve social conscious, why should the act of love be inhibited by the act of love?

Our souls are weighted down by gravity's fibers, twisting till they break in times grip. Yet the light in our eyes stayed steady. Unresolved conflicts, energetic catharsis, reversals, revelations, they are all catalyst to free us from fear, guilt, and shame. These demons that plague my heart consume my creative energies by monstrously dangerous predators. I can barely breathe in this courtroom, as a condemning courtship with one man's ideas enacted in life freely, may be the noose that condemns his freedom forever. My love can hardly bear witness as these outcomes may choke my deepest breath to the voice of my humanistic ideals about equality and freedom forever. I deeply fear these burdens of presence of mind will sway generations to come. That inner union and harmonious state of wholeness can only be designed and designated by men of power, prestige, and public opinion.

Doors will close to human awareness that consciousness cannot breach, because of one person's branding of taboo closing its porthole to divinity. This miracle gift of existence mere folly, along with the merit of a grave heart that has been invited to the light; I have seen its clear glow. I have also witnessed its ecstatic joyous state and know the beauty of this astonishing world from realms only our daring awareness need tread or deny its expression. Ah, this inspired state of humanity atoned by nature, and at its core, truly free until the consequences of the illusion of social norms waylay its proclivities to adapt, react, evolve and expound its truths.

Barristers superciliously exchange words with arching eyebrows, and unscrupulous mannerisms that would blight an army of Hamlets. Vanity is as vain as a weather vane, urging me out of my comfort zone into a dark and stormy night of our fragile souls. I hear the magistrate sharpening his knife to impale the impaler, our master of the night, who has prevailed so long in the streets of London. His charisma was about to dry up as his mask was being ripped from his face to see what pact was made with the devil in his own picture of Dorian Grey. His timeless youth was now sucked from his veins where blood no longer was rich with the liberties of his victims.

"Poor Oscar," I thought to myself, lamenting for his refined intelligence and its necessity to learn and experience this worldly life abundant in sensation, filled with the excitement of adventures to be had. He was a cunning player, unafraid of evil spirits that leached into his carnivalesque escapades of the obscure. He who was bewitched, who had bewitched me, I felt no grudges for as these curses of the world had fallen on us all this day. The souls of mankind have missed these truths, fond of their own folly, I would think love as harmless but we all know the opposite of this is truer. Although these mixing vapors of energy, whether infatuations or not, in the end rids us all of our own foolishness, in this realizations that snatches us all from our pedestals. But, for now, and who knows how many years from now, you will hear the echo's from this day of reckoning that has closed the closet door. So many joyful voices that simply plead to express their hearts in eager outstretched arms now must be quieted. Mine included as this puritanical empire shapes the paradigm of the manifestation of consciousness's quest.

Ironically, the rule maker of gentlemanly battle, Marquess of Queensberry Rules was the kindle for Oscar's demise. Interestingly enough, it makes sense that his son would be attracted to the likes of Oscar as he was just as arrogant, eccentric, and perhaps just as much intelligently imbalanced as his father. This dispute could have been quickly solved if Oscar's outrageousness could have comprehended that while his genius was embraced in his life style, the matter of law was not. The Marquess knew his demands were sugar for the fly, that a public battle would fall in his favor and destroy Wilde, with his son's connection with Wilde only a vague memory. It was too late when Oscar relented and dropped his case of slander, calling Oscar a sodomite, after all, he was so much more than that. I wonder why they call it a cross examination where only the strong can manage in its shadow. You must pledge on the holy book, all these things must have felt like being in the theater of the macabre, unwittingly the reality completely devastating. Yes, dear friends, the train has gone and you are foolishly not on it, now long and grey in the face, your playbills have all been removed.

I hear the nails pounding into the coffin of those whose crime was that they loved too much and could not help themselves from expressing it. You have us slither back into the shadows again, dear Oscar, these things we can't control, our art, passion, effeminacy or overt masculinity all targets for scrutiny. Justice Wills proclaims as the gavel crashes, through eons in a sentence of suffering that shakes the fibers of humanity unknowingly with great malice. "The jury has arrived at the correct verdict and he cannot persuade himself to entertain a shadow of doubt. It was a matter of decency and morality after all and no prejudice could horribly distort anything about the real charges of his distasteful crime against mankind. For under these circumstances only the severest sentence must take place in a law that was designed to protect the chastity of young Victorian women." He frankly told Oscar that people who do these things (love someone) must be dead to all sense of shame. Oscar's mighty pen is silenced at a time of irony, when corruption in the back rooms of English life flourished like the wind without a commentary. Justice Wills (another fitting name) felt the judgment inadequate for the crime but perhaps two years of hard labor would redefine dear Oscar's idea of whom he would love.

Morbidly, I had to be here to witness his soul's death, to grieve a childhood love affair, and to let go of the man I loved and admired. My wife and family, where my cleansed heart focused, needed me to be forthright in all my declarations here forth. With every death, we reflect on the best of times of those passed, who have loved us so much and took us on a special journey to our higher selves. Oscar did so much for my passion as he rinsed through my writing, I had learned that we were both predisposed to love men. I have always struggled against the inclinations of nature but Oscar was there to catch me. Like all boys who are smitten with the immense love for their mates I allowed myself through Oscars help to express my deepest desire to surrender my affections of love. Now it's the laughing eyes of my wife Florence that have enchanted me but is love limited in life to only one? My love is rich and wanting and growing wider every day. My associations are not restricted and these instincts are more than formable. We however are not waterproof, even though heterogeneous, the umbrella we must carry is our only shield against those watchful raindrops.

Grim were his infectious platitudes, or his innocently diseased heart that spread to all his victims including myself. It was a deranged partnership of musty secrets festered in souls like boll weevils eating the seeds from the inside out. What delirium does irrefutable madness come from? What lechery supersedes our responsible nature to guard and protect those that we love? When does the fear of becoming a monster subside with a comfortable skullduggery like a broken in pair of shoes that fit so earnestly? The price we pay for our deceit can be measured in lifetimes, broken hearts, and dreams in our illusions pretending we could never be monsters. One day we look into the mirror and see our reflection is absent and our hearts are cold as death itself. Yet we persist into what the French say, "L'heure la plus sombre de votre âme," (The Darkest hour of the soul) to seek out light to guide us towards our salvation. Oscar Wilde shall serve his time in solitude, angry at a world that seemingly has done him wrong. Yet those enchanted by his covetous act are branded souls, hell bent to perdition until their weariness dwindles into the obscure void where all monsters rest.

Out on the Town

Dare with me, care with me, stare with me into oblivion until someone becomes undone completely, discretely, so sweetly.

Marina was ready to take our love out into the world and we planned to go to a little club in West Hollywood, "The Bayou." First we went to Cleo's Restaurant on near Capitol Records for a perfectly romantic meal that was not our own making this time. Its

Mediterranean tapas style was made to order for our playful way of sharing food with each other. One of those nights that had Oscar excitement still lingering in the air around Hollywood and Vine. You could see it on our way to the club in West Hollywood driving past the Dolby Theater in Hollywood where they were still taking down the red carpet runway. When we arrived, we noticed it was boys' night out, even on a Monday, in West Hollywood. Broadway show tunes were being sung in the evening air, celebrating Les Miserables' win for Anne Hathaway. Everyone was abuzz from the show, talking about the Divas who sang, the dresses that winners or losers wore, and what faux pas brought down the house. This was the fun part of town, where everyone lets their pretentious ways down with lots of hugs and kisses to really party. West Hollywood, known as "WeHo" is primarily filled with same sex couples or those looking to make a special connection. Interestingly enough, WeHo culture isn't affected by the mores of puritanical expectations or the trifles of media. These were people sharing their essence unobstructed by false pretenses. They were there for only one reason and that was to let their hearts soar with love and fun. Soar they did, singing together, and doing contests to see who had the best voice; the winners receiving free drinks. While we so enjoyed this fun, we were looking for something a little bit darker. After all, the moon was full and in Leo, a time to show your flamboyant shades of midnight. We moved to another club where the music was loud with the DJ beats pumping up the night with excitement. The only filter is the one filtering the heart with openness and contact between flirting souls looking for love. Marina and I really didn't stand out here and were accepted amicably among the revelers. In fact, we were received as warmly as everyone who entered this site of pure fun. Rhythm was the catalyst, savage, malignant, and infectious, entrancing all participants to get out and boogie.

The DJ is whetting Marina's appetite, appraising the dance floor. She excitedly entwines our fingertips to entice me to escort her into the throb. Music in all its unspoiled meanings, speaks to her soul in infinite treacherous ways. Musical particles stir a chemical mist rousing tribal rituals and acts of ethos to our dark evening out. Her flirting, intrinsic movements beg my eyes to follow those deep inviting strides and hips. A temptress, a courtesan scarlet body pliable like smoke, floating on rhythmic vibrations, pulsating from heaven and radiating in the flesh of Earth. Her captivating persuasions coaxing me, dangerously, targeting my masculinity, consummately seducing me into ritualistic tribal initiation with my body and soul.

Without hesitation, her feminine wiles transmute her blissful cosmic sky dance to weaving illusions treacherous with loving enticements. Seductively, her expert alluring eyes make suggestive accusations, charming my engulfed flames to ignite in increasing degrees. Nothing escapes a dakini's metaphysical persuasions around testosterone-induced pandemonium. Marina's conjure has enticed the enchantments of all mystic divas in the room, drawing them to sway around her melting, sweating body. Life force is the hub of creation and we desperately hold onto its fringe that blows voraciously in this tempestuous musical wind. She finds herself falling into hands that propel her into my awaiting arms in a beehive. Honey is smothered all over her half naked body with infidelity written all over her revealing dress, high heels, and deep red lips.

Charlatans bewildered in unrepressed expressions of a kind of sexuality, genderless, erotic, and a seeping embezzlement of lust. Clothes whittle down to underwear and the prowess of sweat conveys our inner voice. It communicates beyond physical boundaries subtly singing underneath the breath in cosmic hymns and hums. More join our suicidal pursuits from subjugation to liberation cutting off the physical to whiff the fragrance of another plain of existence in movements. We have all transformed ourselves beyond most people's comfort zone, all willing to display our individual expressions of tenderness in collective pantomime set to music. Original sin lewd and daunting, proclaims in its self-discovery that awareness has consciousness of which we all sacrifice obliviously for clarity to shatter us. Clarity is cunningly maneuvering contrived concepts about identity through brick walls like phantoms to a destination of realizing our connections with each other. We are one tribe, one family tree hanging from the Tree of Life, like apples in the Garden of Eden. This brewing energy among souls acknowledging our aggregate collective selves is unified in Shiva's cosmic dance with Parvati. In high frequency, we sexually move hands and limbs around all our bodies synchronistically on the dance floor unabashed. Participants feel extraterrestrial inebriation lost in the DJ thumps and the thralls of divinity, lifting our spirits higher.

Collectively, our meditations invoke fundamental Love-Will-Wisdom spontaneously as our fertility goddess of enlightenment unfolds in the dark of night. After a sudden burst of light goes dim, everyone only recognizes themselves by an electrical imprint of their mystical communion. Our sacred Tantric cycle of yogi and yogini reaches out like branches of a tree stretching towards every consecrated yoni and lingam. Our collective innate sensitivities are spiritual implications of this shared moment beyond chthonic euthanasia where souls are set free of karma. This is our idealistic moment, risen from inside our cosmic cocoons, opened from the fibers of the Tetrahedral to spread our wings and fly. Lilith's forbidden fruit that has been concealed throughout these unfathomable eons are now visible for all to ingest through all the senses, congealed by a universe to participate, surrendering our sacraments shamelessly for one sweet moment to have fun together without feeling oppression.

While we are all in vogue, playfully in paradise, the music stops. Every one of us begins to realize what just happened and begins to laugh hysterically. In childlike abandon with mirthful joy replacing the futile madness of social distortions, our serene little moment of

279

collective engagement bows humbly. What may seem like taboo is as innocent as innocence can get to a mind that has not been tainted by the hype of media's attempt to put labels on identities. That media's only invocation is to have us believe we need to indulge in everything secretly and be coveted with money until death do you part. Our collective consciousness just wanted to smile and laugh until the next song came on and we could re-immerse our gallant seductive game of chance into the mirthful passion play of life.

Marina wasn't waiting around for the music again and mentioned she was going to the bathroom and winked at me flirtatiously. With her fingertips gliding down my hand I realized that there are many universal languages innately comprehended this evening. Unspoken words have themes that are as varied as the dim light that surrounds us, securing the mood of this anomalous adventure. I claim her hand before it leaves my skin, touching her palm tenderly, allowing her to lead me albeit the commotion we created. This was our simple stir among the brilliant teasing stars begging our hearts to yearn for more.

The next song began to thump the dance floor again and our tribe began to form another communion in deep trances like Whirling Dervishes. A dangerous anticipation followed us into a woman's bathroom stall where the intensity of bump and grind fuels our sexual escalations. Bass tones vibrated the cool tile walls as I push her back up against it to take a taste of her frenzied lips. Masculinity settles through my eyes as my hand finds the edges of her soaking wet dress slipping my hand in to move her G-string to one side. She pushes back, kissing me with carnal desire in a spontaneous combustion validating our connection in sincere aggressive touching, the comportments of royalty. Our Tantric connection of emotional intelligence and sexual communication sent out signals like a shock wave throughout the club. Her unrestricted glances of my virility radiates in her selfless visualization of me inside her fruitful womb. In unspoken verbal teases consummated in dialects only understood in carnal torments, we relish the heat of this cherished instant. I lift her up onto my tactile dark fantasies, pushing her back against the wall as she wraps her legs around my back. A conjugative metamorphosis explicitly overwhelms our adventurous pleasures staining time between these folds of secret fantasies exposed to only us.

A sheer ephemeral cellophane barrier separates a weaving heightening seduction of our colliding skins in serendipitous glides that make it disappear. She adds more ingredients, seducing my fascinations carnally, driving my alpha-male over the edge to animalistic levels and then slows down to a mindful stop. She wants to keep my body burning with only one myopic view burnt into my awareness where she is eventually a lusting prey. I resist, heightened in sexuality to penetrate harder, but she talks me down, assuring me this night is far from over. Rearranging ourselves from obvious intensity, she wipes off the dry spots on my shirt and grooms herself in the bathroom mirror. She cleans up her lipstick and tucks in my dress shirt, brushing back my hair and adjusting my tie. Even though we still have that look of fresh sex on our face she takes my arm to be escorted like a queen back to the festivities still in progress.

Rejoining the revelers, we are immediately hailed with applause from a bevy of spectators who are all expert seducers and speakers of physical, emotional, spiritual love. Their gratification comes from seeing love on our faces and feeling their personal connection to love's radiance. Incredible beauty shared in unearthly sirens from a DJ booth at the edge of sensual seraphic energy captured by tonight's splendor. We all share each other's love as it wavers in the air rolled out like a carpet for all our feet to feel. The Endless Knot, an ancient Buddhist symbol representing the interweaving of every sentient beings' path, where every tug makes for repercussions across the universe. We had shameless fun, with a group of shameless loving souls, whose prime directive is to make contact at all cost. But now it was time for us to go.

There is an art to seduction that unexpectedly carries us away in curvaceous lines, climactic peaks and valleys, vivid, succulent as oozing juices that are succumbed to by passion. Its nectar begs us to taste our fundamental urges unstoppable until all its flavors are inimically perceived. Reinvigorated innocence with a dash of naivety always has a logical conclusion that intuitively always ends with taking your partner home for further exploration. Saying farewell to our new friends with a few teasing flirtatious kisses and loving hugs cherished in goodnights to this adoring crowd of beautiful people.

In our silent pleasures, there are no masters or slaves, no dominance or submissive, not even a naughty child disobeying their parent. There's no role-playing, drama or needed spankings from Daddy. Our mutual concern was the precious time we're given to spend with each other. Swapping orgasms had never been a priority of our intimacy. All these reactions from our bodies merely the results of a timeless kiss we all recall when tasted from a higher source. A sacred language through a sacred kiss, served in crimson red on a plate of unexplainable consciousness. Inside each of our blood memories these human bonds ring true, reverberating back to heaven's firmament. Constantly resurrected in the cycle of birth and death, these collected glimpses of consciousness remind us that there is nothing more important than the love we receive and give.

When you drink it all in, in a pure kiss, it tastes like a long sweet drink of salvation, with a shot of familiarity awakened by consciousness to recognize existence everlasting. Compassion unfurls metaphorically, moving through the motions that have been uttered through lips in memoriam for love's sake. Consciousness is roused, willful, remarkable, emerging from the shadows in acquisition of ancient memories bilaterally connected by our human embrace. We are the overlapping phenomena, spontaneously aligning our spiritual molecules of omnipresence in quantum order. That's when illusive existence attempts to find balance expressed in a binary universe

SOULKISS: TANTRIC TALES OF MAHAMUDRA

where silent pleasures can experience equality in our magnetic attractions. Love will finally find its own equilibrium, to the point that it is hard to discern any separateness in polarity between collective consciousness and self.

The minds skeptical fluctuations percolate rumors and disbelief that gnaws on consciousness's likelihood, confusing it with identity. Our contrived demons and underworlds echo from a well of lost souls, aberrations to logic that just cannot be comprehended in reality. Their murmurs ricochet off foundations, principles, and opinions that are just as unfounded as the notion of existence. Ah, the folly of the source of sensory perception, what is realized and what is real, objective, or objected. These meditators acknowledge that clearly we are deceived, always in the lurch of misguided certainty of what a waking experience even is. Where have we conjured all this iconic imaginary from, composed from, or believed in? How do we make these conclusions at all in this geometric arithmetic of deciding even the meaning of two plus two? What clarity makes truth out of our identity that is always in flux and where is the omnipotent God? Underneath our primal mud, it's impossible to keep habitual opinions and assumptions from surfacing, but is everything we murmur imprinting on our helpless friend named Consciousness? These evil false perceptions are the deceiving demons that nip at Awareness's heels to decide, decide, decide about reality. It's in our mediation where the groundwork for allowing consciousness to subsist at all is contemplated and realized. Those who understand its order, have any kind of clear view that stills the mind first, eventually will begin to sense the shadow surfaces of consciousness.

I ponder on my philosophical metaphysics prejudicially, wrestle with my Aristotelian thoughts that weigh out my perception's view. I realize that I am seduced more by pure dark voids than any labyrinth of mind. Unorthodox opinions may only be coaxed from an intimacy of inception and we empirically get closer to it every day. Universal possibilities, dreams, and proclamations of identity are still as vaporous as the smoke and mirrors Illusionists create with astounding tricks. A cerebral gathering of purges and reformation in infinite array of a purpose to be decided prejudicially by someone called us. Skeptically we doubt, debate, discuss, and transpire to what is probable and may never entirely be ruled out as understanding, ultimately these processes are fleeting. Random reasoning attempts to empirically predict our ability to perceive, when there is no real framework for any claim to consciousness other than it somehow must exist.

The nature of the human mind is resolved to continue its search for certainty, discarding any slightest doubt that rises for its truth quest. It has immovable points that, once figured out, stays fixed despite any reprisals of truth whether shakable or not. What is concealed or congealed, consoled to the mirror of self whether it has essence at all, is determined by a priority list that can't even be obtained by consciousness. Our insidious duality's cognizant argument is that it has special knowledge and answers to all questions for no apparent reason. It's as if we have tasted the halo of consciousness unwittingly and resolved that these attributes must be ours to begin with. Cogito ergo sum. "I think therefore I am." The prestidigitation of this argument that rightfully deserves the most skepticism has become the hypnotic argument of western versus eastern philosophies. "I think therefore I know nothing," is a clearer answer to this conundrum. Syllogistically, we are dissuaded earnestly, wanting to believe that we are something as if nothingness has no substance. Exist, exist, exist, we want to shout it out! I am reason, I can reason, I know reason, walking as a ghost the day we are born with no epistemological legs to stand on. We are the sum of nothing and what is plausible metaphysically can only be seen in the Shaman's vaporous holograms stirred in cosmic primordial soup.

A fine dust shimmers the dawn, the dusk in a constant parade of settling those holographic particles on this planet. In a chaotic wave of ballyhoo, there's tossed up soot from a clamoring population attempting to fulfill their missions of survival day-by-day, year-by-year, century-by-century. A continual contamination we barely notice, meekly cohabiting with a mindless agenda moving in a sea of deadly molecular pollenated broken emotions. These minute particles barely notice going in and out of all sentient life's lungs, trees, plants, and surfaces in contortions. Revealed to us twice a day to those that notice just how infested we are with particles we have created from desires to make money to sustain the illusions of life's goals. Our intentional fallacy like the three monkeys, see no, hear no, and say no evil, yet these fallacies are just the tip of the iceberg of our ambiguous baggage in this contemporary paradigm we insist on. We have developed an entire language dedicated to questionable acts of throwaway words some call oxymoronic and I call toxic. Imagination is a second-class citizen's foolish dream lost in the hope that merit has value and love is the only commodity worth trading. Those that wear the most expensive suits make the rules for all the jeans and tee shirt-wearers in this pretending world of ambiguity and animosity. I dream about the waxed wings of Icarus who dared the sun with ambition, unafraid of the deep blue sea to learn just a bit more to expand his perspective of life.

I'm grateful for effortlessness that has congealed figments of my imagination into a plausible reality. My higher self has made a campaign out of this for years, making treatises with that clever mind that analyze every sliver of common sense. Eventually we reached an agreement, that there was no explaining unexplainable consciousness but to just be thankful it exists. That we would accept its presence in our awareness and embrace its playfulness to constantly delve in its wanting discoveries. No more apprehension about disunity, multiplicity and its competitiveness to decide what is important. We are spiritual beings having a human experience through the aid of consciousness; just hold onto that.

All subliminal meditators eventually reach equivalence in their constant struggle to identify who or what drives our spiritual body's earthly vehicle in this extraterrestrial experience. Delve ruthlessly if you like, but remember what is distinct and clear in your resolve and a careful scrutiny to the importance of this perception. Could consciousness's mission be more than why is there love and what is it for? This is what confirms both our nature that existence is truly ravished not by intelligence alone but the idea that love could be at its solvent core. These are my reflections, my glimmers, pondering my liberation with Marina, but I get philosophical when I get tired.

While Marina and I are certainly intoxicated on the love we feel for each other, I am still capable to drive us back to paradise. She licks my ear, strapping herself into the car and concludes that she wants me inside her again. It's her moaning mantra, caressing its message with each pass of her hot whispers and roving fingers. These acts imply more than a doubtful outside world could ever conceptualize, that consciousness was apt to stretch out within our experience. Our collective visual sensations objectify this apparent intuitive picture where theories of the mind fade away and are replaced by celestial instincts. Divine aberrations drink like ambrosia in our chattel goblets, clinking in the dark, imbibing profound transmissions through a lineage of primordial Vajra lightening. Our synthesis is the contrast that shatters our souls' confinement, expansion without the emotional properties that bind us to time. We are both no strangers to sacrifice, courageousness, or sympathies for raucous assaults on each other's components of consciousness. She is my temptress, my declarations of sentiments of a very restless visceral love that she incites me with every fiber of her being.

She has not stopped stroking the genie's lamp until we've made it back to our lair where she already has me out of my pants licking her lips, inhaling deep. She smiles as I park the car gripping my treasure, toying with my fiery desire to take her in the car before we even get a chance to return to our original sins. Marina tells me, "You're gorgeous!" stroking my chest in front of our new home under the streetlights. She wants to see me desire her as she removes her tenderness from her plunging V-neck dress. She bids me, "I want your desperation, let your desire possess me and haunt my lechery." She knows my capable hands will entice her mischievously surrendering body in our first very playful night out. I move my hand to cup them and looking for her to dip her nipples in my mouth, teasing me incessantly, she begins to giggle. She reaches around me and begins to lower the seat back with both her naked breast covering my face, I begin to laugh covered with her fleshy sculpted appendages. She gets up so I can breathe normally and covers my mouth whispering, "Be quiet or we'll wake the neighbors." My sudden impulse to move her G-string makes her focus solely on me. Her lubrication becomes sticky to my touch as she moves on top of me in the front seat of my car. Completely engorging my member she breathes a breath of satisfaction. She is so stimulated and enthralled she bears down on me like a sex fiend pumping herself in and out erupting, liberating her creamy emulsions.

I see tears in her eyes before she collapses on my exposed chest that she tore the buttons off just before she became overwhelmed. I get my pants up and position her to open the door and lift her limp body up into my arms and carefully close the car door. Carrying her up the stairs, I open the door with one hand, as she holds on tight to our welcoming glistening abode lit by Los Angeles's city lights. I lay her inert body down on crisp clean sheets but like a baby attempting to fight off sleep she attempts to talk. I run a bath for her and then come back to help remove what clothes she has on. She shimmers in the dark, still moist from the evenings sweat. The bath water already smells of lilac oils. I only needed to light a few candles to add to the calm to the end of another night together. I lay her exhausted body gently into its warm abyss to her cooing ah's as every fiber of her begins to let go.

The brevity of this human experience is filled with the powerful and powerless, both are able to do good or be disingenuous. Personal power, however, streams like a river in our veins ultimately expressed in a conglomeration of sexual powers and higher powers of equal strength. Our compunction pricks at consciousness until our gyroscopes find their alignments to a previously unimagined power in our appetite for an experience of supreme love. This has always been a place the eccentric could never buy, although their attempts have been impressive. The Oligarchy have lost their balance, their spin of cherished self, delusions no longer distinguish reality they merely commit to the reality they chose. Collectively we turn the tide but like drowning victims, the powerful hysterically, furiously look to grab onto something to pull down with them to the bitter end. Nature is soaring in this new spring of our lives even with a small sociopathic group that harbor a vile hatred that is now collapsing under the weight of their own rhetoric. The next play for nature's antagonist is sure to describe themselves as dominated victims of social idioms, secret codes, and unseen demons that taint their underlying golden glimmers with opaque varnish. Of course the irony is that we all have access to the autonomous temple of spiritual knowledge and are all a part of the secret chain that connects us all. No matter where their personal wealth may lie, power is restored to those in their practice of this supreme ritual of contact. To recognize our vehicle is a receptacle of divine revelation, a sacred Trinitarian linked with universe consciousness is a grand first step. Human kind must reevaluate where the splinters of tradition strayed and what the common pitfalls we share are in our self-discovery.

Marina, still exhausted, whispers in a trance these thoughts to me in the stillness of broaching morning. "My love, our ideas of sublime beauty are essentially our essence and balance beam in between our epic existence. Our life is extreme and thoughts can be detached from outcomes but let them all go for unconditional love to fill their place. Our language comes from our hearts so let their sacred presence grow naturally. Those extreme conditions are no deterrent when we coexist in harmony. Come; manifest amazing things with me from the center of our accomplishments now that we have invested our souls so completely. This fundamental choice comes from our collective fundamental voice of equanimity vibrating with life in profound happiness. My energetic aura of pure radiation dwells in an inexhaustible source opened by your love so completely we can't forsake it. We have arrived at this crossroad where our narrative can take on another shape that either looks like us being together or us being apart. Right now, today, we have a limitless capacity resting in our field of all possibilities with infinity looking over our shoulders. We have experienced a bliss that has bathed us both in an incredible light more than a soul's greatest desire could wish for. How shall we transcend my love with this passion that has more than inspired us, has enlightened us in so many inconceivable ways?"

I was completely taken with each word that dripped off Marina's dear lips as she rested in the steaming bath. I tended gently to her limbs, washing her body with a soft loofah to release any bits of stress she may be unconsciously holding on to. These deep questions she bids have always gnawed away at my romantic bidirectional afflictions. I always wanted to believe that a real romantic bond was possible but my experience told me that it's difficult to be reciprocated. Our love is much more than a novel sexual experience; we have been reclaimed in unrestricted spiritually. Our connecting emotional bonds are filled with compassion that feels as though it reaches back to the beginning of time. We shared all love's essential ingredients, sublimating sexual desire with subliminal interwoven fibers tying our psyche into one consciousness. Tonight we learned that our sexual freedom is far from stereotypical of feminine and masculine attractiveness. There are far more comprehensive pieces fitting together in a romantic and spiritual attraction sense. She is my perfect romantic interest, sexual partner, and my spiritual guru for traversing time/space. Our sex drives outweigh social pressures, or influences of disapproval, or judging from the outside world in our unique love. Enlightened as we both are, it took working through so much trepidation and risk for our fragile humanness to accept that truth had finally come for us.

Empathy, the crux in Marina's testimony, offered in her sacraments of sacred epiphanies. These natural rituals between female and male have given us more than mere erotic pleasures in our expanding horizons. This has been a communion of ultimate creativity, of a spiritual lusting, of intuitions radiating from original divine creation. Our mystic lust has enabled us to fully experience strength's substance resonating from the seat of unknowable will. After a lifetime independently searching for communion with love's inspirational ways, we have discovered Tantra's captivating muses in each other. Without warning we received the full expression of the sacrament of union from the boundless and measureless cosmic sea where we impossibly found each other. We'd watched ourselves become archetypes of timeless ecstasy, become the aroma of the monastic spikenard oils that ignite heavenly bliss. Our burgeoning realizations balanced our heart charka by reexamining our goals, motives that have solidified our relationship that has walked us through eons. There is no confusion, needing to be right, conflict or defense in our constant state of calm, spiritual centered peace. We are ready now as we have always been ready. It's a responsible pair bonding of mythic ancient tribal prophecy that we must surrender at last.

I have to tell her, "My love, our sacred weaving comes from cocoons spun from the purest thread of love, will, and wisdom. We are harmoniously joined with the skillful means that act like a fruitful womb manifested in our vital sea of life's blood that course through our veins. We are the homeostasis of our metamorphosis, a conjugated epiphany from our individual essence of life force in union. This non-duality rests with us multidimensionally, infinitely in our time-space relationship. We can measure it with the absence of perceptual differences in a sum that has become whole. We are the culmination of positive-negative aspects that have somehow become zero. Our humming emancipation of non-polarity is our systemic natural state where the observer and the observed dissolve. We both have been weary in our tireless pursuit of discovering true love; we have always secretly believed in our unprecedented ways. There was never a doubt that this love was possible, there was only uncertainty if it was possible in this lifetime. We have become the harbor of consciousness once again. Awareness clearly reminds us that our view of each other is divinity. Our transcendence is only possible with our undying devotion from this moment and forever to each other's pure love as its source has offered itself to our consciousness."

Our altruistic intentions of liberating all sentient beings was as natural as visualizing ourselves in an enlightened state. She was my guru, my teacher of wisdom, in an actual engagement of Mahamudra, and finally, a perfect dedication to human virtue. We have rediscovered our good fortune of obtaining this precious human life in this universe of impermanence. The infallible workings of cause and effect, the nature of illusion, and the plight of accepting those illusions as fact behind the eyes of sentinels. We've become our own refuge, the triple jewel of our inner trident where the teachings are awakened in our sacred place of attainment.

Now it is about the practice of purification and the eradication of negative imprints that are notorious for eroding love. We have accumulated a type of merit, of inspired blessings that have taken many lifetimes to achieve. Now we ride on a steed of love and compassion, whose rewards are as boundless as the stars in a desert sky. Culminating from generations, the completion of practices from the highest yogic Tantra, our cycle is now complete. Marina and I have had extraordinary experiences in true states of phenomena, unceasingly fulfilled in the profound quickening of pure nothingness. We are now each other's Vajra teachers, with Tantric empowerments ingrained throughout our true nature of mind and spirit. Devotion is present in our conversations with each other, without delusions or attachment, spontaneously profound and full with acceptance.

I lift Marina out of the tub and lay her on the bed where I have already laid out our big fluffy white towels. She has her arms around my neck again and is smiling wide, with her tired eyes peering into my soul serenely. I wrap her in the towels, dry her body, and start to dry her hair with a blow dryer. Her eyes drift off and then back again, each time reassuringly stroking my frame ever so softly with the little bit of energy she still has. I hum around the frequency of the dryer, some distant melody I discovered spontaneously, caressing her hair until it is completely dry. Her body is also dry and I put on some lilac oil to feed her beautiful skin. Then I remove the towels to tuck her in bed. My temptress of the new world we have created is no stranger to sacrifice; she's courageous and sympathetic to all those in need of her mothering love. Our cause and momentum grew to theocratic proportions, eloquently showing us the way to our hearts desire, as scary as that can be. Gradually, our speculative fears are shattered one by one by our tact, inciting genuine warmth and loving affinities. Our commitment has been waiting for this moment, where the decisions of suburbia and social calendars won't shape our aesthetic to be unspoiled in this moment of our endless love.

Marina, almost asleep, begins to utter these loving thoughts to me, "I see the constellations reflected in your ebony pools when I open my eyes. It's as if we soar across oceans of perpetual gratitude. Your inexhaustible source of all true art is the mysterious power of majestic creation, my privilege to witness throughout the eons of existence. Our human boundaries transcend in our marvelous restructured reality wrapped in a divine likeness of you. I am so grateful for the risk you took to recognize my silhouette in the eternal darkness of an endless void. Teach me more of this love that's evolving in unbound consciousness, where identity disappears in eternal essence." With that she sleeps and I hover over her preciousness, watching as a guardian, until I too spill into her realm, where she awaits my contact.

"It is a singularity," rustles in the wind of my dream state, "primeval antimatter and matter discover their positive negative charges in an instant gathered without time." I see Marina coming into focus at the edge of a pond playing the veena with two of her arms. In her other two arms, there is a book that she is reading out loud and a Hindu mala, counting down Mantras as she reads. She looks away and tells me, "Could you imagine everything squeezed into a single point?" Another deity that looks like me, Brahma, who is resting on a giant lotus petal coming up from the fluttering ebony pond also says, "In an instance." Oddly, as simple as this ancient story is told, even though Brahma was self-contained before the existence of time, he longed for company. Brahma decided to split in two creating a feminine counterpart. When he viewed his mirror image in feminine form love overtook him. He could not stop gazing at her, deeply smitten, in something he couldn't understand. Brahma wanted a place to dwell to understand what this experience might be. He asked his endearment Saraswati if she would help him create the material universe where they may explore his conundrum. She hovered closer to him, as if in procession, moving in increments until her lips met his and at that moment, life was born.

"Insatiable lust is written in your mechanism of curving movements, smiles enchanting my lips closer to yours," Brahma thought.

"This is our vehicle, our symbiosis at the point of zero, where the one electron makes impact with an infinitely dense point of complete devotion," Saraswati professed.

These words cannot be divorced from their meaning when two unknowns become known to each other. Their collision coalesced matter to form the finite. Quantum means a discrete quantity of energy proportional in magnitude to the frequency of the radiation it represents. Sub atomic particles, protons, neutrons ionized in the cauldron of fire from a singularity in the frequency of a radiating kiss. What dire gravity was born in one more particle of matter tilting the balancing scales of antimatter overwhelmed by love? This was the quantum flux, the beginning of the overall theme and scheme of our universe, home of consciousness. I hear the whisper again, "There was a singularity made dense until gravity completely imploded on the curve of zero." I wondered: did consciousness pass through the eye of the needle as an electron animating all matter? The entire observable universe would not be available to any sentient being without consciousness witnessing itself. All these truths become self-evident as the illusion of separateness, in the infinite soup of stellar epochs, clearing away the timeless solar dust to see its own reflection.

Marina's and my spontaneous telepathic induced deliberations beckon our lucid dreams to summon us together in our sleeping realm. If we are all born from a universe that inscribes us all with its code of essence, eventually all the answers will be revealed. Whether or not we misconstrue or miscommunicate these messages determines if we follow down a senseless path of illusion or return home. Grasping the impermanence of our ultimate existences is the only reasonable conclusion of any revealed truth. Funny, once you realize this jeweled gift of fleeting observable life is so temporary, only merit makes sharing time so valuable. Marina and I have this merit and apparently also in our dream state further unfurling our syncretic amalgamation over every spiritual discipline. Evanescence is inevitable. For now, though, we are immersed in our story of conductivity even through the ethers of consciousness itself.

Don't we all want to cry for our salvation, let tears flow from the wellsprings of our immortal souls? Is happiness the illusion of the material universe? That this true love is impossible in our pathetic little lifetimes? I have heard too many gut wrenching cries reverberating through the eons of time, aching to be recognized in existence. I am shattered by love, its quest, its longing, and its desperation to be self-acknowledged and returned to its rightful home. Surrendered and lifeless, everything ends up in annihilation, the perilous outcomes of consciousness, as it deconstructs. Will contact be a disastrous success or an absolute validity of psychic and mystical experience teaching us about our own sabotage of ideology? Can humanity rise above our cybernetics through a proper enunciation of shamanic invocations and ultimately be reborn in promised purelands? Feebly, I challenge known laws of time and space to broach a viscerally innate sensation of familiarity and otherworldliness. I would eviscerate myself to bleed to near death, for a moment of true memory like this. I would immolate my reincarnated lineage to pass along one letter of sacred texts to carry from one life to the next for my contemplative initiate to comprehend. Marina and I are somehow remembering these embodied deciphered codes shamanically understood each little grasp at a time. We are a vivid kaleidoscopic vision transmitting esoterica for all those seeking transcendence inter-dimensionally and four dimensionally. Marina and I now perceive each other's souls in all awakened realms. It becomes more apparent with each second that passes in our new timeline and heroic nature.

Our new life has just begun and even when we are awake in this world of CNN, governmental discourse, or special corporate interest groups, this awakened state will flourish. Before we move from the sleep realm to this timeline, our lives have already changed in our commitment to never leave each other no matter what. We've been shown the pathway to the universe and have a step-by-step plan in how our inner world becomes our outer world. This is what has been revealed inside of us and we've been waiting for so long. It's more than a leap of faith because faith would have you believe in something you've had no experience with. We've had an adept experience unraveling the fibers of the very navel of creation's vortex. The reason for existence has inundated our souls beyond any likeness of our former lives. That unknown hidden hand has rubbed off the soot to reveal the words that have always been written. After all, what can really happen to us all other than sickness, suffering, and dying before our mission has been made complete? Whatever that means in this fuzzy schematic imprint we are lead to believe and what is actually provided for us, we will discover together. I have no laments to utter as all my laments have been surrendered and no more sadness can occupy my heart. This long night of fun and adventure has brought us to a unique crossroads in our narrative that no one but ourselves can deny as foolish as that could ever be. There is nothing in the so-called rational world that can dismiss the aura Marina and I have now acquired in our vigil to discover love. Certainly our Prince/Princess has to come to the rescue, from the lingering suffering, of this unsettled excuse, for living in day-to-day uncertain existence. We are alive in our dreams, in this world and all worlds we have yet to conquer with awareness, as our love is the love we all seek. Somehow, roving around my heart, the heart of a child waiting for Christmas morning, I anticipate the arrival of dawn and my reinvigorated heart to shine once again. For now, I see Marina in my dream as the Tibetan goddess Yeshe Tsogyal smiling and looking deep inside my eyes.

Padmasmbhava and Yeshe Tsogyal

Meant to be lost in nothingness two unwound in magnificent bliss hope dissolves when time is resolved and two magnetically charged can no longer resist.

The lotus born guru and well know Vajrayana Buddhist Padmasambhava had ventured off into the mountains of what is now called Afghanistan. Afghanistan is riddled with caves and a perfect place for deep meditation practice to master the body, mind, and soul. There he reached the Vidyadhara level, or Tantric Magical

297

Empowerment, of Mahamudra by means of Vishuddha, the Fifth Charka Throat meaning sound, and the sharpened blade of the Kilaya. Essentially meaning, becoming a master of the ability to utter sounds whose frequencies could effectively cut through illusion of one's life forever. He knew that this was a practice that would be important for him to have completed in his quest for spreading compassion.

Padmasambhava, also known as Guru Rinpoche or Great Teacher, was born fully enlightened, yet he sought out different practices and accomplished many different spiritual disciplines. He was ordained by another of the eight masters, Prabhahasti, in the ancient kingdom of Zahor where he received the teaching on Yoga Tantra and Vajrakila, the Destroyer of Compassions Obstacles. There are many Vidyadhara levels and Guru Rinpoche had spent many hours in caves attaining them to become a protector of the Dharma. His time at his beloved city of Oddiyana though, was about to come to an end, as he was being called to the Himalayas to the high mountain city of Samyé.

The King of Tibet, Trisong Detsen, was having difficulties building the Samyé monastery. Many types of energies, both man-made and other worldly, kept tearing it down. Erecting Vajrayana Buddhism in Tibet was not an easy task as there were so many other Buddhist forms and disciplines in the splintered towns and villages of this realm. With all of these forms vying for supremacy as the best Buddhism, one could only achieve enlightenment through their practice and lineage alone. The King knew it would take a great teacher to unify his country under one banner of Buddhism for the good of all sentient beings. When Guru Rinpoche arrived he immediately began to create a core group of disciples. Through his teaching, these could be strong enough through sutras, Tantras, and treaties to protect the Dharma. One of these students was Yeshe Tsogyal, Princess of Karchen, who became adept at removing obstacles that were hostile to compassion even in her youth. Because of her fame at this, even at her tender years of twelve, her spiritual practices brought her to the attentions of the King of Tibet, who forced her to be one of his queens. After Guru Rinpoche instructed the King in the Tantric practices, his life was totally changed forever from his enlightenment and he offered anything from his kingdom to the great teacher. Guru Rinpoche asked for Yeshe Tsogyal and the King Trisong Detsen granted her as his consort. Guru Rinpoche began the process of teaching her everything he knew about Vajrayana Buddhism as they began their spiritual sojourn in this lifetime.

From the beginning of Yeshe's life, she was enlightened: aware of the travesty of human suffering and full of compassion. Because of her beauty and intelligence she was fought over by suitors and even abducted and raped by one in order to make her his wife. However, she was not a typical woman by the standards of those times. Or of any times. This was very difficult on her family, whose integrity was always being challenged by her willfulness. She had insights into the Dharma that were transcendental and she had already dedicated her life or death to protecting its cause. Rumors about her austerities and devotion to Buddhism attracted the King of Tibet, Trisong Detsen, to have her brought to him. He was so taken by her that she was placed in his harem, waiting to become another of his queens. She recalled that when the king first summoned her she ran away, destroying anything that would identify who she was and what path she had taken. A young boy carrying a mala, or mediation rosary, came out of nowhere to talk with her about the path she had now chosen and how it would not aid in her destiny. She realized that the boy in the forest on that day was the great Guru Rinpoche as an apparition. There he gave her a special Mantrayana and she sat to meditate with it in this very remote place. He also assured her that this is what she must do and that she would be discovered and eventually have to go into the King's harem, where she would be one of his queens.

Only nine students were chosen and the king, because of her merit, included Yeshe among those original monks eager to learn Vajrayana. She was the first woman student of Guru Padmasambhava and was allowed to participate in his divination process that had been strictly designated for men before. Each student tosses a flower onto a mandala and wherever that flower falls the student gets that specific teaching. Yeshe got the divination for the teaching of Vajrakilaya, which proved that she was indeed already adept at removing anything hostile to compassion.

One of these stories was when the Guru needed her to go to a village in Nepal to free an Acharya, or spiritual guide. Seven road robbers came to steal everything she had brought with her, but she visualized them as deities and gave them all her belonging as a gift. Then they planned to rape her, but out of compassion she had sex with them all, and as a result they were freed from obscurations and negativities. Realizing her compassion, they felt remorse. They apologized for their actions and swore to follow the path of virtue and liberation. Padmasambhava was very happy on her return; her next scared empowerments would be at the cave of Paro Tagtsang in Bhutan, The Tiger's Nest, from Lhasa.

They set out from Thimphu and gradually made their way on foot throughout the whole of Tibet, filling it with blessings. This journey was very perilous across the spines of the Himalayas. Reaching the mouth of the cave was also very precarious for a woman, let alone Guru Rinpoche, as it rested precariously on a cliff on the western side of the mountain. Yeshe had made many journeys in the name of the Dharma for her dear Guru; this was merely another obstacle to be conquered as they ascended. Inside the cave, their mediation room was like a womb. It was body temperature and full of ferns and moss, with water running through grooves cut through the rocks by its stream. It seemed water was cutting through many rocks along the sheer cliffs and spectacular waterfalls came spurting from the sides of these surrounding mountains. They had but a few comforts, a pot to make tea, ritual tools for the initiation process, and paper and ink. They both knew why they were there and would be there for several months, as a great task needed to be completed. Yeshe was to receive all treasured teachings, explaining many concealed doctrines of the Mahamudra and all the Tantras. She was humbled by this journey and reverent toward this great teacher that he would entrust her with such great knowledge.

Yeshe, confronted in this moment with the object of her devotion, spoke, "I, the woman Yeshe Tsogyal, offer you my inner and outer host on this rippling timeless ocean consciousness prevails on. Great teacher, you have been very kind to the many people resting on the Lion of Tibet and also to my humbled soul. I have never experienced anything like this before, nor will I ever experience anything like this in the future. So now, even though my humble graces reside with you and I will no doubt attain enlightenment, I recognize this precious jewel. I know if skillful means and practice vary even slightly, the inclination of attentions will split and many obstacles will cause great disharmony without proper instruction. What is pure in every heart cannot be forsaken because doctrine will not be salvaged by those seeking to destroy the Dharma. From my deepest compassion Vajra Guru, how do we preserve the sacred Dharma?"

Padmasambhava replied, "My loving consort, faithful and full of compassion, it is true, future sentient beings will have many distraction. Yet the spiritual instruction and methods I have offered are immeasurable." He starts sitting in the Vajra position and continues talking to Yeshe, "Heart sphere teachings, Kriya and Mantrayana practices have prepared you for the supreme attainment of Mahamudra. You are skilled in the compassionate means and have unlocked as many Sugatas, or immaculate and indestructible blisses, as there are stars in the sky. You have been my attendant through many lifetimes and in many caves throughout this lifetime."

Yeshe brought him water from her hands to his parched lips and he gently grasped her hands and drank from them saying, "All Tantras are explained when you have obtained the fortune of a human body without straying innumerable eons. You will be freed in the great liberation of enlightenment when you can surrender your form in divine devotion."

Yeshe was dressed in Tantric ornaments but otherwise was entirely naked to symbolically express the beauty and simplicity of emptiness. They were sitting in complete darkness in the cave while Guru Rinpoche was talking with her. She heard her inner self suggesting that only one small candle be lit to signify the luminous nectar of enlightened awareness. Visualizing one as a Buddha is one of the most important practices of Buddhist Tantra and physical aids are helpful to this cause. In Vajrayana, we are all in a beginningless enlightened state, residing in Chenrezig, in complete nothingness. This was a moment of shamanic Tantric transmission between guru and disciple where the practitioner of Higher Tantras partook in the esoteric journey into nothingness. They now sat in front of each other and began reciting mantras while doing visualization practices. It was the channeling of energy in order to realize certain effects through theory and ceremonial magic that awoke their respective sleeping Kundalini. Tantra is the sublime and profound form of spirituality's intrinsic nature and the ultimate mode of existence and phenomenon. It is an intuitive experience where essence and existence become identical. Its esotericism is only caused by lack of proper initiation because Tantra organically runs through the veins of all living creatures.

Sexuality is inherent in the human experience, but the recognition of consciousness and the transformational epiphany of its essence, sublime. Tantra takes cognizance of our crude aspect of

302

human nature and introduces it to our spiritual and truly recherché connections in divine form. The vehicle of union is our Gnostic theocracy that guides us through illusions into the bosom of quasicrystal forbidden light. This fleeting experience is our most intimate contact with Mahamudra, inseparable connected by heart in a meditative state preserved by your higher insight. Diligently, we cultivate this union of bliss and emptiness, detached from desire in our pursuit of great perfection. The sacred weaving of the awakened divine light, the manifestation, the metamorphosis an expression of life force seeking perfect union. When we abandon our philosophies and allow the homeostasis of our non-duality to transcend yin and yang, we find the melding of spiritual hearts naturally. This is the simplicity of Tantra, beyond the metaphors where Padmasambhava and Yeshe Tsogyal dwell eternally in sublime congress at the Tiger's Nest.

Our tests are to feel but not to crave, to experience yet not hanker for more, if anything a sign that spiritually stature has arrived. Being unattached to physical climax is something foreign to the ears of social idioms of today's concepts of sexuality. The rise of attachment can be very subtle and leach into the most advanced and sincere practitioner. Yet when attained, the rewards outweigh the difficult practice. Breath is also a trained empowerment that requires skillful means to attain and purify our inner and outer minds. Ordinary desire for pleasure will not take you to the higher realms where sexual energy cleanses the impurities of common passion and lust. Tantra is not sex in the ordinary sense of the word; it's a form of union whose measurement is discovered by one's commitment to the Dharma. This sorcery is congealed within the nondescript spaces between the Tetrahedral and oblivion where cohesive energy dwells. It's the awakened heart-mind or Bodhichitta; The Practice of Mahamudra that guides us through the flames of sexual identity, surrender, and empowerment. Dualism and sexual distinction fall by the way side in Tantric divination when we coalesced in wisdom and compassion.

Guru Rinpoche knows it's time for Saraswati to reappear, joining Vajra and lotus in countless manifestations. All forms of Vajra enter the guru's hands and all deities who protect and honor the Dharma became every molecule of his being. Embroidered into every fiber of his being, all moving in unison to the will of Brahma, the creator of the material universe. All forms of dakini came in union with his lingam along with all female deities seeking liberation in all aspects of Yeshe Tsogyal's secret and natural form. Every ignited Dorje sends out rays into the nine-fold rainbow path, sparking every sentient being in all realms. Yeshe is transformed into the Tigress, bound to their communion and to all the Guru's bestowing empowerments. There, every detailed prediction, scroll, and oral transmission is recorded into the fabric of the universe.

The steadfast scribing of Yeshe's magic brush continued, stroking the translations onto the papers of Terma's in this extremely powerful Sadhana of the twenty Kilas. Again, the words come off the lips of Yeshe, "I, the woman Tsogyal, performed the practice of Vajrakilaya and have seen the deities of the mandala come to life through the eyes of my guru. I have, by skillful means, acquired the empowerment and Sadhana as described in the Vahrakumara and have become the vision of the mandala of liberation."

Guru Rinpoche replies, "I, Padmasambhava have no teachings more profound than Vajrakila, these attainments must be transmitted, some orally, others concealed as treasure for future generations. It is up to you dear Yeshe to take all these treasures memorialize them on the pages of time and place them carefully for future generations." Suddenly Yeshe looks deeply into Padmasambhava's eyes and asks in the ancient language of Sanskrit, "tvaM kutra asi mAmaka rati" ("Where are you my love?")
She tells him, "I am right here, always in the folds of timelessness awaiting your embrace." Enraptured, their lips locked, their eyes rolled to the back of their heads, as they embraced the

form of Mahamudra. Physically their bodies changed shape into the many god/goddess forms of Shiva/Parvati, Brahma/Saraswati, Vishnu/Lakshmi, Rama/Sita. They transformed into every pantheon in human history until they transformed into each other again still in the great position. Their union had always been transcendental and their chakra petals and channels always branched out intertwining through eons of their divine passion. The little candle goes out but another type of illumination ignites the room. Transforming into holographic rainbow bodies, our purelands existence plunging them deep into the oceans of space-less void in union. All the Tantras inhabit this space of absolute purity, assimilating them into the manna of supreme bliss.

Their eyes roll back in unison and she tells him telepathically, "Great master I have recognized the natural state of awareness of the prana-mind. I've attained all the virtues of clarity of extracting essences and abandon all attachments to be in this timeless moment."

Padmasambhava in all his compassion tell her in his radiance, "You are happy as you have realized your mind, you're happy in our still silence in the union of solitude. Your emotions do not disturb you, as there is no need for longing, yearning or desire. Purified like space, our minds no longer stain as we dwell among nothingness in the bosom of compassion itself. We have discovered great bliss that has cut through misery, illusion, and have become freed from effort or struggle. We have become the Yidams (Teachers of the Dharma) of our own awakened nature, an embodiment of enlightened mind." Submerged in emptiness, their radiant awareness of their visualizations have revealed pure perception of one's own intrinsic relationship to reality. They have become inseparable in the Vajra vehicle, chosen to walk through their adjoining vestibules into a single heart.

An ocean of spiritual flowers burst from every pore in their bodies and every crevice of the cave, raining on them in heavenly

305

scents. Bathed in soft petals of ultimate delight, they caress their naked skin with a nourishing life-giving mystic mist. The vapors feel very fine, like silky electricity wondrously weaving along the outline of their ignited souls, buzzing hums on perimeters called identity. Distinctly written on each electrified electron, a wealth of transmitted akashic truths are revealed through a crystalline receiver to her soul. Innate tasty sips of solar coronal mass ejections stimulate adrenal rushes through her veins, arteries and lymphatic systems merging three magnetic fields forming the Gankyll, body mind, soul, and wheel of joy, in unlimited little symbolic dots. Yeshe's enlightenment is complete, filled with the ultimate wisdom of universal knowledge.

Yeshe immediately took these treasured Termas and concealed them for those seeking the revealed phenomena of Dharma. Padmasambhava predicted a coarsening pollution of the human psyche and a disengagement from the outer universe. So these teaching would only be shown to those who could reignite the Dharma in cognizant epochs of human existences. She became the mistress of all mandalas, absorbing life forces from god/goddess spirit, worldly and otherworldly. Diamond-like, indestructible and invincible, she achieved immortality in all realms, effectively becoming the root syllable MA. She burned her handprint into the volcanic rock to remind us that impermanence surrounds our physical form but not our affinity with consciousness. These messages were scattered throughout the four corners of this Earth, tucked away in volcano's, lightening, fire, on whispers in clouds, winds, and folded into the currents of streams, rivers, and oceans. These phenomena cannot be empirically delineated as they defy sciences based in the material universe. Ultimately, reality is Yeshe's jewel and plaything far from the nihilism of those who cannot see the profound Dharma of existence. Our world is composed of so much more than the apparent; it hovers around us like ghosts attempting to communicate, to the apparitions that claim human form. Yeshe claims that she is there even now for those faithful ones who adhere to the Dharma in the future.

Oh mother of the universe, I hear your breath ebb and flow at the crest of a wave rushing into the shores of reality. Here I sit, mediating on your immortal essence in this impermanence near the shining star under the shade of a bristle pine. Each chirping bird restores my happiness as the smell of salt water refreshes my skin. I live in my omnipotent smile that rests on this temporary harbor of consciousness, on the rippling ebony ocean of nothingness. My wishes are to reside in your presence again as beings, flesh and bone where our singularity resonates and our still presence speaks in familiar whispers.

Come sit with me dear mother, daughter, consort, and fly home to me again so these hollow moments are filled once more. My wishes are that your stoic compassion rinses my heart like a meadowlark restoring spring's promise in our epiphanies of rebirth. I sit here as a man on the edge of the horizon, contemplating your words and promises that one need only remember you to have you return. I remember all too well the timeless kiss in the midst of darkness as light is born in a culminating flash of our eternal electron. MA is at the end of every utterance, mantra, invocation and your sweet coo was your flickering manifestation, absolving through the eons over the ripples of consciousness. Dance with me again and let me remember our reasons for your sublime cause in the scheme of creation.

There is one thing that is clear within this story of love fueled by awareness that has determined that we must be consciousness, nothing else, and nothing more. At the point when you are the source of thought and your eyes no longer turn inwards. When you begin to look outwards in clarity and survey your universe in a pristine view. Only then will you have changed places with consciousness and have the seat of consciousness resting in the timeless unity of pure thought. Our observations have ruled out the absurdity of the unsettled mind and emptiness has replaced its chatter; truth no longer needs to be revealed. We reach into the folds of time and respond to those synchronicities of boundless riddles and questions by pinging echoes in timeless motions traversing time/space. Consciousness has no abundance, tranquility, or immortality to gain, as there is no fixation. Body, speech, and mind have all become equal and virtuous. Karma melts away into the space of a boundless universe.

The myopic eye of awareness is always looking for a purpose to life as if life itself means anything in this short time we are granted. Awareness's first contact during childhood trains the mind by stimulating our five senses with pleasure and that young mind associates that with life's purpose. This is what the outside world is training our minds to do in our adult years, by indulging those senses with tempting sugary delights. However some of those delights are passed through the instincts of parental love that also gets layered among those impulsive desires discolored by our curious mind's filters. This connection with parental love and those five senses sometimes can be blurred due to work and play times being inhibited because of social constructs, i.e. Social Media, Television, and cell phones. Parents generally attempt to make up lost time from parental duties with treats and gifts that convolute those imprints between love and the love for things. As we grow older, our philosophy can get confused if our fundamental connection with the universe is omitted and our spiritual nature shunned because of this disconnect. What gives us happiness and where is the real enjoyment in life itself if our purpose has not experienced what connected love is?

Romantic love while sought after, has a reputation of undependability and even though at one time it flourished, now is perhaps an illogical myth of love. Regardless of this, many still seek its refuge in the hopes of tasting its sublime nebulous sacraments whose flavors are as endless as time itself. Yet today, romantic love's icon represents unrealistic dreams of attaining things that society has deemed worthwhile of determining the value of love. Thus making heroic love as questionable as those intense aching, thumping heartbeats, and a swooning yearning as soon as your object of love is present. It is tirelessly celebrated as the ultimate achievement in our world now governed by rules that inhibit it to take hold and flourish naturally. It seems in our associations to acquire things; romance has been reduced to an iconic object of desire.

This rare craving is relentless; the aches and agony of anticipation that someone will recognize us, and our hearts will become their object of gratifications and their inner vision of spiritual unity. Few question the supremacy of romantic love, but after the movie, the flowers, the dinners out, or even the walks on the beach, what's next? How many have found profound rapture? Recognized the peak of ecstasy? Who is looking for the spiritual insights of claiming a lover for an authentic moving experience? Love by itself cannot be the justification for un-reflected passion as our highest aspiration. It's fathoming the depths of romantic love that we discover its roots lay deeply in the soil of human endearment and compassion realized. Where shedding the bonds of the human coil is our deliverance from a malleable sorrow of unpredictable outcomes, when love is set with conditions. We are all spiritual beings having a human experience in a world of possibilities that include fulfillment of romantic love despite the odds. We have the ability to improve our scope, lessen suffering, and increase happiness when we allow ourselves to view it. Henry Thoreau once wrote. "The only remedy for love is to love more." This is the answer to all questions and our capacity to love and to enjoy love has never left our side even in "… the best of times or the worst of times," as Charles Dickens once said.

Marina and I have looked beyond the teetering universe, capricious infatuation or shallow irresponsibility. Our thoughts have been bathed from foolishness, absolved from ego whose sights grow sharper with every view. Our bravery to meet our fortunes unflinchingly and truly that cool refreshment of wisdom that quenches even the most robust thirst. These promising circumstances of unconcealed truths are the support for our hearts' tomorrows, where quarrels, despair, friends, and relatives become meaningless to our abiding union. The vacuum of our abyss is now filled with knowledge and requires nothing, as our love loves best when we are filling each other with our love. This is not contrived, it need not be prodded or coerced, there are no emotional roller coasters; we are clearly devoted to the notion that we are each other's completion. The challenge is to make our home in this conviction, as there is nothing or any purpose more worthy or higher to live for in the material universe. Merit of our deeds has brought us to this station of the embodiment of compassion, empathy, and fulfillment. We have become the essence of each other's happiness and posses the wish-fulfilling jewel of enlightenment. The XIV Dalai Lama said, "Compassion and love are not mere luxuries as the source both of inner and external peace, they are fundamental to the continued survival of our species." This is Marina's and my cause and we know it can only happen with us spending our lives together in reverence. Practicing love and kindness, sympathetic joy, compassion over cruelty, has made our love a refreshing source of vitality and a wellspring of happiness.

My Heart

Cleansing drenches hypnotize these senseless prayers to realize that dreams are fleeting in vapors that can't be apprehended. My yearning soul can't really know the touch that means so much but comprehends the strength that always mends us.

So many incarnations have been revealed and Marina was still enchanting nothing but goodness from my heart. We woke in splendor, the new love from our Mett☐, or Love and Happiness, state of restful sleep and mutual nurturing in this realm and all realms. She opened her eyes, looked at me serenely and said, "We have to find a way not to ever leave each other's side."

I looked back at her sincere face and told her, "We can't waste another moment ever."

Marina looked back at me, reached her hands up around my neck, and told me in a very soft voice, "Yes, back to the path we have always been on."

So this is our cause, ripened in the fruits of our epiphanies, ready to be engaged and engorged by our serving love. I asked her if I could make breakfast for us this morning so we could sit on the terrace. She said, "I have a few details I must attend to, but I will be back in about 30 minutes or so. Just start breakfast and I will be back before you know it." I noticed her looking at her cell phone worriedly. She raised her head and smiled.

"So?" I asked, "What shall I make us this morning my love?"

Marina threw on her jeans and a sweater, collected a few things and came up to kiss me and said, "Surprise me my love!"

I kissed her back and told her, "We have a lifetime of surprises in store for us."

Then I get an odd feeling. "Don't go my love, let it wait till tomorrow. Stay with me here. Let's never leave each other's side."

Marina told me, "Don't be silly, I'll be right back. I don't want to ruin your day."

"Marina, being with you could never ruin my day. Let me get

312

dressed, it will just take a second."

Her cell phone text message goes off again. She ran out laughing and said, "I'll be right back."

I got up, put on a pair of jeans and sandals and a tee shirt and went to the kitchen to start making some breakfast. Then I heard the sound of metal crunching.

* * *

The sky was ultra-blue, framed in Marina's view with me nestled in a field of wild flowers and tall spring grass. Her long legs stuck out above the green blades and yellow blooms; they became my distraction as my eyes followed them swaying to-and-fro. A nearby brook babbled and tall trees unfurled new leaves, which danced flickering with light in the gentle wind. I could hear the sound of her pranayama breathing along with mine, moving with the ebb and flow of the currents of air surrounding us. It was so blissful, birds chirping in the distant background high above the world, in a mountain paradise basking in the afternoon sun. A dark cloud started to roll in out of nowhere, bellowing like a rushing monster from the abyss robbing us of sunlight. It cast a dense shadow, black as a raven's wing draping over our paradise, giving one the feeling of someone looming over their grave.

Suddenly I snapped awake with this eerie feeling still hovering, not knowing where I was, what day, or what year it is. A flight attendant noticed I am lost and came right up to me to reassure me that I was just fine. "Sir, I have seen that look before. You will be arriving in about two more hours." I scanned my whereabouts in a daze, noticing people with sleeping masks, blankets, and headsets, realizing that I was on a plane, and fell back asleep. Immediately, I returned to where Marina and I were laying. She is shading me with her big white hat that she's desperately holding onto so the wind doesn't blow it away. She is so beautiful wearing a matching white cotton sundress, a new tan and her hair blowing around the edges of her brim. She looks long into my eyes and tells me, "Come to the Tiger's Nest." Her eyes completely dilate, growing so large they become doorways sucking me into their cavernous abyss, cold and empty, swirling me into an endless void.

I wake up again to the voice of the aircraft's captain saying, "Welcome to Bangkok where the time is now 6:00 AM. We hopes you enjoyed your flight today with Thai Airways. Please fly with us again."

Thailand is one of the last bastions of Buddhism in the world, where over 90% of the people are Buddhist. Greetings in Thailand are, "Sawatdee krup and korp koon krup for thank you." These types of facts just rattle through my mind lately. It's been in reprogramming mode for a few years now. I find myself haunted by a dream coaxing me to travel to Bhutan, home of the flying dragon. So here I am getting ready to run to my next flight on Drukair Airlines, to continue my sojourn to The Tigers Nest. I've been walking this Earth like a specter riding a shock wave of meaningless risings and settings of the yellow ball in the sky. Really, Sawatdee Krup means, "I honor the Buddha inside of you," but its intention is too much to explain to foreigners. I have been aimlessly seeking destinations that lead to nowhere from the static chatter of my mind. A feedback loop that derogatorily keeps asking how do I change fate, what is fate, and who is the force behind my destiny? Frankly, I exist in my personal myth that coexists with my personal importance, lost in a plethora of insults that all start with my failure to preserve love. Here I am, in another foreign country, going through a process, seeking a destination for a purpose my thoughts haven't grasped through my agonizing haze.

Horror's deepest gasp cuts to the chase in a spiritual pain whose tears come from the origins of the deepest well-lit harbors. Barely can

314

I speak of its components where each compartment, each dimension, is flooded in an instant with a grief that can't be expressed. There is a pause in the air, in life, in time where nothing can move, where your very breath is snatched away from you and you never breathe the same again, even if it returns. They want to put a word on this to make it something that can never really be identified, "Bereavement." Bereavement means to be deprived of a love, one through a profound absence, but that all sounds so futilely hollow. I contemplated my shattered emptiness, devastation that doesn't wipe off, a stain that permeates through every fiber of the cloth called self. My greedy perspective wants to possess a pinnacle to peer over to view eternity and hold on tight to my love before her soul is sucked away into oblivion. Marina was my apex, my archetypal liberator, whose life was cut short by millions of cascading, colliding coincidences. Who would have thought our communion would be a catalyst of love's unthinkable disaster. I never wanted to let go; I never wanted her to walk out the door that day. Cruel and ruthless, this material universe and words cannot put back the pieces to this puzzle that was about to be solved by our love. I have no way to frame my pain, re-establish stability, integrate, pass through a transition, or cope with change and anxiety of my dearest love. This is not a time of discontentment, it's a grief that loss can't conceive of describing, or the ideas of a spiritual crisis that will never be diagnosed or cured.

I knew no one at the funeral and no one knew who I was, except her mother who knew all her secrets. I could barely glance at her, feeling that our love caused her untimely departure from our world. The reality of her body being lowered into the cold dark ground made me move under a tree in my loneliness, to shed my heart's most sacred tears. Having your child die before you is the worst pain, but her mother saw my broken heart and came to me. She was a divine angel of god as she put her arms around me and we cried together for a rare love that was irreplaceable in both our lives. While she was in her deepest moment of grief and could barely speak a word she managed to whisper in my ear, "You made her happy and I know my daughter experienced true love with you." My knees got weak, but she held me up by her sincere embrace, then others started to come up to kiss and hold her, while I faded into all of their past.

Not too far away, Bob was standing by for me. He had driven me there because he knew that I could barely function. Bob was the only one in my circle who knew just how in love I was and how hard this had hit my soul. He put his arm around me and helped me get into his car to drive off. Bereavement is a word that those who have not suffered loss say, who have not lost a child, or known and lost a love like Marina's and mine. I could not be consoled. Bob knew it and just let me be in pain as the phenomenon of grief is something no theorist could solve.

Shock, acute mourning, resolution, detachment, transition, and re-integration; these are the steps to recovering from someone's death. Multidimensional spiritual pain refracts in every facet of the material universe etched into every fiber of your immediate existence. Pain is a component of birth, death a component of pain that somehow meets in the middle of our timeline and wrenches our heartaches tight. Neither can be rubbed off from life's transitory memory nor covertly put to sleep, as the language of pain is something we all innately understand. Belief originates from our awareness, attempting to justify this process of birth and death as neither of which, like consciousness, can be defined. It's a riddle that can't be solved, or forgotten, pushed back or worked out, it's a pain we carry with us 'til our own days turn to ashes. What's our purpose, our intentions, and existence all about that eludes us at every twist and turn? Awareness attempts to discern and justify its reason. Marina told me once upon a time, "It is so wonderful when you are with someone you want with every fiber of your being. Feeling both present and lost at the same moment, alive, connecting completely and soulfully. Deeply desiring each other with honesty, with an intense, incredible passion. Moving energy and intelligent consciousness that transcends body and being." Now these are reverberations that comfort my spiritual distress. They ping through these facets in multi-dimensions that believe that I can find you somehow, somewhere.

My diagnosis is evident, my spiritual guilt, spiritual alienation, and my confusion in my relationship with creation undeniable. Loneliness' extremities can't be comforted when they reach out at the speed of light in all directions and still find emptiness. I packed up everything we had put together in our love nest and put it in storage because I just couldn't let go. I had the moving PODS© Company come and take everything. I told them to pack it away and paid for a year in advance. These flashback scenes seem like vaporous holographic images from times long ago I barely recall happening. Work stopped for me, I let go of everything to my friends to pursue and they insisted I continue my hard won labors of love. I sold everything else and did what I knew how to do best, which was to travel. I was shut off from everything and everyone who ever knew me and terminated my connection with the universe all-together. My life had no meaning or substance and really I could care less if I lived or died. My existential delve into the complexity of life's struggles and spiritual connection where love dwells, was as numb as I was. Completely spiritually bankrupt, I was a ghost on the solar winds to nowhere, with nothingness as my guiding light.

I felt like we were mere playthings for the universe to toy with, hurtled from one lifetime to the next, as if our experiences where inconsequential. Finally finding our perfect gift of timeless love, only to have it snatched up in an instant like candy from a baby. More than a fleeting brisk singe, a taunt, or a sip, it was a full immersion into the well of my craving heart. Cognizance engulfed in total spiritual anguish, dismissed from my devalued ideology about my

317

mission of selfless servitude, now completely ignored. Paradigms immutable, cause and effect stymied, a fractal empathic non-corporeal agreement where the main clause was left unrevealed. There can't be a validation or intervention for this kind of suffering, when the archetype of human divinity has been stripped from my soul. Pain from death emits a frequency that nothing can transcend, and all life avoids this kind of misery. This is where faith, love, or forgiveness will never cleanse your souls from a senseless assassination of perfection. Many people, in different ways in books, songs, poems, "The treasure of love lasts a moment; the pain of love last a lifetime," have said it. To rise above or achieve a new perspective on human existence, even though it's an absurd wasteland of hoaxes and fake communions, is a fallacy. We are who we are and must endure it, regardless of what shore you come from or discover. Death is final under the maestro's baton. Survivors of our own obituaries as the walking living dead. I am in a pool of demoralized weariness, nervously acknowledging that death is a blank stare that collapses all that you appear to be. A corpse's name eventually disappears after overwhelming tears offered from gut wrenching pain, to smolder the remaining flames of misbegotten love forever. The universe delves ruthlessly, gravely, desperately, without apparent reason, preening its never ending plumage of creation without a thought. Thus, leaving in its wake, carnage of human emotions whose plight is scorned down to their very fundamental core.

Dubious elegies of death's conundrum, my disparaging laments, fiercely tormenting me in a fatal attempt to make sense from senselessness. I am a contradiction, abandoning my generous perceptions that happiness is possible because of a voice, a gesture that needs no explanation. Right now, for me, I need everything explained. My poetry has been robbed and I have been neglected, I have become my own allegory without a suitable ending. I still remember the long run to the bottom of the hill, the mangled metal and the smell of rust. Her face soaked in blood and a message going off on her phone that read, "Your whole collection just sold, you have to come and sign the paperwork now!" That was never going to happen in this surreal madness of screaming sirens, panicked air that had been sucked out to the point of silence. I thumbed through each of the paintings she had just on her phone, telling me a truth that scared my heart. They were portraits of us making love, with our bodies painted, lying in bed, standing in the bathtub, and one of us kissing. Ambulances, fire trucks, and police came in what seemed like a split second but life's spark had returned to the cosmic furnace, a holographic nebula of oblivion.

Even though this was years ago, I still live in that split second. My disparaging descent has stricken me with melancholia. I know Marina would never have wished our poem of love to end this way and I do so desperately want to relive those epiphanies, but I am lost. The sale of the paintings went through anyway and those paintings became very valuable, the profits going to her beloved mother. She sent the money to me with a note that read, "Marina wants you to live. Share your love, I know your pain is great and mine will never leave me, but please don't give up on yourself. Marina told me yours is the perfect love. Don't abandon your heart."

I wanted to give her the money back or give it to charity, but it was Marina's energy attached to it. So I opened my solar sail to the universe that betrayed me, to take me where it willed. My will was surrendered and already turned to ashes. My dedensification centripetal contraction that had sucked my heart into a vortex and fragmented my being, was now compelling me to expand again. Rumi once said, "Since love has made ruins of my heart, the sun must come and illumine them. Such generosity has broken me with shame." I am broken, destroyed by experiences stronger than death where the condition of love and happiness is owned solely by infinity. I ping in silent languish in my brutal suspicions of my own madness, in this reasonless phenomenon of love lost. Yet all the poets proclaim, enjoy the brief time the flame of love warms you, as the night is long and cold. Maneuvered into a folly of misbegotten turmoil that soothed me like a fool, believing my immortal fibers could be as indestructible as hers. Mysterious treasures, coins of endless torments, forged in beating hearts, unforgivable torments that strip away all your intentions. Rigor mortis of the living sets in when every emotion that can be shed is spent on your own numbing obsessions and undoing. My broken heart can't be mended in the celestial crucible of forgiveness, our atmosphere of paradise has been leached out and my only desire is to find you again in the cauldron of oblivion.

It was a two-hour drive to the city from the tiny Paro Airport. The pilots had to have some experience to navigate between the narrow valley and the landing strip. Thimphu Tshechu festival was in full swing in the capitol city of Bhutan and everyone was wearing his or her finest demon killer outfits. This was a time to celebrate the Great Teacher Guru Rinpoche with his healing ritual, the Cham dance. Cham dancers wear Tantric masks and costumes associated with their different sects. These meditative dances have a timekeeper that keeps the musicians and dancers in sync by beating on a brass cymbal. Guru Rinpoche was the first to perform this dance to heal the ailing king, who later spread Buddhism across his kingdom in gratitude. This was a day of pageantry and intense fervor that filled my sad eyes with some joy.

Huge Thangka's of Yeshe Tsogyal and Padmasambhava unfurled making their testament that spiritual love and compassion be known. The driver brought me to the clerk that would prepare my passport and other documents that I needed to move around their beautiful country. I felt alone in this forbidden world, struggling with the language barrier trying to go inside the cave at the Tiger's Nest. Unbeknownst to me, Marina's artwork and my writings of our love story and tragedy had made it to the world stage many years ago. A dignitary from King Jigme Khesar Namgyel Wangchuck, who was a fan of Marina's work and mine, greeted me at his office. The King and his country were no stranger to love stories. Their King is known as the Prince Charming of the Himalayas. The king's great love for his queen and country made him an inspiration to his people, along with his policy of pursuing the "Gross National Happiness," for everyone. His wife and consort, Queen Jetsün Pema, had brought pure love and joy to the land of the Thunder Dragon with her beauty, poise, and charm. Mr. Chenkyab Dorji, a very kind dignitary, saw to my paperwork. He had their department of transportation prepare a very special document so I could visit sacred landmarks unencumbered. He assured me that everything would be taken care of. Then he asked me to collect my belongings and follow him to a waiting car.

Samteling Palace is the fifth kings' home and he had offered for me to stay the night and have dinner with himself and his queen. I was very honored to be between these two loving people. They had succeeded to the throne after his father abdicated from 34 years of ruling; the kingdom was now in the good hands of their capable love. King Jigme Khesar Namgyel Wangchuck is committed to insuring his people stay in touch with nature and that technology and money don't dominate the lifestyle of this simple, undisturbed culture. The consciousness of this happy place was focused on seeing to the collective needs of all sentient entities that inhabited their diverse and beautiful country.

This balance was interesting to me because it seemed in the United States that we have divided our original culture that was farm-based to factories and now services. Once upon a time, we owned land to grow food and we took care of the needs of our community. We saw to the well-being of our neighbors. That was when no one was afraid of what went bump in the night and pre-industrialization of America's Republic. Children would develop under the watchful eye of nature and through their hard work and merit, discover themselves. With this self-knowledge and love they could fall in love and have children of their own. Today, in the industrialized world, jobs have been stratified throughout many countries; paying rent, food, and water, has become our youth's main struggle. Finding time to find one's self to be in love or have a family is almost out of the question without an income. Most can't afford their day-to-day expenses let alone for someone else or a child. I like Bhutan socialization because its citizenry can be self-sufficient yet still participate in technology in carefully measured steps. Those who rule it and its overall ability to bring liberty and happiness to its citizens are the true measure of a successful country. The Western world citizens are made to be concerned with consuming, technology, and survival with little emphasis on real love or happiness in the pursuit of economic wealth.

The king and queen graciously bid me to sit with them and have green tea, while food was being prepared. We overlooked the two rivers outside their palace; Para Chhu River is known as the father river and the Wong Chhu is known as the mother river. Both rivers come from the Goddess Mountains, but where they both converge near the palace is considered a sacred union. The king and queen's marriage is just as auspicious as these rivers joining, a real love story written into the timeless pages of the Akasha, much as Marina and mine were. Both of them had studied in the States, so the queen spoke with me in perfect English, "I love your consort's paintings of your celebration of spiritual love. You must feel that the universe blessed you with this unique experience."

I tell her simply, "It was a miracle that her precious gem touched my soul at all."

The Fifth King tells me, "We all grow from the gift of consciousness, don't you think?"

322

"Yes, your majesty," I insist.

King Jigme smiles and assures me, "We are friends here on the quest for enlightenment, dear friend of the Dharma, so you may call us Jigme and Jetsün in our private chambers. We know why you have come and we are here to help in your quest. Jetsün had a vision of your coming and insisted we make it possible for you to spend seven nights alone in the Tiger's Nest."

Queen Jetsün spoke, "Your weary travels are far from being over, even after the very serious accident that occurred as it radically changed your life forever."

The King spoke," Your role has been to bring a perfect love into this realm that is accessible to all those seeking love."

Queen Jetsün cuts in, "Even though we have been schooled in the West, there are many things my King and I cannot explain about the esoteric nature and phenomena of Dharma."

The King admits, "We have been approached about your coming by Buddhist scholars, astrologers, and His Holiness the 70th Je Khenpo, Trulku Jigme Chhoeda, who all agree there is a divine ambrosia waiting for you at the Tiger's Nest. It is written in the stars."

How is this possible, I thought to myself, 'My consort is gone, the love of my life Marina, how could I be more profoundly affected by love.' Queen Jetsün compassionately tells me as she lays her gentle hand on mine. "There have been others like Trungpa Rinpoche, a writer and poet like you, follower of the Vajrayana. You have come a long way for this moment and we have laid the path."

I am considerably overwhelmed by this and had no idea what was in store for my journey. I had merely trusted Marina's voice that whispered to come to the Tiger's Nest. I heard another voice in my head saying, "Who is Lost? And who has lost? But there remains complete devotion," words from the Abbot Trungpa Rinpoche. There is nothing concealed when it comes to kindred spirits on the path. No one is separated; we are a family recognizing that familiarity is the first step to seeing the hidden fact that we walk the Earth together.

Sadhana, or the accomplishment of Mahamudra, was the imprint left behind in the caves of Bhutan and those sacred chants of ecstasy still reverberated. Queen Jetsün Pema, which literally means, "Revered love," has made the way for this very sacred experience in this holy place where Shakti Shakta is realized. Marina, my supreme experiencer, one with the changeless whole, absolved from duality as consciousness recognized itself through our love. From the point of the finite immersed and expanded into the infinite when knowing goes beyond the many and perceives the whole all at once. This is the attainment of the Sadhana of Mahamudra, supreme knowing of self in utterly clear clairvoyance, shattering illusions in a silent storm of actualization. Spiritual experience is not our self-deception. As we experience, we go beyond that of a believer transforming the super-sensual truth into knowledge.

My affirmation was at hand, I had been poised in my island for too many years alone, until Marina vindicated our exquisite truth into recognition of the great path. Samadhi, ecstasy, transcends all reasoning. This is impossible in the frugal terms of what is considered ecstasy by pop culture. We are fearlessly weighing out what has value and preserving its worth in our day-to-day cause. This is why the gracious King and Queen have brought me here, because of my cause, and I humbly accept their invitation to its effortless ends. Jetsün with her smiling eyes bid me to rise and head to the dinner table, where the cuisine of Bhutan awaited me.

I had that displaced feeling again when I awakened in the still morning of the king's palace. Vishvasara Tantra says, "What is here is elsewhere, what is not here is nowhere," and I still felt in between time and space. The air was brisk and morning light began to glisten on the tranquil sounds of their sacred rivers. Monks who tended to the Palace needs, saw that my eyes were open and helped me to an awaiting tub of water. The King and Queen were already meditating, facing the rising sun, gathering chi, doing yoga, and preparing for a day of service to their people. We all gathered on the veranda for coffee and a breakfast of farm fresh everything. It was a simple, perfect start to this exciting day.

After we expressed our morning greetings, I asked the Queen a question, "Why do they say Guru Rinpoche arrived at the cave riding on a tigress that flew from Tibet over the Himalayas to the Tiger's Nest?"

She was happy that I knew the truth and said, "So you know it was Yeshe Tsogyal's love that flew him to their moment with destiny."

"How could it have been any other emanation," I responded joyfully.

The King also was amazed, "During my time at Oxford, so many wondered why I didn't go out and party like everyone else in college. The answer was simply that I had already met my consort, I recognized her reincarnation, and there was no time to waste. I needed to be prepared for my moment where fate and destiny collided with an education, which would enable me to be a wise king. Understanding history in its metaphors and allegories enables one to discern its ultimate spiritual outcome. There is a universal divine principle, where awareness has met consciousness head on in understanding that human existence is the manifestation of love."

His revelation moved me. I felt I had somehow returned to my tribe after many years of isolation. Jetsün and Jigme's welcome had restored the opening to my heart. Blood was now starting to trickle through my veins again, with molecules attaching to their gentle love vibration. Jigme means fearless in Tibetan, which he represented well, along with having good judgment and the skills to operate the business of a country. Both their names were very fitting to them and now my time had come to part physical company and ascend to the Tagtsang Monastery and the Tiger's Nest.

The king and queen had arranged everything with the National Commission for Cultural Affairs. A couple of monks from the Monastery had come with my paperwork and were now leading me up the mountainside. The trek was arduous, almost going straight up from the valley floor 900 meters from an altitude of over 2000 meters. Land of the Thunder Dragon, this Himalayan kingdom was comprised of lush, green, fertile mountains while strikingly stoic in its awesome beauty. Ascending above the thick forest canopy, the trail was framed with unusual endangered flora and fauna, including the rich Blue Pines. Then we came upon it, teetering on the edge of an abyss a Lost Horizon, a mystical Shangri-La. A sanctum waiting in the mist of timelessness, defying gravity while perilously nuzzled into the cliff's side. It was a testament to the fortitude of Buddhism in Bhutan. It was magnificent to behold these temples that protect the entrances to the caves that many enlightened souls came to bath in consciousness. The first, the Dubkhang, houses the cave where Guru Rinpoche meditated with Yeshe Tsogyal almost 1300 years ago, when the world was having a spiritual rebirth. This is where I was going to stay for seven nights, in the dark, for the sake of the universe that had brought me here in whispers.

Nuns started to prepare me for a Vajrayana meditative journey inside Padmasambhava's sacred cave. Honored and humbled by this opportunity, since no outsiders had been allowed to spend a night inside these sacred caves at Taktsang Monastery, let alone a week. Harmony was settling in on my bones, tended by giggling nuns

326

ceremonially bathing me in tepid Himalayan pure spring water. After which they laid me out on a black volcanic stone, ritualistically shaving my entire body with a Tibetan Vajra Kartika blade. Then, they rubbed my skin with pink Tibetan rock salt, exfoliating every inch of my freshly bathed body with a final rinse of herbs and flowers. The Vajra Kartika symbolizes the sharp edge of wisdom, which strips away spiritual and intellectual defects, such as pride or envy. The rock salt is used to remove dead skin, returning my body to reenter this womb of forbidden timelessness with the purity of a baby.

I fasted along this three-day journey, only drinking special herbal tea my traveling companions the monks gave me. Over the last few years after Marina's death, I had been subsisting at the lowest denominator, losing weight and body mass. Essentially, in the cave there would be no food, some water, but nothing else was required at ten thousand feet other than my skillful means. The Vajra Guru Mantra was etched in henna on my naked body before they would dress me in the traditional meditation robes of Guru Rinpoche. This was a different type of night hunting, the Love Ritual, where my years of practice stilling my mind in absolute darkness, came into play. Their compassion meant to awaken my Kundalini to rendezvous with consciousness in the impenetrable, immutable, indivisible, and indestructible state of enlightenment. Supreme Experience lies just below the skin of all sentient beings; it's just a matter of pointing undisturbed awareness towards the center of the whirlpool.

The Abbot Khen Rinpoche Geshe Yonten Dhamchoe of Taktsang Monastery was to guide me into the depth of the cave to start my initiation in the Tiger's Nest. Kind and gentle, like a grandfather reminding me I cannot be desirous, allow mercy's hand to come effortlessly and it will guide me. He was my promulgator and my spiritual benefactor. He held one candle that became brighter and brighter as we penetrated into the venerable depths of this holy place.

You noticed right away an ominous presence, moist, cool but not cold, as if the rocks were Earth's skin alive and sensuous. Kind Abbot Rinpoche showed me to my perch, where ignorance and attainment are divided, home of Atma with two tools for my time here.

Abbot Khen Rinpoche said to me before he left my company, "I know you are a follower of skillful means, but I want you to hear the words I am about to say. One is a Tibetan word that dispels chatter of the mind called P'et. Use this to keep your focus clear. The other I am sure you know but it is my duty to instruct you so listen carefully my dear traveler. Aum Ah Hum Vajra Guru Padma Siddhi Hum. Let this reverberate here where it was first spoken inside your heart of Sattvapatti, or commencement of realization. Uttara Mimamsa is a single principle transcending the limitations of self-identity to realize unity with the universe."

He removed a mala from around his neck and handed it to me. The beads were made from the deepest black onyx stone. One hundred and eight beads, six for the senses, sight, sound, smell, taste, touch, and awareness, multiplied by thee reactions of each, positive, negative, or indifferent, makes eighteen feelings. Each of these can be attached to pleasure or detached from pleasure making thirty-six passions that can be manifested in past, present, or future. I humbly accepted his kind gesture, placing my palms together in the Añjali Mudr☐ and honored the Buddha that dwells inside his heart. His Holiness smiled at me one last time and turned towards the entrance to leave, chanting the Vajra Guru mantra as the little candlelight was swallowed by darkness. I was left alone in its wake.

The mind is always looking to latch onto something and particles of light spun kaleidoscopically into my dilating eyes. Like colorful shooting stars in fast motion, buzzing like bees until there is no light to hold onto anymore and they all dissipate into the unknown. This is complete darkness where you can come to terms with the mind until its chatter stops and your view becomes distinct. I settled without a task at hand as I was not here to attain anything or become enlightened. I came here because of a voice and without any expectations; I enjoyed the complete silence inside the dragon's belly. I surrendered the rest of my heart, love, and being. With so much behind me and with nothing ahead, this long day took me into the restful bosom of a perfect, peaceful sleep.

Every boy has a moment in their lives when they find spirituality, but it's not one you would expect. It's a very strong contact with something larger than the apparent world around us, almost like a calling from a higher power. Beautiful and sublime in nature, the awareness that springs forth in spiritual rapture. Somehow, the universe recognizes their heart. They see signs, have dreams, and hear voices that all point to the obvious conclusion that there is more to life than the transient nature of Mankind. This is the wellspring of creativity, home of the poet, architect, composer, painter, writer and so many other inventive visionaries. Our lament should be for those boys whose broken hearts cause them to shun this world of hope, turn off this powerful connection in exchange for illusion.

This was me as a child; I had knowledge of self, resonating with life that was buzzing in every facet of my new reality. My head poked through the dreamer's veil in awe and wonderment of the expansion of our marvelous, endless universe. Explorer of the cosmos, adventurer, and unraveller of universal truth, I was fearless to venture out into other realms; all realms. I became a defender of pure joy and happiness, slayer of hostile giants of beauty, and protector of nature with an innocent compassion for all living things. This was my transformation, undisturbed by the petty world of envy, lust, and greed. How could these time wasters even exist or anyone care for them when there was so much to learn, talk to, or hear among the symphony of nature. I would not be alone in the quest, my love, dear sweet Becky was my companion in the discovery of what the universe wanted to play with us on those eventful never ending days. We were five years old and alive with wonder scorching through our eyes, on fire by the passion of what every new exciting day would bring.

Magic brought dear Becky and I together as if the forces of nature used all its powers just so we could sit next to each other and stare at the sky. I was obsessed with her, thinking about what I would say to her the next day and if she would still be my girlfriend the next morning. All the answers to every question would be written in the signs of nature; you only had to look for them. For instance, I would twist off the apple's twig saying the alphabet because the universe would snap it off when I came to the letter of the girl that loved me. Every time it would break off at the letter "B" for Becky or "V" because it was the same letter at five years old. It would reassure me that all the signs were pointing towards us to be together. We would talk for hours, ride our bikes, and take long walks. Sometime her mom would invite me over to have dinner with her family and I always knew there would be something good to eat. It was pure joy to be in her amazing presence. It seemed she knew everything and would show and teach me things about having fun. The true playground oracle that every girl knew how to make was the whirlybird, or cootie catcher that would always tell us who loves whom. Fortunate for me, my name came up when Becky asked the special question, "Who loves me?" or should I say, "Who likes me."

Then, when I was seven years old, my family moved. I wrote her letters and she wrote back, but those childhood things fade with every new developmental phase. I would still think about her and ask the sunsets to send her a message about how I was doing from so far away. I always felt like I would never meet anyone that would make me feel the way I did with her. I always had a longing to be complete with an idealistic dream of finding a woman who would recognize me

330

like Becky and want to play with me. This imprint was what my mind's eye would seek in every woman I would encounter, a part of my perception of my mate. I was blind to it, but having lost my first love, I wanted to believe the universe didn't want me to suffer alone. So I looked for her, swam through my dreams for her, believed that she was out there looking for me just as hard as I was for her. Somehow, we both would find each other and our reunion would take us back to the beginning of time and restore that innocence of pure love. When I hear a meadowlark sing I still remember our little walks through the woods not too far from our parents' voices so we could always hear calling to come home for dinner.

Knowledge of my childhood was on the tip of my tongue when I woke up in total darkness. I was completely unaware of how much time had lapsed or if any time had lapsed. There was a brewing storm of synthesis and assimilation out in the distance, just on the horizon of my purgatory. I could feel it in my dream building and I began to meditate to prepare myself for the shock wave that was brewing inside. This lifetime had been a treasure of kind people assisting my good nature to do well in this world. My voice had always been there to help people in pain through their hard times and even perfect strangers had recognized something special about me. I don't know why the perfect word for the perfect moment comes across my lips but I am grateful to help anyone who is suffering. Perhaps there is just a lack of compassion in our world and pain is thought of as weakness. All truth is relative, all truth will be revealed, and truth is truth and so many other things that don't help a troubled soul. Sometimes an ear, a touch, listening with so much love that their feelings are free to flow because you want them to. At some point we must all face ourselves as time is short and for me this point is now.

P'et! P'et, P'et, P'et. I think to myself as I shoot down all those rushing thoughts on perhaps my second or third day here. My inner voice is restless to be heard and it says, "Still your mind and she will come." Like a skimming stone on an endless pitch-black pond I get a glimpse of my old friend consciousness, lurking in the shadows with great concern. A sphere of calm overtakes me and I begin to focus, staring into the darkness raising my Kundalini one sound syllable at a time. Using Kriya yoga techniques of controlling my breath and channeling it up and down my spine, debris started to clear, and my resolve smoothed out upon the glassy coal black waters of consciousness. A primal process started out like a wounded, trapped animal filled with tormented emotions, trapped, caged, and separated from night and day. Ending with the cobra hood spread wide, oscillating with the rhythm of the universe. Lower, middle, and higher mind all start purging through chakras LAM, BHAM, RAM, YAM, HAM, AUM, in round robin up and down the Ida and Pingala pathways. Veils started to quiver, melting like wax to reveal my own face looking back at me as it emerged from the molten abyss, devoid of duality.

A sprouting evolution of omnipotent quintessential awareness arose, illuminating the ocean of remnants, vicariously dissipating as order appeared. They were never present in a still gaze at everything and nothing, where heat and cold have no value, where there is no up or down. A billion little stars sparkle at the tips of billions of lightning rods that emanate from an essence of unknown identity that casts light. Emanationism, the principle where all things flow from the first reality, struck from our shared hearts of this type of perfected awareness. A sovereign journey started in timelessness for no apparent reason, emerged from a dreamless sleep. Had it all been changeless in this divergence of views where separate has always been the illusion? Un-manifested formless laments at a nexus of creation's potential, the absolute and infinite synchronistically. Brahma's contemplative affirmations of longing, a reason that could constitute reality and ultimately solve this inscrutable riddle of why. "I." This identity I clung to surrenders without authority of the mind or a resolve of consciousness. Somehow it shed itself in the presence of

332

divinity. "What is here is there. What is not here is nowhere." Existence at the end of a long day had always been within the inevitable destruction of the universe. My potential rest in non-judgment on the supreme perfection in unassailable monism, bliss I've only known in the arms of Marina. There is no mystery as to how one can be both as Brahman and Saraswati. That impossibility happens to us from unfathomable nothingness. We are the creators in our foregone conclusions, the stardust in the matter that composes our physical and metaphysical forms that harbor an unimaginable supreme spirit. Being consciousness's bliss is synonymous with compassion's vibratory alliance, floating in a mixture of conscious-unconsciousness. We have always been the almighty substance, a life force co-mingling with particles of the aggregate whole.

Consciousness is consciousness, ominous, foreboding, appearing in a split moment in my transformation, entering its abode of Supreme Majesty of breathlessness. Total clarity consumes my new identity of a totalitarian myopic hyperkinetic awareness that is ruthless in its all-absorbing gaze that takes heed. Echoes manifest from ethers, ethereal apparitions ripple along the surface of consciousness's home of ebony, riffing like music resonating on the surface of its endless pond. "Where are you my love?" roars a tigress's voice across its surface. It's a familiar weight resting on dialectic compassioned knowing: a sound remembered so well.

Those resonating tones yield my view to seek its source to answer this intrinsic question within a deep echoing declaration, "I am right here." Rousing perception, ecstatic in the notion of an imminent reunion manifests its likeness rushing towards me, jumping through the ethos.

My Shakti arrives, popping in transcendental illuminations, pouncing on me like a tigress flying from a continuum of voracious void. Stepping on me like a dakini, fiery red, invoking Samadhi. My state of consciousness is transfixed, hovering in this breathless moment, negotiating pure thought and ecstasy at the same time. I hear her speak. "My boundless love, liberation is not a requirement when one is karma-less. One quiescent point can't exist in two aspects profoundly, there is more for you my love." She profoundly kissed me, making a sound of material manifestation where I can touch, feel, and know her like she had never left. She told me, "Where are you? Here? There? Impermanence tells you, 'You are nowhere.'"

We get into a banter of spiritual sexual salutations when I praised her and she responded, "I visualize your wandering nakedness broaching my wanting strides that enact a forbidden dance that finds me inside a festival of your love. Our shameless discoveries, ornaments of our retreat into our sacred bodies, the expression of our sharing hearts. Replenish my soul along your beaded strains, fibers that connect heaven and Earth." Marina's ravishing fury swallows me as she speaks, "In rapture undulating in sensuous mist and molten fire."

In between our wet, abandoned kisses I said, "Wean my yearning mouth that is soaked with the nectar of your poetic litany."

She responded, "Scintillating waiting in the fortress of love's perfume."

My heightened awareness responded, "Be my emanation that guides me to your ultimate pleasure in one deafening cosmic pinnacle, where we are the eye of the storm. Proliferate my indulgences that are inevitably meant for your liberation into total ecstasy."

In gasps of erotic passion, she ventured, "Intoxicated by your lips, I surrender my yearning and intense divine pleasures."

Divine ecstasy became my soliloquy, "You are my imbibing serenity, each touch, each response, from your cooing heart. Every preexisting morsel of your desire is my instinct to reveal."

Didactically she added, "My senses exalted are lured to the garden of our inception to savor knowledge's forbidden fruits falling in torrents."

Tasting and licking her lips, kissing her eyelids I added, "Your body, my fruit, my desires to procure and dine in the absolute splendor of your majestic beatitude."

Quivering, Marina told me, "Primal drumbeats move through me, feeling you inside."

Engorged in love I said, "You are my esoteric, my mysticism, my wealth, my depravity."

Marina cooed, "How I miss you lover."

My body can't stop delving the depth in wet plunges inside her throbbing womb that tightened and loosened in cosmic rhythms. Marina begged, "I miss your dripping passion dripping wet over my naked folds."

I pleaded, "Fathom further, be my initiator, and show me the mysteries of the very essence of flesh and blood. Let me explore your unconcealed abyss, worship your insatiable wellsprings of love, whimsical and capricious. Let me fill you up over and over lover in everything mysterious and holy."

Marina, resolved, said, "Your throbbing phallus caressing sacred places, holy of holies, is all I seek in our actualization of omnipresence."

I said, from my center, "Marina you are my embodiment of femininity, my ovum of understanding. I have been completed in your complete love. You are free and you have freed me, without our time in paradise I would not be in the presence of pure love ever. My love, I am always with you and you are always with me."

All-pervading consciousness danced me in between the shadows temporally. I am but an instrument of attainment that is only consciousness's to attain. She who is everything, my worshiped love, had never left, merely seeking another vessel to ride the tides again on this ocean of oblivion. Her swirling currents drifted to the shores of my desperation inside this vortex manifesting in a rainbow body, a sublime tease at my awareness. These feelings no longer mattered around my soul because I'd somehow found peace in my waking clarity. I had unfalteringly stayed in the great posture of Mahamudra and recited the Vajra Guru Mantra deep within my silent psyche. A still flame resting in the blossom of awareness and non-awareness, a mystic coition sublime in my liberation from my mortal wound. Gracefully slipping from behind the static background to restore a missed last kiss, a physical embodiment of supreme consciousness takes life. Death is not a barrier of our echoing grief, a statute of our prevailing treatise underwritten in this story called, "our life on Earth." Our ongoing deeds are but the residue we leave on the ripple along the cosmic pond and do not measure a perfect accomplishment.

I ventured deeper into my meditation, surrendering my illumination to be swallowed up again by darkness. Deep in that darkness, I came across his blackened lustrous form outlined in vital youth, contemplating loneliness. Wishing for a magic love to find him so he could live happily ever after in his discovery of true love. Vicariously, consciousness identified itself in a polarization seeking some sort of equilibrium between plus, minus, positive, negative, male, and female to resonate against its vaporous will. Both their poles have always been one-and-the-same, two that are one, a running theme in the ideas of love's perfection.

Woman has always been there for man. Even in Brahma's intense loneliness, it was Saraswati who came to his aid. Yet it is viewed that the Male God is the ruler of all he prevails. In my view, it was Female who supremely come to the aid with ultimate selfless love unconditionally for his betterment. To me, the source of creation was silently listening, manifesting compassion in many aspects of kinetic energy that nurture creatures. There are no partitions to reality; only an imperfect eye whose broken vision does not perceive engendered quintessential consciousness unfolding inside a perfect lotus blossom. Femininity is the harbor of beauty and understanding, the art and sciences of nurturing love, family, and teaches males about the sublime nature of all things good.

In asceticism, positive and negative charges hold each other in check, circling around a nucleus of intention. It's a balance of absolute love resting between anabolic and catabolic energies, momentarily at bay during the actualization of nothingness and the threshold of creation. My mind in this utter void stands there while stillness fills my being and the rhythm of my breath ceases as I hold it outside of my physical body. I hear another timbre in a familiar voice reverberation from a more ancient past, "Where are you my love?" I feel a shift in my identity, the presence of Padmasambhava layers over me like a cloth transforming my persona into his. This enlightened being who was mediating at this very spot so long ago commandeered my physical characteristics and mannerism. I begin to chant mantra out loud as an invocation, summoning all experience in this life and all lifetimes of existence. With a primal force of supreme adoration, love fills the cave in a shock wave recognized by my sincerity in the return of Yeshe Tsogyal.

Yeshe Tsogyal recoils from a black lotus emerging from consciousness's primordial ebony pond. She raises her Kundalini, stretching out her likeness and finally lifting her gaze like a cobra's hood lifting off the ground to look into your eyes. Void drips off her outlines in silhouettes as details fill in, transfiguring a rainbow body apparent to my timeless view. At the velocity of light, her density

337

gathers molecular mass and gravity until her matter reaches its three-dimensional solid form. I begin to breathe again in very deep breaths, autonomically becoming synchronous with her manifestation. My body felt like it was filling up with opiates, tingling every neural fiber's ascension while all transgressions disappeared. This was a remarkable heightened state, the dynamic power of prana saturated with converging intentions along the axis of sublime forgiveness.

Worldly life had long left me from the first moment I met Marina and now my attachments to it were completely meaningless. This was the moment of unchanging reality. Yeshe was its phenomenal flow that engulfed my awaken state with Padmasambhava's consciousness. Yeshe claimed victory of my unhindered awaken state without the limitations of mind. Bliss invades my ethereal body and Yeshe begins to dance, ripening this moment of union in ultimate liberation. Lightning strikes my third eye gaze, my breath is slow, resolved, and controlled, deep and long. I taste the sweet purified milk flower of rapturous devotion of Shakti my consort. She is my feminine deity whose goal it is to offer compassion so righteously, my heart automatically surrenders completely.

Yeshe joins me in Mahamudra, a reflection of the creative act of Shiva, Shakti that seeded the universe. Her fertility is a beacon in absolute darkness. She sits on top of me as if she has never left this moment. The infinite power of consciousness there at last, we are the experiencers of "I Am." Never exhausted, never diminished, and instruments of substance essential and active, both contributors to motion and change. We are the unconscious lost in affirmations, transcendental without identities or gender. Out of darkness in a perpetual motion, life force is realized, undulating, vibrating in my deepest state of meditation. I have shed myself. Male and Female aspects of the same unity that's neither gender dissolves in total darkness inside a sacred cave in the absence of time. Deep in the unconscious before the moment of creation, before wisdom, or knowledge of identity, the flittering undulation of life force begins to gather. Suddenly, there is a high-pitched sound, like a bell with only one ring, piercing the veils of a nebulous existence. Our eyes open in unison to observe each other's spiritual euphoria, in a climax that fertilizes our metaphysical ovum. We are complete, gushing with a love supreme, overwhelmed, as she evaporates into oblivion smiling like a saint in rapture.

My resolve turns my eyes towards the center of my eyebrows. My organs have all been sucked up into my diaphragm. My throat has also sucked in as all the oxygen has been held outside my body in the peak of this experience. My hearing returns and I notice my body shaking and the gasping sound of me keeping myself from inhaling. My belly extends like bellows, slowly drawing in a very deep breath that returns me to normal respiration. Still spinning, exhausted yet revitalized, I've returned and slowly draw in a conscious breath purified of any wanting or attachment.

Unknown to me, outside Padmasambhava's cave, Lamas and the nuns have been reciting mantras and visualizing the goddess in Vajrayana fashion. Compassion assisted my spiritual journey through the wormhole, leading to a bosom of pure consciousness opened by their collective united harmony. Entering the cave in monastic procession with reverently lit candles to retrieve my naked body and lay me down on the cliff's edge to face the dawn. Theirs has been an unprecedented vigil for seven days, focused on restoring love from my broken heart. No one has been allowed to visit the monastery and everyone, including the abbey's children, have been in meditation and fasting with me sympathetically. I'd tasted goddess nectar ripened from the Nourisher's vessel, suckled from her imminent transcendental bosom. By entering into the body of the goddess I had become the goddess and she had become me. This moment, eternal and finite, had not been without merit. The rewards of my emancipation filled my heart with a poem. All the monks had gathered, along with the translators to hear the voice of my rapture as I recite my gift.

Deep into the morning light

No promise was ever kept

Compassion was a sacrament

A pine tree heaven's scent

Miraculous and unforgiving

Nature merely unfolds

Stoic dreams a wanton giving

Hearts are all bestowed

No footstep plotted

No love unrooted

No forbidden after glow

No homages of parody

No cantors can recite

When all the stars come home

The quiet chestnut breaks

The Buddha of boundless light

We become the objects of our worship, transforming into the likeness on which we are set. If you are always thinking of sensual objects, you become sensual objects. If you are focused on a divine pure love, you become divine pure love. These were the thoughts I contemplated on my return flight to America. Marina was now at rest in my heart where I carry her spirit always. I feel freed from the need to become absolved in the world of impermanence now that I understand. We had seized our moment of divine splendor that seemed so fleeting, but life is fleeting, slipping through our hands like cupped water. It's difficult to explain reality or un-reality empirically or transcendentally, let alone consciousness. There is one thing that we can be certain of and that is that we are all feeling-beings who have the capacity to love. Time is fleeting and distractions are plentiful in the barrage against our awareness to decide and take action to survive in the material world. The only measure that seems to be right every time is that mysterious voice under our breath suggesting yes or no when we query choice. Effortlessly and ultimately, goodness always comes for us if we allow for our compassionate hearts to point towards love's cause. Tantra takes into its arms spiritual knowledge, resonating to harmonize our resolve in this matter of compassion. Its purpose is to give liberation, in which monistic truth is reached through this illusion of a dualistic world. Life is all encompassing love, embracing mind, matter, and consciousness in ancient smiles of compassion.

The plane is landing at Kennedy Airport where Gina and Todd are excitedly waiting to pick me up. Who knew they would end up together and start a new life in the Big Apple? Bob is already at the hotel with his new boyfriend, a deep thinker and Icelandic handball star, Olafur Stefansson. Bob has orchestrated a personalized and private dining experience at the Peacock Alley Restaurant for us all. It's an elegant, epicurean journey in celebration of his yet to be announced engagement to his true love. Poised within Manhattan's exquisite jewel, The Waldorf Astoria, this will be a perfect night. It will embed a memory of love and friendship that I am sure will traverse the reels of time. After dinner, Bob is taking us all to a very exclusive dance club called XI where world renowned DJ David Morales is spinning tonight.

At dinner, Gina and Todd tell me about what happened after I left. She ended up returning from an uneventful sleepover with the romance writer that turned out not so romantic. Todd was there and they started talking. They learned that they had a lot in common, other than just preferred sizes and shapes. The icing on the cake came when they both ended up getting work in New York not far from each other. After a whirlwind courtship, they ended up tying the knot while I was in Bhutan because they just couldn't wait. They wanted to find a way to thank me for introducing them, so they got me a flat in Manhattan near Broadway. That's when Bob piped in and also wanted to thank me for sending him on a vacation to Iceland. He had met Olafur at a dance club in Reykjavik called Bakkus. Olafur, with a big smile, came up to me, kissed my cheek, and thanked me for sending his true love to him. I gave him a huge hug and kiss back to show my feelings of welcome. Happiness for those I love is a part of my happiness rekindled and ready to give and receive love again.

It was strange being back in America, especially while the country was going through so much. Yet love was emerging from the streets in ways I never thought possible. For me, I had laid down my sword to pick up the pen again, resolved that love is also possible for me, but perhaps in some new way. Really I don't know what way it will come but I know that Earth is a place meant for the discovery of love. That discovery comes in many shapes and forms derived essentially from that initial spark of what we now know as a 'Divine Kiss.' Not just any kiss, but a kiss filled with intention, exploration, and sublime compassion that remind us all that we are not alone. There is a resonance meant for transforming darkness into light stirring your awareness and burrowing you into awaiting consciousness to embrace the void. Who knows what will happen out on the town with my best friends in one of the most elegant cities in the world?

Great Completion

Love is a many splendored thing that exists inside every living creature. We are so fortunate to somehow recognize and comprehend its various manifestations in our lives and in the lives of those around us. Simply, this is the enlightenment, suspended in the naked clear emptiness, undeviating from the path of compassion and bestowing love to aid in the suffering of all sentient beings. When the attention becomes dominant, refined, and our aspirations and intentions are fulfilled in understanding, then we all belong together. Mahamudra has no cause, conditions, methods, path, or results; it's an innate reaction devoid of belief or faith that happens instantaneously without thought. When we stop conceptualizing and exhausting our minds with trivia, our undistracted instincts make us profound and allow us to be love. It is allowing our voice to be the voice of love, the one that we have heard before coming from those we love every minute of every day. This dreadful epoch of fear is waning because of love's ability to be resilient even in the face of utter disaster. Let the love flow from our hearts and heal our world, its people, and all the inhabitants of our beautiful planet.

We are each others enigmas and enigmas to ourselves beyond the nature of the mind to identify. It's our soul's nature to recognize its inseparable connection with all things and embrace this adventure and beauty with love. Yes, intrinsic nature is the ultimate home of satisfaction, non-duality, and an awakened state where love dwells. This is what our hearts must preserve in the short time we have to make contact in our beautiful affirmation. Nurture this undistracted state of spacious awareness that flows through every corridor of our unfettered self. These poetic aberrations cannot explain the phenomena of 'love only those things that keep us from this human right we are all entitled to.' There is not one of us who hasn't been a child, a baby imprinted and imprinting those around us with our innocent love. This is what must be protected by our collective civilization. Love is supreme and with our unwavering true nature it's no longer affected by the plagues of envy, lust, and greed. I have very high hopes we become our own antidote through the line in the sand that states, "Love is the answer."

I trust in a spontaneous presence where unconditional love will seek me out and wrap around me like a warm blanket. We are the fragrance that attracts a stellar bliss ineffable, a prevailing light within where kisses are the true currency of our heart's desire. These moments in our desert of oblivion, when nothing seems possible, where we are surrounded by mirages and hope seems lost. Love is the immaculate jewel, celestial ambrosia, a binding spiritual pleasure, and an oasis for those to quench their thirst. When indescribable circumstances seem to delude our path, look for luster, for that's where a deserving wellspring of compassion will be your miracle. Love has never abandoned our hearts; it just must be encouraged,

344

coaxed, and welcomed to the waiting arms of our world without fear. We are the true gold, our spirit and our love the only currency worth trading for. May the buds of joy bloom into the passionate patterns of your amazing journey towards pure love.

Sonnet XVIII

Shall I compare thee to a summer's day?

Thou art more lovely and more temperate:

Rough winds do shake the darling buds of May,

And summer's lease hath all too short a date:

Sometime too hot the eye of heaven shines,

And often is his gold complexion dimm'd;

And every fair from fair sometime declines,

By chance or nature's changing course untrimm'd:

But thy eternal summer shall not fade

Nor lose possession of that fair thou ow'st;

Nor shall Death brag thou wander'st in his shade,

When in eternal lines to time thou grow'st;

So long as men can breathe or eyes can see,

So long lives this and this gives life to thee.

William Shakespeare 1609

I would like to thank you all sincerely for taking this valuable time from your life to read my words. They come from my heart to yours. I have a great passion for love in everything I create, and hope this passion has somehow rubbed off on you.

Best Journey Seekers, David Houghton Revelle Hauser

Happenstance and Circumstance

The gunny shire of outward delights bends the willows branches in the midday sunlight. How do thee afterword be fore warned that neither beast nor man's breath be torn asunder from his blazed boast of love. Never truer these charades of budding dreams and masquerades that smell sweet as guilt in an arboretum of curls and blossoms. 'Tis true these complexities of human dignity where immortal men do dwell to talk of deadly shades of gray whilst nary fade this love away. My wander'st glows that shadows fear whose misfortunate sun has darned to block a yearning light, a fragrant lock. When imbeciles miss their watch, rhythms twitter and sacred longings go un-hitherward. My stealing eyes perchance do dwell on thee, romantically, as tide turns west and my thrust of happiness mirrors through your oblique eyes. Ah the foolishness of men who claim these awkward claims of bravado mere characters of their own minds acquiescence. Beloved, my praise does not go un-scorned as dastardly my failing tongue has no better words to emit upon this joyous feeling framed in the etching of your beauty and your loins. Insidious, ridiculous, as sands and hourglasses pang my heart for brief encounters in oblivion where two do dare depart. Come, I quaintly folly to dally in the dark where happenstance and circumstance have not been chosen by a lark. I bray through my ostentatious shattered gall, that somehow you would hear a sweet melody in my call. But witless bumbling fools, these are the dreams we wish to use, of melancholy spice dashed with disparity with omitted words and one broad,"Will you marry me."

About The Author

David was born in Marshalltown, Iowa in 1955 but his family moved to Los Angeles in 1964. For many years, his childhood was split between city life and working on his family's farm during summer break. Fascinated by religion from his early experience with small town churches, he began his religious studies. Hinduism, Philosophy, and Vajrayana Buddhism captivated him on his perpetual spiritual journey. He has had the honor of studying with spiritual leaders, practices and receiving many initiations.

Soulkiss: Tantric Tales of Mahamudra, is a work of love pouring out a life time of experience and study to quantify a difficult and overlooked subject of our spiritual connection to romantic love. "Where are you my love," is the voice of timeless consciousness seeking restitution to it bewildered identity that only wants to know it love exists.

David, a global citizen, currently lives in Los Angeles, California.

Made in the USA
Las Vegas, NV
21 June 2023

73735592R00197